David Paul Brown

Forensic speeches

Selected from important trials

David Paul Brown

Forensic speeches
Selected from important trials

ISBN/EAN: 9783337276072

Printed in Europe, USA, Canada, Australia, Japan

Cover: Foto ©Andreas Hilbeck / pixelio.de

More available books at **www.hansebooks.com**

THE

FORENSIC SPEECHES

OF

DAVID PAUL BROWN,

SELECTED

FROM IMPORTANT TRIALS,

AND EMBRACING

A PERIOD OF FORTY YEARS.

EDITED BY HIS SON,

ROBERT EDEN BROWN.

PHILADELPHIA:

KING & BAIRD, PUBLISHERS, 607 SANSOM STREET.

MDCCCLXXIII.

EDITOR'S PREFACE.

THE following collection, or rather selection, of the Forensic Speeches of the late DAVID PAUL BROWN, are now presented to the legal profession and the reading public, in the belief that such a compilation would appropriately and acceptably meet the wishes of the many admirers and friends of the deceased.

Although a volume, possessing the main features of the present one, was in contemplation at the time of Mr. Brown's death, it is a subject of regret to the compiler, which will perhaps be shared by the reader, that the selections embraced in the following pages, were not in any way indicated by the deceased.

That responsibility, therefore, rests wholly with the Editor and if these selections do not appear always the most worthy of the orator or the reader, the blame should attach where it properly belongs.

No excuse can be necessary for this self-imposed task; yet, if one were needed, it might be found in an earnest desire to revive in some degree that love of eloquence which more particularly characterized the earlier days of the Philadelphia Bar, and made the name of a "Philadelphia Lawyer" proverbially synonymous with the highest excellencies of the profession.

It was this desire, combined with a devotion to his

profession, which embraced the whole "Bar" as one
united family, that induced Mr. Brown to devote the
scanty leisure afforded by professional duties, to the
preparation of the "Forum," in the introduction to
which he says:

"I may be permitted in conclusion to say, that my
chief motive for engaging in this undertaking, is the
desire to furnish some few memorials of the legal profession. If this work be not attempted *now*, it never will
be. Every hour diminishes our recollections of by-gone
days; but a few glimpses remain; and a few short years
will obliterate every view and vestige of what, in the passing and changing pageants of life, has been so interesting to us all."

Of the speeches that follow, a word or two of general
explanation is due from the Editor. This, he believes, is
the only volume of forensic speeches that has ever
issued from the American press, and perhaps the only
volume in the language, if we except the speeches of
Lord Erskine, which are mainly in "State Trials," and
consequently of semi-political significance. This fact the
Editor adverts to, to show that he has had no guide to
direct him in the path he treads, which, to the generous
reader, will be ample apology for the many imperfections
that a pioneers' labors necessarily exhibit.

The chief embarrassment, however, which the Editor
has experienced, has arisen in determining how far he
would be justified in altering in any particular the text
of the following speeches.

A forensic speech, even when it contains the very
highest and truest elements of oratorical effect—and perhaps for that very reason—rarely, if ever exhibits those

merits to the reader. At the same time, the trimming and polishing so necessary in *belle-lettre* composition, would take from a delivered speech one-half its force in the estimation of the auditor.

Upon this subject, Mr. Brown himself thus writes, in presenting an extract from the speech of William Lewis, LL. D.:

" We are aware, that a speech in type is a very different matter from a speech delivered. If Patrick Henry's fame depended upon the report of his speeches, instead of the effects which they produced, we should be at a loss to conceive how he could have acquired such deathless renown. This difference is attributable to various causes, combining to produce dramatic effect. The court, the jury, the issue, the surrounding populace, the interest of the contending parties and their respective friends, the presence of the bar, the natural excitement of the occasion, all tend to impart animation and vigor to a speech, and to confirm the sentiment of Cicero, that 'no man is an orator without a multitude.'" . . . . . "Action, which is said to be the essence of oratory, is utterly wanting. The impassioned declamations, the varied tones of the voice, the fixed and penetrating eye, the spirit that displays itself 'from every joint and motive of the body,' are neither to be appreciated nor imagined. To be understood—to be felt, they must be seen and heard. Still, as we cannot revive the dead, their past works must *speak* for them." *

Every lawyer will recognize the truth of these remarks, which are here chiefly introduced for the infor-

---

* "The Forum," vol. i, pp. 459-60.

mation of the unprofessional reader, and to explain to *all* the motives which have induced the Editor to present these speeches as he has found them, fresh, and almost untouched, from the stenographer's notes.

As it might reasonably be expected, that some biographical memoir of Mr. Brown would accompany this volume, it may be proper to add, in conclusion, that this has intentionally been omitted for several reasons; the chief of which is the reflection that the filial tie is too close a one to admit of that free and impartial criticism of motives and actions, which it is the duty of the honest biographer, boldly to examine and discuss.

PHILADELPHIA, *June,* 1873.

BINNS' CASE.

Commonwealth of Pennsylvania v. John Binns.

ASSAULT AND BATTERY. 1818.

This action was brought against the defendant—a gentleman of very considerable social and political influence—on the information of a young girl—one of a family of German "Redemptioners," who had lately arrived in the United States. The child prosecutrix, about nine years of age, had been indentured to Mr. Binns, at that time Editor of the Democratic Press, and, upon a suspicion of larceny, had been subjected to severe corporal punishment at the hands of her master.

The case presents no feature of general interest at this time; yet the argument is perhaps deserving of its prominent place in the following series, as the *first* forensic effort of its author.

For the Prosecution.
G. M. Dallas, David Paul Brown.

For the Defence.
Jos. R. Ingersoll, Josiah Randall.

SPEECH IN BINNS' CASE.

IN SUBMISSION TO THE COURT, GENTLEMEN OF THE JURY:

The unusual concourse of spectators and auditors here assembled—the interest and anxiety expressed in the countenance of every one—the zeal and abilities of the gentlemen to whom I am opposed—the painfully solicitous emotions of my own bosom—all, refer me to the importance of the cause in which I am engaged. Important, not simply as respects this poor child, or me, her humble advocate, but as regards the jury who sit here to decide, as regards your honors who sit there to adjudge, and as relates to the world. I say it is important in relation to the world, because the principles upon which this case are to be decided are intertwined, I might say identified, with the nearest and dearest feelings of the human heart. Impressed with this idea, I cannot but regret the great and manifest embarrassments under which I labor—embarrassments not simply arising from my youth and consequent inexperience, but resulting, in an eminent degree, from the magnitude of the issue in which I am engaged, and the abilities of the gentlemen to whom I am opposed. Nor is this wonderful; for such is the constitution of the human mind, that our very fear frequently occasions that which we fear, and in proportion as we feel ourselves called upon for great exertions, in the same proportion we are frequently compelled to acknowledge an utter inability to obey that call.

There is also another disadvantage under which I labor

in common with my professional brethren, and which I
beg leave as far as possible to endeavor to remove—I
mean the prejudice too generally entertained by jurors
to whom a case may be submitted, that whatever may
be the force or quality of the arguments of counsel,
they are still entitled to but little weight, inasmuch as
they are the offspring of the pocket, not the heart—or
in other words, the effect of pecuniary influence, rather
than of any inclination to be serviceable to our fellow-
creatures. Whether this be just or unjust—liberal or
illiberal, it is not necessary for me to inquire; but I
conceive it to be a duty which I owe to the profession,
to my client, to you, and to myself, here, upon the
threshold of this case, unreservedly and explicitly to
declare that I am no hired advocate; I appear before
you upon this occasion without any other bribe than
my sympathies; without any other object than disinterested humanity; without any other motive than impartial justice. I have no friendship for this poor child,
but that which arises from her misfortunes and dis-
tresses—I have no enmity to Mr. John Binns, but that
which arises from his barbarity and cruelty. " Homo
sum et humani a me nil alienum puto." This principle is
considered a sufficient inducement; should any excuse be
necessary, I trust it will prove a sufficient excuse.

Having thus endeavored to remove those obstacles or
impediments which stood between me and the case, at
least so far as they were removable, let us now turn our
attention to the more immediate subject of the present
controversy. In doing this, however, I cannot, as the
opposite counsel have done, with perfect propriety, invoke
the political or social importance of my client, in order to
give weight to my argument. Alas! she has neither. I
stand here before you not in behalf of a powerful and
influential citizen, supported by relatives and surrounded
by friends; I address you in the cause of a helpless, hapless and unprotected child, torn by the storms of adver-

sity from the bosom of her parents and her country; a child whose only safeguard from oppression in this land of strangers, is the verdict of an American Jury; whose only unshaken hope of reliance is in the Father of the fatherless. This, allow me to say, is no professional cant; it is the spontaneous effusion of the heart; the sacred voice of sympathy. Indeed, I should abhor myself, could I, upon an occasion like this, where the indignant and impatient soul is struggling for utterance, coolly and deliberately and dispassionately indulge in the vanity of chosen expression. Nature requires not the aid of art, and had you beheld, as I did, the lacerated, mangled, and bleeding limbs of this poor helpless child; had you seen, as I did, the swollen tear of agony that trembled in her eye; had you heard, as I did, the sympathetic and impressible groan that burst from the assembled multitude in the hall of justice, in contemplating her suffering (that groan which was the unerring testimony that nature bore to the barbarity of this procedure), it would be a wanton and an unpardonable trespass upon your time and that of this honorable court, were I to occupy a single moment of your attention. Nothing, says the poet, can be added to perfection:

> " To gild refined gold, to paint the lily,
>   To throw a perfume on the violet,
>   To smooth the ice, or add another hue
>   Unto the rainbow; or with a taper light
>   To seek the beauteous eye of heaven to garnish,
>   Is wasteful and ridiculous excess."

Not less wasteful—not less ridiculous were every attempt of mine to unfold the horrors of this most horrible transaction. The deed—the blushing deed itself, distances every effort of speech, and baffles all attempts at description. The language of man is amply adapted to the common excitements of life; but weak and cold and callous must be that heart; which, upon occasions like this, does not feel more than the tongue can express.

This, then, is the character of the case, which the counsel—adopting the principles and conduct of their employer—have attempted stigmatizing with malice, as they attempted stigmatizing this poor child with theft, and both because they are *fatherless.** This is the case which was to have been ridiculed out of court. But it will not do; thank heaven, honest nature is too true to herself either to be laughed *into*, or *out* of countenance. The smiles that mantled over their features were as superficial as the artifice that gave birth to them; the heart, I am sure, had no concern in either; it was a mere veil, thrown over their wretched cause to conceal its rottenness and deformity. The convulsive laugh of desperation, while tottering on the brink of ruin—the hectic glow of health on the cheek of consumption—the last cheerful effort of their expiring cause.

But, gentlemen, let us not wander—let us not anticipate. We owe something, it is true, to feeling, in such a cause; we owe more to reason; but we will, notwithstanding, endeavor as calmly and dispassionately as possible to investigate and determine the merits of this discussion. The fact of the beating being admitted, or at any rate proved, beyond the necessity or reach of argument, the remaining facts of the case, appear properly and naturally to marshal themselves under these two distinct points of inquiry.

1st. Was any beating deserved?

2d. Was the beating inflicted justifiable?

If either of these inquiries be negatively decided, the defendant must be convicted. If no beating was deserved; then the weight of a finger in anger, is an assault and battery, and we must have a verdict. Or, if the first part be affirmed, and you should be satisfied that a beating was deserved, still if the beating inflicted was unwarrantable and unreasonable, all defence must fail.

---

* The defendant's counsel moved the court to dismiss the case because there was no prosecutor endorsed on the bill.

Have the goodness to keep these points in view, neither
be driven from them by force, nor seduced by ingenuity.
They will serve as guiding stars to your councils. *With*
them you will steer securely to correct conclusions—*without* them, you will be launched at once upon the ocean of
investigation, without helm or rudder—without chart or
compass—to direct you in your course.

In relation to the first point, permit me to observe, that
there has been no proof of theft, nor can any be produced. The honest, artless conduct of this poor child, is
" all the world to nothing " against this foul and unmerited aspersion. They have mangled her body, and with
fiend-like vengeance, unsatisfied with that, they now attempt stabbing her infant reputation.

> " Spotless reputation, which away,
>   Men are but gilded loam, or painted clay."

But even this shall not avail them. I pledge myself to
furnish you with a clear and fair interpretation of this
mysterious transaction. Since the weight of shame must
fall somewhere, let broader shoulders bear it. For my
part, I have not the shade of a doubt—and if you believe
the testimony you must concur in the opinion—but that
the money was really *given* to Anna Maria Martin, which
she is now charged with having *stolen*. Do you call for
the proof? Do you not see that the story of Benjamin
Binns corroborates that of the child in every particular
except one—I mean the *gift;* to acknowledge *this* were
ruin. He tells you that Mr. Binns and his lady rode out
on Saturday—that Anna Maria came for money to pro-
vide bread, and that she afterwards came to call him to
supper. This is precisely the story of the child; but she
goes further, and says that when she called him to supper,
he gave her nine-pence, requesting her afterwards not to
reveal it to his brother. And why this desire of concealment? It is easily accounted for when we remember
that it is agreed on all hands that Mr. John Binns had

forbidden his brother to give money to Anna Maria, as it seems he had prior to this time, been in the frequent habit of doing. Of this you must be fully convinced, that upon a candid examination of their respective stories, there is every reason to give credence to that of the child. She had no inducement, she had no power to misrepresent—from the first to the last, her testimony has been the same; natural, uniform, and consistent; alike free from cunning and constraint. Of his testimony, on the contrary, we may at least say it is suspicious. His connection with the defendant, his dependence upon the defendant, of necessity have some influence upon his mind; added to which, having early asserted her guilt to his brother, he dare not deny it now. Having sworn to it before the mayor, he dare not now forswear himself. To bolster up their case as well as possible, and to withdraw your attention from the proper subject of controversy, they have contrived to drag in the countenance of Mr. Benjamin Binns; I presume, as a sort of rallying-point to their defeated hopes. But, gentlemen, this is not a case of countenance, and if it were, their condition is in no wise improved. Come hither Anna Maria Martin,—lay off your hat,—look at the jury,—poor child, though her features are dressed in sorrow, though the joyless tear bedews her sparkling eye, still I may with propriety say, that she suffers nothing in a comparison with Mr. Benjamin Binns, nor any other member of the Binns family that I have hitherto seen. This then is the relative position of the prosecution and defence. Let us for a moment compare the testimony ; weigh them,—the one clearly preponderates, while the other kicks the beam; test them,—the one evaporates in air, the other assumes a firmer texture, and lays a closer hold upon the heart; analyze them,—the defendant's testimony dwindles into dross, while that on behalf of the prosecution

" Like purest gold, that's tortured in the furnace,
    Comes forth more bright, and brings forth all its weight."

The next witness in the order of merit, adduced by the defendant, is Mary Caldwell, who lived with Mr. Binns, when Anna Maria was bound; and continued living with him a considerable time after. What does she say?—nothing to the purpose: " Anna Maria was not very good nor very bad. I believe there were complaints, chiefly from children in the family, with whom she quarrelled and disagreed. I often saw her have money, about which she sometimes told different stories. I remember no particular instance. There was no money in places she could get it from. Her character was not good." Hence it seems that Mrs. Caldwell did not entertain the most favorable opinion of this child; and the next inquiry is, what opinion shall we entertain of Mrs. Caldwell? She comes before us perfectly unknown, perfectly unsupported, and for what purpose? Not to testify to the general character of Maria ; not to say what reputation she sustained in the neighborhood, which would afford us an opportunity of refutation, but to declare her individual opinion, and thus to blight the opening prospects of this child, without being able to supply us with a single doubtful virtue from which this opinion may have been derived. This is weaker than air, and lighter than vanity. Probably Anna Maria has quite as unfavorable an opinion of Mrs. Caldwell, and how are their respective merits to be adjusted? It was a saying of Agesilaus, the renowned king of Sparta, that " the character of an informer is as necessary to be known, as that of the person informed against," and it is a well settled maxim, both in reason and law, "that the character of every one should suffer, in proportion to the weight of *his* character who bears testimony against it." How then, upon these principles, stands the account? what unquestionable title to belief has the witness produced? What all powerful and mysterious charm does she possess, that is at the same time to prostrate the characters of others, and yet preserve her own unsullied and unharmed? But I will press this matter no further,

it is at all times painful to me to derogate in the slightest
degree from the reputation of any one, or throw upon them
a shade of imputation; and if upon the present occasion I
have violated my general disposition, let the opposite
party remember that to them it is to be imputed, and let
them also remember, to use the homely but forcible illustration of the proverb, that "those persons who live in
glass houses should not throw stones."

The next witness whom you have had examined, is
Mrs. Susan West, who occasionally nurses Mrs. Binns.
(This lady's testimony read.) Here there are petty child-
ish quarrels raked up from all parts of the house—from
the cellar to the garret, from the kitchen to the parlor,—
as the materials of a defence. Nothing is too trivial or
minute to escape their attention—cleaning the knives and
forks is called in to their aid; and even brick-dust itself,
is relied upon as giving color to this defence. She was
not cleanly in her person! Have they shown that she
was well supplied with raiment; that the cause was not
with the master; if not, her uncleanliness does not make
their case the whiter. In short, the evidence of Mrs.
West proves no beating deserved, and if it operates at all,
it is unquestionably in our favor. The story of Kelly—
fifteen years of age—the chit-chat of Magdaline—thirteen
years old; and the say-so of young Nicholas—I consign at
once into utter oblivion, as matter of indifference or contempt. Their representations are probably strictly true,
but they have nothing to do with the controversy; and
if they were clearly all untrue, I should pass over them in
silence, as my province is to *defend* not to *ruin* children;
to *excuse*, not to *abuse* their errors; to *extenuate*, not to *aggravate* their crimes.

Here ends the elaborate defence; upon this slender
basis, for this is substantially all, you are called upon to
acquit the defendant, and destroy this child—to justify
this barbarity, by charging her with theft. And yet all
the charges brought against her—unable to speak and

defend herself, lisping an equivocal, and to her, uncertain language—might with just as much probability and proof, be produced against the children of any one of you.

Leaving you, then, to decide upon this testimony, without further remark, upon the course of reflection already suggested, I think you must be perfectly satisfied that no theft has been proven—no impropriety of conduct established against Anna Maria Martin; and consequently that this beating, was as wanton and undeserved as it was cruel, barbarous, and bloody.

There is one thing, however, that it may be proper here to observe, and which to me is convincing and conclusive as to the testimony of the innocence of this child, and that is, her resolute refusal to confess her guilt, under the giant arm of her cruel master. Neither fear nor hope could induce it. "My brother denies the gift, confess your crime, acknowledge yourself a *thief*, come stab your *soul*, and I will *spare* your *body!*" This is, in effect, the exhortation of the tyrant. What is her reply? " I have told the truth; your brother *cannot* deny it; let him be called—let me confront him." Alas, poor child, you rested on a broken reed, when you leaned upon Mr. Benjamin Binns—when you trusted to the "compunctious visitings" of his conscience. He appears; again he persists in his denial; and again her infant limbs writhe beneath the inhuman lash. They may extort groans, but not falsehoods. The flesh shrinks, but the soul still stands firm. Merciful heaven! can such things be, in a charitable, Christian land? Despots may exercise their power upon the rebellious or refractory, and thereby punish, and subjugate them to their arbitrary will; but there is something in the female character—there is something in *infancy*—something in feebleness and helplessness, that should palsy or unnerve even a tyrant's arm. " How shall we hope for mercy, rendering none?" (Great applause.*)

---

*Stenographer.

But to recur to our proposed arrangement. You must be convinced, I say, that the punishment was undeserved and unmanly, and inflicted even without the shadow of a cause; yet that we may meet the case in every possible aspect, confront it at every point of the compass, and leave them not an inch of ground upon which to plant their defence, let us suppose for a moment, as a matter of argument, what, remember, I unequivocally deny, that this child was *guilty* of the sin imputed to her, and proceed to the second proposed point of inquiry.

2d. Was the beating inflicted justifiable?

You have heard what has been uttered against her,—a mere "mouse from a mountain"—of malice; you know her fault; what was the punishment? Has the defendant produced any testimony that can be relied upon? has he produced a single witness, out of the many who beheld the misery of this child, to testify to his moderation? Not one! Some of the doctors who saw her several days *after* the beating, thought her at that time not "dangerous;" and it is highly probable had they even seen her *before*, when her back was covered with welts, and perfectly discolored with extravasated blood, they might have entertained precisely the same opinion. But the *danger* is not the criterion of moderation; had she been perfectly flayed alive; had, as was supposed by one of the witnesses, a red hot gridiron been applied to her back, it might not in the view of those gentlemen have been dangerous; but I am certain it would have been brutal; I am certain it would have been barbarous; I am certain it would never have received the countenance or sanction of a benevolent and humane American jury.

Far be it from me to impute any natural hardness of heart to those medical gentlemen; but we all know the duties of their profession; we have all felt the force of habit and familiarity, and perhaps it is not venturing too much to say, that men who have spent a considerable part of their lives in the slaughter-house of their species,

surrounded by all the imagery of death and disaster, are
at least, not those whose opinion should govern in the
construction of this case. If a doctor were called upon
to define a "battery", he would no doubt consider it the
loss or injury of some vital part of the human frame;
whereas in certain circumstances, this would be downright murder. A lawyer, however, will tell you that
laying a finger improperly upon another, constitutes a
battery. On the other hand, a lawyer who saw the
operation incident to the extirpation of an eye, a fracture
of the skull, or a dislocation of the limbs, would pronounce them all terrible calamities ; yet a surgeon would
tell you, with a face of perfect composure, with heart of
stone, and nerves of steel, that these are common-place
occurrences,—mere trivial matters unattended by much
danger,—and whisk you through the whole anatomy of
the human system and catalogue of physical ills, with as
much self-complacency and good humor, as he would
lead his partner down a dance. Let us shun both
extremes. I ask you to decide this case neither by the
technical absurdities of the one, nor refined barbarities of
the other. "*Medio tutissimus ibis,*"—the middle course is
safest. Let then the testimony of your unbiassed and
unperverted fellow-citizens govern your deliberations;
they who know that a fellow creature may be injured
and still retain his head upon his shoulders; and yet at
the same time do not carry this belief to such an extreme
as to lead them to consider the wind of the fist as an
absolute assault.

But, gentlemen, I pledge myself to show you that the
evidence of even the doctors themselves, and particularly
that of Dr. Cullen, inimical, as it intentionally was, to the
cause that I espouse, is for the most part illusory, fallacious, and unfounded. Dr. Cullen tells you that he
received a note from Mr. John Binns, requesting him in
company with Dr. Griffiths, to call upon Anna Maria
Martin, to examine her back, and afford any medical or

surgical aid that might be required. Is not this a proof that Binns himself thought the child materially injured? why talk of medical and surgical assistance? why send TWO learned members of the faculty? was not *one* sufficient?—or did he believe the case to be so desperate as to require consultation? I leave you to divine his thoughts and his motives, while I proceed to my anatomical and physiological inquiries. (Reads the testimony.)

"There was," says Dr. Cullen, "no swelling at the time of examination, though the flesh was still discolored." Now, gentlemen, I do not, as the doctor does, pretend to be a complete surgeon or anatomist, yet those branches of medical science formed one of the pastimes of my youth, and although I never wrote a treatise,—although I never committed one to memory,—although I never had occasion to appear in the capacity of a physician before a court and jury in behalf of a friend,—and although I never instructed counsel to ask me questions calculated to elicit my knowledge and conceal my ignorance,—yet I will endeavor to rescue so much of my reading from the grasp of forgetfulness, as may enable me briefly, but I trust satisfactorily, to answer the medical hypotheses (they deserve no better name), which have been forced upon our attention. In the first place then, the want of swelling at the time of examination, as was asserted by the doctors, was a conclusive proof of the want of severity! This I deny; and I throw myself with confidence upon your own knowledge to support the denial. I refer you to that book, which lies open before you all, as a refutation of such doctrine—I mean the book of experience. You have all no doubt observed, in cases of children, where they have received any very severe contusions and bruises, in consequence of falls, that the swelling subsides and the extravasated blood is completely absorbed in the course of a very few days. The absorbents in children, particularly in those of a vigorous constitution, are extremely powerful, and will take up large quantities of extravasated blood in a short time; and will, indeed, remove many other obstructions to a healthy and free exercise of the animal functions, such as decayed bones, &c. These absorbents are certain vessels connected with the internal skin or cutus vera, by means of the cellular membrane, and are wisely provided by nature to supply or remedy the defects or injuries of the veins; as when, for instance, the blood-vessels or veins are ruptured by extreme violence, and are so impaired as to prevent their returning the blood to the heart, here the absorbent powers interfere, assist the wounded vein, and thus prevent mortification or suppuration, which must otherwise inevitably ensue.

The doctors also stated, that the bruised parts bore compressing and rubbing without any symptoms of pain, and this fact appeared to afford matter of considerable exultation to the opposite counsel. But, gentlemen, I defy them, had they ransacked all the stores of their invention, to have produced a circumstance which would militate more strongly against themselves. Why, the answer is plain—the parts were DEAD. The violence of the beating had in some measure, at any rate, destroyed their vitality; this is therefore a proof of the *severity*, not the *mildness* of the punishment.

But they say "there was no laceration or breaking of the outside skin, and consequently no blood." The doctrine of outside and inside, of external and internal skin, upon which the doctors have dwelt with so much emphasis, although by no means obscure itself, has been so wrapped up in technical mysteries, as to require some slight elucidation; and as Dr. Cullen has taken some liberties with the *Common Law*, he must in turn indulge me with a few strictures upon this part of his admirable thesis. The outside or visible skin is known by the name of cuticle, epidermis, or scarf; and I presume is what is vulgarly denominated "the scurf;" as when the hand is grazed roughly by any hard substance we might say the *scurf* is merely rubbed off. This skin is perfectly insensible, and serves as a sort of protection or coat to the inside skin, which is highly sensible. It is to mankind what scales are to a fish, so that you may break the outside skin or cutus vera, or true skin, without destroying or removing the scarf or scales, which form an integument sufficiently close and firm to prevent the emission of blood ;—you may completely crush a fish without discomposing a single scale.

So far, then, from the blood's failing to flow, being an argument for the defendant, it is subservient to the prosecution. The *internal* skin, I have shown you, may be broken without breaking the external skin; and if this take place, the contusion is much more dangerous than in cases of an incised wound, where nature is relieved in a great measure without the tardy and painful process of absorption. But, says Dr. Cooper,* "I do not believe the scarf skin *can* be broken without the flowing of blood." With great reverence and respect for the doctor, I must be allowed to dispute this; nay, I will go further, and broadly assert, that the scarf and the true skin may both be broken and still no blood emitted. As to the scarf, you have often seen it rubbed off without the issuing of any blood, and it therefore requires no reasoning from me. In respect to the true skin, I say with perfect confidence, that although the slightest puncture will be followed by blood, yet when the wound is extremely severe, and the parts are very much bruised, the channels of the blood become choked and there is little or no bleeding. As in the case related in Chesselden† of the unfortunate miller whose arm was torn off by the cog-wheel of a mill, and also in a case cited by Dr. Physick in his admirable lecture, of a similar accident happening to a boy: in both of which instances, though one of the most material arteries in the human system was completely severed, yet

---

* Dorsey's Cooper, p. 63.
† Chesselden's Anatomy, p. 321.

scarcely sufficient blood issued from the wounded body to
stain the linen that was bandaged around it. Go into the
field of battle, examine the victims of war, many of them
almost entirely dismembered, yet struggling in the grasp
of death for days—their arms, their legs torn away—why
is this? the current of life may be exhausted in a single
hour, why then this lingering? because the vitality of
the parts is so destroyed as to prevent the exercise of
their function; and hence the hopeless invalid is for some
time subjected to the horrors of a living death. So much
for the theory of Dr. Cooper; it has no foundation in
fact. As to the case of the dead man's mark, or the
appearance upon the skin of spots resembling iron mould,
which Dr. Cullen has adverted to, in illustration of his
theory of absorption and extravasation, I will venture
to assert that both the name and nature ascribed to them
are equally unknown to the medical world. Those spots
are not the effect of extravasated blood, but probably
arise from the serum, one of the constituents of the
blood, oozing through the veins. The case of Mrs. G.'s
child was also unfortunately alluded to by the doctor in
explanation of his enigmas. What! shall we suffer him
to tell us that the mark on the back of an infant arising
from a slight blow of the mother's hand, is an extravasation of blood. 'Tis silly, 'tis preposterous in the extreme;
every child-nurse knows better; why, according to the
gentleman's notion, every hectic glow of the blood—
every fever—every blush that mantles on a lady's cheek,
is an extravasation. But cast your eyes upon the resplen-
dent pages of Darwin and of Brown, of Rush and of
Physick, and this misty error is at once dispelled. They
will tell you that the discoloration is the effect not of
ruptured vessels but of too much excitement; not of
blood being forced out of its natural channels, but of its
being propelled through these channels with unusual
violence. Feel the pulse during a fever; it will be found
much fuller and stronger than usual, and the same obser-

vation will apply equally well in relation to a blush.
Hope, shame, anger, anxiety,—almost any sudden emo-
tion of the mind—will so affect the physical system, as
to throw unusual quantities of blood in the veins, and
thus of consequence, increase the pulse and flush the features; but no man but the learned doctor, I am sure,
ever dreamt of this being an extravasation. A single
remark and I bid farewell, a long farewell, to physic.

I have been really astonished and disgusted, to discover
so much madness in the sequel of that story, whose preface promised so much wisdom. To leave now this medical jargon, which is as inconsistent with itself as with
reason, "and fall somewhat into a slower method ;" what
say your unbiassed and unperverted fellow-citizens?

Mrs. Maria Welsh tells you that the beating was extremely severe, from the shoulders down to the waist.
Upon inquiring the cause, the child told precisely the
same story as that related in court.

What says Mrs. Brown? "A most cruel beating!"
What says Mrs. Burrows? "The child's back exhibited
the most awful spectacle I ever beheld; no welts could be
distinguished; it was one entire bruise; it resembled
beef's liver; the blood seemed just ready to start from
the skin." What says Dr. Frick? What says his Honor
the Mayor, a man who for many years held the highest
and most responsible station of your city as a magistrate
and guardian, and who has discharged his various and
arduous duties with credit to himself and advantage to
the community? He tells you that never in the exercise
of his functions, either in his office or in the court, has
he beheld so severe a beating on so young a child. It is
unnecessary for me to indulge in a more minute recapitu-
lation of the testimony. To advert to it is, I trust, in
itself, sufficient to destroy all the wire-drawn notions, and
burst all the airy bubbles, that may be blown upon the
case.

After such conclusive evidence, can any man seriously

listen for a moment to a labored argument professing to
show that such beating as this is justifiable, either " in
foro conscientia" or " in foro humano"—in the sight of
God, or in the sight of man? If the child was guilty,
which I deny; her guilt would not have authorized such
gross inhumanity. If the laws were violated; they stand
their own avengers. Let her be charged with larceny—
let her be indicted and arraigned. This respectable jury
shall try, and this honorable court shall pronounce
upon her crime; but, thank Heaven, no man—not the
Governor of the State, not the President of the United
States; nay, not even John Binns himself, can discharge
in this free and happy land, the four-fold office of witness,
juror, judge and executioner.

In the capacity of a master, I admit he had the authority of the law, in inflicting moderate chastisement for
salutary, not vindictive purposes. This is a right possessed by all persons standing in the relation of husband,
father, teacher, captain and master, and which may be
exercised on their wives, children, pupils, sailors and servants. But " in the name of all the gods at once," what
possible operation is the admission of this abstract principle
to have upon the present controversy? In order that they
may enjoy its protection they must bring themselves
within its provision. Moderation is essential to justification; for at the very last session of the court a school-
master was convicted for an assault and battery upon a
scholar, because he had exceeded the limits of propriety
in punishment. Indictments and convictions of captains
for abuse of sailors are frequent, notwithstanding the
rope's end privilege; and but a few days since a client
of mine was deservedly condemned and sentenced to imprisonment, merely for giving his wife a single blow,
though in my opinion, sex aside, she merited a dozen.

To sum up all, then, we say that in our case any punishment, however slight, would have been unwarrantable,
and an assault and battery, because there was *no offence*;

and we say further, that the blackest and most *heinous offence* would have been no justification for a beating so severe.

I have now done my part, feebly and imperfectly, I must acknowledge, but as fully as my feelings and inexperience would permit. It remains for you to do yours. The worldly destinies of this poor child are now in your hands. Her character and her cause are with you; you may stigmatize her with dishonor and dishonesty, or wash her white as snow; you may either cast her like a loathsome weed from the bosom of society, or exhibit her as an example of suffering innocence to the philanthropic and humane. Added to this, you are to-day to declare whether mingled tears and blood are subjects of commiseration with an American jury. Whether .domestic tyrants are to trample with impunity upon the helpless victim whom misfortune or distress may have placed at their feet. Whether your own children, or the children of your friends—of your fellow-citizens—of your fellow-creatures (for who shall control the fickle smiles of fortune?) should they be reduced to the miserable situation of this poor child, helpless, hapless and forlorn—should they be sundered from your fostering and protecting arms, and subjected to the merciless and iron despotism of men like the defendant—which ·heaven forbid!—you are, I say, now to declare, if such were their sad lot, whether they should pour forth their infant lives in irremediable distress, or look forward to your verdict and the records of this court, as the heralds which proclaim their deliverance at hand. I invoke you, then, by that holy tie which subsists between parent and child; by the sacred rites of hospitality; by the immutable principles of justice, to redress the injuries of this injured, friendless, stranger child. Will you hereafter dare to come into this court when your own children are abused, and claim the intervention of the law, and yet refuse it to this friendless girl? Why, your own verdict shall be cast into your teeth; "even-handed justice shall return the poisoned chalice to your own lips;" and the opposing counsel shall tauntingly exclaim, " What! are you, whose flinty hearts resisted the tears and blood of the oppressed ; are you, who sanctioned unparalleled severity in the case of Anna Maria Martin, the friendless German child ; are you, so peculiarly sensitive and alive when your own flesh and blood are concerned? AWAY WITH YOU !" Never, until you obliterate from the pages of that book, by tears of penitence, the record of this day's error—of this day's WRONG, can you expect an attentive ear to the story of your own griefs. REMEMBER THIS. And, above all, remember "with what judgment ye judge, ye shall be judged: and with what measure ye mete, it shall be measured to you again."

VERDICT : GUILTY.

JUDGE PORTER'S CASE.

INTRODUCTION.

The argument in this case, though not strictly embraced by the title of " Forensic Speeches," the Editor has thought proper to introduce here as calculated to show the rapidity with which Mr. Brown rose in popular estimation; and the mark which he—even at this early day in his professional career—made upon those high in position and influence. It appears—and we are indebted to the Hon. Wm. A. Porter for the statement—that in the year 1822 Mr. Brown, with Mr. Hayes, was engaged in a very important case before Judge Porter (a brother of the late Governor Porter), at Reading, Pa., in which they were opposed by James Buchanan, subsequently President of the United States, Mr. Baird, Mr. Biddle, Mr. Dayton, Mr. Frederick Smith and Mr. Charles Smith, the latter afterwards Judge of the Supreme Court. Although quite a young man—and naturally impressed with the matured talents and character of those opposed to him—Mr. Brown conducted his cause in such a manner, as to produce upon the mind of the Judge before whom it was argued so strong an effect; that when, some two years afterwards, articles of accusation and impeachment placed him in the position of a defendant, he at once secured Mr. Brown's professional assistance.

The trial of Judge Porter was fixed for "Tuesday, December 13th, 1825," when the Articles of Impeachment were read, and the respondent's answers filed; but, in consequence of the absence of witnesses in support of the impeachment, and other technical grounds of delay, the trial was not fairly entered upon until December 21st, 1825.

There were twelve Articles of Impeachment investigated, which occupied ten days; when, by an almost unanimous vote of the members of the court, Judge Porter was most honorably acquitted, December 31st, 1825.

As the introduction of the several articles of Impeachment with the respondent's answers, would occupy more space than is consistent with the prescribed limits of this volume; and as an attempted condensation of them would require scarcely less space; the Editor, by way of presenting the main features of this investigation, takes the opportunity of offering Mr. Brown's " Opening Speech," which, at the same time, will elucidate the points in controversy, and give a specimen (the only one contained in this volume) of his style in the original presentation of a case.

For the Managers.

SAMUEL DOUGLASS, ESQ.

For the Respondent.

DAVID PAUL BROWN.

OPENING SPEECH

IN DEFENCE OF JUDGE PORTER.

MR. PRESIDENT AND GENTLEMEN
OF THIS HONORABLE COURT:

The evidence on the part of the prosecution being
closed, it becomes my duty, representing as I do the honorable respondent, to submit ,to you the grounds upon
which he will rely for his defence, if a defence can be
required in a case like the present, where the attack is
in itself suicidal. In doing this I should act in entire
accordance with precedent and example, were I to indulge in argumentative remarks, in connection with a
detail of facts which the testimony will amply supply.
But it is my intention, as far as may be compatible with
the discharge of my duty, rigidly to consult the time and
convenience of this distinguished court, asking only in
requital a patient and attentive hearing. It is a subject
of unfeigned regret that the honorable managers should
have been unable, with all the indulgence which has been
extended to them in the prosecution of this complaint, to
submit the evidence in the order of the charges; and thus
to impart to them, by method and arrangement, a per-
specuity which, under existing circumstances, is solicited,
and sought for, in vain. Philosophy, however, teaches us
not to increase our griefs by the expression of unavailing
regret; but rather to relieve, by boldly confronting them.
The respondent, who from the earliest age has enjoyed
the confidence of the government; and whose fair fame
the breath of calumny has not dared to taint, stands now

arraigned before you upon charges of a highly criminal character; not by the House of Representatives; not by the people of Pennsylvania; but, as I will show you, by individuals—to name even some of whom would be to fail in the respect which I owe to this honorable court and to myself. As, however, he has served the State with fidelity in every situation to which he has been called, and particularly in the discharge of his judicial functions, he is as faithfully prepared to render an account of his stewardship; and not only to vindicate himself from all unmerited assertions, but to vindicate the source whence his authority is derived. Allow me, Mr. President, with a view to this object, to call your attention generally to the charges preferred, in order that we may be the more fully comprehended, in the introduction of the defence. The evil must be known ere the remedy can be applied; the character of the poison must be ascertained, before we can hope for an antidote.

The charges in their nature somewhat resemble indictments, or counts in indictments; certain facts are set forth from which certain deductions or inferences are drawn.

The first of these charges against the respondent, is for corruptly denying a citizen the right to have justice administered, without sale, denial or delay.

The second, for violating the personal liberty of the citizen, degrading the character of the court, and bringing the authority of the laws into contempt.

The third, for attempting to suppress and compound a felony—to screen the guilty from justice; and endeavoring to induce a judicial officer to commit a misdemeanor in office.

The fourth, for allowing a prisoner charged with larceny to purchase his acquittal.

The fifth, for evincing disgraceful passions and partialities, denying justice and bringing the administration of it into contempt.

The sixth, for wilfully and illegally obstructing the rights of the parties.

The seventh, for refusing and neglecting to file his opinions in writing.

The eighth, for unlawfully altering the valuation of property, on which the assessment of road tax was made.

The ninth, tenth, and eleventh, are but specifications of the twelfth article, which charges the respondent with contemptuous conduct towards his associate.

These imputed offences must depend upon the specifications contained in the charges. We say they are wholly unsupported by the facts set forth in the articles; by the facts proved; or by the implication of law arising from either or both. And it is necessary to sustain this prosecution, that the conclusions as well as the premises should be established by proof. The prosecution however have asked you, that if the facts should be proved, you should pass upon them; although they may not support the conclusion drawn from them in these accusations. But let us not anticipate the defence.

These are the charges in the general; in their details some of them are too odious, some of them too ridiculous, and all of them too worthless, to be entitled to a serious reply. But before this highly honorable court, composed of men of character, and who therefore may fairly be presumed to know the value of character—that jewel of the soul, which when once lost never can be regained in its original lustre—before such men, I say, the respondent is willing to lay open the whole volume of his life, and to expose all its blots and its erasures. Perfection in man is not to be expected, as it never has been and never can be attained; but so far as regards purity of motive, and an honest exercise of those intellectual faculties, which the God of nature gave him; and which should therefore be a subject of gratitude rather than boast—so far, through me, he challenges the strictest and severest ordeal. Prior to entering upon our answer to

those charges, to which I have thus generally adverted,
I must be permitted to observe, that there is one difficulty
which we would most sincerely deprecate on this occasion; arising from the indefinite character of some of the
charges, and the remoteness of time to which they relate.
But however embarrassing those circumstances might
prove against the wicked or the weak, they have no
terrors for us. We are so strongly armed in honesty, that
we defy the confederated powers of darkness (at least before this judicious and enlightened tribunal), to cast upon
the respondent a shadow of suspicion of moral or official
impropriety. That he may have failings we shall not
deny; it is the lot of man. That he may have frequently erred, it is not necessary to dispute; it is the
privilege of nature, and by nature it shall be excused if
it cannot be justified. In addition to the difficulty, thus
merely intimated, there is another; I refer to the manner
in which the testimony for the prosecution has been introduced, and the frequent interlocutory appeals on the
part of the honorable managers. Turn to your notes,
Mr. President, and you will perceive, that in the introduction of this testimony—I say not from what cause—
no order has been consulted, except the order of inverse
proportion; no consistency regarded, no legal propriety
respected; but all matters have been heterogeneously
jumbled together in an inextricable and interminable
chaos, from which nothing but divine inspiration—which
I may be permitted to say, has not been sufficiently consulted by our adversaries in the institution of these proceedings—can possibly redeem them. Light may, it is
true, issue from darkness; order may spring from confusion; but the light that shall shine on the darkness of
guilt, would serve only to expose its horrors and deformities; and the order that springs from confusion, is calculated to unfold that which was intended to be concealed.
There is still another circumstance of embarrassment in
this matter, although I admit it is scarcely a subject of

complaint, inasmuch as it naturally arises from the situation of the respondent. I mean the fact of those persons who are arrayed against him, having in the matters to which their testimony mainly refers, been the losing parties; or at least having their professional feelings wounded, by unsuccessful professional efforts. This, I say, is natural, but it is not the less to be regretted in its operation on this cause. Like the wife of the great Julius, the motives of testimony should not only be spotless—as for the most part, I heartily believe upon this occasion they are—but they should be exempt from the taint of suspicion. Man, in his best estate is fallible; reason is weak; and passion powerful; and it requires no ghost come from the grave to tell us, which is to be the subsidiary of the other. We all know that it is no easy matter for counsel themselves, even in their best efforts, to satisfy the desires of their clients, where those efforts prove unsuccessful—and it is certainly still less to be supposed that a judge however impartial, or a jury however just, whose duty it is to determine between conflicting parties, can afford satisfaction to both. Judges therefore have only to satisfy the dictates of their own hearts, and whatever may be their penalties and sufferings, the consciousness of unerring moral rectitude shall bear them through them all.

Having adverted to the difficulty encountered from the cause and character of the prosecution's testimony, I will now call your attention to the remarks of the counsel in his opening, and then conclude by submitting to you a general outline of our defence; reserving it for the testimony, as connected with our answers to the charges, to supply the lights and shades, and more particular features of the cause.

It is said, and although not exactly compatible with the character of an opening, I deem it my duty to refer to it; as, if proper to be asserted, it is worthy of notice in reply; that sufficient time has not been afforded to the honorable managers and their counsel for that elaborate preparation,which,according to his views,the case appears to require. No! Why not? Have we not had adjournment upon adjournment for the accommodation of the gentlemen? Were not these charges preferred twelve months ago, against the honorable respondent? And were not the seeds of this iniquitous harvest, sown—as appears by the proof—nearly nine years since, by some of the prosecutors? And still is it not *ripe?* But I agree with the gentleman; notwithstanding all this, the time allotted them has been insufficient. But it is not the fault of the Senate—it is the fault of the CAUSE.

Will they ask time to reanimate the dead—to impart the rose of health to the wan cheek of consumption?—to cause the tottering and feeble limbs of age to knit with strength, and feel a second youth? In short to do anything most hopeless and impossible? Why then they may crave time to give shape and strength, and form, and feature, to this ricketty and misbegotten offspring of malice and persecution.

It is said too by the counsel, I quote his very language, that "this trial has been urged with very considerable strictness." Who talks of urgency and strictness? Does the respondent? Dragged from his peaceful fireside— from the bosom of an affectionate and endearing family— in a word, from his domestic gods; not loaded with chains, it is true, like a common malefactor, but with worse, an imputation of crime—Does he complain of strictness—of urgency—of severity? No! It is his accusers. Those who have thus brought him hither.

Thus much I owed to the vindication of this honorable court—to the dignity and justice of the commonwealth.

The counsel has also thought proper to speak of his candor and impartiality. Alas! with him it was but a barren and a fruitless theme. For my part I profess no impartiality upon such an occasion. I cannot sir,—I cannot be impartial when I behold an aged servant of the commonwealth buffeting the billows of adversity, and confronting the storm ; not for his *life*, his country shall have that, but for the preservation of the pearl of great price, his jewelled reputation; without which *life* is a burthen, and the world a waste. I say in contemplating such a scene I cannot be impartial. Nay, more, I never shall envy the feelings of that man, who can patiently behold a struggle so glorious as this and—in the consciousness of his own self-security—cant coldly of the sublime virtue of inflexible impartiality.

But, sir, to return to the facts of the case.

In explanation of the defence: the lucidness, ability and accuracy, with which the facts connected with this case, are detailed in the answers to the charges, read to you on behalf of the respondent, have left me but little to say.

The first article charged, relates to the circumstances attending the case of Seitzinger *v.* Zeller, in the Common Pleas of Berks county. We shall explain and qualify certain parts of this article. We will show that Judge Porter was obliged to preside, in consequence of the affinity of one of his associates to one of the .parties interested. That Judge Witman was a relative to Daniel H. Otto, one of the creditors of Zeller. We shall show you that Marks J. Biddle, Esq., is in error, as to more than one circumstance, in that case. That he never discussed the case before the referee, as he has stated he did. That he did not ask the judge to retire, or say anything from which it could be inferred he did not wish him to sit. That at least, if he did make the observation to which he has testified, Judge Porter, did not hear it. That it was not heard by either Judge Witman or Judge Snyder, who were on the bench; by Mr. Smith or Mr. Hayes, who were concerned in the cause, and were at the council table at the time; or by Gen. Addams, the Prothonotary, who sat at his desk between Mr. Biddle and Judge Porter. But even if the observation had been heard by Judge Porter, I by no means admit that he was bound to retire on Mr. Biddle's request.

In regard to the second article, relative to the lecture given to the gambling-house keepers—Beidleman, Young and Haberacker, at Allentown; we shall adduce but little evidence, because the facts alleged, with one or two exceptions, are admitted. We will prove very conclusively that the words "villains" or "scoundrels" were not applied to them by Judge Porter; that if those terms still ring in the ears of those persons, it was their consciences, and not Judge Porter, that applied the epithet to them.

As to the third article, it will appear that the facts set forth in our answer are true. That so far from the judge becoming a volunteer in the transaction, he was informed by both parties, that it was a mere trifling matter of quarrel between neighbors, as it really was. But as soon as he discovered the nature of the prosecution, which was disclosed to him by Justice Weygandt, he said nothing more in relation to it; and on the trial of the accused before him a few days after, she was convicted and sentenced for the larceny.

The fourth article refers to the trial of the case of the Commonwealth *v.* John Mill. It will appear that there was no ground for the prosecution. That after hearing all the evidence, it was discovered by the counsel and the court, that no larceny had been committed. The counsel thereupon arranged the matter, by securing the prosecutor's demand, which had been the original cause of the institution of the prosecution.

The fifth article alleges improper conduct in the respondent, in the case of Wannemacher *v.* Sechler. In that case Judge Porter charged the jury, that as the defendant had pleaded guilty and submitted—in the *indictment* found against him for the same assault and battery—the plaintiff was entitled to a verdict for something; but what the amount should be, was left, as it should have been, exclusively to the jury to determine. The jury disregarding the charge thus given—which was the settled law of the land—most improperly found a verdict for the defendant; and the court—as they had a right to do—granted a new trial. Courts have their rights; and the safety of our institutions depend on their preservation. It would seem, however, from the doctrine now advanced, that juries have a right to trample on the rights of the court with perfect impunity: and if their actions, no matter how improper, are attempted to be controlled by the court, the judge is to be forthwith charged before the Legislature, and subjected to an impeachment for high crimes and misdemeanors! We will show that a motion was made, by the plaintiff's counsel, for a new trial. ,And had no such motion been made, the court possessed the right to grant the new trial, *instanter;* and the judge would have deserved credit for so doing. The jury have no right in civil cases to take upon themselves the decision of the law. The judge did not make use of the expressions charged against him, nor was there any violence or impropriety in his manner. There is certainly an error of impression in regard to this matter. The respectable gentleman who was counsel in the cause for the defendant, was much excited at the time, as he himself states; and is therefore unable to detail the circumstances with that correctness which would, under other circumstances, have been expected from him.

In relation to the sixth article, which impugns the respondent's conduct in regard to the case of Hays *v.* Bellas, we will show, that the words contained in this " article " were actually used in the charge delivered to the jury; and that the judge did not know of the charge having been filed, when he made the interlineation. In reference to the marginal note on the bill of exceptions; we will prove, that it was written on the bill of exceptions before it was signed and sealed by the judge; that it was according to the fact as it occurred; that there was such an agreement between the counsel made, as is there stated ;- that it was so understood by the court: and that therefore the judge was right in making the correction before he put his seal to the bill of exceptions, and would have been criminal had he not done so.

The seventh article charges the respondent with a refusal to reduce his opinions to writing when required so to do.

As to the first branch of his accusation—the case of Helfrich and Grim *v.* Seip's Administrators—if such a request was made by the plaintiff's counsel, it was not heard by the court. It was not heard by Mr. Smith, the attorney general, who was concerned for the defendants, who will detail certain other matters which occurred subsequently in the case, which will put it beyond question, that such an application could not have been made.

In regard to the case of Schwenk *v.* Ebert, it will appear that a mere intimation was given that the plaintiff's counsel was desirous of having the case reviewed, if it should be deemed necessary ; that this intimation was not followed up by any subsequent application to the judge: and that in truth every fact in the case, necessary to its being fully understood, in the court above, had a revision been had, appeared on the record of the cause.

As to the eighth article, if it should be pressed, we will prove the facts averred in the answer thereto, now on your desks. And upon that proof being made we can have no fear as to your decision upon it.

The ninth, tenth and eleventh articles have relation to the conduct of Judges Porter and Cooper towards each other. In regard to the ninth, we will show that the boy Smith was really sick; that humanity called for his discharge; that the court could not sever the sentence of the two defendants; that Judge Cooper's resistance of the application was as unnatural as it was rude ; that if Judge Porter was betrayed into any warmth of expression, it was but human nature expressing its natural feelings, and therefore is rather a matter of praise than of accusation. And permit me here to observe, that this, as well as some of the other articles of accusation, instead of being matter of impeachment, are proud plumes in the respondent's character.

As to the other two articles, the tenth and eleventh, we shall exhibit to you the testimony of some *disinterested* witnesses, who will detail the circumstances as they occurred, accurately: and if they will not entirely justify, they will at least fully excuse the respondent's conduct; and show you, that in pointing out the *mote* in our eye, Judge Cooper forgot the *beam* in his own. We will show you that a disposition to dictate and to arrogate, has uniformly characterized that gentleman's conduct on the bench, which if not submitted to, would uniformly find vent, if not in paroxysms of anger, in at least rudeness and ungentlemanly conduct, calculated to irritate and offend his fellow judges.

In addition to all this we will show; in answer to the charge of corruption, which will be found laid in several of the articles, that the respondent has uniformly maintained an unsullied reputation for honesty of motive and integrity of character.

And having satisfied you of these facts in way of qualification or explanation of the charges preferred; after having briefly submitted to you our views of the case, we shall rely upon this distinguished court, for a prompt and honorable acquittal.

ARGUMENT IN

IMPEACHMENT OF JUDGE PORTER.

WITH DEFERENCE TO THIS HONORABLE COURT:

Enfeebled and exhausted as I am, by the protracted investigation of this cause, I arise to address this honorable court, not in the vain expectation that I shall be able fully to discharge my duty and do justice to the subject of inquiry; but in the hope that by those efforts which I shall bring to bear on the matter which has so long occupied your attention, I shall at least partially discharge my duty, and thereby facilitate the performance of yours. I shall endeavor to treat the respectable counsel for the managers with that courtesy which is his due; and I wish in the observations which I shall make, as far as possible, to separate the counsel from the case in which he has voluntarily embarked. Should that, however, be impossible, if he has taken his passage in a vessel which is unseaworthy, let him take his fate; I never can nor will permit my feelings, or my wishes to prevent me from a rigid performance of duty.

Never, allow me to say, did a more important question than that which now occupies your attention, employ that of a State or Nation. The object of our convention, on the question of national liberty, was not, in point of importance, of greater interest than this. The achievement of liberty itself was not of greater moment to our fathers, than its careful preservation is to us. What, sir, is liberty, when it is not found on its march hand in hand with justice? The moment you sully the ermine of justice you take from liberty itself, all its valuable properties—you cease to live in a land of laws, and have no more security for the enjoyment of your rights than the savage who roams the wilderness.

To say, therefore, that I approach this discussion with diffidence, is to say only what I am sure will be readily believed. I cannot as has been done by the opposite counsel, boast that I represent the majesty of the people; but I advocate the majesty of justice—the supremacy of the laws—without which the majesty of the people is an idle tale—"a barren theme, an airy sceptre grasped in sleep." It is not merely in respect to the honorable respondent who is upon his trial, that this case is important; but to the country at large and to posterity. The example of this day shall stand recorded as a blessing -or a curse, to those whom you now represent, and to those who shall follow you. If you regard the welfare of the public, if you desire the streams of justice to flow pure and untainted, let your determination be established and placed imperishably upon record, by your decision this day. The cause is one of magnitude in point of principle. To the respondent the result of this investigation is a matter of anxiety; to the commonwealth also, although in a less degree: he has suffered from being unjustly accused; the commonwealth suffers in the suffering of each of her citizens. When the good suffer in the cause of justice, the commonwealth cannot be indifferent. The struggle of the respondent is not for station or for life—it is for reputation, which—although at his advanced period of life, it cannot be long enjoyed—yet is dear to him still as a parent, descending as a rich legacy to his issue. "The purest treasure mortal times afford is spotless reputation." Character may aptly be compared to a fair and fragile flower, that blooms only and exhales its fragrance while surrounded by a pure and wholesome and heavenly atmosphere; the moment it is assailed by the poisonous breath of calumny it withers, pines and dies.

The respondent does not merely ask at your hands, that after a lingering deliberation, he be cleared of the accusations; but he asks, that this court shall join in a solemn lustration of his character. For months, nay for years has he been held forth to the world, as a sort of byword and reproach. I have before said, and I repeat it, that this is not a prosecution originated by the House of Representatives, but by individuals. That it is not instituted upon the suggestions of public justice, but for the gratification of private malevolence. I will nevertheless drag these accusers from their lurking places, and exhibit them to the merited contempt and abhorrence of a virtuous community. How salutary often is the lesson to be drawn from vice! While virtue is ever open as she is honest; vice seeks the covert and concealment and would cloak its cloven foot in modesty. Alas! the effort never can avail. Mountains may cover, seas may hide the guilty, but the arm of justice shall still fathom their retreat. Let them dive if they will into Tartarian darkness; the radiant eye of truth shall beam upon them and exhibit them, in all their naked deformity, to the indignation of a hissing world! Such I will show you are the prime movers of this nefarious scheme—such are those who would be prosecutors in this case, but who are now in truth actually at your bar, morally at least, as respondents—these are they who, by way of promoting the equality of man, would reduce the respondent from the height of well earned reputation, to their own vile level.

Not to anticipate, sir, I propose in the first place to reply to the ingenious counsel for the managers; and, secondly, to call the attention of the court to the articles of impeachment, having particular reference to the respective charges; and here permit me to return my thanks to that learned gentleman for the many compliments, ill deserved as I fear most of them are, which he has been

pleased to bestow upon my humble self. If he really be
that admirer of eloquence which he professes, he must be
truly a happy man ; for he has always the source of his own
gratification within himself. But to return to the notice
of his arguments. I might admit every principle which
he has advanced as law; and still stand unshaken as the
foundations of this noble edifice. What is the position
he has assumed—touch it with Ithuriel's magic spear, and
see its character.

The gentleman has advanced as one of his principles—
although he seemed to say that its discussion was not a
matter of great materiality in the present issue—that
matters might be *impeachable* which would not be *indictable.* It is not necessary to controvert this proposition for the purposes of our defence; but I do protest
against such a doctrine being established as the law of
the land. It is at war with the Constitution, with the
law, and all the decisions upon the subject. The case of
the Commonwealth *v.* Wilson, to which the counsel clings,
with as much desperation as does the shipwrecked mari-
ner to some chance-found plank, so far from bearing him
out in his doctrine, defeats him in it. Judge Duncan, in
fact, lays down the law, that the offence charged against
the defendant, in that case, " was impeachable *because it
was indictable.*"

He has, moreover, referred to cases of impeachment in
England. There is one important feature which distin-
guishes the practice in England upon these subjects, from
that which obtains in this country. There, the individual
impeached, if guilty, is subjected not only to the loss of
his office, but to be punished criminally for his offence;
and that, too, by the same sentence. Here it is otherwise. If the honorable respondent be guilty, your sentence may deprive him of his office; but it cannot deprive him of his liberty or inflict upon him criminal
punishment. The Constitution of the United States provides that:—" The impeachment of the President, Vice

President or any other officer of the United States, shall
not prevent, in case of conviction, their trials before
courts of criminal law." Con. U. S., art. 2, sec. IV ; art.
1, sec. III, 7. The authorities, therefore, drawn from
cases in England, are not applicable here; and they are
by no means calculated to prove, what the counsel endeavored to show by them, that offences which are not
indictable may be impeachable. The clause in the constitution of our own State, which has been more than
once referred to, establishes the contrary ; for if we are
to understand that the offences therein contemplated
were indictable offences, it was idle and silly—and, indeed, worse than both—to point out the mode in which
the offender was subsequently to be tried. " The party,
whether convicted or acquitted, shall nevertheless be
liable to *indictment, trial, judgment* and *punishment*, according to law." But we are told that the Constitution
of Pennsylvania does not mean anything but a *misdemeanor in office*—granted. But what is a misdemeanor ?
The gentleman says it signifies misbehavior, and *mere*
misbehavior. According to his interpretation it means
any *faux pas*. In truth, he says it means any "error." If
this be the legal doctrine, sir, why have we courts of ap-
pellate jurisdiction ? To what purpose or with what intent have we established a Supreme Court ? The law
knew that man, even in his judicial station, was liable to
err in judgment, and therefore provided courts of error
for the revision of judgments of inferior tribunals. But
if what we now hear is law, let judges beware ; for every
reversal of their judgment in the Supreme Court will
furnish ground for an article of accusation and impeachment against them.

When I speak of a legal term I speak of it as a lawyer ;
and as a lawyer I understand misdemeanor to signify any
public offence, less than felony, for which a man may be
indicted. The moment you give any other than a legal
signification to a legal term, to suit the views of a rotten

cause, there is an end to liberty and law. We should be much at a loss to know to what length the doctrine of the gentleman would carry us.

Misbehavior is a very flexible term—you may bend it to suit what you please; it varies as the mind varies, or, what is perhaps still more capricious, as the manners change. Suppose any judicial officer, in opposition to the habits of the present day, should think proper to retain his hat upon his head, instead of remaining uncovered; this might not be exactly consistent with the gentleman's ideas of good breeding; this, in other words, might be misbehavior, but it is not a misdemeanor. It is not indictable; and, therefore, is not impeachable. A misdemeanor is a criminal offence; a criminal offence proceeds from a corrupted heart; sin is the offspring of the heart; and there is no authority to be found, either in law or in ethics, to punish a man for the mere fallibility of the head. Misbehavior does not mean misdemeanor. Would the commission of an assault and battery by an officer, during the tenure of an office, be a misdemeanor in *office*, for which he would be impeachable?

There is a difference between the Constitution of Pennsylvania and that of the United States, in regard to the mode of removing civil officers. In the former, besides the provision already stated, that "all civil officers shall be liable to impeachment for any misdemeanor in office," there is another provision which declares " that the judges of the Supreme Court and of the several courts of Common Pleas shall hold their offices during good behavior, but for *any reasonable cause, which shall not be sufficient ground of impeachment,* the Governor may remove any of them on the address of two-thirds of each branch of the Legislature." In the latter there is no such provision. Under it the judges hold their offices during good behavior, and all civil officers are liable " to be removed from office on impeachment for, and conviction of, treason, bribery, or other high crimes and misdemeanors."

Under this provision in the Constitution of Pennsylvania, the matter is rendered perfectly plain.   What is the purpose of the provision for removal for reasonable cause, which shall not be sufficient ground for impeachment? If the gentleman be correct in his views, they are entirely superfluous ; since, if the first provision embraces all sorts of misbehavior, from the highest crime to the merest peccadilloes, there is nothing upon which the latter clause can act.   I tell you, sir, that removal, by address, is the remedy intended for the lesser evils, and impeachment is that which is designed for indictable offences ; and there is no other mode in which those constitutional provisions can be reconciled with each other, or with themselves. The one is intended as the remedy for *crime*, the other for *misbehavior* not amounting to crime,—such was the intention of the framers of the constitution ; and had this not been their view of the subject, they would have made the latter clause of the third section, 4th article, read : " the party whether convicted or acquitted shall nevertheless be liable to indictment, trial, judgment and punishment according to law, *where the offences are indictable in their character.*"

To show that I am not singular in my views on this subject, I will cite Judge Chase's trial.   Not the argument of Mr. Nicholson, which is merely speculative theory ; and was unsanctioned either by precedent or by the decision of the court in that case : but the opinion of Luther Martin, that giant of the law, with whom the court accorded in opinion.   Mr. Martin, pages 137–40 of the trial says " I shall now proceed in the inquiry ; for what can the President, Vice President, or other civil officers ; and consequently, for what can a judge, be impeached ?   And I shall contend that it must be for an *indictable* offence.   The words of the constitution are, that ' they shall be liable to impeachment for treason, bribery or *other high* crimes and misdemeanors.'

" There can be no doubt but that treason and bribery

are indictable offences." We have only to inquire then, what is meant by *high* crimes and misdemeanors. What is the true meaning of the word "*crime?*" It is the breach of some law, which renders the person, who violates it, liable to punishment. There can be no crime committed where no such law is violated. The honorable gentleman, to whom I before alluded, has cited the new edition of Jacob's Law Dictionary: let us then look into that authority, for the true meaning of the word "misdemeanor." He tells us—

"*Misdemesnor or misdesmeanour, a crime less than felony. The term misdemeanor is generally used in contradistinction to felony, and comprehends all indictable offences, which do not amount to felony, as perjury, libels, conspiracies, assaults,*" *&c.* See 4 Comm. chap. 1, p. 5.

"*A crime or misdemeanor*" *says Blackstone,* "*is an act committed or omitted in violation of a public law, either forbidding or commanding it. This general definition comprehends both crimes and misdemeanors, which properly speaking are mere synonymous terms: though in common usage, the word 'crimes' is made use of to denote such offences as are of a deeper and more atrocious dye; while smaller faults, and omissions of less consequence, are comprised under the gentle name of misdemeanor only.*"

"In making the distinction between public wrongs and private, between crimes and misdemeanors and civil injuries, the same author observes, that '*public wrongs, or crimes and misdemeanors are a breach and violation of the public rights and duties, due to the whole community considered as a community in its social, aggregate capacity.*' 4 Comm. 5.

"Thus it appears, crimes and misdemeanors are the violation of a law, exposing the person to punishment: and are used in contradistinction to those breaches of law, which are mere private injuries, and only entitle the injured to a civil remedy."

"Blackstone's Commentaries, 4 vol. p. 5th is cited by

Jacob, and is as there stated. I shall not turn to it. Hale, in his pleas of the crown, volume first, in his *Præmium*, which is not paged, speaking of the division of crimes, says,

"*Temporal crimes, which are offences against the laws of this realm, whether the common law, or acts of Parliament, are divided into two general ranks or distributions in respect to the punishments that are by law appointed for them, or in respect of their nature or degree ; and thus they may be divided into capital offences, or offences only criminal, or rather and more properly into felonies and misdemeanors, and the same distribution is to be made touching misdemeanors, namely, they are such as are so by the common law, or such as are specially made punishable as misdemeanors by acts of Parliament.*"

"Thus then it appears, that crimes and misdemeanors are generally used as synonymous expressions ; except that 'crimes' is a word frequently used for *higher* offences. But while I contend that a judge cannot be impeached, except for a crime or misdemeanor, I also contend that there are many crimes and misdemeanors for which a judge ought not to be impeached, unless immediately relating to his judicial conduct. Let us suppose that a judge provoked by insolence, should strike a person : this certainly would be an *indictable*, but not an *impeachable* offence. The offence for which a judge is liable to impeachment, must not only be a crime or misdemeanor but a *high* crime or misdemeanor. The word 'crime' as distinguished from misdemeanor, is applied to offences of a more aggravated nature. The word ' *high*,' therefore, must certainly equally apply to misdemeanors and to crimes. Nay, sir, I am ready to go further, and say, there may be instances of *very high* crimes and misdemeanors, for which an officer ought not to be impeached, and removed from office. The crimes ought to be such as relate to his office, or which tend to cover the person, who committed them, with *turpitude* and *infamy:* such as show there can be no dependence on that integrity and honor which will secure the performance of his official duties."

" But we have been told, and the authority of the State of Pennsylvania has been cited by one honorable manager (Mr. Rodney), in support of the position; that a judge may be impeached, convicted, and removed from office, for that which is not indictable—for that which is not a violation of any law."

" What, sir, can a judge be impeached and deprived of office, when he has done nothing which the laws of his country prohibited? Is not deprivation of office a punishment? can there be punishment inflicted where there is no crime? Suppose the House of Representatives to impeach, for conduct not *criminal;* the Senate to convict; doth that change the law? No, the law can only be changed by a bill brought forward by one House *in a certain manner; assented* to by the other ; *and approved by the President.* Impeachment and conviction cannot change the law, and make that *punishable* which was not *before criminal.*"

In considering the term "high" used in the Constitution of the United States, the gentleman seemed at a loss to understand its meaning. It is a term used by sovereign governments; and its legal effect is very satisfactorily explained in the extract which I have just read. The gentleman has suggested the case of "fatuity." It was an unfortunate case. I meet him on his own grounds, and I deny everything like authority under the laws to proceed in such cases by impeachment; for errors of the head must be remedied by "address," when they will be probably destructive in their consequences. Impeachment rests upon the errors of the heart alone; and the case from 10th Sergeant & Rawle, instead of overthrowing, supports this idea. Judge Duncan did not therein determine, as he could not have determined, that the offence was not impeachable. He merely decided that it was indictable.

The case of Judge Pickering, cited, is a mere abstract of the proceedings referred to in an elementary treatise—we have not the details, nor if we had, could the decision in the Senate of the United States, under the Constitution of the United States, alter the law or the Constitution of Pennsylvania.

The same observation—that they are mere abstracts—taken in connection with the observations heretofore made on the authority of British precedents in cases of this kind, will apply to the cases of Lord Bacon, the Duke of Buckingham and Lord Finch, with this answer to the gentleman's question; that bribery and the corrupt purchase and sale of offices, charged against Lord Bacon and the Duke of Buckingham, are indictable offences.

But the opposite counsel infers from the case in 10th Sergeant & Rawle, that the offences contained in these articles of impeachment, or the greater part of them at least, are indictable; and consequently impeachable: which leads me to the consideration of this, his second position. In reply to that, I in the first place say, that the two positions of the counsel are mutually destructive, or at all events imply a want of confidence in the mind that suggested them; for, if the offences are impeachable, though not indictable, why occupy your time in the attempt to show that these offences charged, as contended, are indictable? Why engage in a laborious effort to show that, which is alone necessary to be shown, in case the law were otherwise.

Let us now turn our attention to the remarks of the counsel, brief as they were, upon the different charges, in the order in which they are exhibited. After all the display which was made on the other side of professed candor and impartiality and frankness, has a single charge been abandoned, until we bearded the prosecutors in their den? True, when we were calling our witness to the bar, then and not until then, was the 8th article abandoned, and it is the only one which has been withdrawn. The 12th article, although not urged, has not been abandoned. But, sir, as to the 1st article which we have swept from its foundation, the counsel passes over it simply by saying that he would not rely upon any particular law to support it, but upon the law generally. This reminds me of what a learned gentleman once called "amplifying to a point." If I understand the rules laid down by the honorable court for the government of its proceedings; upon the conclusion of the testimony, the argument upon the part of the commonwealth was first to be made, and then the argument on the part of the respondent; and in conclusion, the reply on behalf of the commonwealth. Under this view of the subject, I was entitled surely, to the gentleman's argument on the case, in order to enable me to answer, if necessary. He has the advantage of the conclusion, and the reason why he was required to sum up first, is, that he may lay down the legal principles at least, upon which he rests his case, that they may be open to the observation of the succeeding counsel. I can fight a wind-mill, sir, because it is visible and tangible; but I cannot fight the wind by which it is driven. If, however, upon the present occasion, he knows no particular principle upon which he can rest this part of a sickly cause, I hope I shall be able to satisfy even him, that there are many principles upon which it can be resisted.

In reference to the second article, we are told that the rights of personal liberty are sacred. That the judge had no right or authority to arrest Beidleman, Young and Haberacker; and that his having so done, was an official misdemeanor. I am not now discussing these articles. I am merely glancing at them in a hasty review of the gentleman's arguments. But for the present, my answer is, that there never was any arrest. If, instead of reading authority upon authority, to show what is a legal, and what an illegal arrest; the gentleman had established that there had been an arrest, it would have been much more satisfactory. Everybody who invites a gentleman to a party, would be guilty of an arrest, according to the counsel's new version of the law. But, sir, it is abusing the time and patience of the court, to dwell longer upon it; and I shall pass from it, observing that the course of the opposite counsel reminds me very strongly of a circumstance which is alleged to have taken place in the time of Charles II. That merry monarch, it is said, with a view of selecting one of the wisest men in his kingdom for some special purpose, called together most of the learned of the realm, and proposed to them this question, "What is the reason, that in placing a fish in a bucket full of water, the water still will not overflow?" A variety of reasons were suggested by the candidates for royal favor, all very ingenious, no doubt, until at last the King put the inquiry to a sagacious Scot, who replied, "I deny the fact, your Highness;" and the Scot was right. I will leave it to my friend on the other side of the question, and the members of this court, to apply the story. I deny the fact, as alleged by the opposite counsel, and until it is established, time is too precious to discuss the empty theory alone.

As to the third and fourth articles, which have been jumbled together in their consideration by the counsel; and in relation to which, we have had an ingenious dissertation upon the ancient doctrine of *theft-bote;* it is not necessary for me to say more at this time, than that the fact of compounding, or attempting to compound a felony, is not made out. In one of the articles, he is charged with attempting to induce a magistrate to violate his duty. Although this is also wholly unsupported by proof, it would seem that in view of the prosecution, there is no difference between the act itself, and the attempt to do the act.

The law in regard to these matters is well settled. It is no subject of dispute. Every tyro knows what constitutes larceny, and what is the meaning of compounding a

felony. And every man who contemplates with an un-
jaundiced eye, the features of this case, so far as relates
to those articles, must at once perceive that the case is
not brought within the provisions of the law. If all the
facts alleged in those charges were true, it would not
avail the prosecution. It is therefore unnecessary for me,
untrue as they are in all material points, to attempt establishing the invalidity of this portion of the accusation.

All the remaining charges appear to me to be similarly
circumstanced; either the facts, if true, do not support
the conclusion attempted to be drawn from them; or the
facts alleged are untrue, and of course the conclusion falls.

This case is said by the opposite counsel to be in the
nature of a criminal prosecution. What does this mean?
I understand it to signify that it is a case in which the
same principles and rules must govern, as in cases of indictments at common law. I ask for nothing more. For
this doctrine is in the teeth of three-fourths of the arguments to which you have listened this morning. Suppose
the case of an indictment for larceny, would it not be
necessary that the word *feloniously* should be introduced;
or could the prosecuting counsel succeed upon merely
proving that the goods were taken? Certainly not. If
so, any member of this honorable court may be convicted
of larceny, either for taking his own hat, or that of
another, through mistake. It is essentially necessary
that the indictment should set forth the facts, and should
set forth the motive; and in returning your verdict, you
cannot find the one without the other. I lay it down
to be a principle, which alike governs human and divine
tribunals; that no man can be guilty of a crime, where it
does not clearly appear, that the act from which the crime
is attempted to be inferred, was *intentionally* committed.
In the present case, therefore, it is not enough that facts
should be found, although there we are thrice armed; but
you must find the legal conclusion also, which goes to the
establishment of corruption of heart. These remarks are

particularly applicable to the case of Hays *v.* Bellas, contained in the sixth article, which imputes forgery to the honorable respondent. But as it is my design fully to discuss these articles in their order, I will not now occupy the time of this honorable court, in more particularly referring to them. The system which I have prescribed to myself, and which I now merely mention to facilitate the comprehension of my views, is this: *First*, I shall consider the case, as exhibited by the prosecution; and *secondly*, by the defence. Under the former of those two heads, I shall advert to the charges as contained in the articles, and to the charges as established by the proof. Under the latter general division, I shall refer to the answers of the respondent, and to the evidence by which they are supported.

The first article charges the respondent with official impropriety in the case from Berks county, of Seitzinger *v.* Zeller. And here, permit me to observe one circumstance in this prosecution which is not a little remarkable; and which is calculated to excite feelings little short of superstition; and it is this: the first name which ought to have been uttered in this prosecution; that of him who has been the prime mover of all this mischief; he who, to use a simile borrowed from his own vile vocation, has *shuffled* every other witness in turn to the top of the *pack*, and with his characteristic *modesty* has kept himself on the back ground; I say, this name is—after a ten days' investigation—the last word uttered by the last of the witnesses examined in the cause—JACOB W. SEITZINGER!!! He, sir, who battened on the public for weeks during the last session; he who has regularly been called every day since this court has been in session, and regularly *answered* to his name; he, sir, who hired counsel before the committee of investigation, and who, it would seem, was to carry counsel, committee, commonwealth, and all, on his Atlantean shoulders; who is alleged to be particularly interested in the matters referred to in the first charge, never condescends to appear in person as a witness:—Nay, so successfully does he seek to conceal himself under the mantle of ill affected modesty; that it is not until the last moment of the testimony, and then, not without great reluctance on the part of his friend and confidant (Mr. Bellas), that we are able to identify him with this nefarious plot—a plot against the respondent and the State. Here then, I arraign you—Jacob W. Seitzinger, Hugh Ross, and Henry Jarrett—as public conspirators; the first, as principal, the two last, as accessaries before the fact.

Let me, without proceeding further upon so odious a theme, direct the attention of this honorable court, to the more particular subject of inquiry.

The first article after setting forth the matters of complaint, concludes: "Thus wilfully and corruptly denying a citizen the right of having justice administered to him without sale, denial or delay." These are very pretty, specious, high sounding words, picked out of Purdon's Digest for the occasion, to round off this elegant and classically written specimen of legal and literary erudition. "Sale," of what? "Barter!" for what? I should like, soberly to inquire, what has appeared in the whole of the evidence, like inducement to the respondent to act otherwise than fairly and honestly? I agree, if you please—and it is according all that can be required at my hands—that sacrifices are frequently made by men in elevated situations, to objects altogether insignificant and disproportionate in point of consequence or character. Doctor Dodd, we are told, surrendered all regard for his character, his family, his friends; and meanly consented to become a worshipper at the shrine of Mammon, "that least erected spirit that fell;" Lord Chancellor Bacon, "the greatest, wisest, meanest of mankind," sacrificed the mighty space of his large honors "for so much gold as might be grasped thus!"—Nay, not to confine ourselves to the corrupted currents of more moderate times; Esau sold his birth-right for a mess of pottage—and to sum up all, Judas, the traitor Judas, basely bartered the Saviour of the world for " thirty pieces." But *this* it seems—in opposition to everything like reason, like reputation, like example—is a *sale* forsooth, without purchaser or price. Is it, or can it be supposed, that the honorable respondent, whose character for honesty and integrity has been emphatically admitted to be without spot and without blemish, would immolate himself, destroy his reputation, and entail infamy on his family, without motive—without inducement?

Is there " denial? " why, the very complaint is, that he adjudged the cause. Is his judgment erroneous?— why has it not been reviewed in the Superior Court. Has there been " delay ?"—the objection is, that he would not delay. Let these terms then be wafted on the idle air for proper company. But, take every fact alleged in the article to be fully sustained by proof; admit it to its utmost extent, yet the prosecuting counsel could not sustain it as matter of impeachment. As well might he attempt to swim with fins of lead, or hew down oak with rushes. (Here Mr. B. read the whole article.) He never could have hoped to sustain it—the article in its composition is about as legal as it is classical. There is no offence or impropriety alleged, which has a particle of truth in it; and if it were all true, I care not.

I admit that he presided on the argument, upon the exceptions filed to his report, in the case of Seitzinger *v.* Zeller. I admit that he had previously, with reluctance, consented to serve as a referee; and that he reported every farthing that was due to the plaintiff. I deny that he was requested to leave the bench when the argument came on. Mr. Baird could not say whether the expression of Mr. Biddle " that Judge Porter could not sit, or ought not to sit," was intended for the ear of the judge, or a mere intimation to himself. Mr. Smith, Mr. Hayes, Gen. Addams, and the two associates did not hear it. Mr. Biddle, it is true, says, "I mentioned to Judge Porter that it was our wish that he should not sit;" and "I have every reason to believe he heard it." But, sir, he is mistaken in saying he addressed the observation to Judge Porter; or why would not some one else have heard it. If, however, he *did;* his enunciation at best is indistinct, and there is every reason to presume that it was not heard by the respondent. But, if it had been distinctly and openly addressed to the judge, and as distinctly heard by him, I care not a feather. It cannot affect or injure the respondent. Has it come to this, that because one of the parties, or his counsel, requests a judge, whose integrity and stern justice do not suit his views, to leave the bench, that the judge is bound submissively to comply? Are your judges to be made mere puppets, to be shoved on or off the scenes, at the will of the counsel. Sir, had he submitted to this, he would have been culpable. He would have abandoned his duty. He then would not have been "administering justice without denial or delay." He was not bound to go; he was bound by the law, and by the obligation of his office which he has sworn to perform with fidelity, to remain on the bench and fearlessly discharge his duty.

But it is alleged, that the judge refused to produce his calculations, on which he founded his report. Suppose he had; no injury was sustained by it—the exceptions to the report, by the rules of the court, must have been filed within four days after the reading of the report. The report in this case was filed, as appears by the record, upon the 15th day of November, 1823. The exceptions were filed upon the 17th day of the same month. The judge was asked for his calculations at August Term, 1824. So that the exceptions had to stand on their own merits; and could not be aided or amended by any statements or calculations produced nine months afterwards. The exceptions were dismissed because they were defective and insufficient.

The respondent did not, however, refuse to give his calculations. Although from having been present and concerned in the cause, I might, with the chaste poet of Mantua, say: "all which I saw, and part of which I was;" yet I will take the evidence adduced before you, as it essentially corresponds with my own recollections. Mr. Biddle does not pretend to say, that the judge refused to give his calculations; but that he alleged that he had not kept any, or had none. Mr. Baird does not say there was any refusal to explain. Mr. Hays says, that "the judge stated he had not preserved his calculations, that he had made them on slips or pieces of paper which he had not kept, *but that he was ready to state the grounds of his report.*" Judge Witman says the same in effect. Judge Schneider says he appeared willing to give them every satisfaction; and Gen. Addams says, that when Mr. Baird said they would be under the necessity of examining the judge, he said he was very willing to be examined.

When the judge came upon the bench, he ceased to be a referee. He was then a judge of the court: bound to decide all questions that legally came before him in his judicial character, in which he was not personally interested—or to the parties to which he was not connected by ties of affinity or consanguinity. The case before the court, to which I have been referring, was not one of those exceptions; and consequently the respondent was bound to sit, and to adjudicate upon it. When a judge of the Supreme Court sits at *nisi prius;* and tries a cause; and a motion is made for a new trial; and the case comes on to be argued in *banc*, the judge always sits on the argument. Nay, more, he always furnishes the facts on which the argument is founded. Such too, was the practice on motions for new trials and appeals, under the old Circuit Court system. But the respondent here had an additional necessity imposed upon him to sit, from the circumstance of his associate (Judge Witman) being the father-in-law of Daniel H. Otto (one of the active creditors in taking defence), who had told him, that in consequence of that relationship, he could not sit upon the argument.

With regard to the institution of these proceedings against the respondent, it would seem that the charges had been slumbering seven or eight years in the tomb of the Capulets. Hugh Ross had taken notes (of that, however, more anon), but I am glad to find that to him—the obliquity of whose moral vision is so notorious—the respondent seemed to act with *impropriety.* For virtue would not be virtue if it received the approbation of vice. But, why do not these charges slumber still? The problem is solved—Seitzinger had obtained a judgment for five or six hundred dollars more than was due him, to the prejudice of the honest creditors of Zellers. *This judgment the respondent reduced to what was honestly due him, to wit:* $576.63, *instead of* $1,100 *claimed.* Seitzinger felt his pocket touched; he breathes revenge; he finds some kindred spirits willing, like himself, to sacrifice the respondent at an *auto de fe.* He communes and consults with Bellas, and with him impeaches the respondent in his absence before the committee last year; and then gets the worthies from Northampton and Lehigh' to join in with him; yet he does not now come forward to testify before you. He has looked within, and fearing that if he made his appearance, all that there rose to his own view would be exposed to the world, he shrunk from the spectacle.

I submit to this honorable court, that this is a trial between the justice of the land, and those who would wield the thunders of the commonwealth for their own vile purposes; and I leave this article thus, with a full conviction that there can be no difficulty in your decision upon it.

The second article is worse, if worse can be, than the first. Can I have read rightly? Is it seriously true, that the respondent is impugned, nay, arraigned, for a high crime and misdemeanor—for doing, what? For reprimanding men who had violated the law in the worst form. But, says the counsel, the arrest, and not the reprimand, is the offence—and is it so? What says the article, "that the said Judge Porter, sitting on the bench in the court, did reprimand and insult, &c., *for suffering gambling in their housse.*" What said the counsel himself but just now. He said "these persons were brought up before the court in public; and exposed to ridicule and contempt; and made a laughing stock to the whole country." And is this honorable court to fight the battles of Beidleman—Young—Haberacker—Scitzinger, and every other gambler in the county or commonwealth? Suppose the respondent had termed them "villains;" he would have but called them by their own right names; but he never used the term. Beidleman alone, was examined as to this part of the charge. He speaks and understands the English language but imperfectly, and could very readily misapprehend the expressions used to him; more especially as his conscience told him that the expression was applicable. He was asked before this court, whether, at the time, he suffered gambling in his house? And he answered not, but shielded himself under the protection which the prosecution claimed for him, from proclaiming his own infamy, guilt and disgrace. So, sir, when called before the Court of Quarter Sessions of Lehigh county, and informed of the complaint which had been made against him, he denied them not; but by his conduct, admitted that he had so offended. Col. Hutter and Judge Fogel, who were both present, and saw and heard everything which passed, tell you that the word "*villains*" or "*scoundrels,*" was not used; and they add, that it could not have been used, or they would have observed it—that they never heard such words from Judge Porter's lips.

Will you believe the one biassed and prejudiced witness, and whistle the others to the wind? Does the

Senate sit here to protect gamblers—the vilest and most worthless depredators that infest and prey upon society? Is this parent of all vice to receive sanction and encouragement at your hands? Are the gamblers of the land to assemble and hold a jubilee on the success of this cause? Are ye fathers? Have ye children? Do ye owe it to them, do ye owe it to your country to protect gambling? And can it be, that the Senate of Pennsylvania, sitting in sober judgment, as the highest court of judicature known to the laws, is seriously called on to do this? It is monstrous, I can scarcely have patience to endure the thought of it.

Are not your public functionaries, your judges, to be administrators of the law? Are they not called upon by every principle of duty, human and divine, to be a terror unto evil doers? Is it not in proof to you, that the vice of gambling was prevalent, even to an alarming degree, at Allentown; at the times referred to? And was it not necessary for those, sworn to administer the law, to interfere and save the morals of the country from prostitution? Aye; but says the counsel, he should have received information on oath, issued a warrant, and had them indicted. This mode of proceeding would be less effectual than the one adopted. Who was there willing to take upon himself the character, at all times odious, of an informer? The venerable Judge Hartzel, now no more, seemed to shrink from it—although one of the judges of the court— because they were his neighbors. Should they have selected, or sent for one of the clan; he might have either not sworn the truth, or like the culprit here, *stand on his privilege.* Sir, the stand which the respondent took on the side of morals and virtue, was worthy of himself, and of his own fearless and exemplary character; and I should have thought less of him than I do, had he failed in doing what he has done.

The simple facts in regard to this article, are, that gambling prevailed openly and publicly in Allentown.

That the vice was spreading ·its devastations over the place; the widow and orphan felt it; the stranger, setting his foot in the place, was liable to become the victim of the sharpers who infested it. The tavern keepers, licensed by the court, and necessarily under its control, gave it countenance and support; in violation of the law and morality. The respondent interposed his authority, and having desired those most notorious for their transgressions, to come before the court, they voluntarily came forward; and the respondent openly and publicly informed them of the complaints which had come to his ears, the truth of which they admitted ; and he then cautioned them to beware how they again transgressed ; for if complaints should be again preferred, they should be punished with all the severity of the law.

If the respondent be censured for conduct like this, instead of injuring him in the estimation of the only part of mankind whose estimation is worth having—the virtuous and the good—it will be the brightest gem in his coronet. And if the lawgivers of our land; if the highest and most dignified tribunal of the commonwealth, shall think this a matter of accusation and of crime; why then you may as well turn your hall into a *gambling den;* appropriate your sacred desks to *faro banks;* and let justice depend on the hazard of the die.

In the third article of impeachment, it is charged against the respondent, that he interfered to screen a culprit from justice; and endeavored to induce a judicial officer to violate his duty, in her favor. But the facts are not proved, to sustain any part of this allegation. As to the evidence of this man, Reese—whose testimony, taken alone, must have convinced you that no dependence can be placed upon what he said—even *he,* has not dared to say more, than that the respondent told him the case could not be settled before the justice, unless he could certify that Mary Everhart had not committed a larceny. But it is evident, from the testimony of William White and Jacob

Weygandt, Jr., Esquires, who are gentlemen of character
and standing; that the respondent did not know the nature of the prosecution or charge, until he was informed
of it by Justice Weygandt, who emphatically says:
" when I observed to Judge Porter that it was a clear
case of larceny, he did not press the matter." Taking the
facts, given in evidence, it appears, that upon a sudden
quarrel, and in a moment of excitement, Jacob Reese, Jr.,
and Mary Everhart instituted proceedings against each
other, simultaneously. The one for larceny, the other for
slander. That they both repented what they had done,
and were exceedingly anxious to settle their disputes and
to pay off their respective costs. That Reese was particularly desirous that it should be done, although before
the court, he equivocated a good deal about it. That at
his earnest solicitation, the respondent accompanied him
to the office of Justice Weygandt, who, he represented,
was anxious to see him; that the respondent did accompany him, having been informed both by him and by Mr.
White, that it was a trifling quarrel, which they were
both anxious should be settled. That the respondent,
until informed of the nature of the case, was disposed to
give his aid to restore peace between them; but, that so
soon as he found it was a prosecution for larceny, he declined having any thing to do with it, and said, " the
law must take its course."

Suppose, if you please, that the judge did what he was
not bound to do. Suppose he was disposed to be merciful.
Was there anything criminal; was there anything
wrong in what he did? Are you to pass the judgment
of the law against a merciful judge. It is the first instance in which I ever heard of a judicial officer being
criminally arraigned for possessing too much of that,
which is most truly styled, the divine attribute of justice. Judge Chase was impeached for issuing a warrant.
Judge Porter for not issuing one. Judge Chase for being
too severe. Judge Porter for being too merciful.

> "No ceremony, that to great ones 'longs,
>   Not the King's crown, not the deputed sword,
>   The Marshal's truncheon, nor the Judge's robe,
>   Become them with one-half so good a grace,
>   As mercy does."

But in the disposition to practice mercy, you find no disposition in the respondent to interfere with justice. The moment he discovers that its exercise would interfere with the due administration of the laws, that moment says he, "let the law take its course." But, what are we to think of Reese. He first calls upon the respondent to do him a favor, and when he has done it, with the blackest ingratitude he accuses him of crime.. Ingratitude has ever been considered the parent and associate of all other vices, and it is the worst of all; he who is ungrateful has no sin but one, all other crimes may pass for virtues in him. Reese has been ungrateful, and deserves the treatment inflicted by Philip of Macedon upon the soldier, who, ungrateful for the preservation of his life and his restoration to health, robbed his benefactor of his possessions. He was branded on the forehead with the words, "The ungrateful Guest."

Had the defendant, upon her subsequent trial, been acquitted through the influence and interference of the respondent, then indeed might some complaint have been made against him. But you will find, that on her trial the facts and the law are all submitted to the consideration of the jury; and she was convicted and sentenced, and has expiated her offence by undergoing the penalty of the law. Instead, I say, of interfering in her behalf, you find that the respondent says, "Let justice be done, regardless of the consequences"; and the sentiment is re-echoed by a member of this honorable court.

The evidence, as I have already stated, disproves the charge contained in this article, and consequently there can be no reason to apprehend that you will doubt in relation to it.

[The court here adjourned until the next morning.]

Mr. Brown, at nine o'clock A. M., resumed his argument.

MR. BROWN.—While I gratefully acknowledge the obligations I am under to this honorable court, for the indulgence granted me yesterday by an adjournment, I trust I shall show my sincerity in expressing it, by the shortness of my further trespass upon your attention.

In the course of my observations yesterday, I observed that the respondent's case was one of peculiar hardship, as regarded the motives with which the prosecution was instituted. In this allusion, sir, I had no reference to the motives of the honorable the House of Representatives, or those on their behalf immediately conducting this prosecution. The allusion was to those who instituted—who originated, this *persecution*. I make this explanation now, to correct or counteract any misrepresentation or misunderstanding which may have been made, or entertained, in relation to that which I did say. But be the motives of its originators what they may; the proceeding has been instituted, and the respondent must endure and meet it. I know ("uneasy lies the head that ·wears a crown;" and that the stubborn and unbending oak will suffer more beneath the fury of the storm, than the yielding and more time-serving myrtle. But we honor the scathed and riven tree for its assimilation to that integrity which never yields the right, to the expedient.

I had proceeded so far as to have concluded my observations upon the third article. I shall now approach the consideration of those which remain, and although they be great in quantity, in quality they are nothing.

The fourth article has relation to the case of the Commonwealth *v.* John Mill. It has relation to a transaction which should have taken place at January Sessions, 1819—seven years since. There is no doubt that, in consequence of the great lapse of time, this court are not in

possession of as full and complete a history of that transaction as they might have been, had it occurred at a
more recent period. But who should suffer from this?
Not the respondent, surely. He could not time the institution of these proceedings ; and if either party is to be
prejudiced, it ought to be the commonwealth ; because
it was at her option to institute the proceedings at what
period she pleased. This honorable court is not to convict upon want of proof, when the deficiency is attributable to the prosecution itself. (Mr. B. read the article.)
It concludes, " In violation of the legal and constitutional
right of every citizen to have justice administered according to law, and against the peace and dignity of the
Commonwealth of Pennsylvania." Here, again, we have
another of the many specimens with which these articles
abound, of *legal* and *logical conclusions*, drawn from *classical* and *grammatical premises*. This, however, is the charge
—how, and by whom is it attempted to be sustained? It
is by George Levers, the prosecutor, and by Hugh Ross.
Levers does not support it. His recollection of the circumstances is at best like a dream. He no longer is able
to recollect the parties to the bill obligatory, the alleged
subject of larceny—nor the amount. He says he understood the proposition to compromise to have originated
with the counsel ; and that the court merely assented to
it. He was put, as it were to torture, by the opposite
counsel ; but to no purpose. All that Levers—who worshipped at the shrine of Mammon—wanted, was his
money ; and he got it. But who is the other witness?
Hugh Ross ; another member of this triple, gorgon-
headed, league. The judge " was very pressing," " very
urging," says he. He does not presume—with his notes
and all—to give the respondent's language. He is confirmed in this, his own jaundiced impression, by no other
witness. . I asked him what he was doing. His reply
was, " I am not bound to answer." " Not bound, sir !
Why, are you not sworn to tell the whole truth ? Your

oath has been recorded here, and in heaven." He claimed
the protection of the court to be excused from answering.
It was not afforded him. He said he was "taking notes."
Taking notes! For what purpose, as you were not
concerned in the cause? His trembling motive skulked
in his coward eye. Again he claimed to be excused from
answering, but in vain; again he hesitated, but at length
it came out—" With a view to its being a charge against
Judge Porter, some day." Here was an occasion and an
employment worthy the amanuensis of Prince Lucifer
himself; noting down the foibles and the faults of human
nature. Such testimony should scarcely be adverted to,
much less relied on, for any purpose. But, sir, although
we here unveiled him, we stopped not with that. He
was obliged to own that he travelled miles to procure
signatures to the complaint against the respondent. He
sought a public dance house to procure signatures. And
then, some time after he had confessed this, he again asks
to be permitted to come before you, to give the reason
why he did so. He says that he did it, so that he could
send the petition by Jarrett, and save postage. Here, sir,
is a fellow, according to his own account, hunting down
the reputation of his fellow-man; putting his hands in
his pockets, and coolly calculating the cost of twenty-
five cents postage which he might save by sending on his
precious document by Jarrett, the special messenger of
the league. A man who has battened last year—a
month; and this year—a fortnight, upon the coffers of
the commonwealth! But, be it remembered, that this
saving was to be of the funds of the commonwealth, for
she pays the postage on all letters to the members of the
Legislature.

Ross is unsustained and unsupported in his evidence by
Mr. Levers, the other witness for the prosecution. He is
contradicted by James M. Porter, Esq., the deputy attorney general at the time; who had a right, if he chose,
to enter a *nolle prosequi*, even against the consent of the

court; because it was previous to the passage of the act of 20th March, 1819, restraining the attorney general's power, relative to the entries of *nolle prosequi*. (Mr. Brown here read the indictment, Commonwealth *v.* John Mill.) It appears by the indictment, that the bill obligatory never was assigned by Mill, and from the evidence before us, it is manifest, that he had merely deposited it with Levers; and had not received full consideration for it; nor parted with the property in it; and that he took it under a claim of property. But why, as this was the act of the whole court, is it to be charged against the respondent alone; both the associates, Judges Cooper and Wagener concurred; and the latter tells you that he does not now recollect all the circumstances, but he remembers that he did not think it was an indictable offence; and of this he is certain, that had there been anything improper, he never would have consented. The jury too, concurred in the opinion of the court, and without a moment's hesitation, acquitted the defendant.

I do not apprehend that there can be a loop upon which to hang a doubt, in relation to this article.

The fifth article relates to the case of Wannemacher *v.* Sechler. In that case there had been an indictment, in the sessions, for this same assault and battery, for which the civil action was brought in the Common Pleas. Upon that indictment, the defendant pleaded guilty. On the trial of the civil action, the respondent, as every judge and lawyer would have done, charged that the plaintiff was entitled to recover. The amount he left entirely to the jury. The jury, disregarding the law as laid down to them by the court, and assuming to themselves the province of the court, brought in a verdict for the defendant. If the respondent had refused to receive this verdict, he would have done right. But he did not refuse to receive it. He advised the jury again to go out; repeated to them what the law was; and instructed them that the law of the land was part of the evidence upon which they had sworn to decide the cause, and that it ought not to be disregarded. The jury received the recommendation of the court, and agreed to go out again, and did go out. Was this an insult to the jury? So far from it, I say, that the jury in again bringing in the same verdict, nay—in finding the first one—insulted the court. If the interference by the courts with the rights of the jury, be an insult to them; surely, an interference by the jury with the rights of the court, is an insult to the court. We are entitled to the one side or the other of the argument; for that rule is a bad one which will not work both ways. Sir, the jury were bound to take the law from the court, and the respondent in so instructing them, acted as he always, I am proud to say, acts—with entire judicial propriety. Never, I trust—much as I prize the inestimable right of trial by jury—shall we live to see the day when the jury shall take the law into their own hands, in civil cases. They have not, and they ought not to have, the control of the law. Injury and distress beyond conception, would be the result, if they had; because, should they err in its construction, the parties would be remediless. There could be no revision, no correction of their errors; whereas, if the judge, who decides the law, errs, the law has given the means whereby you can revise his errors.

But it is alleged that the respondent set the verdict aside without a motion. The fact is not so. I will grant that Christian F. Beitel, the prothonotary, did say that no motion was made for a new trial, and he is the only witness that says so. This court will recollect, that the court at which this transaction took place, was the first one at which Mr. Beitel officiated as prothonotary. A competent man would probably be somewhat awkward at a new business; and much more so, consequently, would one who was as little qualified for the situation as Mr. Beitel. He may therefore easily be mistaken, especially as twelve months ago he knew nothing about it; as appears by his evidence before the committee. But Mr.

Smith expressly contradicts him, and says, that he did move, not for a rule to show cause, but at once for a new trial; that he did it as soon as the verdict was recorded, and while the jury were yet in the box; on purpose that the jury might hear him, and learn that they ought not to disregard the law. Apply to this testimony the rules of evidence read by the gentleman from Swift's Treatise; and where does it leave the testimony of Mr. Prothonotary Beitel.

I almost wish, however, for the respondent's sake, that no motion had been made, and that he had himself set the verdict aside, without request. He was sworn to administer the laws, to do justice without fear, favor or affection; and was he to sit quietly by and see those laws trodden under foot, and that justice trampled on and disregarded by a jury? The greatest judge who ever sat upon a bench in the United States—and who still sheds lustre upon the high and dignified station which he so usefully fills in our judiciary—has granted new trials without motion, where the jury have flagrantly violated the law, and usurped the province of the court. I should be the last man who would encourage encroachment upon the rights of the jury; while I would be the first to resist an encroachment by the jury on the rights of the court. Each has its appropriate sphere; each, in its own province, has its exclusive and appropriate duties to perform, and each should move in its own orbit.

But it is said, that the respondent used improper language to Mr. King; that he told him "not to attempt to make the jury perjure themselves." Mr. King, who has testified with great propriety, admits that at the time, he was considerably excited; and that, from that cause, or the lapse of years, he cannot be certain even in his impressions; and will not undertake to say what the language used by the respondent was. All that he is certain of, is, that the impression upon his mind, was, that the judge charged him with acting improperly, when he told the jury they had a right to persist in their verdict. Mr. Beitel, who never recollected anything of this matter before the committee of investigation; and whose knowledge has been produced by reading over the printed charges and conversing about the matter, since April last; tells you: "that the judge told Mr. King he wanted to make the jury perjure themselves." Upon the other parts of his evidence, I have animadverted sufficiently in my observations on the preceding parts of this article, and will therefore not observe further upon it. But the attorney general, Mr. Smith, was present; he was cool, and understood his business, and therefore able to give us a correct statement of the facts as they occurred. He tells you, that when the jury were about retiring to reconsider their verdict, Mr. King told them that they might find the same verdict—or persist in their verdict—and that the respondent observed to him, "Oh! Mr. King, do not endeavor to make the jury do what is improper—they are sworn to decide the cause according to law and the evidence, let them do so." That there was nothing remarkable in the respondent's manner—that he saw no passion in him—that Mr. King was a little warm, and in the opinion of the witness, richly deserved all the judge said to him. This venerable and respected officer of the commonwealth, was present, and saw, and heard, all that took place; and has related it as it occurred.

I must here be permitted to remark upon the little respect or regard paid to many, if not all our witnesses— no matter what their age or standing—by the opposite counsel, in the manner of propounding his questions. When they had related their knowledge, the counsel chose to cross-examine them, by saying, "will you undertake to say," or "will you venture to say, sir," that this, or that did not take place, or was not said. The witnesses (and I now allude particularly to the attorney general), would not undertake to say what did *not take place;* but they undertook to say what *did take place,* and

what the respondent *did say.* With such witnesses, we
tread on holy ground.

But, sir, if the judge had said so, it is no ground of
impeachment; because, if the respondent had even been
in error, he committed no offence, he was guilty of no
misdemeanor. But I deny that he would have been even
doing wrong, had he used the language imputed him.
Are counsel to be at liberty to insult the court with impunity, and must your judges quietly submit, as though
they were tongue-tied? The judiciary is everything to us.
It is entitled to, and should receive our countenance and
support. It is easily assailed, and if its character and
standing be lost, your property—your liberty, is gone.

The sixth article is next in order. That was the case
of James Hays *v.* Hugh Bellas; the suit, in which case,
was brought to November Term, 1815, and was tried at
April Term, 1818. It is now ten years and upwards since
the suit was brought, and nearly eight years since the
cause was tried. And here again, I must be permitted to
advert to the lapse of time which has intervened, and to
ask you, that anything arising from want of evidence in
consequence of it, shall operate against the prosecution,
and not against the respondent. There are two matters
of accusation contained in this article. The first, is the
interlineation of the following words, in the charge of the
court after it had been signed and filed; to wit: "a man
may, if he pleases, buy an imperfect right, and if he is not
imposed upon, but buys with a knowledge of the imperfections, he shall in law be held to the performance of his
contract."

The second is for writing on the margin of the bills of
exceptions, the following words:—"and the same papers
were objected to, for want of proof of the handwriting of
the said Henry L. Clark, and for other causes; but it was
finally and mutually agreed, that the whole correspondence between the parties should be given in evidence, and
that the third exception before mentioned, be therefore

withdrawn, and the last mentioned papers were read in evidence accordingly."

Let us approach these charges boldly, and "take the bull" at once, "by the horns." I will however premise, that there has not been a solitary witness examined on the part of the prosecution, who has not been disappointed or displeased in some personal matter, or professional pursuit, and who does not come forward with all the bias incident to poor weak human nature, when operated upon by such causes: and this observation applies with peculiar force upon the present article, as the attempt to sustain this part of the case, is supported alone by the evidence of Hugh Bellas, the defendant in the cause, who, according to his own acknowledgment, has been reflecting upon the circumstances ever since; thus giving additional strength to the original bias of his mind, in relation to it. Mr. Bellas is, no doubt, a respectable man, at least, when compared with the other inciters of this prosecution. Yet, he is but a man, and one who has his full share of personal feelings to be operated upon. That they have been operated upon, is manifest from every part of his testimony.

As to the first branch of the accusation—the interlineation in the charge of the court—we admit that the respondent made the interlineation, and made it after the charge was filed. But sir, we say, and the evidence bears us out in the assertion, that the matter interlined was actually delivered in charge to the jury, and that when the interlineation was made, the respondent was ignorant that the charge had been filed. What is the evidence on this subject? Mr. Bellas says, that the words interlined were not in the charge when signed by Judge Porter; that the judge delivered the charge orally:— (and by the by, I never heard of one that was not so delivered) that notes of it were taken down by Mr. J. M. Porter, who was his counsel,—that from these he wrote out a charge, and the next morning handed it to the respondent, who read it over and signed it; and that he knows nothing of the interlineation or how it was made, as he left Easton the day the charge was signed by the respondent.

This is the only evidence adduced in support of the accusation; and Mr. Bellas on his cross-examination, says he has not sufficient recollection of the charge of the court to say that the judge did, or did not, use the language interlined, in his charge to the jury. Taking it up on this evidence alone, what is there in it? That upon subsequent perusal, the respondent discovered that a sound legal proposition which he had laid down to the jury, had been omitted in taking down the charge; he therefore interlined it in the charge. But when he did it—whether before or after it was filed—by no means appears. The law will presume it was done before it was filed; because that is the natural presumption, and the presumption in favor of innocence. For you will recollect the charge here is FORGERY; and yet we are told that the character of the respondent is not assailed.

But when you come to consider the evidence of Capt. D. D. Wagener, who was one of the jurors in the cause; and Mr. James M. Porter, who was the counsel of Mr. Bellas; all doubt or difficulty on the subject vanishes: and we have no occasion to call in presumptions, or even the bulwark of character to aid us in our defence. Capt. Wagener tells you that he was a juror in the cause; that Judge Porter did use words in his charge to the jury, to the effect of those interlined; and he tells you the reasons why he feels positive that the respondent did so charge the jury. He says, that after having heard the evidence, he and Mr. John Horn had adopted the idea that the plaintiff ought to recover, as he had not deceived the defendant; and that the defendant had bought the patent right in controversy at his own risk: and that when they retired to their room to deliberate, after receiving the charge of the court, he remarked to Mr. Horn, that Judge

Porter had taken the same views upon that part of the case, that they did; and he adds, that it was upon that very ground the jury founded their verdict.

Again;—If you examine the issues which had been joined, and the points propounded to the court; you find that the matter interlined had a direct relation to the cause; and surely no one will say that it is not sound law; and thence it must fairly be inferred, that it was the subject matter of charge. So much then for the proof that this language was actually used to the jury. Now, as to the time and manner in which they were interlined. Mr. J. M. Porter says, that it was the first cause he tried in Northampton county; that he labored with zeal for his client, and fought every inch of ground; that he took notes of the charge as it was delivered; that on the same evening he transcribed it and on the next morning handed it to the respondent, who looked over it hastily, signed it, and *gave it back again to him;* that before the term had ended, he went off to the West-Chester court: and previous to leaving Easton, he handed the charge of the court to General Spering, the prothonotary. On his return to Easton in June following, he was informed that the bills of exceptions drawn by Mr. Bellas, were too informal to be signed. That he then procured the charge of the court from the prothonotary, drew up the bills of exceptions, attached them and the charge of the court together; and at the ensuing August Term, handed the whole to the respondent; who then examined them, corrected any errors which he discovered so as to make the papers conform to the truth of the case; and then signed the bills of exceptions; and they were then for the first time, as the respondent believed, filed of record. So far, as regarded the* bills of exceptions, such was the fact; and how could the judge suppose, as all the papers were appended together, that part had been filed and part had not? From all the circumstances we have a right not only to infer, but positively to say, that the language interlined was actually used to the jury; and that the judge was ignorant of the paper having been filed, when he made the interlineation. But had he even known it; he did no more than the Supreme Court, on a suggestion of diminution of record, would have compelled him to do. He but placed the truth upon the record. Truth would never tarnish the books of heaven itself. The judge was bound to hold the scales of justice even between the parties; and he could have had no motive but that of perfect honesty in doing what he did.

But it is said, that the letter of Mr. Porter to Mr. Bellas, says "the judge's conduct was improper." You will remember that this letter was written nearly eight years since; when a partial feud existed between Mr. Porter and his brother, the respondent. Mr. Porter was a young man just making his *debut* in Northampton county: it was his first cause there: he and his colleague, tyros as they were in the profession, had gone through a long and a fierce contest with veterans of the bar: they had been defeated: and under the warmth and feeling of the moment he wrote the letter, which is here introduced by the prosecution; and serves, to use the beautiful and figurative language of a distinguished author, " like a moonbeam on a thunder cloud, to make the storm more dreadful." But what does this letter—the writing of which was far more commendable than its dishonorable publication—say? That "the conduct of the judge in putting it (the interlineation) there, was highly improper." This declaration is made, as I say, under the influence of irritation and excitement; and the witness expressly states—" in the belief on his part, that the judge knew the charge had been filed." Upon mature reflection, he says now, that he believes he did Judge Porter injustice in that supposition, and in the consequent charge of impropriety. Shall Mr. Porter not be permitted to correct his errors? Must he, like Hugh Ross and others (and I beg his pardon for even naming him with them), grow older and grow worse.

As to the second branch of accusation; I shall confine my remarks principally to the allegation on our part, that the marginal note to be found on the bills of exceptions was according to the truth of the case; because it is perfectly clear, that the note was placed there before the respondent signed it, and of course, before it became a record. Mr. Porter tells you that the bills of exceptions were handed to the respondent at August Term, 1818; and when he next saw them, they were signed, and contained the marginal note in question; and the marginal note, and the other corrections, must have been put on, in the interim. This is also confirmed by the allegation in the letter, of which, no doubt, much will be said. He there acknowledges the receipt of Mr. Bellas's letter (dated 22d August, 1818), a few days after its date; and says: "the bills of exceptions, were signed at August court, a few days before the receipt of Mr. Bellas's letter. The August Term, 1818, commenced upon the 17th day of the month: The letter might take three days or a week to go from Sunbury—where Mr. Bellas lived—to Easton; and the bills of exceptions may have been signed during the first week of the court."

This is all the evidence we have, as to the time when the marginal note was placed there, and when the bills were signed.

Then—on the subject of the truth of the fact stated in the note—Mr. Bellas only says: "he has no knowledge of any such consent, as is there stated, and he feels confident no such consent was given;" and here permit me to say, that in this Mr. Bellas is unsupported by any witness whatever, and is contradicted first by the record, and secondly by the evidence of Major Hays and Mr. Porter. Nay, the strong presumption to be drawn from the whole of Mr. Bellas's own testimony, taken together, is, that he is wrong when he makes that declaration: because he

says, that he and his counsel were willing that the whole
correspondence should go to the jury, and that the reason
why the third exception was taken, was, that the opposite counsel would not so agree. But when he subsequently offered on his part, the remainder of the correspondence, we find it admitted—not *without* objection, but
by *consent*—after objection taken and withdrawn; and
even letters produced by the plaintiff without notice; and
unproved copies received where the originals could not be
had. According to this statement alone, how do the facts
strike every member of this court? why, that certain
letters passing between Henry L. Clark and Hugh Bellas,
were offered in evidence. They were reciprocally objected
to. The first one admitted, is excepted to by the defendant; not for want of proof of the handwriting, but because it was only *part* of the correspondence. Subsequently the defendant offers certain other of those letters
in evidence, to which the plaintiff objects, because *they
were not proved.* Then, how could they be admitted in
evidence? Mr. Bellas says he did not prove them, and
that he was willing to waive all objection, provided the
whole correspondence went to the jury. It, did go! It
could go in no other way but by consent; and if there
were no actual and absolute declaration on the part of
the defendant that the third bill of exceptions was withdrawn, could the court do otherwise than suppose such
was the intention of the parties, and such their understanding. But the testimony of Major Hays and Mr.
Porter, puts the matter beyond doubt. The former tells
you that letters from Bellas to Clark, and from Clark to
Bellas, were offered in evidence; that the attorneys on
both sides disputed the letters; that they had a very hard
argument, and after they spent a good deal of time, the
judge said, " I think, gentlemen, you had better let all the
letters go to the jury." *Finally they agreed,* and he thinks
all the letters and papers went to the jury. Mr. Porter
tells you, that when the letter from Bellas to Clark (dated

10th December, 1813) was offered in evidence; the court
compared the handwriting with that of Mr. Bellas to the
article of agreement—which had been already proved—
and said it might go to the jury for them to compare it;
that Mr. Scott and he then opposed the admission of the
letter in evidence, on the ground of its being only a part
of the correspondence. After argument, the court admitted the letter, and the third bill of exceptions was
taken. While this matter was before the court, Mr. Bellas instructed his counsel, and they so informed the
court, that if the other side would agree to admit the
whole correspondence, he had no objection to admit this,
as part of it. When the plaintiff closed his rebutting
proof, of which that letter was part, the defendant's counsel offered in evidence, some letters from Clark to Bellas.
I presume they were those of the 2d November and 2d
December, 1813, and 15th and 23d August, 1814, mentioned in the bill of exceptions. To the admission of
these the plaintiff's counsel objected; and Mr. Sitgreaves
charged the defendant with blowing hot and cold; first
in denying Clark's authority; and then in endeavoring to
make his letters prejudice Major Hays. The judge then
advised both sides, to waive all captious objections and
admit the correspondence, and that after some observations by the counsel as to who was in the right—as is not
uncommon, they agreed on both sides to admit the whole
correspondence, and it was accordingly given in evidence.
It is true, Mr. Porter says, there was no *express* declaration on the part of the defendant, that this third bill of
exceptions should be withdrawn; but the assent to the
proposition by the court, was a waiver of all exception in
relation to that part of the case. Shall the party be entitled to the benefit of the agreement to admit the whole
correspondence, and yet hold fast to his exceptions as to
part?—Certainly not! But it is enough for us, that the
court understood such to be the intention of the parties;
and if so, even if in error, there can be no impropriety

imputed to the respondent for stating the fact as he understood it.

The court will remember, that the charge under this article, is forgery; that it imputes to the honorable respondent—who for three score years has maintained an unsullied reputation—whose character, it has been admitted, is unimpeachable—and of whom the counsel for the managers, has declared in relation to this prosecution, "that there is not a single charge that imputes dishonesty" to him: I say, that this charge imputes to him "the false making or alteration of a writing, with intent to defraud another," which is the legal definition of forgery. How this charge is to be reconciled with the declaration that "there is no imputation of dishonesty," remains for the learned counsel to show. But this we know; that where there could be neither motive nor object for so doing, it would require proof, strong, clear, and undeniable—upon which no suspicion could cast a shade—to convince any tribunal that an honest man, who maintained a high and respectable standing in the community, would commit a crime, which betokens a total dereliction of moral rectitude, and would consign its perpetrator to infamy for life. There can be no stronger breast-plate than a heart untainted.

The seventh article contains two branches of accusation. The first branch has relation to the two alleged cases of Schwenk, administrator of Schwenk, *v.* Ebert—in which it is said : " the respondent neglected or refused to file his opinions, although required so to do." It turns out that there was but one case of that name in Northampton county, and on referring to the evidence, how do the facts appear before this court ?

It appears that an appeal had been taken from the judgment of a justice of the peace on the 7th of March, 1822, which was not tried in court until the 1st of May, 1823. Between the time of taking this appeal and its being tried, the Legislature passed the act of 1st of

April, 1823, repealing the ninth section of the act of 1820, which altered the rule on the subject of costs, in cases of appeal. A number of questions arose under these acts, in the various cases tried in Northampton county; and it would rather seem from the evidence, that when the judge gave his opinion in this case a conversation took place, in which nearly all the members of the bar participated, in which it was stated, that it was desirable that the opinion of the Supreme Court upon the construction of these acts, should be taken. In that conversation, it seems to have been agreed, that a case should be taken up which would embrace all the questions which had arisen. In the course of this conversation, a request was made of the judge to file his opinion in this case; but it seemed agreed that the filing it in any case, which would carry the question fairly up, would answer. The case of Grace *v.* Altemus, decided shortly after, did embrace all the points which would be likely to arise under those acts; and in that case Judge Porter delivered and filed an elaborate opinion; and the case was removed to the Supreme Court, where it is yet pending. No subsequent request ever was made of the respondent, to file his opinion in the case of Schwenk *v.* Ebert; had such a request been made, it would have been filed; although for obtaining a rehearing, it was not necessary, as all the facts appeared upon the record. There, therefore, could have been no motive for withholding it; nor was any injury sustained: because even Mr. Charles Davis, himself, says that his client immediately abandoned all idea of removing the cause to the Supreme Court.

I will merely add, that the utmost that is made of this, is a mere *oral request*. The language of the act is not *request*, it is *require*. The judge was not *required* here, to file his opinion; there was a mere intimation given, that the party might perhaps ask a review of the decision, in which case the judge was requested to file his opinion.

This review never was had; nor was the respondent's attention ever again even called to the case, until it was made a matter of accusation against him, by Mr. C. Davis last winter. It is a miserable plan for the *young* to attempt to build their hopes of eminence or elevation upon the prostration of the aged or distinguished. It is generally as unsuccessful as the snail's attempt to destroy the beauty of the statue; and has about as worthy a motive for its origin, as the fable imputes to that reptile.

The second branch of this article, is most satisfactorily refuted by the respondent's answer to it, which has in every respect been sustained by the evidence. (Here Mr. Brown read the answer.) The actions were instituted on joint bonds against the administrators of the surety, and were tried the last time in 1820; at least, they were to be considered as joint bonds under the decisions which had then been made; and in accordance with those decisions, the respondent charged the jury in favor of the defendant. Was the charge right, or was it wrong? I care not what the decisions of the Supreme Court have been since; I know what the decisions uniformly were prior to 1823, when the case of Geddes *v.* Hawk was determined, giving us the new law on the subject. My inquiry is as to the *motive*. Is there anything to impeach his motives in charging? It is sought for in vain in the evidence! It has no existence even in the charge! Shall we be told, because a different determination has since been had in your Supreme Court; that therefore, the respondent has been guilty of a misdemeanor in office? Sir, the laws of Draco and Caligula, were humane compared with such a construction of ours. Be it remembered too, that Mr. Binney, who was consulted by the plaintiff, concurred in opinion with the respondent. But the allegation is, that the respondent did not *file* his charge. We say, he never was requested so to do, or if requested—never heard the request, which is about the same thing. What is the evidence on this subject?

Mr. King thinks the point in the case was, whether the bonds were joint or not; that perhaps there might have been others, but that he does not recollect them; that the court charged the jury, that the bonds were joint, and therefore the plaintiff could not recover; that it is fully impressed upon his mind, that the judge was requested to file his charge, but whether that request was made by himself, or by his colleague, Mr. John Evans, he cannot say. That having directed a writ of error to be taken, he requested Mr. Binney not to issue the writ, unless he thought the opinion wrong. That on examining the records, he did not find the opinion filed. At the succeeding term, he or his colleague, Mr. Evans, mentioned the matter to the court. Judge Porter did not seem to have a distinct recollection of the application having been made, and desired that the matter might go off until Mr. Smith would be there. That at the following court, Mr. Smith denied that any application had been made to file the charge; and that Judge Porter having no recollection himself of the request to file the charge, refused to do so, contrary to Mr. Smith's consent. That upon consulting Mr. Binney afterwards, Mr. B. said the charge of the court was correct; and the parties abandoned all idea of taking the case up.

The testimony of Mr. Daniel Helfrich, the plaintiff in the suit, amounts to nothing; for in truth, according to his own account, he knows nothing, except that he lost his cause; and he seems to think that the respondent was the occasion of it.

The attorney general, Mr. Smith, to whose cool, deliberate and candid testimony, I have more than once had occasion to refer with pleasure, gives us a very clear and distinct account of this matter. He is able to give you all the particulars in relation, as well to the nature of the actions, as to the defence taken, and the facts which transpired at each trial. He tells you that there were two points made:—1st. That the bonds were joint,

and the defendant's intestate, a mere surety; and 2d. That
the plaintiff had given time to Knerr, the original debtor,
without the assent of Seip.   From his evidence, it must
be clear, that no request to file the charge was made.   He
says he did not hear it ; that his opportunities of hearing
were at least as good as those of the respondent; and
what induces him to believe it could not have been made,
is the fact, that when he cited the authority from 2d
Browne's Reports, Mr. J. Evans gave up the case, saying,
if that be the law, our case is lost; and at the ensuing
May Term, 1821, Mr. Evans appealed to his liberality,
and requested him to consent to the charge being filed.
Mr. Smith refused, and the respondent not recollecting
either the request or the language used in his charge, declined doing anything except by consent.   Mr. King will
not say the respondent heard the request.   He is uncertain as to who made it, if it was made.   Mr. Smith says
he did not hear it, and he thinks he must have heard it,
had it been made.   The respondent says he did not hear
it—and the subsequent conversation of the three counsel,
resulting in Mr. Smith's refusal to consent—all show
that there could have been no legal right existing to
require it.   What said Mr. Evans?   He appeals to the
attorney general's liberality, which he need not have
done, had it not been a favor asked of him.

Some of the jurors, it seems, had, in one of Mr. Evans's
odd humors, been subpœnaed to attend at the May Term,
1821, to inform the court what had been given them in
charge, in the December preceding.   The jury are to be
the Magnus Apollo, it would seem, throughout this business.

I dismiss this subject with observing, that the facts
charged, have not been substantiated ; and that if they
had, they exhibit no wilful violation of duty, no corrupt
or evil motive.

The eighth article has been abandoned by the prosecution.

The ninth article embraces all the remaining matter; for the other articles are but specifications of the general charge contained in the commencement of this: "that the respondent threatened, intimidated, and insulted his associate, Justice Cooper, on the bench in open court."

[Mr. Brown here read the article.]

This tribunal, permit me to say, does not sit as a court of etiquette, to regulate matters of form and punctilio; to settle the vain and empty, and if you please, the uncourteous, or even disgraceful disputes, between men in high stations. But the respondent claims, in the subject matter of this accusation, to have acted with strict correctness of intention, and pure benevolence of motive. And if a due regard for mercy is an insult to an obdurate associate judge; then indeed is the respondent guilty; and he will be found to be the first judge, that ever was condemned for possessing the dearest attribute of justice.

Of what kind of stuff must this worthy associate (to whom it would seem the respondent should in all things submit himself with due humility) be made, who with a dying boy, an aged grandmother, and a weeping mother before him—circumstances which should almost have softened a heart of adamant—pertinaciously insists that the boy shall lie in jail. He wants time—day after day— to make inquiries, and talk the matter over with Dr. Swift; in the meantime, says the respondent, the boy may die, and we will then discharge him—but to be buried. The associate at length agreed to discharge *one;* which he knew, or ought to have known, could not be done; as it was impossible to discharge the one without the other. Judge Cooper should remember, that he gives twice who gives early; and that reluctant charity has but little to recommend it over actual refusal.

That Judge Cooper is in error in this matter, is evident, as well from the other evidence, as from his own testimony. He admits that he was in a passion; that passion too, did not vanish,—when *he* took occasion to vanish from the court house—as he saw Judge Wagener coming down the street. He assails him out of court; tries to prejudice his mind, and prevent his joining in the legal, humane and merciful course recommended by the president. But to the honor of Judge Wagener, be it told; that, disdaining the cold hearted persuasions of Judge Cooper, he came into court, and concurring with the respondent, discharged the boys. The act is proud and honorable in its aspect, and calculated to redeem the character of the administration of justice, from the imputation of cruelty, with which Judge Cooper would have stained it.

It is exceedingly doubtful from the evidence, what the expression used by Judge Porter to Judge Cooper, was, whether;—"if the boy dies in jail, his blood be on your head," or "if the boy dies in jail, I wash my hands of his blood." Be it which it may, it was provoked; as well by the inhuman conduct, as by the aggravating and irritating manner of Judge Cooper; and it but bespeaks the honest hearted integrity of a man, too noble to disguise the ordinary feelings of nature: and for this, surely, he is not to be arraigned as a criminal.

What then of this bushel of chaff remains?

Article tenth. [Reads the article.] An action of ejectment between Witchell, plaintiff, and German and Levers, defendants, is tried—a number of legal questions arise in the progress of the trial. Judge Porter, the president judge, who has been a lawyer for forty years, delivers the charge of the court. Judge Cooper, a practitioner of medicine—who perhaps understands something of fractured bones and heads—is on the bench during the trial, and assents to the charge delivered by the president. The jury fly in the face of the charge of the court; and the associate declines interfering when an application is made for a new trial. The counsel behave indecorously to the court; and Judge Porter reprimands them for their behavior. Judge Wagener, the other associate, is sent for;

and comes into court, and concurs with the president in granting a rule to show cause why a new trial shall not be granted. The case is subsequently argued, and Judge Cooper assents to granting a new trial, assigning as his reason for so doing, that he did not wish to give an opinion unfavorable to Mr. Levers.

When, or where have we heard of the respondent ever founding his opinion upon the effect it was to have on an individual? No, his eye has ever been steady to justice—knowing no distinction of persons—punishing what was wrong, and approving what was right, without regard to the actors in the scene.

As to the second branch of this accusation, it can only be heard, as this court have decided, when taken in connection with the respondent's answer. If the respondent's answer is to be used for any purpose, it must be used for all; and taken altogether, it shows that Judge Cooper deserved, upon the occasion alluded to, more than was said to him. It appears that Judge Porter was holding the court alone; that the counsel concerned were about adjusting a cause upon the trial list; when in comes *doctor* Judge Cooper—after, perhaps, a morning round among his patients—and without knowing what the court was doing; but disposed to display a great deal of zeal for industry; very insolently demands of the respondent, why he did not attend to the trial list. This, sir, was in effect charging the respondent—who had been assiduously attending to his duty—with neglecting the public business; and the charge made too, by one who only made his appearance in court, as the intervals of his own vocations gave him time to look in upon the court, and take his temporary station on the bench. Why, sir, had he been a master workman, and the respondent his mere journeyman, he could not have assumed more authority over him. What was the respondent to do under these circumstances? Was he to humbly submit himself to Judge Cooper; and mutely set about obeying his commands, no matter how injurious to the public business then transacting? Or was he to act as an honorable, high minded officer, entitled to at least an equal voice in the administration of justice? He acted upon this occasion, as he usually acts—with propriety and becoming dignity. He mildly informs Judge Cooper that "he would thank him for less of his dictation;" and the respondent informs you (and Judge Cooper cannot deny it) that he (Cooper) apologized for his rudeness. I know that Judge Cooper, and his worthy coadjutor, Henry Jarrett—who, although an old man, is but a young lawyer—endeavor to give this matter a somewhat different coloring. Who, pray, constituted Henry Jarrett a judge of manners?—and who, if there even were incivility or rudeness proved, constituted the members of this court judges of manners? But the truth to be collected from the evidence, and the known urbanity and courteousness of Judge Porter's behavior, bear me out in the statement which I have given you of this transaction. Judge Cooper says he was abashed. I hope he was, for if so, it shows he is yet capable of being convinced of error, and evincing a becoming regret for outraging the feelings of others.

The eleventh article charges the respondent with improper conduct to Judge Cooper, while the case of Reese *v.* Sigman was trying in the Common Pleas of Northampton county, at January Term, 1822. In the first place, permit me to say, that the testimony of Dr. John Cooper and Hugh Ross—the only witnesses for the prosecution on this article—do not bear out the facts as charged against the respondent. The amount of their allegations is—that Judge Porter and Judge Wagener, adopted one view of the case, and Judge Cooper another. That the two, being a majority of the court, the opinion delivered by them was "*the opinion of the court;*" and that when Judge Cooper said he was of a different opinion, Judge Porter observed, that what *he* had delivered was the opinion of the court. Ross says, Judge Porter's manner

in making this observation was angry; such as a superior
would use to an inferior. Judge Cooper, although no
doubt he and Ross have compared notes on this subject,
is more cautious. He says, "I think the judge—*rather*
in an imperious tone—in a manner that excited a *little*
awe on my mind—observed, that it was the opinion of
the court." I should be cautious of giving much credence
to the evidence of these witnesses as to *manner*, were
there no other proof. We have seen them throughout
this cause, detailing matters of impression, seen through
the jaundiced medium of their own biassed feelings; and
in such matters it would be dangerous to rely on either
of them.

But Colonel Ihrie, who was concerned for the defendant, Abraham Sigman—who was her son and agent, and
attending to the cause for her; and Judge Wagener, who
was on the bench during the trial, and participated in
the proceedings; all tell you that there was nothing offensive, indecorous, or improper in the manner of Judge
Porter to Judge Cooper; and that had there been anything of the kind, they must have observed it. Divest
this matter of its false coloring, and the charge.against
Judge Porter is, that he had no right to deliver the
opinion of a majority of the court contrary to that of
Judge Cooper; in other words, that reversing all the
principles upon which our government is founded, the
majority shall submit to the minority, and that Judge
Cooper's *ipse dixit* is to be the law in Northampton
county, no matter what may be the opinion of the two
other judges.

The twelfth and last article of impeachment has been
properly abandoned, as being too loose, vague and uncertain; and also, perhaps, because all the evidence that
could have been produced under it, has been embraced
under the three preceding ones.

In taking a retrospect of this cause, the circumstance
cannot well have escaped the attention of this court, that,

with a few solitary and honorable exceptions, the witnesses on the part of the prosecution have come forward under a marked bias of feeling, which has disclosed itself in almost every stage of the proceeding.

Judge Cooper, Hugh Ross and Henry Jarrett, have been ringleaders of this prosecution in Northampton; the first, the party preferring the complaint in at least four of the articles of accusation and impeachment;—the second, disappointed in the decision of several suits; of a naturally envious and jealous disposition, and always "hating that excellence he cannot reach," indulging a rancorous malignity for years against the respondent—making and treasuring up jaundiced notes and statements of transactions which escaped the observation of others, to gratify the foulest feeling that disgraces the human heart. The third, the messenger of the league;—and in regard to all the evidence he has given, I may make one passing remark, and leave him to that infamy he has so richly merited. By comparing his evidence with the articles of impeachment, you will find that he has just taken up the articles to each matter to which he has testified, and sworn exactly to the matters charged; but when cross-examined, as to time or circumstances, he knows nothing; and what is rather singular, no one of the witnesses on the part of the prosecution or defence, saw him in court at the times the transactions should have occurred to which he has testified. From this, and the known character of the man, it is fair to presume, that the first knowledge he ever had of the matters to which he testified, he derived from the articles of impeachment themselves; more especially as he was in attendance last year when the committee of inquiry sat, and never testified to a word of the kind. Much has been said of the respectability and so forth of Judge Cooper. For aught I know, he may be considered a respectable man; but surely it can add nothing to the respectability of any man's character to find him the fellow, laborer, associate and boon companion of *Jacob W. Seitzinger*, *Hugh Ross* and *Henry Jarrett!*

Mr. George Stroud and Mr. Charles Davis, were both professionally disappointed; and like many others of their profession, would endeavor to cast all the odium or fault of their want of success, upon the judge who decided against them. '

Reese need scarcely be mentioned, but he was a party in Reese *v.* Sigman, Commonwealth *v.* Mary Everhart, and Everhart *v.* Reese; poor fellow, he is calculated to do little harm to any one, no matter what his wishes may be.

Beidleman and Haberacker, are the two respectable Allentown gambling house keepers; they yet feel the lecture they so properly received.

Hugh Bellas comes before you, as I have already had occasion to observe, with all the feelings of a losing party; and has given vent to his embittered feelings to such an extent, as to leave no room for candid and impartial recollections of what actually did take place.

Even Mr. King, who is not to be named with the others, has had his professional disappointments and personal differences.

Against this evidence we have adduced a host of candid, dispassionate witnesses; who have satisfied you, I trust, as to every matter of charge, which was susceptible of refutation, or necessary to be refuted.

And in conclusion: I put the character and public services of the respondent—from his early youth, when he was found in his country's ranks fighting for that liberty we now enjoy, to his present venerable age—during all which period he has been found without spot and without blemish—in opposition to charges thus made, and thus attempted to be sustained. They who would grapple with him, grapple with a brazen wall. He has discovered throughout his judicial career—nay, throughout his life—a steadiness of purpose and an inflexible integ-

rity which never could be shaken ; and—with perhaps a
solitary exception—that courteousness and urbanity of
manners—which is sworn by several of the witnesses
to be his characteristic—has never been departed from in
sixteen years. What other judge in the State could
stand a similar inquiry, with equally triumphant success.
A firm and inflexible judge, is a blessing not to be lightly
prized ; for if he, who is to administer the laws of the land
is to be a pliant tool, have an eye to your own rights!
Once establish this idea, and you infuse into the bosom
of society a deadly poison, which carried throughout
your system, relaxes, enfeebles and ultimately destroys
the whole. Have a care!—The decision of this cause is
not a mere matter between the respondent and his persecutors. Its effects will be felt upon society at large.
Offer up the respondent on the altar of vengeance, and
sate the prosecutors in their desire of his destruction ;
and mark me, less pernicious would be the consequences
to the respondent and his family, than would be the result upon the country and the world, which now look
on.

CASE OF THE

JOURNEYMEN TAILORS.

COMMONWEALTH v. JNO. M. MOORE AND TWENTY-FOUR
OTHERS.

In the Mayor's Court for the City of Philadelphia, September Sessions, 1827, Hon. JOSEPH REED, Recorder, presiding.

CHARGE—CONSPIRACY.

The indictment in the above case contains eight counts, and under each count numerous overt acts are set forth. The following argument, however, sufficiently explains the points of the case, to meet all the requirements of the intelligent reader, without any prefatory remarks.

For the Prosecution.
JOHN WURTS, ESQ., JOSEPH R. INGERSOLL, ESQ.

For the Defendants.
WILLIAM B. REED, ESQ., DAVID PAUL BROWN.

(93)

SPEECH IN

JOURNEYMEN TAILORS' CASE.

WITH DEFERENCE TO YOUR HONORS:

Your time and attention have been so largely drawn
upon, in the investigation necessarily incident to the trial
of this cause, that it can scarcely be expected, gentlemen
of the jury, that you should accord to me a very attentive, much less an indulgent hearing; but I do expect—
although I found my claim rather on your liberality
than my own merits—I do expect a *patient* and an *impartial* hearing. The importance of the case, upon which
you are called to decide, requires it; the interests of the
conflicting parties, which are committed to your charge,
solicit it; the laws under which we live and of which
you are the well approved ministers, demand it; and the
solemn obligation which you have assumed—*an immortal
tie*, which at once binds you to this world and to the
next—imperiously enforces it. In thus adverting to *your*
duties, the advocate is, not altogether involuntarily, referred to the discharge of his own. And I regret much
to add that, however safely I may speak in your behalf—
however confidently rely upon the fulfilment of your
duties, I am neither willing, nor do I feel competent to
say—without assuming that to which I am not entitled
—that I can so securely speak of my own. The case
upon which you are to determine is, notwithstanding
all the efforts of the eloquent counsel opposed to us to
establish the contrary, one of great magnitude and

importance. Its consequences are not to be decried, nor its character degraded. You are not to be told that the result of this case will be nothing more than the imposition of a trifling, or perhaps a nominal penalty, upon these unfortunate and oppressed men. Whatever may be the penalty, it is unquestionably to be estimated with reference to the situation and circumstances of the individuals upon whom it is to fall; and we request you to remember, what it appears has been forgotten by the counsel, that it is " the last hair that breaks the camel's back." Suppose the pecuniary penalty which the gentleman has thought proper to affix to the alleged offence, were even unimportant; are there no other penalties acknowledged than those which reach the purse? Is it no penalty to trample on a fallen man? Is it no penalty to taunt the feelings of a lacerated and bleeding heart? Is it no penalty to take from the poor man that which is the pride of the rich as well as the poor—the prince and the peasant—his jewelled reputation? To take from his children the priceless inheritance of a good name—to brand him with a mark as indelible as that of Cain, and to stigmatize those who shall follow him with infamy—are these no penalties? When the gentleman looks to the pecuniary imposition, it may, indeed, as he said, be unimportant; but when he connects wounded feeling and the destruction of reputation, dearer far than life, and to the poor and the humble doubly dear; because with them there is no cure for a bleeding heart in the weight of the purse: when the cause is considered in these more extensive views, allow me to say, the penalty so lightly anticipated, is scarcely to be borne. Let us not then, have this matter undervalued.

Without treating any part of this prosecution either with indifference or want of candor, allow me to say, that the levity assumed on the part of the prosecution, is no unusual mode of crying "*peccavi*" in a cause. "We have," say they," brought a case before you—it

has occupied your attention, and estranged you from
your families and your business for an entire week; but
it is of little consequence, the punishment will be
nothing; jump at once to a conclusion, favorable, nomi-
nally favorable to the prosecutors—and we are content
—justice is satisfied." This is, indeed, a happy method
of sporting with your time, your duty, your consciences,
for the benefit of the commonwealth. If the case be
thus worthless, thus contemptible, its objects so mean
and disproportionate, why has it been originally wrought
up into such a storm? Why have they thus,

> ——"ocean into tempest toss'd
> To waft a feather, or to drown a fly."

With these preliminary remarks, let us address ourselves more immediately to the subject before us.

This is a charge of conspiracy, and may be divided, as
may most subjects, submitted to this tribunal, into,

First, Matters of Law.

Secondly, Matters of Fact.

With reference to the first division of the subject, let
us briefly consider the character of the offence, the
principles governing in the construction of the indictment, and the general law relating to conspiracy; under
which last head, we may aptly embrace the authorities of
the opposite counsel.

Under the second point of inquiry, we shall discuss the
facts relied upon to support, and to resist the prosecution;
not being unmindful in our course, of the situation of the
parties—the consistency and veracity of witnesses, all of
which, as the court will tell you, are proper and legitimate subjects of remark. It is not my intention rigidly
or severely to quadrate my course by these points; but
merely to resort to them as stars by which to steer upon
this dark, and doubtful, and perilous ocean. Arrangement and system are ever the friends of truth; and if
they deserve, will secure success.

What, then, is a CONSPIRACY? It may be defined to be "an agreement between two or more persons to do an unlawful act, or to do a lawful act in an unlawful manner, or by unlawful means." And the requisites of the indictment are implied by the definition of the offence; and in all reason, as well as all law, the indictment must conform thereto. It is not sufficient that the witnesses should prove a conspiracy—that conspiracy must be exhibited upon the face of the *record*. Nor is it alone sufficient that the indictment should be perfect; the facts must also be so—they must mutually impart and imbibe strength—reciprocally borrow and reflect light. One offence is not sustained by proof of *another*, any more than it is supported by defective proof of the *same*. When the indictment is insufficient—it matters not what the facts may be—it may be demurred to, or taken advantage of upon the trial; or after the trial, upon a motion in arrest of judgment.

Overt acts may or may not be important, according to the character of the charge; if the offence consist in unlawful means or manner, the overt act is generally necessary. At all events, the means and manner must be set forth. When the act alleged is clearly unlawful, unlawful means need not be stated; and if the act be not illegal, and no illegal means stated, there is no conspiracy. If this doctrine requires support, it will be found in the City Hall Recorder, vol. 3, page 59.

Again—a conspiracy to do impossible acts is not sustainable, unless when rendered culpable from the means contemplated. Hence an agreement to extinguish the stars—to blow up the moon—to swallow the ocean—to darken the sun, or to do any other impossible thing, unless the means to be used are illegal, is a subject for a commission of lunacy to decide upon, and not a criminal court.

Further—a confederacy is not necessarily criminal. A conspiracy to maintain the laws—to resist oppression—to protect rights, though that protection may interfere with the views of thousands—to discharge our duty to this world and the next, is neither illegal in the act contemplated, nor, in the present case, in the means adopted.

All this even by the common law—but let us recross the Atlantic, and come nearer home. The common law upon this subject must be received here with great caution—with abundant allowance—and so modified as to be adapted to the principles and policy of our government. It is part, and in criminal cases, the worst and most barbarous part of our inheritance from our parent stock. In Great Britain it is a necessary engine of power. It is essential to check and subdue their mechanics—their manufacturers—their artisans; otherwise every man would swell himself beyond his assigned limits. The law, in its administration, is somewhat swerved to their purpose—"to do great good they do a little harm," and too often build up the throne of the monarch upon the bleeding hearts of his subjects. Upon the contrary, no such restraint is required by us—here every man is a monarch legitimately crowned by the laws under which he lives—here people of the classes referred to are rather to be encouraged and sustained, than depressed. They are of the utmost importance to the character and wealth of the State—of the United States. But what says Judge Gibson? The authority referred to upon this subject by our opponents, is exactly what we contend for.

If therefore, I say, this portion of the common law is to be engrafted upon the law of this land, it must be modified and regulated by the policy of the laws of this land, and then it may be adopted. And when adapted to the character of the people here, it may then be said to be equally cogent, here as there. That reason, which operates without regard to difference of circumstances and situations, becomes madness.

Why, may it please your honors, conspiracy, as considered in England, is scarcely less grievous than impressment, and neither has anything to plead but necessity and expediency—neither reason nor justice will sustain them. But if, as I have said, this doctrine were to be extended to this country in all its force, and with all its majesty and might, the defendants could not be convicted, plainly for the reason suggested by my learned friend, the opposite counsel, who has quoted Judge Gibson's opinion, from the Journal of Jurisprudence.

The gentleman has turned to page 226; and that is the page to which I will call your attention.

" In no book of authority has the precise point before me been decided. Rex *v.* The Taylors of Cambridge is found in a book (8 Mod. 10) which can claim nothing beyond the intrinsic evidence of reason and good sense apparent in the cases it contains. In the trial of the *Boot and Shoemakers of Philadelphia*, there was no general principle distinctly asserted, but the case was considered only in reference to its particular circumstances, and in these it materially differed from that now under consideration: And in the trial of the Journeymen Cordwainers of New York, the mayor expressly omits to decide whether an agreement not to work, except for certain wages, would be indictable *per se.* There are, indeed, a variety of British precedents of indictments against journeymen for combining to raise their wages; and precedents rank next to decisions as evidence of the law; but it has been thought sound policy in England to put this class of the community under restrictions so severe, by statutes that were never extended to this country, that we ought to pause before we adopt their law of conspiracy as respects artisans, which may be said to have, in some measure, indirectly received its form, from the pressure of positive enactment, and which therefore may be entirely unfitted to the condition and habits of the same class here. An investigation, then, of the principles of the law which declares the offence, becomes absolutely necessary to a correct decision in this particular instance;

and I at once proceed to it: Whether there are not questions of fact proper for the considerations of a jury, as material to the relator's defence, may, in case I find myself bound to remand them, be a fit question for consideration.

"The unsettled state of the law of conspiracy has arisen, as was justly remarked in the argument, from a gradual extension of the limits of the offence; each case having been decided on its own peculiar circumstances, without reference to any pre-established principle. When a combination had for its direct object to do *a criminal act;* as to procure the conviction of an innocent man (the only case originally indictable, and which afterwards served as a nucleus for the formation of the entire law of the subject), the mind at once pronounced it criminal. So where the act was lawful, but the intention was to accomplish it *by unlawful means;* as where the conviction of a person known to the conspirators to be guilty, was to be procured by any abuse of his right to a fair trial in the ordinary course. But when the crime became so far enlarged as to include cases where the act was not only lawful in the abstract, but also to be accomplished exclusively by the use of lawful means, it is obvious that distinctions as complicated and various as the relations and transactions of civil society, became instantly involved, and to determine on the guilt or innocence of each of this class, an examination of the nature and principles of the offence became necessary. This examination has not yet been very accurately made; for there is, in the books, an unusual want of precision in the terms used to describe the distinctive features of guilt or innocence. It is said the union of persons in one common design is the *gist* of the offence; but that holds only in regard to a supposed question of the necessity of actual consummation of the meditated act; for if combination were, in every view, the essence of the crime, it would necessarily impart criminality to the most laudable associations. It is said in Leach's note to Hawkins, b. 1, ch. 72, § 3, that the conspiracy is the gist of the charge, and that to do a thing lawful in itself *by conspiracy* is unlawful; but that is begging the very question, whether a conspiracy exists, and leaves the inquiry of what shall be said to be doing a lawful act by conspiracy, as much in the dark as ever. Mr. Chitty, in his Criminal Law (vol. 3, page 1139), the best compilation on the subject extant, very truly says there are many cases, in which an act would not be cognizable by law if done by an individual, that would neverthe.ess, be the subject of an indictment, if effected by several with a joint design: yet he too, says the offence depends on the unlawful agreement and not on the act which is to follow it: the act when done being but evidence of the agreement. From this it might be inferred that the act can operate only to show that an agreement of some sort has taken place, but not by its nature or object to stamp the character of guilt on it; but Chitty himself admits that it is impossible to conceive a combination, merely as such, to be illegal. It will therefore be perceived that the *motive* for combining, or, what is the same thing, the *nature of the object* to be attained as a *consequence* of the lawful act is, in this class of cases, the discriminative circumstances. Where the act is lawful for an individual, it can be the subject of a conspiracy when done in concert, only where there is a *direct* intention that injury shall result from it, or where the object is to *benefit* the conspirators to the prejudice of the public or the oppression of individuals, and where such prejudice or oppres-ion is the natural and necessary consequence."

In the trial of the Journeymen Shoemakers of Philadelphia, the recorder, a lawyer of undoubted talents, instructed the jury that it was "no matter *what the defendants' motives were,* whether to *resist the supposed oppression of their masters,* or to insist upon extravagant wages ;" but this, although perfectly true, as applicable to that case, where the combination was intended to

coerce—not only the employers, but third persons—is not
of universal application.   A combination to resist oppression, not merely supposed but real, would be perfectly innocent: for where the act to be done and the means of
accomplishing it are lawful, and the object to be attained
is meritorious, combination is not conspiracy.

Now I will change the sides of the question, and if I
do not convict Robb & Winebrener, then the defendants
deserve to be convicted.   And we will furnish ourselves
with arms and ammunition out of the enemy's own camp
—the very means which our enemies had themselves provided.

Well, but, says the gentleman, certainly if you will not
allow us anything from Judge Gibson's opinion, you will
not deny us the Pittsburg case.   But I will deny it; for
that case and ours are the very antipodes of each other.
They were journeymen to be sure, but they might have
been readily mistaken for the masters in the present case.

I say Robb & Winebrener were the men indicted there
—virtually the men, not the men in name nor quality;
but in point of principle they were the same.   And to
show that it was the case of Robb & Winebrener, I refer
to the indictment.   The Pittsburg indictment may have
been copied by our friend, but it does not follow that
they copied the Pittsburg facts; for after setting forth
the names of some score of individuals, it proceeds:
" that they unlawfully conspired and agreed together,
to form and associate themselves into a society or com-
·bination, and then and there did with like force and
arms and in' like manner, form and associate themselves
together, in pursuance and furtherance of said combina-
nation, conspiracy, confederacy and agreement, into a
society and combination, and did enact certain by-laws,
rules and regulations, by which it was agreed by them
the said conspirators, that they would not work in the
employment or shop of any master cordwainer in the
said borough, who had in his employment any journey-

men cordwainers who were not members of their said society; and who did not conduct himself according to their said by-laws, rules and regulations—that they would not do or perform any work as journeymen cordwainers, unless for such prices as they the said conspirators should agree upon and regulate—that they would not permit any journeymen cordwainers who were members of said society, to work in the employment of any person, unless for such wages as the said society should agree upon and regulate. And that they the said conspirators, would withdraw from the service and employment of any master cordwainer in said borough, who would not pay them such wages as they in their said society might agree upon and regulate, or who would employ in their shops or service, any journeyman cordwainer who was not a member of their said society, who had been expelled therefrom, or did not comply with all their by-laws, rules and regulations."

But, the gentlemen are so led away with the idea of a society, that, finding societies in both cases, they took it for granted the offence must be the same.

I think in the course of the proof it was made to appear, that they had changed the price of making boots, from $1.75 to $3.50, thus raising the price and departing from the old bill. Now will any man tell me that journeymen entering into an agreement to do that which they were legally bound to do, will meet a case of this character Robb & Winebrener occupy the place of these men who refused to do work, unless upon payment of higher wages.

They insist on cutting these men into mincemeat—they insist on crushing them with the hard hand of vexatious need. They had conformed to this agreement, they had ratified it by their practice; and now they think proper to depart from it, and to indict these men for not submitting to their imposition. Suppose they had reduced to six cents their daily wages; these individuals, I suppose, must either submit, or starve, or be prosecuted : they would have said, " if you demand seven dollars, we will pay you seven dollars, but the penalty of poverty shall be your portion—we will advertise you, and all master tailors shall close their doors against you." The law should be more severe with masters than with men, and that in proportion to the means of individuals to encroach upon its sacred limits. The masters are more dangerous than the men, as was well observed by my respectable colleague ; for although it does not bear directly upon this case, it bears upon the opposite party, and is therefore perfectly apposite.

There is no resisting the groans of a wife and the cries of her infants—this is a law which nature has inscribed on our hearts, and which it is neither in our inclination nor ability to resist ; yet the counsel for the commonwealth has ventured to appeal to your feeling. The plaintiffs are the offenders—they have conspired to reduce the wages, and nothing saves them from punishment but the want of an indictment.

I was about to observe that combinations of this sort are more dangerous in masters than in men, because poverty is a law which man cannot resist. Masters have the means, and though they may exact from their customers any price which they please, there is never a thought of their being conspirators, while they are grinding down the men whom they employ, to little more than nothing, and pocketing their services. They can hold out, they can persist in their determinations ; for they have already accumulated a sufficiency to confirm them in their obduracy. And again, the effects are more pernicious because they are more generally felt ; for one master may perhaps, have twenty journeymen. The suggestion of this cannot be too much dwelt upon, for even journeymen will some day become masters, or they look to become so, for " hope bears us through, nor quits us at the last." Every journeyman expects to become a master—it is the regular line of preferment; but few masters expect again to become journeymen. The journeymen, therefore, having a view to their subsequent elevation, are less dangerous in their opposition to the laws —they take care not to affect their character. But when the masters form a combination, they have no regard to the situation of their journeymen, because they never expect to share with them in their perils, nor pains; nor can they sympathize with them in their liability to evil, or susceptibility of good.

I know, and am happy to say it, that I address those who have, in all probability, many of them, passed through the different grades to promotion—and a promotion which they now enjoy as they ought. But will you kick down the ladder of your own greatness—will you turn your backs upon those who are engaged in the same virtuous struggle? Is it not much more magnanimous for you to avow to the world, that you have erected your own fortunes, and have not forgotten it, but that you sympathize with those who are erecting theirs, in the same laudable pursuit.

Again, we are turned to another indictment in a sister State—we must be assailed somewhere, and if Pittsburg won't reach us, New York must. But let us see the indictment; what do the counts set forth? These resemble strongly the Pittsburg case—but ours not at all. The charge is—having enumerated the persons by name—of: " designing and intending to form and unite themselves into an unlawful club and combination, and to make and ordain unlawful by-laws, rules and orders among themselves, and thereby to govern themselves and other workmen in said art, and unlawfully and unjustly to extort great sums of money by means thereof." Second. " That none of the said conspirators, would work for any master or person whatsoever in the said art, &c., who shall employ any workmen, &c., who shall thereafter infringe or break any or either of the said unlawful rules, orders or by-laws." Third. "That they would not work for any master or person who should employ any workman, &c., who should break any of their by-laws, unless such workman, &c., should pay to the club such sum as should be agreed on, as a penalty for the breach of such unlawful rules, orders or by-laws; and that they did, in pursuance of the said conspiracy, refuse to work and labor for James Corwin and Charles Aimes, because they, C. and A. did employ one Edward Whitess, a cord-wainer (alleging that the said E. W. had broken one of such rules and orders, and refused to pay two dollars, &c., as a penalty for breaking such rules and orders), and continued in refusing to work, &c., for C. and A. until the said C. and A. discharged the said E. W.," &c., &c. Fourth. " Wickedly, and intending unjustly, unlawfully, and by INDIRECT MEANS, to impoverish the said Edward Whitess, and hinder him from following his trade, did confederate, conspire, &c., by wrongful and indirect means, to impoverish the said E. W., and to deprive and hinder him from following his said art," &c.

Thus, without a single observation, you perceive that the charge there and here are of an opposite character.

Having inquired into the nature of this offence, the general principles of law bearing upon it, and the particular character of the charge against the defendants, let us next inquire,

What are the facts of this case—in other words, how is this volume sustained by the evidence? For after all, this is the most important branch of the cause—" To this complexion we must come at last." Upon casting the eye here, placing the indictment out of sight, and forgetting who are said to have committed the offence, honest nature at once asks, who are the alleged conspirators, the master, or the men? Let us, in answering this inquiry, look to the origin of the transaction—the more immediate origin. Is this prosecution founded in the pursuit of justice, or in the gratification of avarice and

revenge?—two of the meanest, as well as the worst passions that agitate the human breast. Why is it that Mr.
Winebrener is thus clad in the panoply of the law, and
mounted upon the broad shoulders of the commonwealth ;
is it to spy into abuses that have been practiced upon
the State, or is it to convert the thunders of the law to
his own selfish purpose?—I say it is the latter. He
commits an outrage upon Mr. Boner, one of the defendants, upon a mere " cock and bull story " of the naval hero
Mr. Chamberlain, who permits no opportunity to escape,
from the beginning to the conclusion of this case, of exhibiting his fidelity, at the expense of his courage. Mr.
Winebrener is the first offender, and is bound over : then,
and for the first time, as his counsel admit, he thinks
of binding over the defendants; he first charges six, next
twelve, and increase of appetite still growing by what it
fed on, he finally charges, twenty-five. After this, although it certainly cannot be said of him as was said of
Paul, that too much *learning* has made him *mad*—undoubtedly, we cannot but perceive, that too much *malice*
has.

Having swayed dominion over his own shop, he en-
larges it to his pavement—then extends it to all Chestnut
street ; and not satisfied with this, carries his authority
to assail and beat these men wherever they may be
found—holds them all in subjugation ; and emphatically,
at last becomes the self-created "Lord of the Bright
City." Chamberlain is confederated with him, as well
as his partner, in this assumption of authority—in this
oppression of the defendants—in this violation of the
laws ; and still we are told that they are no conspirators,
but that the offence should be charged only to these unfortunate men—men who, for aught that appears, are
much more " sinned against than sinning."

Let us for a moment, while upon this part of the case,
turn our attention to the *particulars* of the affair with
Mr. Boner. Induced, as I have said, by Chamberlain, he

(Winebrener) approaches Mr. Boner, and tells him he had better go about his business.—Why do you volunteer your advice, Mr. Winebrener—is not Mr. Boner pursuing his course home—is he not engaged in his own business? Certainly. Has he interfered with you or yours? No. He is a poor man, it is true—and you have wealth—he is a cripple, and you have not only strength, but you are supported by Mr. Chamberlain, who has the Nemæan Lion's nerve—but still you have no right to trample upon legal privileges — nor personal sanctity. Mr. Boner replies, you are not to dictate to me; I am on my road home, but I'll walk where I please. Upon this Mr Winebrener shoves him, Boner raises his stick—which he carried for his support, being lame—merely as a defence; upon which Winebrener knocks the stick out of his hand, and as an additional proof of magnanimity, strikes him over the head. Well was it that night had spread her dark mantle over the blushing deed. Not contented with this outrage—which, remember, he relates himself—he adds injury to injury, by preferring a complaint, some days after, against the man he had assaulted, before one of the neighboring justices of the peace; for the praiseworthy purpose, no doubt, being under the direction of counsel, of counteracting the testimony, which otherwise must overwhelm him. The binding over of Boner bears strongly upon other parts of this case—it indicates the disposition of the prosecution—it shows an activity and vigilance of spirit equal to any emergency that may be encountered. The disposition and ruling passion of men being once ascertained, it serves as a key to unlock all the intricacies, and unfold all the mysteries of the human heart. The cruelty practised upon Mr. Boner, is in accordance with the prosecutor's deportment toward the other defendants. Having dismissed them from his employment, and taken *measures* (I mean no pun) to prevent their being employed elsewhere, he is offended that they should convene together in the vicinity of his shop. "I have shut you out of my house, and out of every other house by my influence—and now the *wonder* is that you should be found together in the street"—*most reasonable surprise* truly! As well might every unfortunate individual, who is a disbanded officer, be indicted for high treason against the country for which he bled, because the United States may have left him nothing to do, or to hope for, but to congregate with his former associates in arms, in endless idleness, and sympathetic misery. But further—these men are not even permitted to assemble in the region of the post office—not even upon the Rialto. One is supposed to have a private pique against Mr. Chamberlain, and is not allowed to speak to him. They are not allowed to communicate their own grievances to an individual, to whom Winebrener had communicated his. He can go to Mr. O'Neil and relate the story, but these men may not. That is the simple explanation of this great matter; they have character, and they depend on it for employment, and when Robb & Winebrener had been to stigmatize them with O'Neil, they thought proper to vindicate themselves. But more than this—he will not let them stand, or walk, or speak, without his leave; but he will speak himself, and boldly too! He comes to the door when Radford is walking peaceably by, and commences an attack upon him; and I wonder that in your attendance here, passing by the residence of this gentleman, you had not been assailed and indicted also. It was a public street and Radford had a right to be there; but this gentleman was not satisfied with restricting them; he claims a privilege which he denies to them. He comes up to Radford, and tauntingly asks him, " A'n't you tired of standing guard, won't you have a chair?" Now this is frivolous, but it deserves punishment. But it is said, by way of enfeebling the evidence, to which I have referred, that the witnesses for the defence are all journeymen tailors except some three or four; and these we are told, although they are not journeymen tailors, are master tailors, and are supported by journeymen tailors and apprentices. I ask you to notice the shop of Messrs. Robb & Winebrener—this northern hive—this *officina gentium*—that pours forth this host of witnesses. If you take the testimony of those who stand in close relation to the prosecutors, out of this case, it has not a foot to rest on. Mr. Winebrener is the first—the former prosecutor and aggressor. Mr. Chamberlain, the Messrs. Robb—Charles, Samuel and William, the one a partner and the other his brothers—O'Neil, who is employed and gets the work intended for these men—Ramsay the runner—and he follows so close after his master that he brings before you, as Mr. Winebrener did, a memorandum; and asks you to affix your seal to his *Scroll of Fate*. There you have the most important witnesses in this case, every one, I was about to say, from the self same shop-board—nay, every witness, I might almost say, is a party to this very cause.

For all the purposes of testimony, the defendants are dead; their lips are as effectually closed, as though the ponderous and marble jaws of the tomb had devoured them; and nothing is to be heard but Robb and Winebrener—nothing seen but that bright galaxy in which they, the primary planets, are surrounded by a host of twinkling satellites. All this is matter of consideration; the inconsistencies of the prosecution are to be more rigidly scrutinized, their dispositions more closely examined, inasmuch as they have an unlimited power of doing wrong, and their antagonists are debarred of all opportunity of counteracting that wrong. But the prosecutors have not only sealed our lips, but they at the same time complain of our want of witnesses. They say we should have produced Mr. Alderman Barker—for what? To establish what had already been abundantly confirmed by at least three or four witnesses. Was not the transcript of Mr. Barker offered by us and opposed by them? If they did not like the act, it is not probable the man would have met a better reception; or if he were desirable, why did not they produce him? If he could gainsay the defendant's proof, they had but to step across the street, requiring no seven league boots, to secure his attendancè. But while upon the subject of evidence omitted, allow me to inquire from our friend, who conducts this charge—where is Mr. Ross, who applied to the Messrs. Watson for the price of the riding habit? Mr. Winebrener's statement unquestionably required his support; he is among the missing. Where is Mr. Burden? a gentleman of undoubted character, and who could at once have placed the impress of unequivocal truth upon those transactions, in regard to which, we have at present nothing but the scambling, scattering, and unsure observance, of the redoubtable naval hero, Mr. Chamberlain. Mr. Chamberlain! whose sight is so jaundiced either by fear or favor, that the most common and familiar courtesies, are subject to be misunderstood by him. Shaking hands, itself, with him is a badge of deliberate treason; there is not a smile but lurks a devil in it; and in short, all the charities, and sympathies, and civilities of life, are dark denotements of the most deadly and destructive hostility. The eloquent counsel, chiming in with the witnesses, solemnly apostrophizes a pair of thread-bare "breeches," in the course of his interlocutory appeal; and finally, they are by joint effort magnified into something but little short of a nine pounder at least, and paraded before the commonwealth upon this occasion, with all the pride, pomp, and pageantry of a military triumph.* Now, though some men, as we are told, when the wind is north-northwest, may distinguish between a hawk and a handsaw, I respectfully submit to you, that after this, Mr. Chamberlain is not entitled to rank of that number: however this may be, permit

---

* This refers to Mr. Chamberlain having mistaken *a pair of pantaloons*, in the hands of one of the defendants, for a murderous weapon. —ED.

me nevertheless solemnly to congratulate the hero upon his escape from all those toils and perils past, those " hair breadth 'scapes, and imminent adventures." Had it not been for the timely, critical interposition of Mr. Boner—one of these nefarious conspirators—had it not been for his merciful, all-imposing, irresistible injunction, addressed to Mr. Parkinson, in the mystic and magic words " NOT YET "—the wide world would have had to lament the premature death of the illustrious Mr. Chamberlain, in a manner scarcely less deplorable or infamous than that of suicide—*A tailor killed by the untimely explosion of—a pair of pantaloons !*

I have no more inclination, though much more cause to assail the witnesses in this case, than the opposite counsel, and as much confidence may be reposed in the candor of this declaration, as in his ;—neither, I hope, having any view to *ulterior* results.   But allow me to say, it is the policy of the commonwealth to abstain from considering the veracity of the evidence, and particularly that of Chamberlain, as it could terminate in nothing but discomfiture and disgrace.   With us, however, as I have said, the matter stands differently.   The prosecuting testimony I will show you is assailable wherever it is tangible, and vulnerable wherever it is assailable.   And we are bound to say—at the same time that no man should be wantonly attacked—that that delicacy which would protect a witness from merited odium, in a cause like this, would imply an abandonment of duty, and so far from being a *virtue*, would be a *crime*.   Let us then, proceeding upon this principle, approach somewhat nearer to the witnesses, and touching them with the celestial spear of Ithuriel, deprive them of their masks and exhibit them to the world in their true features.   First, in the first rank, comes the redoubtable Mr. Chamberlain, to whom I have already generally referred.   The *Hero* comes! after having sustained a friendly blank cartridge fire from the gentlemen engaged for the prosecution, for about an hour, with most undaunted bravery! Did you observe the moment the battery of the defence was brought to bear upon him, how utterly the scene was changed? Upon being cross-examined, he was simply asked—Have you been to sea? Do you remember how at once he floundered and fluttered like a winged widgeon; first declining, and afterwards demanding whether he was bound to answer the question? In this dilemma his confusion is increased by a friendly attempt to diminish it—Mr. Wurts tells him he may answer it, and "say also whether he had not seen Mr. Reed in South America." This is too much, and everything like composure is at once put to flight. At length, however, mustering up his scattered spirits, he, after a prodigious effort, succeeds in saying, he had once been on board the United States ship Macedonian. The question related to other matter than that—but explanation on our part was not allowable, and upon theirs not advisable. But was it not evident to you, not only from the manner, but the answer, that there was more in his recollection than either reached the eye, or ear? Why, sir, are you ashamed of your naval glory, of having been defending, and defended by, the wooden walls of your country—why, above all, would you disclaim even a single leaf of the Macedonian's laurels—a single ray of that lustre which she reflects upon the nation? Why! there was not a splinter in the ship, either considered in connection with herself, or in relation to her great original, that might not have lighted up more courage in your heart, than even all your *imaginary* exigencies and impediments could possibly have required! —Fear, however, is always the spontaneous offspring of crime—"suspicion always haunts the guilty mind; the thief doth fear each bush an officer."

But to his story—having escaped the *murderous weapon* of Mr. Parkinson, he takes shelter under the friendly roof of Mr. Burden; while here, he sees, or fancies he sees enemies upon all sides; three men nearly opposite to the door—and several others approaching—Falstaff's men in Kendal Green, I suspect—*buckram men*, certainly, even according to his own statement. To relieve him from this state of incalculable peril, the magistrate and Mr. Milliman who had been sent for, at length arrive; and under the charge of the latter he is induced to resume his way home—and what is remarkable, none of these beleaguering enemies, according to Mr. Milliman, molest, speak to, or apparently notice them. When they reach the vicinity of South street, Mr. Winebrener arrives in breathless anxiety—calls to the constable, and then, instead of passing on to the residence of Mr. Chamberlain, which was within a short distance—wonderful to relate, and the more remarkable, as it is entirely forgotten by the hero of this episode—at the instance of Mr Winebrener, they all three retrace their steps—encounter Mr. Boner and Mr. Donahue in their return, which results in the unprovoked assault and battery upon Mr. Boner, to which I have already adverted. Mr. Milliman, a perfectly respectable, as well as disinterested man acquits the individuals accused by Mr. Winebrener and Mr. Chamberlain, of everthing like impropriety; and conclusively shows that this most horrible and appalling scene of outrage, and probable murder, was but the sheer coinage of an over-heated brain.—In short, this man appears to have been wrought up, by some internal and unaccountable agitation, almost to a pitch of madness—or at least, he centres in his make such strange extremes, as to render his conduct perfectly inexplicable upon the common principles of human action—he first flees from danger either real or imaginary, with little or no apparent cause; and then, with no more cause, he voluntarily confronts that danger. He sees a man at eleven o'clock at night moving about his door, and is terrified at the treacherous designs of which he suspects him; and yet leaves his house for the purpose of pursuing the enemy and subjecting himself to the very crisis that he dreaded.

This shows the spirit of the cause, and it is for that purpose mainly, that I have taken the liberty of occupying your attention with these transactions. And is it at all extraordinary that thus situated, the opposite counsel should attempt making a virtue of necessity, by professing a disinclination to comment upon the character of the proof, when the proof which they have exhibited, for the most part shrinks from the test of comment.—Their profession is too thin a veil to conceal the true character of their liberality—it resembles the kiss of Judas the betrayer—the compassion of the crocodile, who mingles his tears with the life's blood of his expiring victim.—If men are to be assailed, let it be done openly, with full opportunity of resistance. Why is it, notwithstanding all this mercy—this theoretical mercy—the prosecution is still so cruel, even to some of their own witnesses—Saturn like, devouring their own offspring. In regard to O'Flaherty, who was called by them, it is plainly intimated, without any inducement being suggested, that he is perjured—nay, more—that by way of protecting himself in that perjury, he had torn a leaf out of the minute book of the society. Notwithstanding the witness—with a promptness and frankness that did him honor—gave for explanation, that this book had originally been appropriated to other purposes; and that, as he did not slumber amidst hoards of gold, and had no money to lavish upon unnecessary purchases, he converted the book to the uses of the society; having previously torn out the leaves which appertained to other matter. From the severity, with which Mr. O'Flaherty has been treated, we may easily preceive that, whether friends or foes—if the individuals who have been invoked into this trial, stand in the way of Robb & Winebrener—they are equally liable to persecution.

But to return to the consideration of the prosecuting testimony; Mr. O'Neil, who follows upon the heel of Mr. Chamberlain, and who was encouraged by our friends on the opposite side, in rather more impertinence than be-

came the solemnity of the obligation under which he
appeared—Mr. O'Neil, I say, showed his disposition to
convince you, that, as the other was not a prepared witness, he at least *was*, and that he came purposely prepared
to answer me—it is true he was prepared to answer *me ;*
but he was not prepared to answer *himself*. He should
have come prepared to swear to what he had sworn to
before—to swear to the same men, and to vindicate his
statement before the magistrate; while he should have
forgotten his studied argument for Robb & Winebrener,
or left that with the *other* unfinished garment—at home.
He tells you at this time that Mr. Hough, the man sworn
to before, is the man that called at his house in company
with Radford ; yet at the magistrate's office, as we have
shown by three or four incontrovertible witnesses, he
swore positively to Radford and to Miller, and to the best
of his belief as to Scott.   What then is the argument?
Without at all designing to convict Mr. O'Neil of falsehood ; if at different times he swears to different men,
his testimony is too imperfect and unsatisfactory to furnish anything like a basis upon which we may safely rely.
If Mr. Radford and two others, being participants jointly,
in a criminal design—in pursuance of that design, called
at the house of the witness, we are entitled to know who
they were; and *that* we cannot ascertain, from the evidence of any man who swears on different days to different persons.   To entitle testimony to our reliance, it
should exhibit at least as much truth as zeal.

If you cannot rely upon Mr. O'Neil as to the person,
much less can you confide in his remembrance of the conversation ; but even if you could accord your belief fully
to both, what is to be the result ?—What was the offence ?
These men having understood that Mr. Winebrener, Mr.
Ramsey, and others, had related their stories to O'Neil,
and had also employed him ; thought proper to wait upon
him, and to submit an account of their grievances, and
concluded by asking if he thought it right to join in a

confederacy with Robb & Winebrener to do the work of
the journeymen, and thereby to deprive them of their
wages, according to their contract.

Had not these men authority to remonstrate against an
encroachment upon their rights?—Or is that encroachment to be justified, and the remonstrance itself to be considered culpable? O'Neil, and Robb & Winebrener, and
Ramsay, and Chamberlain were all conspirators—integral
parts in the great scheme—to reduce journeymen to submission or starvation. Yet they have so managed their
cards as to shuffle the poor and unfortunate to the top of
the pack, while they themselves are screened from observation, and protected from animadversion by the very
individuals whom they have abused. I put it to you,
without the fancy of the advocate, that these are the
plain, unsophisticated facts of the case. The next witness is Mr. Ramsay, the compeer of Mr. O'Neil. What
shall be done with these men—though they are in gears
together, they refuse to pull together. Mr. Ramsay even
now denies that Hough was one of the companions of
Radford, but upon the contrary still adheres to Miller and
Scott. Then you have Ramsay in opposition to O'Neil.
There is, in short, such inconsistency and contrariety in
this portion of the testimony, intrinsic and relative, that
it is almost impossible to accord your confidence to either
of them. If there were any explanations that could assist or reconcile these statements, it was in the power of
the opposite party to supply them by the evidence of the
magistrate; and they stand confirmed by the omission on
their part so to do. But there are still greater discrep-
ancies. Winebrener, O'Neil and Ramsay—with the benefit
of their memoranda to boot—tell you that there was never
any instruction to the alderman to discontinue the prosecution against a number of these men; but that it was
determined to pursue it. Notwithstanding which, the opposite counsel gave you to understand that the defendants
were merely on their good behavior, and to be discharged

or tossed in a blanket, as the whim, will, or pleasure of
the prosecution might suggest. Four witnesses for the
defendants state, that three of them were actually discharged at Mr. Winebrener's own request; and we have
offered the records and the returns of Mr. Barker for the
purpose of confirmation. The same witnesses swore that
a commitment had been prepared for Bates, Skeegs, and
Scott; and that it was only upon their counsel declaring
that they would not give bail, but should submit to imprisonment, and that a suit should subsequently be instituted against Robb & Winebrener for a malicious prosecution—that, from a fear of punishment, and not a love
of justice, the case against these gentlemen was dismissed, on simply their own recognizance. Notwithstanding this, they, and some dozen others, for the
purpose of depriving us of testimony, and transferring
the responsibility of this prosecution to the shoulders of
the grand jury, are subsequently embraced in the indictment. If this shows nothing else, it at least betrays
a conscious fear on the part of our antagonist; and dis-
closes the state of mind by which they have been, and
still continue to be influenced in this proceeding. There
has also been the most unnatural obliquity, not to say
perversion of intellect and vision, that ever crept into a
cause. It would appear as if every one of these gentlemen had, like Foy, employed a telescope; with this difference, to be sure, that it was so inverted by them, that
every thing appeared erroneously, and the world was
turned topsy turvy. Mr. Robb tells you—and his testimony and deportment are entitled to much greater respect than some others—that one of the individuals not
now upon trial—taking the name of the Deity in vain—
swore he would enter into the shop in despite of Robb;
whereas the very individual referred to, upon his examination, says, that the language imputed to him was used
only by Mr. Robb, who accompanied his profanity by
levelling a lapboard at the head of the witness, and pur-

suing him down stairs with threats; although he had previously offered willingly and peaceably to leave the premises. This man has no interest in the present controversy, and he is strengthened by being opposed only to those who have.

Last, though not least, comes Mayhew. How does he stand? He was formerly in the employment of Robb & Winebrener, and *now* under the promise of future employment from them. Heaven forbid—though I am not in the habit of invoking anything sacred in a cause like this—I say Heaven forbid, that, because he has been in their employment, he should be thereby biassed, or swerved from the truth. While we condemn the suspicions of others, let us not fall into the same error; but will you turn your attention to him and examine his claims to belief. He is one of those who suppose that somebody always wants to buy them; and for the very reason that they are always willing to be bought. He supposes that these journeymen wished to purchase him, and he says they endeavored to dissuade him from going to Robb & Winebrener's. Now what is the plain testimony of those who are not journeymen tailors? What say they? Why that they endeavored to dissuade this headstrong young man from getting himself into difficulty, and adding the twenty-sixth man to this conspiracy; but never dissuaded him from going to Robb & Winebrener's. But what is very strange is, that he throws up his work, not from any dissuasion of others, but from some domestic broil; and still it is imputed to these men.

It seems there was some unhappy family disturbance, and that disturbance was pursued by our friend, under the hope that it might be traced to the defendants; but it turned out to be purely a domestic disturbance, and was subsequently avoided by me, as indelicate and improper. He states, when put to the torture, that in consequence of this difference, he turned Pickering from his house. Pickering says he never saw him there, that he never was in his house but once, and then he called to mention that he had some work for him. He mentioned it to his wife, Mayhew not being at home; and the next day the man came down to the shop. Do you suppose, if it were true, that he expelled him as he has said, that he would come down to Pickering's shop and ask his advice? Does not this fact show, as well as the evidence of Miller, that all this story about his wife and Mr. Pickering (which nobody can understand), was merely resorted to, to extricate him from a difficulty which he could not otherwise escape; and that it had as little foundation as three-fourths of the other statements from the same quarter. Mr. Mayhew is next seen at Mr. McGuire's, where the society met. Here he saw some of the defendants—converses with them—tells them he is willing to be idle if he can get money enough to support him—never receives any money, and finally, finding no other bidders for his services than his old employers, he communicates all, and *more* to them; and again enlists under their banner. It would be safer to rely upon the fidelity of the winds and the waves, than upon testimony so loose and unsatisfactory as this.

As to the charges, or rather reasons, why these men should be considered conspirators.

First, because they belong to a society which has adopted illegal laws. It is not so charged in the indictment—that is my answer. All the time that is employed in discussing the affairs of this society amounts to nothing. You discuss the laws of the society as if the society had been indicted; and, as if the crime consisted in confederating and forming these laws. But that is not charged. It is attempting to argue that there was a conspiracy, which can amount to nothing unless embraced in the indictment. For you can no more punish a crime without an indictment, than you can punish upon an indictment without a crime. But allow me to rescue the society—though I have no interest therein but that which every man should have—from unmerited reproach.

We are told by the gentleman on the opposite side, in relation to the book of this society, that he did not take it home, because he supposed that he should be suspected of taking out the leaves. He might have taken it home, I assure him, without any such suspicion—nay, we should have rejoiced in it; for had he known more of its principles, he would have condemned them less.

If, may it please your honors, this society had been indicted, the cause could not have been sustained: undoubtedly, then, the society not having been indicted, the cause cannot be sustained: at least, so far as relates to the proof bearing upon the society alone. There is not an illegal principle in the whole book. The first, however, adverted to, and that which gives a more dreadful note of treason than the rest, is an enactment, that any individual who shall move to convert this society into a beneficial society, shall be *fined* for the first offence, and *expelled* for the second. I have not much knowledge of this subject, but I presume that most of you have belonged to societies of a similar kind. And every man knows perfectly well, that this portentous and ominous rule amounts to nothing—nothing at least in support of the gentleman's apprehension. Now what is the evident object in this? Here are men who have associated together for the protection of their rights: and ever since the allegory of the bundle of sticks, it has almost been reduced to a proverb, that the wheat should combine for protection against the storm. They have done it, and they are bound together by a silver cord ; securing the object for which they have united. Now that provision is to prevent lawless individuals from coming into the society in large numbers, and turning the public coffers to their own benefit; in contravention of the design which forms the basis of the institution.

Have you not been told that it is a *beneficial* society ;

that they bury their own dead; that they pay the expenses of the funeral: and are not those benefits lasting which survive the grave? Nay, is not one of the charges, that it is a beneficial society, virtually? I trust the gentleman will excuse me for saying, that he has been blowing hot and cold with the same breath; first, it is a beneficial society, and therefore to be repudiated; and the next instant to be condemned because it is *not* a beneficial society. How shall we steer to catch a favorable breeze? How shall we at the same time shun Sylla and Charybdis? Let him take it as if it were not a beneficial society, armed with lawful objects; but if it be a beneficial society, let it never be said, that the benevolence or beneficence of its character should take from its legality. But we are next exultingly turned to the 14th article, as the respectable counsel supposes it means mischief; but neither he nor any one can tell *how.* At the time when journeymen are standing out for their rights, against the oppression of overweening masters, or opposing despotism and force—if any man desert his brother—if he desert him in a struggle like this, he is a coward, and a traitor, and he deserves no better name. The law says that men shall stand out for their *rights*— and it is only when they stand out for their rights against the encroachment of others, that they are vindicated or sustained; and I am willing to read the article to you a hundred times if you please, as the best encomium that can be pronounced upon a body of men so grossly abused— so miserably misunderstood.

" *Article* 14. Any man going to work at the time of a turn out, and at a time when young men are standing out for their rights in this city, or any of the principal towns in the United States, if it shall come to the knowledge of this society, the parties so offending shall pay a fine of five dollars; and after paying the same, if any member shall upbraid him with his former conduct, he shall pay the sum of one dollar."

Observe the justice of the law—Solon himself could not have framed a wiser law. *And after paying the money, if any man should upbraid him, that man should pay a fine of one dollar.* You have erred and returned again, like the prodigal to your duty—you have erred, and we, who are all liable to err, forgive you; "to err is human, to forgive divine."

But nothing being found in the book, the gentleman resorts to his fancy, to an imagination of what might be; and you are to convict upon a prospective or possible evil. Although it is not contained in the book, yet how do we know, that they have not made provision for it by a shop rule? We offered to tell them what were the shop rules; but having shut their eyes to the light, they should not now complain of darkness. We have offered to show them that it was not a shop rule—they refused; and we are bound to believe the truth of the case is against the surmise. You have heard many instances where journeymen—individuals, not members of the society—have not been disturbed; and you have had no instance in which they have. There may, it is true, be the "pitcher law," governing their little convivialities; but they do not drink treason on the admission of every new member; and they are not to be convicted on mere hints and innuendoes—we ask for stubborn and unequivocal facts. I say the witnesses, or some of them, have clearly established that there was no illegal confederacy at all. But what is the answer again? We answer, you have not charged us with the "pitcher law." We have spoken to that law, not that from any interpretation we can be affected by it, but to show that we ask no quarters; but are ever ready to encounter the alleged charges, whether suggested by the record or imagination. We come prepared to meet you, armed against the offences of which you have accused us; but we do not refuse to meet anything and everything—although it is illegal and unjust to expect it. So much then for the society—we will now throw out of the question that which does not belong to it; and for which our opponents must be our apology if it has constituted the burthen of our song.

What, then, is the first charge in the indictment, and the facts relating to that charge? We will endeavor not again to refer to that which is not essential in this case; although it was necessary that this should be remarked upon, lest the jury should suppose the subject unanswerable because unanswered. I only ask you to exercise your own reason, and I will be perfectly content to leave the cause to its unbiassed results. But do not understand that in being somewhat unwilling to extend your time and protract this case; it is with any other disposition than to abridge your labors, that I have omitted to answer some of these arguments; but rather impute it to its true source—a proper regard to you, and a perfect conviction that they are answerable, in your own unassisted minds.

What, then, are the first four charges? They are charges of conspiracy on the part of these men, *to do an unlawful act*, or *to do a lawful act by unlawful means;* and I care not which. The act alleged to be in contemplation by the conspirators, was the increase of their wages beyond the usual price of wages; and not accepting the usual price of wages which Robb & Winebrener, and others, had been accustomed to pay. These are the first four charges. I allege that the prosecution cannot succeed on the establishment of a doubtful case—they cannot succeed by rendering it difficult to decide whether the defendants did in fact exact more wages, or whether Robb & Winebrener offered less. They must show clearly—the burthen of proof being with them—that we demanded more than the usual wages. It is not incumbent on us to show that they wished to pay less; but we intend to show that these men are the sufferers, though not the complainants. Instead of their demanding more wages, Mr. Winebrener himself introduced the attempt to reduce the wages below their proper legitimate level—(turns to bill).

Is this your bill, Mr. Winebrener? Yes. Is this your bill, Mr. Robb? Yes. Is this your bill, Mr. Watson? Yes. Well, is it the bill by which you work, or by which journeymen work for you—and does it govern the prices in this respect? It does. This being the bill, and placed in Mr. Winebrener's book, and displayed publicly in the shop of the journeymen—now how did it become the bill? By express contract and agreement between the parties. And, strange as it may seem, this is an indictment of men for endeavoring to keep their contract. You may have been led away and bewildered by the learned counsel; and they may hope to succeed by the mystery in which the subject is involved: but stripped of all its borrowed plumage, it is an indictment against twenty-five men for wishing to keep their contract against—I do not know how many—desiring to break it. This being the bill, we have nearly arrived at the conclusion of our labors, and allow me to congratulate you upon the subject. What was the work done? It was a pongee riding dress, requiring five or six men to complete it, as it was wanted almost immediately, and to be finished in a particular way. Well, what were the appendages, and what were the extras? In the first place, it was a dress with hussar skirts—in the second place, it was stuffed in the breast—it had wadding in the heads of the sleeves, and vents at the wrists. It had hussar skirts rantered at the body—flies at the breast; and all this, in conformity with the bill, is charged seven dollars. It is said that there were no extras, but every man examined has proved that there were extras; thus making the prosecution the worse, by giving them a *bad habit* in story telling, as well as in other matters of their vocation. I put it to the jury, and ask if they know any exception, besides that of Mr. Winebrener. The other witnesses all stated that there were extras. But the gentlemen seem to have abandoned the extras, while relying on the difference in price. With the extras, the job amounted to seven dollars six and a quarter cents, and what did the journeymen demand? Did they demand eight dollars, or ten dollars? No such thing; though they might have demanded something above the usual price, they demanded exactly seven dollars. And what did the masters offer to pay?—One dollar less than the regular price. They insist on departing from the regular and usual price, and turn round and indict these men because they are not willing to submit to the imposition. Corrupt motives are not to be causelessly assigned; the defendants are supposed to act purely, particularly as there is sufficient reason here to induce us to believe they were right. The price is authorized by the bill. Were there any distinction designed, it is not introduced; and when it is not introduced, you are to take analogy for the guide. They might as well say their making a blue cloth habit should be but six dollars, because there is a difference in colors. The question is whether the work was done, and intended to be paid for. Thin coats, coatees, and jackets are distinguished in price from thick ones, because there are more seams in the one than the other; because there is a difference in the seams, and no wadding, as the object of the dress is to prevent being overheated. The wadding is excluded, and they are made in the most simple and airy style. What is the analogy? It is " marked " in one case; and in the other the absence of the mark shows that no distinction is to be made.

Now, in the first instance, how is it with a pongee habit? is it as with a thin coat? Not at all. There is in the first place a very evident distinction. But I mean in point of fact, not in principle—the one is intended for a lady, and the other for a gentleman. But that is not very important. In the next place, it is made of stuff half a yard wide, and contains more seams—the one having five, the other two or three; but it is not necessary for me to go into an actual calculation, for when I tell you all, I can say no more than the witnesses have expressly sworn to.

The man who has been stigmatized with being a gardener and sexton—(I am wrong) a "clerk" of St. Stephen's—I beg pardon, your honors, not being so well versed in *church history* as the opposite counsel;—The clerk (it shall be) of St. Stephen's would rather make *two cloth habits* than *one pongee*—independently of the price or profit—he would rather make two cloth than one pongee. And did they not all say that it was as much or more work? But it is said, perhaps from the charge in the book of Mr. Watson—a most respectable gentleman, whom no man will disparage or accuse of improper participation in this matter—that on one occasion Mr. Watson had paid but six dollars.

[The court adjourned till half past three o'clock.]

Upon the reassembling of the court, Mr. Brown resumed as follows:

WITH DEFERENCE TO YOUR HONORS:

At the time of the adjournment I was about closing my remarks, and of course I have but a moment to claim an extension of your indulgence.

The subject under discussion at that time was the price charged by these journeymen for their work. And we contended, and I hope satisfactorily, that this was the only matter embraced in the first four counts of the indictment. The unlawful act with which these men are charged is their having combined to enforce the payment of prices beyond the usual and established wages. I had proceeded so far as to invite the attention of the jury to

the testimony introduced on the part of the defendants,
and that part of Mr. Watson's testimony, said to be sustained by the book of original entries; whereby it appears
according to his own declaration, standing aloof as he
does from this case—and if possessed of anything like
sympathy, certainly that sympathy is naturally with the
prosecution—that the amount paid by him for a bomba-
zett riding dress for a lady, was six dollars, which is the
precise sum charged by the defendants, independently of
the extras.   The difference between four dollars and fifty
cents, and six dollars—one third—would scarcely have been
paid by Messrs. Watson, liberal as they are, if not sanctioned by the bill.   We are told, however, there should
be a difference—they *supposed* there should, as between
summer and winter clothing!   But I say there should not,
because the bill precludes the idea—the bill makes a distinction expressly, in cases of men's attire; and not doing so in relation to women's attire, shows that such a
distinction never was intended.   Six dollars, Mr. Watson
has told you, was paid by him for making a riding habit
which had *flies in the breast*—here, say the gentlemen, is
an extra not charged.   Grant your attention to one small
circumstance—I desire you to bear in mind, that one of
Mr. Watson's journeymen was examined but a moment
before he (Mr. W.) was called.   This journeyman states
that the habit referred to, was made in his shop; and the
only reason—there being flies in the breast—that they
were not charged was, that not being very conversant with
his rights, he omitted to charge the twenty-five cents.
Here is a thin habit then for which was paid six dollars;
and the only reason that the journeyman did not receive
six dollars and twenty-five cents, was, that he did not
charge it; and still he received the price for making a thin
habit, the same as if it had been a cassimere or broad-
cloth, without the extra, which he only failed to receive,
from omitting to mention it.   But it appears on the book

according to the testimony of the gentleman, speaking of a remote period of time, that there is a charge also of six dollars and seventy-five cents, for a thick riding dress : but he at the same time tells you, that since this bill became the law governing this establishment, he has no recollection of any other; and he does not recollect whether that contained extras or not. It is pretty clear that it did contain extras, or otherwise six dollars and seventy-five cents could not have been made out. There must have been vents ·in the sleeves, and hussar skirts, which were charged, and which were paid for. I claim no credit for this, it is perfectly evident from the bill itself, as compared with the book exhibited. He who runs may read.

Then here we have all that we contend for, ratified by practice. For if the prices of summer clothing *generally* were to govern in ladies' habits, Mr. Watson would have offered some four or five dollars for that for which he paid six, and for which he might have paid six and a quarter, if there had been any attempt to claim it; but he paid what was on the face of the bill, without adverting to the extra. I apprehend the matter is perfectly clear. Nay, Messrs. Robb & Winebrener themselves finally paid the price as it was demanded ; and here is another confirmation of the propriety of the charge. If they had thought it really an extortion, would they have paid it? They allowed their minds to cool, and paid the bill; but yet their malevolence remained unimpaired. This attempt was an indirect mode of saying, reduce your prices—we have offered you six instead, of seven dollars, and we will, by and by, offer you five instead of six. And still they turn about in the face of all these facts, and tell you that the conspiracy was on the part of these men, and rely upon the master tailors to bolster them up. They invoke their interposition—they confederate actually, as well as constructively, to bring these men into subjection to their will, and for what? For the purpose of violating an express contract with these men, to which they were mutually bound to adhere; and for departing from which the law would have punished them. I say that Robb and Winebrener are the men contemplated in the indictment to which the counsel have alluded—that they are the conspirators—and that they are not alone in the confederacy. The legal offence—the moral offence, if there be any, as suggested, is in the defendants raising their wages, and *that* not being well founded in fact, they cannot be convicted, for the facts do not sustain the indictment. It may appear monstrous on paper and nothing on proof. And I shall insist on that with which I first set out, namely, that the indictment without facts ; or facts without an indictment, can claim nothing at your hands, but to be considered, as specious, legal amusements and toys— " mere sound and fury, signifying nothing."

What then remains, but a single charge, which has been exhibited in various ways, but the design, as alleged, is still the same—to injure Robb & Winebrener, and their thrice valiant champion—the peerless knight of the *pantaloons*—who mistook a pair of simple " galligaskins " for a *pair* of pistols—just twelve inches long—duelling size— hair triggers, doubtless—percussion locks, and loaded to the muzzle. *O horribile dictu—O miserabile visu!*

But we design to embarrass and impoverish Robb & Winebrener, Chamberlain, O'Neil and a number of others!!—have they shown the design? for that is the gist of the charge. The defendants did assemble, it is true, at the corner of Third street. This is offensive to the prosecutors, but not to the laws of the land. Messrs. Robb & Winebrener dwell at such an immeasurable distance above them in point of character, that they are not allowed to look at them—even with a *telescope.* But notwithstanding this prohibition, we are told that some of them did undertake to look through Girard's bank with a telescope, into the back window of Robb & Winebrener's shop. But from their location, I should have supposed, that they would require a telescope that would enable them to look, not only through the marble walls, but through all the loaded coffers of Mr. Girard:—a fine prospect truly—and you are asked to enjoy it in fancy—believe it you cannot. But why was that an offence? Did they halloo? Yes.—They hallooed to Winebrener, and Winebrener hallooed to them. Is it the play of children that is seriously employing intelligent men, invoking the interposition of the law, and sacrificing the time of hundreds?—We are again told that they made noises that are not to be described ; wonderful! but it is not for what *cannot be described*, but what *is described*, that they are to answer. Did you hear them make a noise? Yes, they hallooed through the windows, and looked in with a spy glass. Well, is looking through a spy glass, and hallooing in a manner that can't be described, a conspiracy? Again—they stood at the corners:—they had a right to do so. It is said they intercepted the men, and told them that if they did not continue in the service of Robb & Winebrener, the society would support them. If they had a right to enact such laws they had a right to promulgate them; that they had such a right, I trust we have shown.

It does not appear that one-half of the defendants were connected with the matter at all, by the proof; or connected with each other. They were shown to be members of the society, it is true; but not even shown to have been *on* the pavement—it is necessary that they should be identified in this transaction. I protest against doing justice by *wholesale ;* when the facts on which it must rest have been so miserably *retailed* from the beginning to the end. Well, but Mr. Radford is certainly to blame! This goes to all the counts, and with this I conclude. He ventured to pursue Mr. Ramsay or Mr. Chamberlain—I don't speak certainly (the argument is the same). Mr. Winebrener followed along Third street, down Fourth street, and then turned up, and then down; thus having a real wild goose chase in pursuit of Mr. Radford, while Radford was in pursuit of Chamberlain. But what is the amount of this? They thus pass up one street and down another; and give their courses and distances, going and returning: all of which serves only to remind one of Goldsmith's compliment to that honor and glory of her sex, Madam Blaze.

> "Her love was sought, I do aver,
> By twenty beaux or more;
> The king himself has *followed* her,—
> When she has walk'd *before*."

Winebrener walked after Radford, and Radford after Ramsay—but he stopped at a watch box, or lamp, and that too is become a matter of conspiracy—if so, it must have shed more light than we have yet seen.

Mr. Ramsay next encountered some half dozen opposite the post office, and was asked where he had been—he said in answer, what was not true—I hope it was the first time—I am sure it was not the last.

Here were Messrs. Robb & Winebrener sending clothes all over the city; and if Radford did follow, Winebrener followed also. He must not impute the consequences to us when he is the cause. I don't pretend that one conspiracy justifies another; but what I say is, that there is no conspiracy but in the prosecution itself, and that the means of resistance adopted were necessary; and are sanctioned by the opinion of the judge referred to by the opposite counsel, upon the principle of self-protection.

Gentlemen of the jury, you have now the whole case submitted to you: my duty is discharged, so far as my ability, humble as it is, will allow. A still more important and responsible duty remains to you; it is for you to determine that, which it devolved upon me merely to discuss; to determine it, even under all the influence of that eloquence which you have already heard, and which you will again hear from our opponents. You have been told, among other appeals to your feelings, that you cannot sleep soundly or safely upon your pillows, unless you convict these men—nay further, that it is necessary to the happiness and welfare of the community. If this be so, you are virtually parties to this proceeding; and while the prosecutors are to be allowed as "large a charter as the wind," the unfortunate defendants are to be bound hand and foot, and offered up as an atoning sacrifice, upon the altar of the violated laws. Well, if you cannot sleep soundly, and acquit these men; and you dare not encounter, for the preservation of your consciences, these phantoms of the gentleman's imagination; why, I suppose you must sleep soundly, and the defendants must be convicted. Their conviction shall not disturb your slumbers; the groans of these men, and of all those who depend upon them, shall be uttered, but you shall not hear them; their tears shall flow, but you shall not see them; their children shall be reduced to beggary, and worse than beggary, they shall be blurred and blotted with inherited crime; but still the peace and tranquillity of your domestic retirement and repose shall not be disturbed: *you shall sleep soundly*, and the gentleman shall have his way!—Time shall roll on, until in the grave, the last pillow of repose for the oppressed and the wretched, the poor man at least rests from his labors, and throws off his griefs! The earth closes over him— the grass springs from the kindred sod, the only monument of the miserable—moistened by no tears, save the dews from heaven! The night wind, while it wings its flight across "the narrow house," sings his last—sad— only—requiem—HE WAS—he is gone, and all that appertained to him, *is forgotten* forever! The events of this cause are no longer remembered, the reproach which you affixed to him, is no longer felt by their intended victims, but *you* and *yours*, those whom you represent, and those who shall come after you, shall feel it. The verdict of this day, shall be imperishably inscribed upon the records of this court, " and many an error, by the same example, will rush into the State."

CHAPMAN CASE.

Commonwealth of Pennsylvania *v.* Lucretia Chapman, otherwise called Lucretia Espos y Mina.

In the Court of Oyer and Terminer; held at Doylestown, Bucks county, Pa., February Term, 1832.

SKETCH OF FACTS.

This remarkable case which excited popular attention throughout the whole country, may be condensed in the following statement: Mr. Chapman, a prominent school teacher of great respectability, and the head of a family, consisting of a wife and five children, died, after a slight indisposition, on the 23d July, 1831. Reports of foul play having been extensively circulated, the body of the deceased was exhumed some three months after its interment, and upon the report of medical experts engaged in the post mortem examination, a charge of murder, by poison, was preferred against the widow, and a young Mexican, by the name of Lino Amalia Espos y Mina, who had been domiciled in the family at the time of Mr. Chapman's death.

Through the efforts of her counsel, Mrs. Chapman, who had been jointly indicted with her alleged paramour and accomplice, was given a separate trial, which resulted in her acquittal, on the 25th February, 1832.

The following named gentlemen appeared as counsel:

For the Commonwealth.

Messrs. Thomas Ross, and William B. Reed.

For the Prisoner.

Messrs. Peter McCall, and David Paul Brown.

SPEECH IN CHAPMAN CASE.

WITH DEFERENCE TO THE COURT:

Laboring as I do, and as you gentlemen of the jury must perceive, under a severe, painful, and distressing indisposition, although permitted to commence my remarks, it is far from being certain, that I shall be enabled satisfactorily to conclude them. As respects the advocate, this is a matter of indifference, compared with the all-absorbing interest of the defendant. However, if fate should decree this speech to be my last, I do not know that my professional or earthly career, can be more happily or more honorably terminated, than in the just defence of an oppressed fellow creature—a woman—hapless, helpless, friendless, and forlorn.

This case is one of no ordinary importance, I may venture to say, even in *your* consideration; and to *me*, it is a subject of awful and overwhelming interest and responsibility. Your position, however irksome it may be, is far less painful than mine, since it is within your power to do, what I can only solicit; since you are able to avoid, what I can only deprecate.

I appear before you, gentlemen of the jury, a stranger in behalf of a stranger; but I rejoice in the reflection that justice knows no distinction, either local or temporal or personal; but is the same at all times, in all places, and to all persons. The only distinction that she regards, is the distinction between virtue and vice—between innocence and crime; and it is upon justice, as thus understood, that we confidently rely.

If, indeed, it were necessary that your sympathies should be appealed to, what subject more fruitful than that which is here exhibited; what more sorry or more solemn perspective, than that by which we are now surrounded and appalled? An individual who has run more than half the race allotted to mankind, stands here accused of the highest offence known to the laws of the land; that individual a *female*, with whose character we are ever accustomed to associate all that is lovely in tenderness, affection and fidelity. That female a *wife!*—charged with the deliberate murder of the husband of her affections—the partner of her bosom. That wife a *mother!*—stigmatized and denounced as the fell destroyer ·of the father of her infant children.

There can, I say, be nothing in reality or fancy, to add poignancy to the accumulated and unparalleled afflictions of such an occasion. Did I say nothing? Alas, gentlemen of the jury, there is still one step further ere the soul is " supp'd full of horrors "—the conviction of the defendant. Let us pause and maturely meditate ere that awful step shall be taken—ere we deprive a fellow creature of that life which we cannot give, and which when once taken,·we never, never can restore. Such a conviction completes—consummates—all that can be conceived of anguish on this side of the grave; and therefore it should be founded upon the most indubitable proof. If the evidence be questionable or equivocal, if the probation bear a hinge or loop to hang a doubt on, the obligations—the sacred obligations of the law, throw a vast and inevitable preponderancy in the scale of the defence. I say an inevitable preponderancy; and in saying this, let us not lose sight of another legitimate subject of preliminary remark and reproach, which has obtruded itself upon this cause; namely, the storm, the tempest, the whirlwind of prejudice, by which the unfortunate though guiltless defendant, has been assailed and surrounded, from the moment of these charges having been preferred. No ear

has been protected from the accursed hebanon—the lep-
rous distilment of pernicious rumor; of busy and active
fabrication—presenting every variety of aspect, and unit-
ing only in the obvious tendency, to injure and destroy an
unhappy woman, whom it is our imperious duty to believe
to be innocent, till her guilt shall be established. That
storm of prejudice still rages, and still let it rage. Thank
Heaven, there is yet *one* refuge left for the innocent and
oppressed; there is one arm at least that is powerful to
save. That refuge, is the sacred temple of justice; that
arm, the omnipotent arm of the law; directed as we are
bound to believe, even in its wordly influence, by a sovereign and overruling power. There is a special providence, we are informed by the Book of books, even in
the fall of a sparrow; and it may therefore readily be
conceived, that the agonies, the throes, the torments of
the human heart, are not altogether unnoticed subjects of
regard, to the great Creator of earth and heaven.

Yet still, gentlemen of the jury, terrible as it would be
that the life of the defendant should be wantonly and
unjustly sacrificed, it would, nevertheless, be comparatively
unimportant. Time, the great physician, may heal the
wounds inflicted upon the bosom of social or domestic
peace; the life and the death of the prisoner may be
alike forgotten; but avert if you can the sacrilegious
blow, that is aimed at the maternal bosom of the law; the
pillow where we must all repose in the hour of peril and
distress—claim safety there, and have that claim allowed.

The life of one, or of fifty individuals, may be considered as a mere unit in the vast sum of human existence—a mere pageant upon the extended theatre of human
action; but beware of the corruption of the sacred sources
of justice, " the fountains from the which our current
runs, or else dries up "—the streams whereof, in the circling eddies of life, we are at one period or another all
compelled to drink. Beware of this, if not for the hapless being now upon her trial, beware of it for yourselves,

for the community, for a helpless and an endless posterity. We do not ask you to acquit an offender; but we *do* ask you, and the hardest heart cannot refuse us this, not to substitute the charge for the offence—the rumor for the evidence—the suspicion for the guilt. If you permit the sacred ermine of justice to be once stained or polluted by the blood of the guiltless, not all the spices of Arabia shall ever purify it; not all the rivers of Damascus shall ever wash it clean.

That there has been a death, no man denies; and in this valley of death, no man has a right to wonder; the wonder rather is, that we should live. We appear in the morning, and are cut down; and we wither ere the setting sun. But the laws of the India Empire, have no existence here. The unoffending widow is not, with us, dedicated or consigned to the funeral pyre, as the barbarous penalty of survivorship. The loss of one member of the community, is not diminished by the unjust sacrifice of another. Absolutely the evil is doubled, and relatively its consequences are incalculably increased; as the example largely contributes to enfeeble and impair the general tenure and sanctity of life.

But, gentlemen of the jury, if the mere death of a husband, *were* to subject his relict to such bodily tortures, upon what principle is it, that her character and her hopes, and the hopes and happiness of those who belong to her, are to be eternally blasted and destroyed?

The prosecution, not content with this single victim, embraces all that is dear to her "in one fell swoop." The daughter who has been examined before you—as through the perjury of the child, the life of the mother only can be reached—may be considered on *her* trial. There is no difference between extirpating the tender ivy, and hewing down the parental oak, to which it clings, for its nurture, its shelter and support. There is no difference between sacrificing this artless and interesting girl—tearing the tender flower from its native stalk, and destroying a loving and beloved mother, at the very period of life, when of all others, her attention and protection are most required.

Nay—the ravages of the commonwealth, extend even further than this. To say nothing of the aged parent, of whom she so pathetically speaks in one of her letters, and whom she so forcibly compares to the patriarch Jacob, on the loss of his son Joseph, whose sorrows were so great that he refused to be comforted ; those prattling innocents whom you have here seen in their mother's arms, smiling as it were, at the glittering sword of justice, suspended over a mother's head, neither plotting nor fearing harm, even *their* fate depends upon the issue of this cause.

The time shall come, and that ere long, when your verdict, should it affix crime to a mother's name, will enter deeply into their souls ; the worm that never dies shall prey upon their hearts through life ; and the curse that never spares, shall stigmatize their memory when dead. And long—long after their. bodies have quietly mingled with their sister clods of the valley ; long after the eternal doors of the narrow house shall have closed upon them, their reputations, dearer far than life, shall be blurred and blasted, by the odious, and recorded imputations of this day.

But, say the learned counsel, these children are merely introduced for effect. We can only say, that they were not introduced by us. We require no such aid against the prosecution ; but as I have not requested their presence, neither have I opposed it. It demands a bolder spirit than mine, to defy the laws of nature, or to stand between the children and the yearning bosom of an afflicted mother, at that awful moment, when you are about to determine, whether or not, they shall be separated—ay, separated *for ever.*

I agree, however, with the learned counsel, that thus horrible as the consequences would be, nevertheless, if guilty, those consequences supply no defence. I advert to them only for the purpose of securing a becoming and just estimate of the amount at stake. Though we decide like fate, let us feel like men ; and if the defendant were ten times guilty, where, let me ask, is the man, and who would envy his feelings, that could resolutely and recklessly pursue the prosecution of such a case, while with every step he takes, he tramples upon the feelings of a bleeding heart.

Having said thus much of the outlines and general character of this case, and of those emotions which belong to it, let us approach more nearly, and at once proceed to examine its more particular and essential features, which array and present themselves under the following inquiries :

I. Was the deceased poisoned ?

II. By whom ?

There was, as I have said, a death ; not sudden—the deceased was ill nearly a week : Not in the prime of life,—he was advanced in years, and his sun was fast descending to the dark horizon of the grave : Not unexpected—expected by himself, calculated upon, as appears by his letter to the parson a short time after he was taken ill ; and by his conversation with Mr. Vandegrift, a few days preceding his demise.

But before we enter regularly upon the discussion of those inquiries, there are some other features of the argument or address of my ingenious adversary, to which I must invite your attention. This cause has been managed for the prosecution with great ability, and I am compelled to add, with unexampled zeal. The gentleman closed his remarks last evening, with a beautiful passage from Anastasius, exhibiting the reliance of guilty parents upon the pure petitions of their infant children at the throne of Divine Grace. The passage was well chosen, and most admirably applied. But I marvel much, that the same gentleman who so strenuously deprecated the influence of sympathy in behalf of the friendless prisoner, should have condescended so frequently to invoke it in support of himself and his colleague.

You are told in the very outset of his discourse, that unless this prosecution should prove successful, the fault will be attributed, not to any deficiency of proof, but to a deficiency of ability on the part of the officers of the commonwealth; that they forsooth will suffer in public estimation. They have given you "the ocular proof" of their unquestionable capacity. But suppose it were otherwise; has it come to this, that for the purpose of gratifying vaulting ambition—for the purpose of inflating professional pride—for the purpose of avoiding individual mortification, the majestic bark of justice shall be driven from her moorings, and the liberty and lives of the community set adrift? If they have harnessed themselves to the car of the commonwealth, and its massive weight is beyond their strength, are you to listen to their supplications for help?—are you to apply your shoulders to the wheels? If Phæton will assume the reins, and direct the chariot of Phœbus, he deserves, and should endure, the fatal consequences of his temerity.

The counsel have not, it is true, invoked the aid of little children in their distress; it would have been wiser had they followed the Egyptian example; yet they have prayed most lustily for themselves, but Justice is inexorable, and deaf to their entreaties;—entreaties, which, permit me to say, to my untutored ear, resemble less the mild and mellowed plainings of a contrite spirit, than the wild shrieks of a famished vulture, just pouncing upon its prey. I ask no sympathies for myself; I had almost said I disdain them; but I openly protest against their enlistment for the prosecution. Where is the man so reckless and so lost to honor, who in this momentous struggle against all odds, for the life of a fellow creature, will cast the sword of Brennus into the scale of the commonwealth? If there be such a man, let him deny his *name*, as he must long since have abjured his *nature*.

Notwithstanding this appeal, the counsel assure us—assure our client of their kindness, their tenderness, and commiseration. *Timeo Danaos—et dona ferentes*—may it please your honors: this is the kindness of Judas, kissing to betray—the tenderness of the vulture, covering to devour—the commiseration of the crocodile, mingling his tears with the life-blood of his expiring victim. We will endeavor to protect ourselves from their open hostility, but we earnestly implore you, to guard and defend us, against the *tender mercies* of such a prosecution.

As a specimen of their deep condolence with the prisoner, they at first attempt by the assistance of police officers, to deprive her of the safeguard of character; and miserably failing in this, you are next told by them, that character is the very worst defence that any cause can have. Will this court and jury recognize that doctrine? Can they reconcile those inconsistent attempts? Character is always a *good*, and sometimes an *only* defence, in doubtful cases; and surely it is conceding enough to our opponents, to admit that this is a doubtful case. Character is a broad and secure shield, against which the pointless shafts of suspicion break themselves in vain. If the advantages of a spotless reputation, be at all proportioned to the difficulties encountered in its acquisition, it may be confidently relied on. The attainment of character is an uphill work; the ascent is difficult, laborious, and treacherous; but when we reach the glorious summit, after all our toils and perils past, Fame, with her own hand, arms us at all points in celestial panoply, which, like the polished mirror, *reflects* without *retaining*, the calumny, reproaches, and odium that assail it. Reputation, it is true, may be gradually lost; its safeguards gradually impaired; but whatever may be the particular and hackneyed exceptions which human nature supplies, I hold it to be a well established general rule, that it is never suddenly surrendered or abandoned, without some inducement or temptation, either actual or imaginary, commensurate with the importance of the sacrifice.

There is one other subject of comment, before I return to the systematic consideration of this case, under the inquiries proposed; and that is, the inference of crime from the supposed existence of motive; an inference from an inference.

In human tribunals, we generally ascertain the motive from the act, and not the act from the motive; and this improvement in moral philosophy, for which we are indebted to our learned friends, serves to remind me of a story related, not of an "Egyptian," but a Turk, which I may be pardoned in recounting. Conforming to the sublime ordinances of the Koran, the Turks, it seems, had forbidden under severe penalties, an indulgence in wine, or any other intoxicating beverage. An officer of the government observing an individual with a jar upon his head, and discovering that it contained the juice of the grape, summoned him forthwith before the Mufti, and there preferred his complaint. The alleged offender acknowledged the wine, but denied the offence; whereupon the accuser rested his charge, as the prosecution here does, upon the probability of guilt, from the strength of the temptation or motive to commit it. Upon which, the prisoner observing in the hand of his adversary a glittering scimitar, immediately turned to the magistrate, and accused the officer of murder; and when called upon to sustain his charge, relied upon the reasoning that had been urged against himself. "That shining blade," said he, "is an instrument of death; I find it drawn and naked in your hand; if the mere ability to commit crime, be an evidence of crime committed, you stand arraigned and condemned upon your own principle." It is almost unnecessary to add, that the Turk was discharged.

"Man is prone to evil as the sparks fly upwards;" but we should be careful, not too far to confirm this doctrine, by its unthinking application. The object of evidence is the establishment of facts; those facts, when established, are what we denominate proof. But if from mere liability or inducement to evil, we are to draw satisfactory conclusions of crime, why, then, to be sure, all mankind are flagitious offenders, and *we* the *most* of all. You have nothing to do but to read the indictment, to run over a string of truisms, or popular brocards on the subject of human iniquity, and the business of destruction is done. Your courts of justice virtually become slaughter houses, and you yourselves, the ministers of the law, instead of being sacrificers, are converted into butchers.

There is another view taken by the counsel of this case, which, for its novelty, is deserving of attention. He contends that you must either find the prisoner guilty, or pronounce her entirely innocent. If he mean that the charge contained in the indictment cannot be qualified or reduced, so as to admit of a conviction for any inferior offence,—if, in other words, he meant that she must be capitally convicted, or not at all, I concur with him. But if he intended to signify, and so seemed to set the current of his thoughts, that you must either absolve her from every act of imprudence and indiscretion, or else convict her of this heinous offence, I deny it totally. Even a general want of innocence would not be in itself, sufficient evidence of the perpetration of a particular crime. If the mysteries of the case, as is said, cannot tally with the idea of innocence, they must cease to be mysteries, and become self-evident facts. If they are *mysteries*, they *may* comport with either innocence or guilt, and in that event, the condition of the defendant is the best.

Aware of their difficulties, you are told that crimes of this description are always committed in such a way as not easily to be discovered. So are most offences; but does it follow therefore, that where they are *not discovered*, we are to guess at a verdict, and thereby entail upon our consciences a heavier crime than that which we unjustly

condemn? What can we reason but from what we know?
It is possible, it is true, that there may be guilt even
where it cannot be ascertained ; but it is also possible
there may *not be*, and all that it is requisite should be
said, is, that the benefit of the possibility is with us, and
the necessity of distinct and conclusive proof, with them.
If they fail in this, the cause, for all worldly purposes, is
ours ; and the punishment of the offender must be left
to that omniscient Power, to whose vision all the depths,
darknesses, and recesses of the soul are revealed. "Vengeance is mine, saith the Lord, and I will repay." Let
not sublunary tribunals audaciously and impiously presume to invade the sacred sanctions—to usurp the high
prerogative of heaven.

To return now, from this discursive flight of the counsel—in which I confess I have been compelled to pursue
him—to the more essential and substantial merits of the
charge, I will in the first place proceed to show you—
instead of adopting the chronological order of events—
which probably would have been the most perspicuous arrangement—that there was no poison; and without making it an independent ground of observation, I shall also
endeavor to satisfy you, should I even fail in my reliance
upon this first broad shield of the defence, that there is
no sufficient reason for believing that this defendant participated in the offence.

It was a practice adopted by Sir Matthew Hale, one of
the greatest ornaments that ever adorned the criminal
jurisprudence of any country, never to allow any man to
be convicted of a murder, until it was at least distinctly
shown that a homicide of some one had been committed.
Our own experience has furnished an ample illustration
of the wisdom of this rule. In a sister State, two men
were accused of the death of a third, and upon being
arraigned, they both pleaded guilty to the charge, willing, no doubt, to terminate the horrors of remorse, of
which they had long been the prey. The plea of guilty

to such a charge, is an unusual one ; the public journals teemed with various accounts of the case; the day appointed for their execution rapidly approached, when lo! the murdered man appeared in their behalf, not like " blood-bolter'd Banquo," " with twenty trenched gashes on his head," but in the possession of full health and vigor, and with far better prospects of protracted life, than those by whom he was alleged to have been slain. The explanation is this: those two men who stood accused, had lived in the same neighborhood with him, they had encountered him in an adjacent wood; and having had an ancient grudge against him, they proceeded to wreak their vengeance, and left him, as they supposed, lifeless.—This, however, was a mistake, for gathering himself up, after they had left him, and unwilling again to confront them, he set out forthwith to some of the Southern States, as he had previously contemplated, where he remained, until apprised of the peril to which his alleged murderers were subjected; when he generously presented himself, at the scene of trial, and afforded the ocular proof of their innocence.

The dead body is not more necessary, than the corpus delicti,—I adopt Dr. Togno's doctrine in its greatest latitude, when he says "no poison—no poisoning;" and it will afford me infinite pleasure also to show, that this conclusion of a most estimable man, and intelligent physician, is not only obviously correct in itself, but is in entire consonance with undoubted authority, and with the development of every feature, in the course of this important and protracted investigation.

Montmahou, in his " Manuel des Poisons," page 9, says, " the physician will not .pronounce that there has been a poisoning, until he has found the poison, and can designate and name it." And again, in page 11, " all the medico-jurists agree in thinking, that in order to pronounce with confidence, it is necessary to have found the poison." And further, in page 13, he observes, after stating the importance of a chemical analysis, " we ought to use the greatest attention in the execution of the various processes employed; it should be severe, complete, and have for its result the reduction of the metal. Indeed, we have arrived at the present day, by rigorous analysis, to discover the thousandth part of a grain of poisonous substance, mixed in liquids, in solids, or even combined with our own tissues. It would be criminal to neglect the means which chemistry offer us, in order to hold to appearances often deceitful."

The learned counsel has told you, however, that as to his chemical tests, he does not rely upon them—you may throw them entirely out of the case—Wonderful condescension! If you throw them out of the case, do you not at once perceive, that the condition of the prosecution is infinitely better, than if they are permitted to remain? We insist upon them—we rely upon them as a practical refutation of three-fourths of the hypotheses and theories, which cling around the trunk of this charge, " like ivy to old oak, to hide its rottenness." The doctors all agree that no arsenic was reduced, upon the great and final test being applied. Every body that has written, and all who have spoken upon the subject, admit, that the reduction of the metal is the only infallible proof of its existence ; and that it can always be reduced, even where the sixth part of a grain, or one-thirtieth part of the quantity necessary to produce death, remains in the system. Now, as it is admitted on all hands that the chemists were skilful, and that all proper means were resorted to by them for the purpose of discovering the arsenic—as it is admitted on all hands that it might have been discovered if it existed—and as it is also admitted that it was not detected, can anything be plainer than that it did *not exist*— and that all the reasoning derived from equivocal pathological symptoms, and an imperfect anatomical examination, are totally vague and visionary ?—more particularly, inasmuch as I shall have occasion to show you, that the appearance of those symptoms, and the results of that examination, are not peculiar to cases of poisons, but belong also to many cases of death from natural causes. To strike the chemical analysis from the evidence, therefore, is no stretch of magnanimity on the part of our ingenious adversaries, but upon the contrary serves only to show, that in the pursuit of blood, they have taken one step too far—one important step, and thereby redeemed us from the operation of all that had previously been attempted.

But, say they, if we cannot gratify your *eyes*, by producing the arsenic in its metallic form, we can at least tickle the *nose* by the alliaceous odor, which one of the experiments emitted. But, gentlemen, you are not to be led by the nose in a case of this character; much less are you to be governed by the noses of *others*. Mr. Clemson, the gentleman who titillated his olfactory so often during the cause, with the pungent and fragrant Natchitoches or Maccouba, and who was the only individual who arrogated to himself a superiority in the sense of smelling, did, it is true, pronounce boldly upon the alliaceous odor, as an infallible arsenical test; but he at the same time conceded, and Dr. Mitchell proved, and we all know, that the faculty of smelling is the most fallible and treacherous of all the human senses,—confounding different odors—affected by the state of mind or body—the nature of the atmosphere—the condition of the health— and an infinite variety of influences unnecessary to be considered. It is admitted the world over, that the sight, which even itself, as Macbeth says, is often " made the fool of the other senses," is in point of accuracy and perfection, very superior to the smell. We perhaps may be able, therefore, best to ascertain the value of Mr. Clemson's olfactory, by testing it by the accuracy of his vision. You all remember, when asked by me, whether he could tell the arsenical ring by its appearance, he answered promptly, "yes." I like a prompt answer, even in a case of

life and death, when it is promptly right. I immediately
produced the glass tube furnished by Dr. Mitchell, containing the arsenical ring, which was as immediately declared by the witness to contain mercury. Dr. Mitchell
was then called again, and explicitly stated, that it contained *no mercury ;* and he had a right to know, as it was
his own preparation. Now after this failure of Mr. Clemson's best sense, what would you give for the rest ? I
oppose this dumb witness [*exhibiting the tube*], against the
nose of Mr. Clemson, and his eyes to boot. It is small,
it is true, but it has a giant's strength. It is mute, unquestionably, yet it speaks with most miraculous organ.

But, again, suppose the alliaceous odor had been perceived—I deny its infallibility—I deny its probability.
All writers agree, that however it may be considered
sufficient as a mere chemical indication of arsenic, and
for mere chemical purposes, it is utterly unworthy of
regard as a matter of conscientious reliance in a judicial
proceeding. Even Christison,* the god of their idolatry,
declares it should be utterly discarded; and Berzelius,
Orfila, Montmahou, and a host of other distinguished
men, consider it as reproachful in the present state of
chemistry, that it should be quoted as a satisfactory,
or even a reasonable test.

In page 357 of Orfila, the most celebrated toxicologist
of the age, we find this language: "It often happens
that doctors charged with making reports before a judicial tribunal, affirm the existence of poisoning by arse-
nious acid, because they have found in the alimentary
canal, matter, which exhales an alliaceous odor upon
being placed upon burning coals. We severely condemn
this conduct; in effect, the alliaceous character belongs to
other substances, and it is not impossible that there
should be developed in the stomach, during digestion,

---

* Christison, 184. Med. and Surg. Jour., vol — page 80. Cooper's
Med. Jurisprudence, 424.

substances which exhale a similar odor when heated. Besides, does it not often happen, that we are mistaken in the character of odors? Mr Vauquelin and myself, were appointed reporters in a case of poison. The suspected matter was placed on burning coals, at four different times, and twice only, we thought we recognized the alliaceous smell, and we became assured soon after, that it did not contain an atom of arsenic." The character of which we treat, ought therefore to be considered as an indication, and not as a proof, of the presence of arsenic.

Berzelius, notoriously the greatest practical chemist in the world, and to whom—by common consent of all the most experienced and skilful manipulators either in England or France—the proudest distinction has been accorded, thus expresses himself, in relation to this subject.*

"The reduction only, is to be regarded as a certain proof, and renders all other evidence superfluous. When the reduction does not succeed, the result must be always doubtful, even when we think or believe we recognize the arsenical odor, upon heating with a blow-pipe or charcoal, the calcareous precipitate, obtained according to the method of Rose; for an operator, little habituated to such essays, may often imagine he recognizes in the odor of animal matters contained in the precipitate, the presence of arsenic, while in truth there is none."

In addition to these great authorities, you have the direct testimony of Drs. Bache and Togno; gentlemen who, it is true, have in all probability, run not more than half their career of professional usefulness, yet who have, nevertheless, in the Spring of their fame, afforded ample assurance of an abundant harvest of future eminence and distinction. Modest, yet decided; skilful, yet cautious; they draw at once a broad and obvious line

---

* Berzelius, Traite de Chemie, Tome ii, page 451.

between the evidence, which will be sufficient to direct
their inquiries after mere medical treatment, or chemical results; and that *proof* upon which they would be
disposed to rely in a solemn judicial investigation. If,
as medical men, or chemists, certain observations or experiments may have regulated their practice or opinions,
in ordinary matters of doubt; they prudently consider
them too imperfect and fallacious, to form the basis of
absolute and conscientious reliance, upon a subject so
awful and vital as this. They require, as the law requires, that the best evidence the nature of the case
admits of, should be produced. They require that the
symptoms should be unequivocal, or that it should be
reasonably ascertained that no natural cause of death
existed—before they feel themselves prepared to peril
the life of a fellow creature, and their own salvation,
upon the confident assertion of poison. " We would not
be willing," say both those gentlemen, " to decide upon
the presence of arsenic without reduction, because we
would not be satisfied by any evidence except what we
considered the best.—The alliaceous odor is not to be
depended upon."

. But further; if the alliaceous smell indicate arsenic, it
must be, of course, because arsenic is there.. These fumes,
we are told, are the fumes of arsenic;—these fumes, *we
know*, become condensed, and form the arsenical crust on
the upper and cooler part of the glass. If, therefore,
they were sufficient to prove its existence, they were
sufficient, with proper process, to form the metal in its
crystallized shape. I agree that it is possible, that the
odor should be perceived, without arsenic being detected; because it is probable that the odor may arise
without the presence of arsenic, and from other substances, as has been shown; but I deny that the odor ever
arises from arsenic, so powerfully as is here described,
without the cause—namely, the arsenic, being satisfactorily ascertained and detected in its metallic form. Hence

I infer, that as zinc, onions, garlic, the phosphates, and other substances may produce that smell,—in other words, inasmuch as it is not the peculiar effluence of arsenic, that it was produced from other substances, and *not* from arsenic.

But say they—there are the liquid tests, which although all imperfect, and equivocal, still make against the defendant, with the other proofs What are these tests? Let me *test* them; for without pretending to be a proficient or expert chemist, I do profess to know enough of the science for this case, and I should be wanting in my duty if I did not. I have gone through all those experiments myself, with my own hand; bestowed months of attention and reading upon them, and I can only regret, that still greater time has not been allowed for my researches.

The first test applied, as an almost universal detecter of metals, is the sulphuretted hydrogen. This test, in arsenical cases, exhibits a flocculent appearance, and throws down a light, clear, yellow precipitate. In the present case, the test was very doubtful, as is stated; the yellow produced was a darkish and dirty yellow, and no precipitate was perceived. The other test was by the ammoniacal nitrate of silver,—in other words, nitrate of silver dissolved in liquid ammonia. This test should have produced a still darker yellow precipitate, attended by the same flocculency. It failed to do either; and even if it had done both, it is allowed to be a very insecure test, unless amply sustained by those that follow, and precede it.

The third test applied, was the ammoniacal sulphate of copper, which presented an olive green instead of the *Scheele* green, which is about the color of verdigris. The olive green may be obtained much more perfectly by this test, from ginger, stramonium, rhubarb, chromate of potassa, and onion juice, than it was obtained in the present instance.

I conclude then, this branch of my remarks, by saying again, that the restoration of the metal is the only infallible test—I should rather say *proof;* it is the *corpus delicti* itself. The tests, as they are called, and as they have been referred to, are mere presumptions; and apart from the result, are not to be relied upon. Wherever there is metal enough, unequivocally, to abide those tests, the metal may be restored; and chemists have succeeded in reducing less than the 300th part of a grain; and wherever there is not enough thus to abide the test, there is not enough to guess at. The mode of restoring the metal, is perfectly simple, and I will take leave to explain it to you. Having evaporated the liquid containing the suspected matter, to dryness; the dry matter mixed with pulverized charcoal, is placed in a glass tube hermetically sealed at one end. To this end you apply the spirit lamp, until the red heat is produced, when, if there be the slightest portion of arsenic, fumes of the smell of garlic will issue therefrom, and the metal itself, will, instead of fusing, evaporate, and form again in a condensed shape on the upper and cooler parts of the tube.

But, say the gentlemen, "even had the prosecution succeeded in showing that the metal was reduced, the defendant's counsel might still argue the insufficiency of that fact." Reduce what metal? I agree, any metal, mercury for instance, would not be sufficient, but *metallic arsenic* would be; and no argument, however ingenious, could possibly avail against it; and no argument, in that case, would have been attempted. We unite with him, in saying, that you could not pretend to determine, because you saw something glittering on the inner surface of a glass tube, that it was arsenic; for even Mr. Clemson, with all his eyes about him, and after having imbibed the benefit of all the schools of France, most egregiously blundered in that very particular, and has thereby afforded us a salutary lesson of prudence, from a lamentable example of indiscretion. But the counsel forgets, if he

ever knew, that it is not the mere *appearance* of the metal,
upon which skilful chemists and judicious men would be
disposed to rely; but that the metal being first detected,
and its general nature defined by the success of antecedent tests, it is upon reduction subjected to other and subsequent tests, which present its character in a totally
unquestionable shape; not dependent on the sight alone,
the smell alone, the original tests alone, the reproduction
alone, or the final tests, but upon all combined, and with
all the clear denotement of its deleterious and peculiar
arsenical properties. It is in vain, to tell us, that were all
these evidences united, and each perfect in itself, errors
might still be contended for; since authority, experience,
and reason concur in the utter impossibility of such
errors. 1 admit, if you please, as the counsel alleges, that
no *one* chemical result would be conclusive, and it is for
that very reason that we require the evidence of various
and combined results—all conducing to the same conclusion. If, as is contended, we should dispute the evidence
in its aggregate, so much the stronger was the necessity
for sustaining its particular items. Nay, if no one
chemical result can form unerring proof, how much less
can there be unerring proof where, as iu this case, there
was *not one* such result.

But we have shown, exclaim the gentlemen triumphantly, that an individual of that house purchased
arsenic in Philadelphia, a few days preceding the indisposition of the deceased, and the prisoner was in town at
the time of the purchase. That the purchase of arsenic,
in relation to this charge, is a circumstance of guilt, need
not be a subject of dispute, provided it be connected with
the present defendant. It is not so connected. The allegation that Mrs. Chapman was in town on the day the
arsenic was purchased, is no evidence of participation in
that purchase. But the fact was otherwise. She was in
the city with Mina, it is true, upon two occasions, but
neither of those visits was on the day of obtaining the

arsenic. Indeed, it was perfectly inconsistent and absurd, to suppose that an individual entirely conversant as she was, with all parts of Philadelphia, and embarked, as she is said to have been, upon a dangerous and deadly voyage —should have landed, from choice, upon this perilous and Ausonian shore—should have selected, for the first scene of iniquity, an establishment in the very centre of notoriety, and within fifty yards of the residence of an old acquaintance of herself and Mr. Chapman. Was there no Romeo's apothecary—no caitiff wretch to vend this poison to her—no remote and obscure "culler of simples," upon whom she could have more securely relied in the purchase of this deleterious drug? Is she to seek the open and blushing face of day, for the purpose of concealing an object or danger?—to believe it were madness—or fatuity, at least.

Yet, say our opponents, "admitting even that Mina purchased the arsenic without the defendant's immediate participation, it was, nevertheless, in prosecution of a common intent, agreed upon between them." If so, how do you dispose of the argument that the forged letter, written under the instructions of Mina, days after the purchase, and purporting to be from that excellent and accomplished gentleman, Mr. De Cuesta, was communicated to her for the sake of whetting her almost blunted purpose? Where was the necessity for it? If she had been previously so ripe and ready for this fell deed, as to cherish the damning thought of, taking her husband's life—as even to be active in procuring the means of death—the fallen one had already marked her for his own—the last feeble struggle for redemption had passed —and she was so deeply steeped in guilt as to require no further lures to vice—as to defy all further inducements to virtue. If then this forged letter were intended by Mina to deceive her—it was not, as the gentleman imagines, to confirm her in iniquity, but rather to *win* her to iniquity; and if *thus to win her*, it must have been because she was not already won—and if not already won, she could never have been a participator in thought or act, in obtaining the poison, which was procured several days before the letter in question was exhibited or prepared.

Taking leave of this portion of the case, and glancing with comparative civility at the testimony of Dr. Bache, the learned counsel next springs with the fury and rapacity of the hyena, upon that of Dr. Togno—impugns its credibility—denies its modesty—defames and defiles its purity ; and to say nothing of unmeasured language, luxuriously indulges in deliberate, cold-blooded, unqualified, and, allow me to add, unwarranted aspersion, for which the meagre apology is offered, that there is left to him but this alternative, either to abandon his own witnesses, or speak *plainly* of ours.—As to abandonment, so far as relates to the party colored crew, drawn by the prosecution from the prisoner's household, they were, in one sense, *abandoned*, before they became retainers in this cause. In regard to the scientific gentlemen examined by the commonwealth, they have been treated by us freely and fearlessly, it is true, as became the nature of the occasion, but, nevertheless, frankly, and fairly and respectfully, as was due to their talents and their virtues. We spoke of no " volunteers "—we assailed no motives—we impeached no principles, though we liberally discussed the various opinions expressed, and the means and opportunities from which they were deduced.

If by " *speaking plainly*," the counsel mean contumeliously, his remarks have been as plain as a sunbeam, and almost as bright; but if, upon the contrary, he would be understood to signify, a just adaptation of thoughts and language, to the immediate subject of discussion ; he will excuse my saying, he has been guilty of a vast and unpardonable mistake—a mistake in first substituting himself for Dr. Togno, and afterwards applying to that highly respectable gentleman, those observations and rebukes, which, as counsel, he himself so richly merited—though so sparingly received. By what principle he has been influenced—by what master spirits he has been prompted or directed, we shall not deign to inquire, but proceed to repel the attack, and, in doing so, the learned gentleman must not complain if we resort to weapons similar to those with which it has been made—" 'tis fit the artificers of death should die."

I should be a foe to fealty and to friendship, could I dispassionately stand by, and complacently behold the counsel glutting his vengeance upon an unassuming and unoffending individual, who, actuated alone by justice and philanthropy, has imparted the valuable aid of his testimony to the present defence.

And is it not most monstrous and unheard of, that a learned gentleman—himself a volunteer in pursuit of blood—a soldier who has eagerly enlisted in this magnanimous war, without even the temptation or inducement afforded by the *bounty*, should for the purpose of proving his loyalty and submission to the power he serves,—not satisfied with wreaking his wrath upon the devoted head of the defendant,—venture even to grapple with the integrity of a highly honorable man, for no other reason, than because, forsooth, his evidence presents an impenetrable and insurmountable barrier, between the commonwealth and her intended victim.

Dr. Togno's testimony, I cite the counsel's very language, is " *obtrusively adverse*," and therefore, the witness, we are told, shall have the melancholy consolation " of dying on his own sword." Heaven save the mark? The doctor could not die upon a more unsullied sword, or in a nobler cause. A sword, allow me to observe, that cannot even be dignified by the illustrious hand of the distinguished advocate, by whom it is proposed to be wielded. But let not the counsel talk of slaying, until he has, at least, first established his lofty claims to valor, upon the ruins of this wretched, persecuted, and oppressed family.

Let him first, I say, wage a successful and exterminating war, against helpless women and unprotected children. " Discretion is the better part of valor." If he will play the falcon, he must not only fly a "higher pitch," but make his first experiment upon harmless doves, ere either his beak or his talons will prove subjects of alarm to the towering and majestic eagle. Enough of this—I almost owe Dr. Togno an apology for having breathed a word in his support—he is above all assault—he requires no defence, but clothed in the protection of a spotless and irreproachable character—stands self-dependent and self-sufficient.

" The gentlemen examined for the prosecution, do not remember to have seen Dr. Togno at Dr. Mitchell's laboratory." Wonderful oversight! and, therefore, I suppose Dr. Togno, who swears he was present upon that occasion, partially describes what took place, and particularly mentions the individuals engaged in the experiments—must have drawn all these matters from fancy and not from fact. Can any man doubt his presence—if not, the circumstance of its not being remembered by our other scientific friends, may show their own want of memory, but cannot impair the recollections of his. Ah! but says Mr. Reed, he would give us to disbelieve that the stomach was the seat of any inflammation at all, after a very hasty and unsatisfactory examination. I put him in opposition to Dr. Coates—intelligent and respectable as he is, who decided that the internal surface of the stomach was highly inflamed, without ever opening it, upon a very slight examination of the peritoneal coat, and I am content to abide by your decision between them. I put it in opposition to the statement of my friend, Dr. Hopkinson, who was satisfied that the stomach contained the cause of the untimely death of the deceased—without ever having seen its contents, or examined other most important parts of the body. I put it in opposition, even to the highly and deservedly lauded testimony of Dr. Mitchell, who, from a skilful and miraculous combination of a variety of uncertainties and fallacies, rendered everything so perfectly evident, "that it would glimmer through a blind man's eye." I put it, in short, in opposition to everything to be derived from this portion of the case, with the exception, let it be always understood, of Mr. Clemson's refined and delicate sense of smelling, and his unrivalled—his transcendent powers of discrimination, between *arsenic* and *mercury!*

Passing from the chemical to the anatomical part of the examination, we are by no means relieved from the doubts and difficulties by which the understanding is clouded and embarrassed. Upon visiting the grave yard, what are the circumstances attending upon the exhumation? The body, which was disinterred about three months after its interment, was found, we are told, in a state of perfect and unusual preservation. Unusual—how do we ascertain that? Not a physician who has been examined has ever seen a body after an interment for three days, much less three months; they have, therefore, no experience upon the subject in relation to which they speak. This preservation is imputed to the effect of arsenic. Miraculous!—arsenic enough to preserve this body, and yet not enough to be detected subsequently by all the accomplished and skilful chemists employed! It is true, as they say, that arsenic is considered an antiseptic, and is thus used in the preparation and preservation of birds after death, but the quantity thus required is very considerable,—small as the bodies may be,—and can easily be detected. It is no answer, therefore, to the argument already addressed to you in relation to the failure of the chemical experiments.

Further—the best opinions of the ablest writers, inculcate the belief, that only that portion of the body which is more immediately affected by the arsenic is liable to be preserved. Yet, in this case, the whole of the human frame was equally preserved. It would be useless to refer to authorities for this principle, as it will hardly be denied.

It is unnecessary, however, to dwell longer upon these theories, when the facts connected with the interment sufficiently explain the phenomenon. The pastor of the church has told you, that having found fault with his sexton for digging his graves too shallow, the sexton afterwards fell into the opposite extreme, and dug them of an extraordinary depth. In addition to this, the soil was of a dry, sandy character, covered with a stratum of clay, which protected it from moisture, which protection was increased by the declivity of the surface of the ground. Now Orfila, in his treatise upon exhumation, and even the scientific witnesses who have testified in this cause, show conclusively, that this cause is entirely sufficient to account for that preservation, which, by some, has been attributed to the influence of the poison.

The next ground of reliance on the part of the prosecution, is the anatomical investigation. It seems that the body was opened, and the stomach removed, under the impression that "the cause of death," in the language of Dr. Hopkinson,—whatever it may have been,—"was contained therein." The lower intestines were found perfectly empty, and appeared "as if they had been hung up to dry."

The rectum was not examined—nor the brain—nor the heart and larger vessels—nor the liver. I will not pause to show you how essential it was, that the examination of *all* should have taken place in a case of such vital importance. I will not dilate upon the habits—conformation, and constitution of the deceased, and the probability or possibility of death from natural causes. I am satisfied to take the examination as it was—to try it by itself—for "none but itself can be its parallel." The stomach was removed—it was not opened—and yet Dr. Coates, one of the physicians, from its external appearance, ventured to pronounce upon its internal state. He saw through the covering, the peritoneal and muscular coat, and undertakes to tell us, from this superficial view, not only the character of the inflammation of the mucous membrane, or lining of the stomach, but also to distinguish between congestion and inflammation. I aver this to be utterly impossible, and I regret exceedingly, that a highly respectable man, and a meritorious physician, should have been betrayed by the excitement of the occasion, into such unnatural perspicacity. I have not the least question of the entire honesty of the doctor's intention; I can have none—but he must pardon me when I say, his opportunities of observation were entirely too limited to be depended upon.

While on this subject, what says Orfila? "The existence or non-existence of cadavaraque lesions—the extent and seat of disease, are never sufficient to enable us to pronounce whether there *has* or *has not* been poison ; and they can only serve to corroborate the conclusions derived from a chemical analysis of the suspected matter."*

Nor is the testimony of Dr. Hopkinson a more legitimate source of reliance, skilful and accomplished as he is acknowledged to be, in the science which he professes. He ingeniously concedes the fact, that his anatomical inquiries were very imperfect ; that it was the first occasion of this nature in which he had been employed; and that supposing that the stomach contained the deleterious or poisonous substance, he considered it to be useless to proceed any further. I wish it to be understood, once for all, that I find no fault with these gentlemen, but I protest altogether against the attempt to infer poison from what did not appear, when they had it in their power by sufficient care and attention, to have decided the question one way or another; and having omitted to do so, we are entitled to argue that a further examination, would have removed, rather than confirmed, their previous suspicions.

In regard to the "herring " or fishy smell, issuing from

---

* Orfila (last edition), Tome. i, page 379.

the body when opened, it is hardly necessary to say anything. Without attempting to be witty, it affords at
best, but a *scaly* reason for a conviction. Its only recommendation to attention, is, that the doctor never smelt
anything like it before. I presume he must before have
opened stomachs containing arsenic ; and if so, not having met with a similar smell, confirms the idea that
this was not arsenic. But if the fact were otherwise, his
never having encountered a similar effluvia, assuredly
does not show that this smell was peculiar to arsenic.
There is no book that confirms or suggests that idea. He
never before opened a body after three months' interment,
and in like circumstances, and the similarity of facts failing, the reason also fails. Dr. Mitchell, it is true, having
introduced arsenic into a dead stomach, after some
months detected a similar odor. Yet we know nothing
of the state of that stomach,—of the nature of the disease
which produced death,—of its cadavaraque appearances ;
and therefore it affords us no scope for analogical inquiry.
But an answer to all this, is derived from Dr. Coates, who
tells us that the smell did not seem to him to resemble
that of herring, but rather that of tanner's oil. Now I
leave you to decide between the noses of these doctors,
while I proceed to consider the other portions of this case.

Inverting the natural course of things, and pursuing
that adopted by our antagonists, from a desire of grappling with them on their own ground, we come next to
the chamber of disease and death ; and let us approach it
with a gravity that becomes the scene. On the night of
the 17th of June the deceased was first attacked. He
continued ill until the morning of the twenty-third, at
about two o'clock, when he expired. During his illness,
he made violent attempts at vomiting, which but partially
succeeded. He complained of burning pains in his
stomach. Towards the close of his career, he became
delirious, and in his last hours his pulse was feeble and
fluttering ; his mouth was dry, and his skin clammy and

collapsed. After his death, a small quantity of what was called " bloody serum " by Dr. Phillips, was found on the sheets, and supposed to have been involuntarily discharged per anum. Some time after his death, say three or four hours, an unusual rigidity of the body was observed by Mr. Boutcher, who, upon that occasion, performed the last sad office of an undertaker. These are the dark denotements, which, together with the other circumstances, must supply the evidence of poison. By whom administered, is another question. If there were no poison, there was no poisoning, which goes to the whole charge.

Dr. Mitchell, for whom as a physician, a friend, and a man, I have the highest regard, informs us that the chemical tests were equivocal; that the anatomical examinations were imperfect, and not to be relied upon; that the preservation of the body was fallacious; that the symptoms themselves were not peculiar; but, nevertheless, that from the combination of all, he had arrived at the conclusion "that William Chapman died from poison." This is is a home-thrust, and we must parry it or die. I deny then, in the outset, that by the combination of other things, each in itself imperfect, perfect proof can be arrived at. I deny that a chaplet of fallibilities, however artfully strung together, can form an infallibility. On the contrary, the concatenation renders imperfection less perfect, and fallibility more fallible. " The mind," says Lord Bacon, " has this property, that it readily supposes a greater order and conformity in things than it finds. Although many things in nature are singular and extremely dissimilar, yet the mind is still imagining parallel correspondences, and relations betwixt them, which have no actual existence."

But without being an admirer, much less a disciple of the Bobadil school, let me encounter some of these theories in detail. The symptoms, for instance—the nucleus of the whole hypothesis. They are symptoms that belong to cholera morbus, to violent indigestion, some of them to dysentery; none of them peculiarly to poison. But, says the learned counsel, as any and all of them may be found in arsenical cases, you have therefore the right to presume, from their existence here, that this was a case of death by arsenic. Not so, my learned friend: if they are also to be found in natural diseases, you are bound to presume, influenced by the benign principles of the law, that they were the effects of natural causes. Show us, says the counsel, triumphantly, any one of these symptoms, which is not to be found in cases of poison. I fearlessly answer, we cannot; for the phases of arsenic are as various as the constitutious and tempers of men. They put on the semblance of every disease, and chameleon-like, change while you describe them. But let them show *us*, if they can, any symptom not to be found in other cases of disease, and they will have established an important point, in the detection of arsenical poison. Nay, more—not relying merely upon their inability to do this, I will satisfy you, that the main and characteristic indications or symptoms of arsenic, even according to Dr. Mitchell himself, are wanting in this case.

Dr. Mitchell has given us some of the grounds, from which he deduces the notion of poison. The involuntary discharge of bloody serum; the absence of delirium; the rigidity of the corpse; and last, but greatest, the diseased rectum. When, wonderful to relate, there is no certainty of any involuntary emission; and there is a difference between Mr. Boutcher and Mr. Phillips, as to the bloody discharge. And even had it taken place, there are various complaints which would produce it. As to the absence of delirium, not a witness has mentioned it; but Dr. Knight and Dr. Phillips both state, that he *was* delirious from time to time, for twenty-four hours before his death. If, therefore, absence of delirium be an indication of arsenic, the presence of delirium is evidence against it. The *rigidity* of the limbs—if admitted by us—is easily accounted for, the body having been permitted to remain several hours in the bleak air of the morning, before any attempts at laying it out were made. But it is still less to be regarded, when it is understood, that Mr. Boutcher, so far from being, as the doctor supposed, an experienced undertaker, was but a neighboring individual, accidentally performing these rites; who, perhaps, had never seen a dozen dead bodies in his life, and who tells you himself that although he had sometimes done these things, he had ceased to do them for several years before. He perhaps had never performed the service in similar circumstances, and his vague impressions in respect to the stiffness of the limbs, are too flimsy and indefinite to be entitled to much respect.

As I have said, the last and greatest argument for poison, is the diseased rectum. This is establishing a disputed fact, from an inference; when the fact might itself have been ascertained, instead of drawing an inference from facts. Nay, more—and worse than that: an inference of poison is derived from an inference of a diseased rectum. Not a witness has proved it. Not a witness who was present, has mentioned it. No complaint was ever uttered by the deceased about it, though the circumstances attending his illness, as particularly described by Dr. Knight, were obviously such as to induce complaint, had this imaginary cause actually existed. So that you perceive the process, by which these learned Thebans arrive at the conclusion of poison, is by first stating the general symptoms of poison; and secondly, imagining correspondent symptoms in the deceased, some of which never appeared; and the very opposites of others, having been abundantly established. A single remark, and I bid farewell—a long farewell to physic. I have been surprised and astonished at the silly sequel to that story, whose preface promised so much wisdom; and I think I utter your sentiments, when I say, that however skilful our scientific friends may be in *preserving* life,—and I know no men in whom I would more readily confide,—with such evidence as this, they are utterly incapable of *destroying* it. I respect them all —I honor them all; and to Dr Mitchell particularly, I have confided, and would still confide, the health of those much dearer to me than myself. But experience has taught me this salutary lesson of human nature, that whatever may be the gradations in refinement, whatever may be the immeasurable difference in intellect, whatever may be the advantages of science, still, in the essential constituents of the human character, men are at last but *men ;* alike subject to passion, to prejudice, to error ; and perhaps more strongly confirmed and sustained in all, by that very refinement of reason, and expansion of thought, for which, in general, they are so justly celebrated and admired.

Pursuing the course marked out by our learned friends, though by no means that which I had proposed myself to adopt, I now pass from the pathological, anatomical, and chemical inquiries, to what is termed by them, the circumstantial proofs in this case. Circumstantial evidence it should rather be called, as the term *proof* implies a higher claim to regard than belongs to this species of testimony, even in its best estate. I will consider it in the *order*, perhaps I should say *disorder*, in which it has been presented.

As to Mary Ann Palethorp, the little girl of twelve years of age, who served as a modest and ingenious pioneer, for the introduction of bolder and more reckless spirits, scarcely anything need be said. She is a child— an artless and an interesting child—and far, far be it from me, to impugn or impeach her in the slightest particular. I believe what she has said to be as sacred as though an angel spoke. But were it otherwise, my flight is winged above the heads of children, whatever may be their imperfections or inconsistencies, and has for its object and its prey, those who by the maturity of their crimes, are no longer protected from impunity.

First, in the first rank of those, stands the redoubtable Ellen Shaw—*dux fœmina facti*—an Amazonian Queen—a modern Penthesilea; sustained on the right by the peerless Fanning, on the left by the blushless Bantom, and leading on a host of other worthies, in this charitable crusade against a woman—a mother—and a benefactor. It has been the melancholy fate of the defendant, to nurse vipers in her bosom; to warm them into life, and to be the victim of their venom. Her very charities are converted into implements of assault. The abandoned profligate, Mina, the great exemplar of this wretched crew, after having been discarded with revilings and reproaches from every other asylum, presents himself at the door of the defendant about the middle of May, in the evening,—a beggar and an outcast. He solicits alms— he craves a night's lodging. Under the twofold influence of pity, and that duty which is enjoined by divine authority, her house and her heart are opened to him; and she contemplates with the anxious and melting eye of a mother, the friendless condition of her own children, in beholding that of the *wanderer*. In the language of divine inspiration, as impressively quoted by my colleague, "he was an hungered, and she gave him meat; he was thirsty, and she gave him drink; he was a stranger, and she took him in; naked, and she clothed him; sick, and she ministered unto him."

But, returning from this episode, to the testimony of Ellen Shaw, we find a blister on the very forehead—an odious blot on the very title page of her evidence. She informs you that she was in the yard when Mina first arrived; that "the dogs barked at him as he passed by them;" that he knocked at the kitchen door, and she told him that he had better apply at the hall door, which he accordingly did. That Mr. and Mrs. Chapman came out, and that the former observed to him in answer to his inquiries, that there was a tavern a short distance below; that Mina replied he had already been refused assistance at that tavern, and that Mrs. Chapman then took him into the room, and began to talk to him, and that the door being shut, the witness went into the kitchen. Now one-half of this story is the very coinage or her brain, for Mary Palethorp, another witness for the prosecution, distinctly says—without speaking of the testimony of the little Lucretia, who is worth a host of Ellen Shaws—that Mr. and Mrs. Chapman were tranquilly sitting in the parlor; that Mr. Foreman went to the door; that he returned, and told Mr. Chapman there was a stranger at the door; that Mr. Chapman requested Mr. Foreman to show him in; that he was then introduced into the parlor, and *there* the conversation just referred to, took place.

Thus, you perceive, Ellen Shaw not only states the fact of Mr. and Mrs. Chapman's presence at the door, which was not true; but relates a conversation as having taken place at the door, which actually took place in the parlor, and with closed doors, while she, Ellen, was in the kitchen. To place the mildest interpretation upon this story, it is either imaginary, or she has totally confounded that which she knew, with that which she derived from other and illegitimate sources. The inconsistency, however, does not rest here. She states to you, that Mina, upon his arrival, had on a dark, or black suit of clothes, and a long coat; while Mary Palethorp says he wore a light roundabout. This, though I admit it is unimportant in some of its relations, still shows how little dependence is to be placed upon the accuracy of the witnesses.

But Ellen proceeds yet further, and says, preserving the same spirit which she manifested in the outset, that Mrs. Chapman, a day or two after his arrival, accompanied Mina to Count Bonaparte's; they went in the carriage in the morning, and returned in the evening. She omits altogether to mention that Mr. Ash was their companion in the journey, and that it was with the entire approbation of Mr. Chapman. That this was an intentional omission, can hardly be denied, when we remember how remarkably tenacious her memory appears to be, in regard to the minutest circumstance that is calculated to operate in favor of the prosecution

"It was during this ride," says the learned counsel, "illicit love lighted up his unholy fires in the bosom of the defendant." How delightfully—or frightfully romantic! The first attempt, evidently, on the part of the prosecution, was to show the acquaintance between the prisoners, anterior to the arrival of Mina at Andalusia; and, therefore, was it that Mary Palethorp was asked: "who appeared best to understand him when he arrived?"—to which she answered: "Mrs. Chapman." But being driven from this position by their own witnesses, the next effort is, as I have shown you, to infer a criminal alliance between them, from the period of visiting Bonaparte's; which was but two days after the reception of Mina, at Mrs. Chapman's hospitable abode. This is a fancy, unrivalled in all the legendary lore of outrageous fiction. "The Libertines," "the Monk," "the Black Forest," "the Mysteries of Udolpho," and all the other *mysteries* that the world ever heard of, saw, or wondered at, never presented to the human mind so shocking a monstrosity as this. A beggar—"a cut-purse of the empire;" a vagabond, who in personal appearance was not the "twentieth part the tithe of her precedent lord;" a wretched tatterdemalion, fit only for a scarecrow, wins at first sight the defendant from her loyalty—from her husband, with whom she had lived in harmony for thirteen years—from her children, upon whom she doated—nay, even from *herself!* Where, except in the prolific fancy of the ingenious counsel, do you derive support for this notion? Even Ellen Shaw tells you, that upon her return she spoke of him as a son—as a brother, to her children; and I ask you whether it is possible for illicit love to mingle his lurid fires with the hallowed flame of maternal tenderness and affection.

The next part of Ellen Shaw's testimony, is that which relates to the conversation between her and Mr. Chapman, during the absence of Mrs. Chapman with Mina, at the city of Philadelphia, for two or three days. Now, whether any such conversation took place with her, is exceedingly doubtful, as Fanning says she was not present; but take it as it is. This female Iago tells you, that upon the husband's complaining of his wife's absence, she hinted to him, that it was probable they had gone to Mexico, as she had heard them speak of such intention. Yet she never heard them, and *admits* she never heard them; and thereby she convicts herself in the first place, of falsehood; and secondly, she shows—from what cause we need not stop to inquire—that her feelings towards Mrs. Chapman were of the most hostile and malignant character.

Without pausing to notice her various anachronisms— the allegations of her desire, and that of her children, that she should leave the place—her confounding spiritual and temporal songs together—her pious ejaculations on the subject of family prayer—her abominable perversion of the true state of the facts in respect to Mr. Chapman's having been compelled, by his wife, to make the beds— all of which matters have been brushed away from me, by the friendly hand of my colleague—I say, without making these separate subjects of remark; let me merely ask, while thus glancing at them in rapid review, whether there is a man on that jury who would be satisfied to abide by that test, which worthless, discontented, and discarded servants, might be disposed to apply, to the least questionable, to the most laudable of all his domestic arrangements. The language—the manner—the matter—when tortured in her intellectual or moral crucible, lose all their value—their gold is turned to dross.

Again, in speaking of her visit to Mr. Wright's, a visit

made for her own personal gratification, a few days before she left the house at Andalusia, she mentions that
Mina, " pretending to be sick, threw himself back upon the
lap of Mrs. Chapman, who supported him in her arms ;"
and yet she omits to mention altogether, that Mina also
rested in *her* lap, though it was obvious to all, that she
was a perfect antidote to the tender passions. Nay—this
is not all : upon arriving at Mr. Wright's, she informs
you that Mina and Mrs. C. took a walk in the woods, forgetting altogether the fact extracted from her upon the
cross-examination, that they also invited *her* to walk;
and that the house of Mr. Wright, upon their arrival,
was in such a state, as to be unfit to receive them; and
that, therefore, they were compelled to walk, as they had
no opportunity of sitting. If you choose to be suspicious,
why, to be sure, you may perceive impropriety in this, as
you may in any other step in life; but, in itself, it is entirely harmless, and totally consistent with the most immaculate virtue.

The malevolence of this witness towards the prisoner,
was clearly to be inferred, from her promptness in answering, whenever her answer was unfavorable to the defendant; and from her mental reservation—her suppression
of the truth, in those particulars which were calculated
to explain what otherwise might exhibit a semblance of
guilt. But we are not left to mere inference of malevolence. You have it in distinct proof—in proof from Ellen
Shaw herself, who, if she can establish anything, it must
be her own unworthiness. When injudiciously called a
second time by the prosecution, we took the liberty of applying the touch-stone " to see if she were current coin
or not." She was asked whether she had had no difference with Mr. and Mrs. C.; she answers none. But were
you not dismissed from their service? " Well," said she
in reply, "didn't I go?—and they got an old drunken
wretch from the road in my place, but she did not stay
long." Can you have any doubt, gentlemen, after this,

that her malice, thus engendered, has for the last twelve-month been confined like subterranean fire within her bosom, at last thus to burst forth and spread a ruin around. She presents before you the shocking anomaly of a human volcano, breathing nothing but flames, devastation, and death.

Let us turn from this disgusting picture to the next witness presented on the part of the prosecution—Mrs. Esther Bache. Her testimony is of but little importance. She relates what took place between Mina and Mrs. C., and says that Mr. C. having attempted joking with him, he gave Chapman a very ill look. It is somewhat hard to find fault with this, as he certainly had no other look to give. But, says the witness, Mrs. C. apologized, and laughingly said, "Mina does not understand a word Mr. Chapman utters." This, to be sure, was wonderful, and bears its own comment with it. I only ask Mrs. Bache what she would have done, and wherein consisted the supposed impropriety?

But the witness says, that Mina sat on the right hand of Mrs. Chapman at table. Where should he sit?—at the head?—at the foot? If he had taken either of those places, it would have been downright treason! Which side Mrs. Bache sat, we have not learned, but considering she never sat down but twice at the table with Mina; and never was in the house with Mrs. Chapman beyond a day; and then in the capacity of a seamstress; her observations, critical and explanatory, of the domestic regulations of the family, were truly remarkable and surprising. Mrs. Bache has every appearance of a respectable woman, and no doubt is so; but she is one of those ladies with whom Ellen Shaw, and Ann Bantom, have been talking, and what, independently of their communications, she would have considered as every day trifles; when connected with, or engrafted upon their stock of knowledge, produces to her mind a ripe harvest of forbidden fruit,

> " Whose mortal taste, brought *death* into the world,
> And all our *wo*."

Ann Bantom, who modestly takes the third place in this melancholy procession, but who has strong claims to be first, will now be introduced to your notice. She, I suppose, has been brought forward to give some *color* to their case. Thus it is, gentlemen of the jury, " black spirits and white " are conjured and raked up, from the vile recesses of the kitchen and the garret—and arrayed here before you upon this trial, like Milton's devils—" fierce as ten furies, terrible as hell." The day darkens at their approach, and the radiant smile that beams from the brow of innocence, fades away beneath their withering and demoniac charm.

Ann Bantom is the pivot upon which the whole case, exclusive of the medical branches of it, must rest. The *second* proposed general inquiry, relies entirely upon her for its solution, at the same time that her testimony materially affects the *first*. Thus important, I fearlessly plant the standard of my defence upon their own soil. I am content to encounter them with their own arms, and submit unmurmuringly to the issue of the conflict. A word or two, for the general recommendation of Ann Bantom to our regard. She was employed as an out-door servant; occasionally, though not often, had attended on Mondays to assist in washing; and without, for aught that appears, any other connection with the family. Having generally been there on Mondays, how she at this late period, iden-tifies the precise day upon which the events which she relates took place, I know not, and I care not; but I will consider them as they have been communicated; and for that purpose, I am sure you will accord me a patient and attentive hearing.

Ann Bantom says she was at Andalusia the Monday after Mr. C. was taken sick; and it is not a little remarkable, having no kind of acquaintance with Mr. Chapman, that she should have gone uninvited into his chamber in the morning, to inquire after his health—to find him *better ;* and that she should again go up in the afternoon of the same day, to make similar inquiries—and to find him *worse*. I pronounce this remarkable in itself, but it is rendered more so, by the recollection that it does not appear she had ever spoken to him before; and that on the next day after the Monday referred to, she neglected altogether paying him a visit, though she knew he was worse; and at last was urged up into his chamber by his wife, for the purpose of being convinced how important it was, in the helpless state of the family, that her services should not be withdrawn. This may be all true, but much of it is extraordinary Those two visits on the morning and afternoon of Monday, bear strange denotements. The prosecution required that somebody should see him in the morning, to observe that he was better, and then see him in the afternoon, to find that he was worse; while in the interim the soup is to be given to the patient, and the deduction of poison is complete. All these matters are derived from the witness whose testimony we are now considering. Let us turn particularly to her statement.—[*Notes of her testimony here read.*]

"Mrs. Chapman," says the witness, "boiled the chicken and prepared the soup." That the hand of the wife should minister to the wants of the husband in the hour of disease, is assuredly no subject of legitimate complaint:—yet such is the dilemma of Mrs. Chapman, if she gave her husband nothing, she is branded with unparalleled cruelty, and if on the contrary, she comply with the express directions of the physician, and prepare his food or diet, it is only for the purpose of infusing poison into it. Had she for a moment contemplated so horrible a deed, might not the soup have been as well prepared by any other hand? The introduction of the arsenic, was the work of an instant; and it is alleged to have taken place some time after the soup was made. There was every thing to deter her, if actuated by the imputed purpose, from unnecessarily connecting herself with a transaction, from which such direful results were

to spring. It was not usual, we are told, however, for
Mrs. C. to attend to culinary concerns. It may not have
been, but this renders our reasoning the stronger, even as
applied to this condition of facts

One small circumstance, however, has escaped the
memory of our friends, and it almost escaped that of
their witness; which is, that on this very Monday,
Juliana, the cook, had been taken sick; and Ann Bantom
being engaged out of doors, nobody remained to attend
to the preparation of the soup but Mrs. Chapman. Yet
still, perfectly as this portion of the case is explained; if
you choose, as the counsel do, to take it for granted she
is guilty, even this circumstance makes against her. But,
if you are to decide upon the testimony, I will not say
it is irreconcilable with guilt, but I do say, it is perfectly reconcilable and consistent with entire innocence.

To resume the course of the evidence:—The soup having been made about dinner time, after putting salt in it,
it was taken up by Mrs. Chapman into the parlor, for the
purpose of seasoning. I cannot understand this exactly,
and perhaps it is not necessary that I should. Ann Bantom follows Mrs. C. into the parlor, where she finds
Mina. She does not remember what she went up for,
but having fulfilled her purpose, she returns again into
the kitchen. In the afternoon of the day, the soup, or
what remained of it, was brought down by Mrs. C. and
placed upon the kitchen table; and the chicken was subsequently taken up, and afterwards brought down almost
entire, if not quite, and also placed upon the same table,
where they both were permitted to remain, until thrown
out untouched, by this faithful and economical servant.
After this, the ducks of Mr. Boutcher, to the number of
twenty, died; and the argument was intended to be—
nay, was—that the poisoned soup produced their untimely end. Now let me consider this, and if I do not
totally demolish the reliance of the prosecution, upon
their own testimony, I will never open my lips again in a

court of justice; but ever hereafter, shroud my diminished head in obscurity and oblivion. This soup, say they, was poisoned soup: how can you for a moment reconcile with that idea,—or rather with the idea of Mrs. C.'s *knowledge* of the poison,—the resistless fact of the poisoned chalice having been permitted to remain for nearly half a day, upon the table in the kitchen, in the very centre of her children, who were there at play; and subject also to the appetites of her servants? Do you—can you suppose, that she designed the destruction of her entire household, little ones and all?—Nay—do you suppose that she designed directly to contribute to her own inevitable detection? Both sympathy and selfishness alike revolt at the idea. If poison had been infused into the soup without her knowledge, she is free from crime; and if it existed at all, it is only by supposing it to be without her knowledge, that you can account for these extraordinary measures. For all the uses of this argument, I care not whether Lino purchased two ounces of arsenic, or two pounds, a day or two preceding Mr. C.'s death. It may make against himself, but not against the present defendant, for, whether the deceased died from natural causes, or from his hand, is alike to our defence—the prisoner being unacquainted with the cause; and that she was a stranger to the cause, if contained in the suspected soup, is perfectly manifest and unquestionable; and if the cause were not contained in the soup, then was the soup made and salted—the chickens died, and the ducks followed—all to no possible purpose; and we have been entertained here for a half a day in the examination of kitchen concerns, to be told in conclusion, that they have nothing to do with the case. Had she borne with her the consciousness of guilt, what was to prevent her disposing of the soup in a thousand ways? —throwing it into the fire, throwing it out of the window, emptying it herself in the sewer, where no human power could have discovered it?—Nothing. Yet say the gentlemen, perceiving the force of this argument, "but a portion of the soup that was taken into the parlor, was poisoned, and afterwards carried up to Mr. Chapman; and that which was brought down into the kitchen, had not been drugged." This is ingenious; but it has no evidence to stand upon, and is self-destroyed. The only soup thrown out, was the soup brought down. The soup that was thrown out, is that to which the death of the ducks has been attributed; and if that did not contain poison, how was the death of the unfortunate ducks produced? They talk of challenges!—I challenge *them* to reconcile these conflicting hypotheses.

Mr. Hellings, and several other witnesses, state, that the death of large flocks of young ducks, is not unusual. That fish water, lime water, and various other matters, will produce that result; and it deserves to be remembered, that Mr. Chapman having been recently engaged in building, large quantities of lime were scattered over his little domain, and perhaps that circumstance may reasonably account, for the timeless fate of these almost unfledged trespassers.

A word or two more, ere I take leave of the ducks. I am not fond of *quackery*, which must account to you for a very brief obituary notice of these long lamented *ducks*. On Monday morning, before the soup was made, three of Mr. Boutcher's chickens rolled on their backs and died. On Tuesday afternoon, a whole day after the soup had been thrown into the aqueduct, the unsuspecting ducklings followed their example; so that, you perceive, the chickens died by *anticipation* and the ducks forsooth by *retrospection*. They were all decently buried, no doubt, with becoming ceremonies; yet we cannot but drop a passing tear of pity for their fate, when we are told that their rights of sepulture have, but yesterday, been barbarously invaded; and their canonized bones have burst their cerements, and been produced as a sort of *memento mori* in this open court, for the purpose of corrupting the wholesome and heavenly atmosphere of justice. I can wish the prosecution, however, no worse fate, and they deserve no better, in requittal of this unhallowed deed, than to be daily haunted at the festive and convivial board, with the awful apparition of a brace of fat ducks. So shall they ever remember the history of this day's error, and be taught a solemn and salutary lesson of becoming reverence for the departed.

We have thus far contemplated the evidence of Ann Bantom in itself, and found it altogether too weak to sustain itself. What then shall become of it, when opposed to the resistless current from other quarters, that sets against, and overwhelms it? The little Lucretia, with a purity unsurpassed by the great original of that name, and with a beauty and simplicity that won all eyes and hearts, informs you, that the soup in question was brought to her by her sister Mary, while she was attending at the bed side of her sick father, and that she gave it to him; that the chicken was brought up at the same time; that he drank some of the soup, but ate heartly of the chicken; and not having had her dinner, at his request she joined him in both, and afterwards carried the little that remained into the kitchen, and placed it upon the table. What now becomes of the statement of Ann Bantom, that Mrs. C. brought down the chicken and the soup? What now becomes of the notion of the learned counsel, that the portion of the soup that was given to Mr. Chapman, was poisoned, and that that which was returned into the kitchen was not the same? There can be no mistake in the time—it was on Monday, while the father was sick, and Ann Bantom in the kitchen. There can be no mistake in the circumstance—it was the only soup administered. There is no refuge left, therefore, to the prosecution, but to ground their arms, and march off at once, without flourish of trumpet or beat of drum.

I come now, in almost the last place, to an analysis of Fanning. This eastern mountebank—this peddling bookseller—a fellow, vending his salt-and-water physic, and his milk-and-water literature through the land; one of a wandering tribe, as numerous as the locusts of Egypt, and as great a curse. He arrives at Andalusia, a beggar, with an empty head, an empty heart, an empty stomach, and an empty subscription list; and with the same generosity as was displayed in the reception of Lino, she charitably supplies all his wants. Her house is open to him, her table is spread for him. His list of subscribers enlarge daily, even beyond his hopes, under her fostering care; and in kind requital for all this, when by the death of her husband, she was left without a protector or a friend, in a strange land; this viper, who had so long coiled in flow'ry ambush, deliberately attempts stinging her joys to death. He causes it to be rumored through the neighborhood, that he is the sacred depository of some dark and darkling mystery. He leaves word with Capt. McIlroy, that there were deadly doings in that house; and having left his address, desires to be sent for, if anything of importance should transpire. If he knew anything that his conscience forbade him to conceal, why did he not speak out like a man?—why shroud himself in the darkest mystery? If he knew nothing—and it appears he really did know nothing—why did he thus contribute to give wings to wild conjecture and unjust suspicion, against one who never harmed him? For the latter part of his cunning, I could suggest a cause:—Being about to depart for some remote part of the United States, and always having a crafty eye to business, he dexterously manœuvres to be conveniently recalled, and throw the expenses of his journey upon the broad shoulders of the commonwealth.

And now we have him here, was there ever a more ridiculous farce than that which he exhibits? He opens his pedler pack before this court and jury, and while every man stands aghast, with the idea that like Pandora's box, it will pour forth all kinds of evils to afflict the human race, lo, and behold, it presents an empty void!

From the moment of this disclosure, the flood of prejudice began to ebb; the thronged avenues to your court, were literally deserted ; and the rapacious hounds that pursued the defendant, even here to her last refuge—with Blaney at their head—all lost the scent of blood, and sneakingly, though reluctantly, relinquished their prey.

Little, however, as is derived from Fanning, it may not be time unemployed—as he is the Magnus Apollo of the case—to take a bird's eye sketch of his testimony. He first introduces himself, by referring to that period of time, when Mrs. Chapman, her son William, Mina, and Mr. Ash visited the city, and remained absent about three days. On the night of the second day, he says Mr. Chapman was much agitated, and displayed a great deal of passion, declaring that he had had no peace since Mina came into his house, and swearing by the Deity that he would shoot him. After all this storm of rage, however, according to his account, Mr. Chapman quietly and tranquilly retires to his repose, leaving the witness, as a sort of Hesperian Dragon, to guard his honor during the soothing hours of slumber. What a mass of inconsistencies have we here. A husband, publishing to a comparative stranger, the story of his wife's dishonor—raving this moment in all the torments of the damned, and the next, silently seeking the repose of his *thorny pillow*—the consolations of his *violated bed*. But the climax of this absurdity, is the appointment of Fanning to stand watch and ward, and like night's sentinel, Silence, to challenge every sound. This situation, however, was not active enough for the curious and prying disposition of Fanning, and he therefore soon followed the example of his commander, and slept upon his post.

The next day, the plot thickens; the wanderers all return; the death of Mina's sister is communicated ; and Mr. Chapman accompanying Mina into the parlor, instead of pronouncing him as an impostor, as he had alleged him to be to Fanning—instead of blowing his brains

out, as he had awfully threatened the night before—he
takes a seat with him on the sofa, embraces him, mingles
tear with tear, and as Fanning himself says, in the language of scripture, " mourned with the mourner." This
is not all: Mr. Chapman immediately writes to Messrs.
Page and Watkinson, ordering them to prepare a splendid
suit of black for his faithful friend Don Lino, and to
charge it to him. Nor does he stop here: even a few
days before his sickness, he draws an order, in his own
proper hand, upon Mr. Fassitt, and requests him to pay
the balance of his account to his confidential agent Don
Lino. And when you connect with these circumstances,
the tender epistle written by the deceased to the parents
of this Don Lino, or Don Devil, you must inevitably arrive at one of two conclusions, either that Chapman was
a madman, or Fanning a liar.

The pedler, having after the scenes above referred to,
absented himself for some days, again returns a day or
two before the close of his patron's earthly career—namely,
on Monday morning, about nine o'clock. With his characteristic modesty, he makes his way immediately into
the sick chamber, where he found the deceased, very ill,
and vomiting excessively; this, however, he afterwards
partially explains by saying, " he made violent attempts at
vomiting, but with little effect." The witness saw Mrs. C.,
who requested him not to communicate the condition of
Mr. C.'s health to his brother's family. On the night of
the same day he is desired by Mr. Chapman to remain
with him—" for," said Mr. C., " I am very sick; when
Don Lino is sick, all attention must be paid to him; but
now I am sick, I am deserted." Before I turn to other
portions of the testimony, allow me to bestow a few remarks upon that to which I have thus adverted. Finding the deceased very ill on Monday morning, is in the
teeth of Ann Bantom's testimony, who states he was
much better; you must decide between them. The request of Mrs. Chapman that he would conceal the state

of her husband's health from his brother's family, unex-
plained, would operate against us. But we have shown
you that there was an unhappy fraternal feud—that Mr.
C. had not been permitted to see his brother during that
brother's illness; and that in consequence thereof he had,
on the very day preceding the pedler's arrival, written to
his pastor, and spoken to Mr. Vandegrift, to the effect of
excluding his brother's family from all participation in
his funeral rites. He knew that his widow would be
liable to reproach for this, and therefore it was that he
thus publicly exculpated her. As to the complaints
made by Chapman to Fanning of the attentions to Don
Lino and the desertion of himself, uttered no doubt in the
way of bitterness; even if Fanning speak gospel, how little
are they to be depended upon. We all know the fretful-
ness, the whims, the caprice, attendant upon disease; we
know that shortly after this period, Mr. C. was in a state
of delirium—and it would be cruel in the extreme, to
permit his loose and scattering remarks, which owed all
their prosperity to the ear of Fanning, to be visited against
his absent and injured wife.

It was said by the opening counsel for the prosecution,
no doubt anticipating the support of Fanning's evidence,
that Mrs. Chapman drove her husband's attendant from
the room in his last hours; that she refused to send for a
physician; and that she withheld from him the medicine
prescribed. How ungenerous and unjust is such an imputation, it will be for you to determine, after having
heard the evidence upon which it is built. How did she
drive the attendant from him? Her house being a perfect
hospital—her cook sick—Mina laboring under his fits,
either real or affected—her husband dying—she is even
compelled to assail the sympathies of Ann Bantom, by
describing her distress, in order to induce her to remain.
Whom did she drive from the room? Not Bishop, for he
remained in attendance. If anybody, it must have been
Fanning; and how did she expel him? She came into

the chamber about eleven o'clock, where finding Fanning, she expressed her obligations to him, and told him she would not trouble him to remain through the night; and this perfectly simple and usual occurrence, is distorted into a glaring circumstance of guilt.

"I requested," says Fanning, "to be allowed to go for a physician, again and again, and was refused by her." What a cowardly concealment of the true state of the facts do we here perceive. Dr. Phillips had been sent for on Saturday, and visited Mr. C. on Sunday as the family physician; and upon the cross-examination of Mr. Fanning, it appears that it was not Mrs. C. alone that declined sending for another physician, but that it was also opposed by Mr. C., on the ground that it might offend Dr. Phillips.

In regard to refusing, or omitting to give the deceased the medicines prescribed; Dr. Knight, who attended the patient four or five times, gives you no reason to believe it. I think he gave him some of the medicines himself. The prescription of Dr. Phillips was rigidly pursued, and wonderful to relate, forms part of the charge against us. Even Fanning admits *salt and water* was promptly administered; and yet after all, as I have said, the argument is, that when anything is given it contains concealed poison; and if nothing be given, it is an evidence of barbarity.

In conclusion upon these points, I say, the whole course of the defendant's deportment during those painful scenes, was attentive, kind, and wife-like. Dr. Knight, it is true, thought she was not as much in the room as she might have been; but Dr. Knight knew but little of the helpless condition in which she was placed, and of the various avocations to which she was reluctantly condemned. Dr. Phillips, on the contrary, whose evidence was a model of manliness and propriety, distinctly informs you that the conduct of Mrs. Chapman was becoming and decorous; that as death approached, as they all required rest, he led

her and the children out of the room; that he retired also
himself, desiring to be called if any change should take
place; that he was called about one o'clock, and that
Mrs. C. and the children surrounded the bed of the dying
man at the moment of dissolution. After this, all proper
and becoming measures were adopted for his interment;
matters were managed in the usual way on such melancholy occasions; the relatives and friends of the departed
were invited; the curtain fell, and the last scene of this
sad drama forever closed.

The post mortem events, so far as they have not been
already examined, remain to be briefly reviewed. Your
patience and my strength are nearly exhausted, and I
therefore hasten to the termination of our mutual toil.

The marriage with Lino, within a fortnight after her
husband's decease, is considered as a damning spot upon
the escutcheon of this case. If the doctrine be true, that
"none wed the second, but who kill the first," we are,
indeed, driven to despair; for the second marriage is unquestionable. But I deny the doctrine; and although I
admit that there was nothing to justify this unholy haste,
there was, I allege, much to excuse it. The defendant
was left with a large family, with limited and precarious
means, and without a single friend upon whom to rely in
the hour of adversity and distress. Up to this period of
time, at least, she had every reason to believe in the representations of the destroyer. His story was sustained
by the information derived from the steward of Count
Survilliers; it was further corroborated by his reception
at the abode and at the table of the Mexican Consul; by
the grateful expressions of Miss Romana Cuesta in behalf
of a distinguished though unhappy Mexican; by the
munificence of the stranger as exhibited by his will; the
promise to allow six thousand dollars for his instruction
in the English language, and the allegation of his immense
wealth, and that of his family. But above all, it was
confirmed by the confidence manifestly reposed in him by

her husband; as is clearly established by irrefragable documents, notwithstanding all that has been said or surmised by some of the witnesses in this case. Connecting with all these circumstances the declaration made to her by Mina, that it was the dying request of his friend that he would prove a protector to his widow, and a father to his orphans; his further declaration of his intention almost forthwith to return to Mexico ; of the impossibility of their travelling except as husband and wife; of the customs of his own country in regard to disparity of age; of the importance of being so united, that his father, a proud Spaniard, should not be able to dissolve the bonds, or deny to her the advantages of survivorship in case of his death ; of the gratitude which he felt towards one who had sheltered him in poverty and nursed him in disease; of his intention to bestow the place at Andalusia upon those relatives who were most dear to her ;—take, I say, all these combined influences into consideration, and then decide, if you can, that she was not infinitely more sinned against than sinning.

It is perfectly true, that hearing, as you have done, all these falsehoods exposed, it may excite some surprise that they were not earlier detected. But we are to determine upon her conduct with reference to what was actually represented and believed, and not with regard to what subsequently took place. It is the privilege of but one Eye, as has been said, to dive into futurity, and to lay open the dark recesses of the heart; she was human, and therefore fallible ; but there is a vast difference, in the contemplation of this court, and of a higher court, between human error and human crime.

The marriage ceremony having been performed at New York, on the 5th day of July, 1831, Mina returned to Andalusia, and the defendant, in pursuance of the previous arrangement, proceeded to Syracuse on a visit to her sister, Mrs. Green ; the object of which was to place that sister in the possession of her establishment in this coun-

try, while she and her children accompanied her husband
in the projected voyage to Mexico.

Several letters were written by her during her absence,
which have been subjects of severe commentary on the
part of the prosecution; and which are said to contain
nothing but an expression of the wildest and most irregular passions. It is not very easy to say exactly what
should be the character of a letter from a wife to a husband; it must depend very much upon circumstances—
upon the age, constitution, temperament, and condition
of the parties. I have read those letters, private and
confidential as they were, and you will have an opportunity of reading them; and I take leave to say, that they
exhibit nothing that is incompatible with the most entire
purity of the heart, or with a judicious exercise of the
faculties of the head. They were not intended for public
exposure, and therefore, to us, who cannot enter precisely
into the feelings of the parties, they may appear somewhat unreasonable and extravagant. But test them, if
you please, by letters which you have either written or
received in a similar relation, and you will at once perceive that they are neither extraordinary nor remarkable.
It is the privilege of married life to speak and to write
unreservedly; and your own experience will be sufficient
to satisfy you, that in this instance that privilege has not
been carried by the defendant, to a licentious or culpable
extreme.

There is one letter, however, written by the defendant
to Mina, while at Washington, which is said to contain
at least an equivocal passage, and to afford ground for
the belief, in the language of the opposite counsel, " that
all was not perfectly right." In passing to the consideration of that clause, we must be allowed to premise, that
it is not sufficient, that all was not perfectly right; it is
incumbent upon the prosecution to show to your satisfaction that all was perfectly *wrong*. I agree that all was
not perfectly right. It was not right that she should

marry within a little month after her husband's decease.
It was not right that Mina should sell her jewels, her
plate, her horses, and her carriage, or that he should give
away the trunk and books of her deceased husband. It
was not right that he should take two ladies to the
United States Hotel, and that, remaining there with
them, he should pay their expenses and his own out of
his wife's honest earnings. It was not right that he
should squander her means in the journey to Baltimore,
under the false profession that it was for the purpose of
obtaining a legacy of forty-five thousand dollars, left by
his friend Casanova; and it was manifestly wrong that
he should practise all sorts of frauds and falsehoods, upon
this unsuspecting woman, during his absence. I agree,
therefore, as I have said, that all was not right; but I
deny that writing under the influences fairly attributable
to these manifold outrages, the clause referred to in her
letter, is to be considered as an evidence of her having
aided in the destruction of the deceased.

It is a well settled principle in criminal jurisprudence,
and it cannot be too strongly borne in mind, that where
the acts or language of men admit, equally, of opposite in-
terpreptations, that construction shall be adopted which is
most favorable to innocence. With the benefit of these
impressions, let us turn to the objectionable paragraph.
I quote it from memory, and shall willingly submit to
correction, if I quote it erroneously: "When I reflect,
Mina, I am constrained to acknowledge, I cannot believe,
that God will suffer either you or me, ever to be happy on
this side of the grave." Was not reflection upon the
events just referred to entirely sufficient to induce these
expressions, without imagining the perpetration of an
offence so heinous as that charged against the prisoner?
She had been imprudent; she had been imposed upon;
she had been impoverished, together with her children,
to whom she was tenderly attached; and if this were
not a state of circumstances, calculated to produce such a

reflection, I am utterly at a loss to conceive what would be. *On this side of the grave*, indicates worldly suffering for worldly indiscretion. If she had been guilty of the imputed crime, her fears would not have fallen short of that punishment which awaits the wicked *beyond* the grave.

Taking these letters all together, and carefully perusing them, nothing can be found inconsistent with the consciousness of innocence. , Can you suppose, if this woman had committed so odious and hateful a crime as that imputed to her—writing as she did, under the sanctity of a seal, and to her partner in iniquity—she never would have allowed a single word to escape her, in which the lynx eye of the prosecution could perceive a semblance of guilty remorse or timidity. If we are determined to suspect crime first, and then to distort and pervert everything to the support of that suspicion ; no man, innocent or otherwise, can escape punishment. I defy the counsel, with all their learning, skill and accuracy, to write a letter upon any subject, in which I cannot detect, being suspiciously disposed, either an intention to conceal some motive that they entertain, or a disposition to convey some idea that they do not. If their composition be loose, it will be indefinite and equivocal, and admit of a vast variety of constructions. If it be terse and precise, we may plausibly infer, from that very terseness and precision, that they are anxious to guard themselves against the disclosure of some lurking motive.

In reference to the letter written from Erie to Colonel Cuesta, I have but a remark or two to make, carrying with me the benefit of those observations upon the previous correspondence. That letter, be it remembered, was written several months after her departure from Andalusia. It contains this passage : " When I reflect that it is possible that my dear husband died of poison, and that I myself am suspected of being an accomplice, I am shocked, I am paralyzed." Now, says the opposite counsel, "why should she dream of being suspected ?" I answer, for the most obvious reason ; because the public journals throughout the United States, to which she undoubtedly had reference, uttered nothing but the most malevolent and unfounded reports of her participation in this crime. She must have closed her eyes, her ears, and her understanding, against every passing wind ; if she had not discovered, long ere the date of that letter, the weight of obloquy and suspicion that was heaped upon, . and crushed her.

In the same letter, she mentions, among various other matters, the inferences that may be drawn from her unfortunate flight ; and although that subject is not now presented in the exact order of time, I perhaps cannot do better than briefly consider and dispose of it.

The reasons which she herself gives for abandoning the protection of her household gods, and temporarily deserting her children, for the purpose of avoiding the violence of the gathering storm ; are such as to carry conviction of their truth to every bosom. She was a teacher—and had been for years—of a large and highly respectable seminary ; her reputation was her stock in trade ; exposure was but another word for death ; that she should shrink from it, therefore, was natural—was excusable. That she contemplated but a temporary absence, is plain from her conversation with Mrs. Smith ; from her communication to Justice Barker at the time of drawing up the power of attorney ; and from the situation in which she permitted her family to remain.

But two matters remain, ere I surrender this cause to you. The first is the state of things a few days after the funeral ; and the second, the interview between Mr. Recorder McIlvaine and the defendant. Let us take them in their order.

Mrs. Smith, who is a lady in every sense of the word, called at Andalusia, I think, the day after the funeral : Mrs. Chapman, apologizing for the want of servants, an-

swered the door herself. She was dressed in black, with
a white turban bearing a *lilac* border; and this little
matter struck Mrs. Smith with some surprise; I really
don't know why. Grief displays itself very differently
in different persons, and in different circumstances. It is
not in "customary suits of solemn black" alone, that the
heart exhibits its afflictions. Many of the gentlemen
whom I have now the honor to address for the first, and
perhaps for the last time, are disbelievers in external
mourning; and whether they are or are not, they would
hardly convict a lady of murder, from the color of
her turban. Rely upon it, if she had been the wicked
thing they would make her, there would have been no
deficiency in what may be called dramatic effect; her
error would have been in *excess;* like the Ephesian dame,
she would have swept the very earth with her widowed
weeds, and veiled her face in sorrow. Her dress was not
affected, her agonies were not eloquent; but they were
not the less poignant or sincere:

> " The grief that cannot speak,
> Whispers the o'erfraught heart, and bids it break."

There was one expression, however, of hers, which
breathed volumes—that rather escaped from the laboring soul than was uttered by it—that was addressed to
no one, though in the presence of Mrs. Smith—and that
sounded like the knell of departed hope; departed, never
to return. Casting her eyes involuntarily upon the heavens, she exclaimed in a stifled and subdued voice: " The
sun—the sun—looks gloomy." This simple touch of
nature unfolded more, much more, than all the studied
forms and ceremonies of woe.

Again: Mrs. Smith, though surprised at first, must
have been entirely reconciled to her deportment, as she at
that time placed her child under the care of the defendant; and shortly after took up her own residence, and
that of her husband, under this very roof. I will not

weaken these facts by bestowing upon them a single comment.

On the afternoon of the 29th day of August, the recorder, accompanied by High Constable Blaney, and Mr. Reeside, waited upon Mrs. Chapman, at her house. The object, as it is stated, was to discover traces of Mina; with reference to his impositions, malpractices, and forgeries while at Washington. Mrs. Chapman, at the time of their arrival, was at church with her sister, but shortly returned; and the recorder being invited into the parlor, immediately communicated the purpose of his visit. He knew nothing at this time of her second marriage, and therefore much of her conduct, which with that knowledge he would have easily understood, appeared to this intelligent gentleman to be extraordinary. He spoke of Mina's character—of his falsehoods, of his frauds—and inquired whether she herself had not been plundered and despoiled by him. She hesitated, and denied it—until her letter, which had been intercepted, was produced, recounting a long catalogue of injuries to which she had been subjected. She even then rather appeared to evade or to extenuate the evils she had suffered. But will you here allow me to inquire what course she should have pursued? Irrevocably wedded to a felon—the officers of justice upon his crime-covered track—was she to join in the general cry—was she to hunt down one, to whom, bad as he was, she had plighted her faith? She gave no other information than was extorted from her—and I openly rejoice that she did not. Fidelity is the brightest jewel that adorns the female character; it is the *last* that woman loses; and it would have been an eternal reproach to her *sex*—it would have been perdition to *her*, when her vile husband's fate was poised before her, if the whole police of the city, with all their mental racks and tortures, could have extracted from her heaving bosom, a single groan to guess at. Had she then betrayed Mina, infamous and abandoned as he was, it would have supplied to the prosecution the most unanswerable argument of her previous guilt: to *betray* or to *destroy*, is but the same principle, differently developed.

Still not knowing the marriage, the recorder proceeded, fixing his keen and inquisitorial eye upon her at the same time, to inquire whether she had any reason to believe that Mina had contributed to the death of her husband. She changed color—her face assumed a livid hue —and she appeared for a moment as if she would have sunk to the earth. She recovers, however, and replies: " No—he was his faithful friend; I cannot think it possible he should do anything so diabolical!" And yet it is thought this is not a becoming expression of surprise. According to my experience in human nature, it at once expressed surprise, doubt, affection, horror, and all the violent and conflicting emotions which the question was so eminently calculated to excite. But whether it did or not, you do not sit here to decide upon comparative strength of nerve—upon the various results on various individuals, of sudden and unexpected shocks—upon the change of the complexion—or the still more variable forms of passion or expression; depending as often for their character upon the mind of the *observer*, as upon that of the *observed*. Mr. Phillips, in his valuable essay upon the theory of presumptive proof, speaking in reference to the celebrated case of Captain Donnellan, in which it was alleged that the defendant displayed more uneasiness than was even natural to one in his situation, makes these appropriate remarks: " It is a delicate thing to decide this question; it is a nice thing to fix the standard of human feelings, and to say what degree of perturbation an individual already branded with guilt or conviction shall feel, when placed in circumstances which make him to be suspected of a capital crime. Lawyers, and those accustomed to see and advise with persons in that unfortunate predicament, can only tell the terrible apprehension that every one feels at the idéa of being brought to a public trial ; it is altogether a new view of human nature, and we seldom estimate rightly, feelings which we have never experienced, nor expect to experience in our own persons, nor have witnessed in those of others.

'To thee no reason !
Who good has only known, and evil has not proved.' "

But I go further than Mr. Phillips, and utterly deny even the *competency* of those who, from their office, are in the habitual communion with guilt, to decide from the expression of the face or the features, upon the impulses of the heart. Nay, more than this, their very knowledge of the worst part of mankind, with whom they are so frequently brought into contact, imbues the mind with jaundiced and unfavorable impressions of our nature, and leads them to detect a felon in every face:— if you are bold, it is the hardihood of confirmed guilt— if you are fearful, it is the timidity of crime. I do not mean to say that every judge of a criminal court may become a Jeffries ; because, thank heaven, at this day the moral influence of public opinion provides a salutary restraint ; but I do mean to say, that whatever may be the theory of our rights, experience abundantly instructs us, that the moment a charge is preferred against an individual, he bears the stamp of Cain upon his brow ; and inverting the best principle in criminal jurisprudence, he is almost uniformly considered to be guilty, till his innocence shall be established ; and perhaps even afterwards. In these remarks, no one can suppose that I speak in reference to any individual, much less to the highly respectable and amiable recorder, for whom I entertain the sincerest personal and professional regard. I speak to human nature and common experience, and I do it the more confidently, as I acknowledge my own liability to the influence I thus deprecate.

In further illustration of this doctrine, I need only

advert to the case introduced by my learned and eloquent colleague, of the unfortunate Thomas Harris, as reported in Phillips. In that case, though the defendant was utterly innocent, the fact of his changing color, and appearing confused, was relied upon as a strong, if not conclusive evidence of crime; yet that very confusion was produced, partly from the consciousness that the fact referred to might operate against him, and partly from the shame incident to a disclosure of his avarice. If, therefore, different causes entirely consistent with innocence of the particular charge, may create shame and consternation—and if sufficient independent cause can be shown, as in the present instance; how obviously unjust must it be, that it should be construed into evidence of the imputed crime. It is like the attempt made by the prosecution in respect to the symptoms of the deceased; inferring, as they have done, an existence of poison, from indications of disease, which were altogether consistent with other, and natural causes.

As to the evidence of Blaney, but little need be said. It would rather seem, from what he says, that Mrs. Chapman apprized him of the direction of Mina's journey,—though the recorder does not mention it,—as Blaney, it seems, soon after this conversation, wrote to Boston, and succeeded in arresting the offender. But I protest, once for all, against the testimony of such men as Blaney, whether for or against us. He is a police officer, speaking from police reports, or rather from the report of Mr. McClean, who was here, and did not condescend to lend his support to the commonwealth. It is the business of a constable to suspect—and no one can escape him; carrying, as he always does, suspicion in one eye, and a search warrant in the other.

Thus, gentlemen of the jury, have I attempted showing; in the first place, that no poison was administered; and in the second place, that at all events, it was not administered by this defendant; either of which is sufficient for the purposes of the present case. If the defendant be innocent, it is not for me to show who may be guilty; that is the business of the prosecution. It can impart no gratification to me wantonly to travel out of the strict line of my duty, to load, or trample upon a fallen fellow creature.

In conclusion, allow me to observe, that to those who have been engaged in this discussion, and to those who shall be engaged in the determination of the present question, this matter of life or death may be a subject of utter indifference and contempt, as it is contemplated in relation to *others*. Clothed in our own imaginary infallibility, what sympathy can be expected from us, by that isolated, hapless being, upon whom your irrevocable decree is about to be pronounced. Sympathy is ever the offspring of a common liability to *evil*, or susceptibility of *good;* and what penalty do you fear, or what privilege do you enjoy, in common with an individual who is presented before you, suspected and accused of the most horrible of crimes. The very circumstance of her being placed at that bar, is calculated to provoke involuntary prejudice; and however we may be taught that both justice and mercy should incline us to the belief of innocence while passing upon the fate of a human being; experience, as I have already intimated, frequently establishes a widely different practice.

The law tells us—nature tells us—and humanity abundantly instructs us, that whenever a prisoner stands charged with an offence, and such an offence; instead of substituting the busy rumor, the misty moonshine of malice or prejudice, for the meridian light and fulness of truth; we should patiently await the disclosure of facts which the evidence itself, and the evidence only, can legitimately disclose; thereby placing our verdict upon a substantial foundation, which, hereafter, in the hour of deliberate and calm reflection, may remain firm and unshaken. Pause, now while the opportunity is afforded—

now, ere it be too late—now, while reflection comes with healing on its wing. Hereafter, years and floods of penitence and remorse can never obliterate or wash away the consequences of an error, which seals forever, and irretrievably, the defendant's melancholy doom. Considerations of this kind all plead, "like angels, trumpet tongued," in her behalf, and might almost " persuade Justice to break her sword."

The charge in the indictment is most horrible and atrocious, it is true: a husband's murder! The strength of the testimony, should be proportionate to its enormity. It can never diminish the horror of the charge, that the innocent should suffer. The defendant, nevertheless, bows submissively to your pleasure : if such be your terrible decree, let the axe fall; consign her to an ignominious grave, and her children to pitiless orphanage. Return then to your own domestic circle—to your own firesides ; and, surrounded by your partners and your offspring, recall and relate the lamentable occurrences of this day's trial; tell them that the popular clamor was too loud and too general to be escaped—the popular prejudice too powerful to be resisted; tell them, that under those influences you have consigned a mother to a timeless grave, and her children to endless ruin; and thereby give them to understand, how frail and feeble is the tenure of human happiness—human character—and human life.

I have now done, gentlemen of the jury, and the future destinies of the prisoner are committed to *your* charge. For herself, conscious as she is, of her own innocence, and advanced as she is in life, she feels comparatively but little. But you will pardon a sister's—and a daughter's—and, above all, a mother's emotions, while confronting that awful tribunal, upon whose stern sentence must depend not only her own prospects, so far as they remain to her—not only her own existence—but, as I have said, the hopes and very existence of those to her more precious far than life. To your hands, however, we

confidently resign her. You are the ministers of the
law—the standard-bearers of justice—and she feels assured you will sustain the balance with a firm and
unwavering hand—let which scale may preponderate.

My duty is at last discharged—feebly and imperfectly,
I acknowledge; but as fully as my health and limited
abilities will allow. It remains for you to fulfil *yours.*
In doing so, let not, I again beseech you, the client suffer
for the faults and deficiencies of her counsel; but generously incline your ear to the pleadings of your hearts,
and ever bear in dear and sacred remembrance that
"mercy is twice blessed—it blesses them that give, and
them that take."

DR. FROST'S CASE.

The People of the State of New York v. Richard K. Frost.

In the Court of Sessions for the City and County of New York, held December 13th, 1837.

CHARGE—MANSLAUGHTER.

Present, Recorder Riker, and Aldermen Acker and Taylor.

Counsel for the Prosecution.
Mr. Phenix, District Attorney, and Mr. Griffin.

For the Accused.
John A. Merrill, Esq., of New York; David Paul Brown, of Philadelphia.

INTRODUCTION.

This case, which occupied ten days in the trial, excited great interest,—not so much from its intrinsic importance, as through the intense feeling and bitter animosities which it engendered between rival schools of medicine, viz.: between the Medical Faculty and the Thomsonians.

Each system had its advocates and organs, and the battle between them raged even more fiercely in the journals of the day—both medical and miscellaneous— than in the court room.

The facts were simply these: Tiberius G. French—a young man of promise—being slightly indisposed placed himself under the care of Dr. Frost, who was at the head of the Thomson Infirmary in New York City.   After being subjected to the Thomsonian treatment for five days, a " regular" physician was called in, at the suggestion of a brother of the deceased; but despite every effort, the young man died on the night of the fifth day after his entrance into the infirmary.

It was alleged by the prosecution that the accused had no medical education, and was ignorant of the nature and operation of remedial agents,—that he had administered deleterious herbs, and poisonous decoctions made of lobelia, &c.

The defence, on the other hand, advocated the treatment according to Thomsonism; denied the use of deleterious drugs; and very strongly intimated that the introduction of the " regular" physician (Dr. Cheeseman) was the immediate cause of the death.

The trial resulted in a verdict of " Guilty of manslaughter in the fourth degree."

Motions in arrest of judgment, and for a new trial, were made, and the accused was allowed to go at liberty until these rules were disposed of.

SPEECH IN

DOCTOR FROST'S CASE.

WITH DEFERENCE TO THE COURT:

After a long and perilous voyage, gentlemen of the jury, we have at length steered our little barque into a safe harbor, where we may venture to cast anchor—where, with your favor, we may ride securely—laugh at the billows and defy the storm. If, may it please your honors, my learned colleague has felt himself called upon to express his gratitude to the court, for favors conferred upon *him ;* what must be *my* obligations, for the kindness, the courtesy, the unmerited distinctions, bestowed so freely, upon a comparative stranger, in *my* person? My acknowledgment shall consist, not in vain thanks, but in acceptance bounteous—in other words, I shall endeavor to discharge the debt by facilitating the labors of the court, and requiting benefits by desert.

In approaching the consideration of this cause, I must be allowed to congratulate my brethren of the bar, here and elsewhere, upon the certainty that their professional engagements and emoluments shall never cease, so long as medical science and its professors shall continue to flourish —may they, therefore (I say it with all my heart), be immortal. From the time of Hippocrates down to this moment, the feuds and bickerings, the private quarrels, and open hostilities among the medical family, have been such as to form a proverb—a by-word and reproach. If such be their intestine dissensions and divisions ; you may readily imagine how deadly and destructive must the conflict be, when the whole of this irritable race, in their aggregate of fury, come into direct collision with an *opposing* system. How terrible the concussion! how appalling the result!

Some opinion may be formed of the relentless nature of this strife, from the daily display of vindictiveness to which you have been the unwilling witnesses. "The trial by wager of battle," now grown obsolete even in England, where it so long prevailed, however brutal in its character, was less offensive to the eye of justice, than the course here adopted by these "potent, grave and reverend seignors." Their business, rightly understood, is to cure, and not to kill; but they have inverted, by practice, the philosophy of their science, and here magnanimously unite (almost the only union they have ever been guilty of) for the philanthropic and generous purpose of offering up an unoffending victim upon the altar of vengeance. We are informed upon classic authority, which the ripe and ready memory of the court will at once recognize—I think the account is contained in Herodotus, though it has also found its way into other authors—that a wonderful artist, of Greece, constructed a brazen bull, of such curious and exquisite workmanship as to astonish every beholder. This bull he presented to Phalaris, his sovereign, assuring him at the same time, that if heated, and a human being placed within it, the dying groans of the victim would resemble the roaring of a bull, and thus render the illusion complete. "It is well," said the monarch, even more shocked at his cruelty than delighted with his skill, "it is well—the bull shall be heated, and you yourself shall be placed inside of it, for it is most fit that the artificers of death should die." Shall I point the story—can you not make the application? This prosecution is the brazen bull—the medical faculty are the inventors—you, gentlemen of the jury, are the sovereign—the defendant is the intended victim, and I boldly ask you to

imitate the example of royal justice to which I have referred—to protect the innocent, and doom the artificers
of death—*to death*.

Why should they thus attempt hunting down a fellow
citizen struggling in self defence, in a tribunal of justice?
Why should the defendant's rights be entirely disregarded, and the adherents of these opposing systems be
permitted to " hack each others' daggers in his breast?"
Does such a course, to say nothing of justice or charity,
redound to the credit of the medical faculty? Does it
improve our estimation of their learning or their talents?
" Dwells there such rage in heavenly minds?" Persecution
ever defeats its object—the bruised and broken flower is
more redolent than when flourishing on its parent stem;
and the virtues of the Aloe tree are rendered more apparent by the perfume which it imparts even to the axe that
fells it. The glorious temple of Christianity is founded in
persecution; and its fabric is cemented and sustained by
the blood of martyrs, and of the Prince of Martyrs, the
Redeemer of the world. Still how natural does it seem
to oppress the humble, to trample upon the fallen—how
tempting to the foot of arrogance and ambition is everything that may form a ladder to their lofty hopes.

The struggle in which the medical faculty is here engaged is not regulated by sympathies, or charity, or
humanity—it is a struggle for self—they are determined
to bear no rival near their throne—whole hecatombs shall
perish that they may prosper; and when they have once
succeeded in obtaining a sort of sovereign sway in the
land, Wo unto all who shall oppose resistance to their
overweening strength.

Having thus adverted to what must have forced itself
upon the attention of the most casual observer; and
which, in the temple of justice, should not be allowed to
pass without remark and unqualified reprobation; we
come now to the consideration of these points in this
cause, which, although much more pertinent to the issue,

will, I fear, exert a less vital influence, upon its decision, than those subjects which I have thus briefly adverted to, and unhesitatingly condemned. Let it be established— I, say it once for all—that a body of physicians are the only individuals authorized to prescribe—to cure or to kill —and you create a despotism, the pernicious results of which exceed all imagination. They shall make their own terms with you—the rich and the poor shall be alike subjects to their sway; and the instance which the testimony has exhibited of a physician who exacted from a patient racked with disease and pain—and balancing as it were upon the pivot of destiny—a fee of five dollars as an inducement to a visit, will not be a solitary or a startling instance, but be rendered familiar from its frequency, and almost laudable from its moderation.

Without further prelude, let us inquire what is the indictment. It contains three counts. The first, charging the defendant with having produced the death of the deceased, wilfully, maliciously and feloniously, by administering a certain drug or herb, called lobelia; and by also administering cayenne pepper, and applying the steam bath.

The second count, charges the defendant with producing death by the medicines.

The third count, charges him with causing death by the bath, and some of the medicines comprised in the prior counts.

The law of New York, under which this indictment is framed, provides for four degrees of manslaughter; and to which particular degree this prosecution is directed, it is our business to ascertain, and no information has been given.

Such, then, is the indictment—the chart by which we have steered. It charges the defendant, you perceive, with felonious homicide; and it is founded upon statutory provisions, upon the subject of manslaughter, contained in the revised code of the laws of New York. For what earthly purpose those provisions were framed, I confess my inability to perceive: at common law, all the offences embraced by them are clearly prohibited and punished; and that which was plain before, is rendered somewhat doubtful and mysterious, by this legislative effort to improve it. Philosophy, however, teaches us not to increase evils by unavailing regret, but rather to overcome by boldly confronting them: I, therefore, address myself to my task.

The district attorney—unwilling to rely upon any one degree of manslaughter—has converted this act, embracing four degrees, into a sort of sweep-net; in some one of the meshes of which he expects to ensnare, or entangle, and secure the defendant. I have called upon him, as I had the right to do, to state his specific charge, in order that time might not be unprofitably employed in attacking where there is no resistance, or resisting where there is no attack. This he has declined, as he had no right to do, and thereby subjected me to the necessity of travelling through the four orders of manslaughter, for the purpose of showing the defendant's entire innocence of all; or rather, to speak more technically and critically, for the purpose of showing that he has not been proved guilty of any. (Mr. Phenix here rose, and said that he should rely upon the nineteenth section of the law, and maintain that the defendant had been guilty of manslaughter in the fourth degree.)

The fourth degree of manslaughter is embraced in the general clause; it is all that the defendant can be guilty of, and I deny that he is guilty of that. This, therefore, forms the only legitimate issue between the commonwealth and myself.

We set out on the part of the defendant by averring that no act of mankind can be criminally punishable, without being accompanied, either actively or constructively, by a corrupt motive. In other words, that the heart is alone the abode of crime; that the act and the motive must cohere; and that in no case is the *act alone* punishable: and there is but one class of cases in which the motive or agreement to do an unlawful act, or to do a lawful act in an unlawful manner, is subject to the criminal penalties of the law, and that is the class to which *conspiracies* belong. The law there interposes, as it were, by anticipation, to forestall the offender ere yet he come to fall. To crop crime in its germ or in its very bud, and thereby to prevent its growing into a luxuriant and pernicious harvest, and finally spreading ruin and disaster around. This is the doctrine in regard to illegal combinations—but as respects individuals, the maxim is " Non est crimen voluntas sine perpetratione."

In saying that there must be an actual or constructive corruption of design, we may be inferred to mean, that where there is a culpable negligence, or a gross want of skill, in a case like the present, the law may imply an evil design, and thereby render it criminal. If, therefore, in the present case it should appear that the ingredients as charged in the indictments were *not* administered; or if administered that they did *not* produce death; or if they did produce death, that there was no criminal neglect or culpable ignorance: the prosecution rests without its pillow, and the defendant must be *acquitted.*

This is certainly presenting the question in the most favorable shape for the commonwealth.

The defendant hereby assumes—upon the evidence— to negative, or disprove the charge: whereas he has the right to call upon the district attorney to establish— clearly and beyond the reach of a reasonable doubt—the allegation of guilt; and without this the case can neither be embraced by the statute, nor the common law.

In 1 Hale's Pleas of the Crown, 429, this doctrine will be found—no higher authority can be required—" If a physician give a poison without intent of doing any bodily hurt, but with intent to cure or prevent disease, and contrary to the expectation of the physician, it kills

him, this is no homicide—and the like of a surgeon—and
I hold their opinions to be erroneous that think, if he be
no licensed surgeon or physician that occasions this mischance—then it is felony; for physic and salves were before licensed physicians and surgeons, and therefore, if
they be not licensed according to the statute, they are
subject to the penalties of the statute, but God forbid,
that any mischance of that kind should make any person
not licensed, guilty of murder or manslaughter."—Sir
Wm. Blackstone concurs in the doctrine—and in But-
chell's Case, 2 C. & P. 632, it was ruled, that it made no
difference whether the party was a regular or irregular
physician; Baron Hallock adding, that in remote parts
of the country many persons could be left to die if irregular surgeons were not allowed to practice—and in Long's
Case, 4 C. & P. 398, Parke, J., observed, " that whether
the party was licensed or unlicensed, is of no consequence,
except in regard to his liability to pecuniary penalties for
acting contrary to acts of Parliament."

It is not my intention here to discuss the merits of the
indictment—they are subjects of law, and belong to the
court. For although it is perfectly true as the court has
taken occasion to tell you, that you are the judges both
of law and fact; it never yet has been necessary for me,
in the course of my humble practice, to enjoin upon the
jury the propriety of disregarding the opinion of an enlightened judicial tribunal—and I trust it never will be.
I have no greater fears of the court than I have of the
jury, upon this or any other subject when rightly understood; and I trust therefore you will listen with all
proper attention to the learning and wisdom which may
fall from the bench—yielding to it not a servile, but a
rational and conscientious obedience; not surrendering
the exercise of your own mental faculties, but allowing
them to be enlightened, invigorated and enlarged by the
genial influence of superior science and experience.

The court and the jury appear to the greatest advantage, and best discharge their respective duty, while mutually borrowing and imparting aid to each other—and it is thus, and thus only, that the advantages of criminal jurisprudence can be fully enjoyed or preserved.

Let us concede for the sake of the argument, that the ingredients as specified in the indictment were administered by the defendant to the deceased in the manner and form as charged. The proof scarcely warrants the concession; but I wish to avoid all higgling and chaffering about trifles, and to come at once to the attractive metal of this case. The only two inquiries then will be—

First. Did the medicines thus administered produce death?

We have no wish to charge others with that offence, of which we deny our guilt. But if regular physicians are not to be considered the only class privileged to kill, it really would appear that Dr. Cheeseman—one of the witnesses, most earnest and eager in this prosecution—can hardly escape censure. I know that when the patient dies, the doctor is generally in the wrong; as when a cause is lost, its loss is often attributed to the lawyer; but making all allowance for this want of generosity or charity on the part of those who are writhing under the affliction of a painful bereavement or remediless injury, there is still much to condemn, even with an impartial observer, in the deportment of Dr. Cheeseman, as unquestionably established by the evidence. He is certainly entitled to no favorable consideration from *us ;* as his mind seems to be imbued and embittered with the most extraordinary prejudice from the first to the last against the individual now upon his trial—a man who had never done him any wrong; who cheerfully relinquished the patient into his hands and who prudently communicated or caused to be communicated to him the course of treatment previously resorted to. In requital for all which, without any personal knowledge of the defendant, the doctor expresses the opinion that he has fallen into dangerous hands; and leaves the patient to die while he runs after a consulting physician to serve him (Dr. Cheeseman) in the amiable capacity of a witness, rather than an adviser. What cause had he for suspicion—unconscious of wrong, what should alarm him—

> Why should the innocent
> Tremble and quake with fear,—the guilty fear,
> For cowardice and guilt appall each other,—
> But virtue ever wears a lion's heart
> Beneath the downy plumage of the dove.

Dr. Cheeseman is, I understand, a physician of some eminence—he is a man of unquestionable respectability—but the current of prejudice has with him overcome all the kindlier feelings of his nature; and induced him in this case, in which a young man is engaged in a holy struggle, not for life, it is true, but for liberty and reputation—without which life is nothing—to volunteer as un‑generous and pernicious a sentiment, as ever tainted the atmosphere of justice from the lips of a witness. I regret to speak harshly of this gentleman. I regret more that he should deserve it; but I trust I shall ever advance fearlessly against any opponent, where duty points and leads the way. It has fallen to my lot, in the course of my professional career, to examine many distinguished physicians, and to be present at the examination of more; and, although there may have been some exceptions, I am proud and happy to say, that their testimony has generally been characterized by a tenderness and humanity towards the accused, which would naturally be inspired by a science, which necessarily and daily, enlists all the sympathies and charities of the human heart.

Dr. Cheeseman, called in, as he says, while the patient was in "*articulo mortis*,"—never having seen him before,—without making inquiries into his complaint or his treatment, ventures unhesitatingly to say, that the disease of which he died was *not* typhus fever, although he cannot tell what it *was*; and pretty plainly implies, that the medicines administered by the defendant caused the death of the patient. How ungenerous! how unjust! The patient dies under the assiduous efforts of the defendant to restore him; gentlemen adopting an opposite system are employed; they reject everything that is incompatible with what is called regular practice; and the enemy, becoming the judge, Dr. Frost is to be condemned. Why, upon this principle, the good Samaritan himself might have been indicted, had the wounded traveller died upon his hands. How would Dr. Cheeseman, or any other of this learned faculty, be content to abide by such a test. In the most successful practice *some* will be lost. The doctor's "prescription" cannot withstand the *fiat* of fate. The disease may be mistaken; the remedies of course misapplied; the calculations of the physician defeated by latent and adverse causes; the constitution misunderstood—a thousand accidents or contingencies may operate to resist the most consummate skill. What then!—is a medical gentleman, entertaining opposite, or different views of practice, to pronounce condemnation upon the course thus adopted. Some physicians resort to bleeding in almost *all* cases—others, in scarcely any: some administer calomel freely—others, not at all: some refuse cold drinks to a patient under the parching influence of a fever—others, stuff, and surround him with ice: some in cases of cholera, particularly, introduce foreign substances into the veins—others, hold it to be certain death: some adopt cathartics — others emetics. Each, in short, has his favorite mode of expelling disease, and each, to a certain extent, at least, condemns the other. Is it then fair, is it honorable, that the temple of justice should be converted into a bloody arena; and that the dignified professors of an illustrious science should here publicly engage, in *ostensible* support of their several theories, but *actually* to the destruction of them *all?*

But to return to the inquiry. Did the intended remedy produce or cause death ?

Before we examine the treatment, let us turn our attention to the state and circumstances of the deceased for a few days prior to his entering the infirmary of the defendant. On the evening of Monday, preceding the Thursday on which he applied to Dr. Frost—for it was his own voluntary application—Tiberius' G. French was engaged at a convivial party—where he indiscreetly, I do not say improperly, indulged himself. Next morning while at breakfast with Mr. Whiting, he complained of serious indisposition and spoke of his imprudence the night before. His disease still continued, and on Thursday morning had very considerably increased. The cause of its exacerbation, as was stated by himself to Mr. Whiting, was his having been employed on Wednesday night till midnight in drawing a will for a dying man, in a cold chamber; which had affected him so much that—in his own words—"he was only able to write a few lines at a time." On Thursday afternoon he resolved to go to the infirmary—the disease no doubt having taken a deep root in his system:—for when he left Mr. Whiting's he was almost unable to walk, and appeared, as the witness said, to "drag himself along." He seemed to have inherited a preference for the Thomsonian system, as his mother it appears in her lifetime entertained very favorable impressions of it. He consulted his brother —left his brother's office—and on the evening of Thursday we find him at the infirmary. In what condition is he there? In the presence of the sister of the defendant, he draws nearer and nearer to a large coal fire; and finally to express the severity of the chill under which he labors, he tells her, that it appeared as though if he were to lay himself upon the coals they would scarcely heat him. This is the individual who was said to be the picture of health. At that time, at least, it was a *melancholy* picture. The icy fingers of disease, if not of death, were already grappling with his vital energies.

I have said that it was his own voluntary choice to place himself at this infirmary—that no inducements were held out and no persuasion resorted to: and I further maintain it was a most judicious choice. He left his boarding house, where he could have had but scanty attendance; with an occasional visit from a physician of five or ten minutes in a day; with no nursing, or perhaps what is worse, bad nursing; and he places himself in an establishment where he is the very focus of attention, and has nurses around him of whom an emperor might be proud:—the mother of Mr. Frost, Mrs. Rae, Mr. Roleston, and last and most important, Miss Frost herself.

> " Oh ! Woman,—in our hours of ease,
>   Uncertain, coy, and hard to please,
>   And variable as the shade
>   By the light quivering aspen made ;
>   When pain and anguish wring the brow,
>   A ministering angel thou.''

This is the lady to whom Ulysses French expressed such unbounded gratitude, and whom he has attempted so abundantly to requite by the conviction of her brother. This is what I suppose they call paying a debt in kind— she watches *night* after *night* in sleepless anxiety on the pillow of anguish and subsequent death—and to repay these attentions, Ulysses D. French watches *day* after *day*, with equal vigilance, to convict the defendant of gross ignorance or culpable neglect.

I entertain the kindest feelings towards the witness, Mr. French; his deportment towards his brother was every thing it should have been. I speak its true character when I say it was fraternal; it is at the same time a consolation and an honor to him, and he may rejoice in its remembrance, when the vanities of this world shall have passed away. Still, it is a subject of unfeigned regret—though certainly not without its excuse—that he should so far have permitted the storm of feeling, or of passion, or of prejudice, to sway or swerve his mind from its true moorings, as to compel him, apparently at least, to unite with this prosecution, and to join in that hue and cry which has for its object the destruction of the defendant.

I have shown you the condition in which the deceased came into the infirmary; and suggested the reasons by which he was probably influenced. It has been said from the symptoms described, that Doctor Frost was doubtful whether he labored under an idiopathic, or symptomatic fever; in simple words, whether the fever was of that character which precedes small pox, or was typhus fever; he, however, settled down upon the opinion that it was typhus, that "*ungenteel* disease," which, as Doctor Manly says, never assails the aristocracy—but riots alone among poverty and rags. The learned professor, therefore, I suppose, infers, that as Mr. French was a *gentleman*, Dr. F. must have been mistaken. It is true Dr. M. never saw the patient in his life, and therefore, merely relies upon a sort of sweeping theory; and even in that theory, I will show you, runs a-foul of some of his professional brethren. Dr. Smith, of Rochester,—who appears not to know that there is more than one class of typhus fever according to modern science, and who would seem to consider it rather a *genteel and gentle* disease—says that in its ordinary course, it would not kill under one month, and in many cases not under three months.—And when I asked him to explain how it happened that in the year 1812, the typhus fever devastated the United States from Maine to Georgia, and almost invariably terminated life in less than a week; he chivalrously got rid of the difficulty by declaring the disease then so called, was not typhus fever; thereby routing the whole phalanx of regular physicians.

Dr. Manly does not exactly concur in this—particularly in regard to the grades or classes of typhus. He acknowledges the typhus mitior, and the typhus gravior—under which head he ranks what he calls the congestive typhus; and the latter or severer disease, according to his experience, might kill a man in from three days to a week. The disease of which Tiberius G. French died, was exactly what Dr. Manly calls congestive typus—Dr. Rogers, who conducted the post mortem examination, establishes this almost beyond question. When, after four days, he raised the body—not as that of Lazarus was raised, to reanimate it—but to furnish evidence *against* the living, he says: "I found that the internal parts exhibited great vascularity—the right lung was ruptured—a quantity of serous fluid was effused through that lung, and the appearance of the external coats of the stomach was more vascular than ordinary," &c., &c.—all evidence of congestion. The ingenious mode of reasoning, by which the medical faculty support this charge is, first, to deny that it is typhus fever at all, without being able to say what *was* the technical character of the fever—having never, let it be remembered, seen the patient until the disease and the victim were both spent,—and, in the second place, they attempt showing that typhus fever would require from one to three months to destroy life. What is the corollary of such reasoning? certainly not that the patient necessarily died of the treatment; but that the disease, whether typhus or not, was of a *graver* order than the common typhus; and therefore probably embraced by the class of cases referred to by the venerable Dr. Gilbert Smith and Dr. Manly—as speedily terminating life.

If these views be sound, everything is left in doubt as to the cause of death. There is not a physician out of the many examined already—always excepting the perspicacious Dr. Cheeseman—who pretends to the ability to determine upon the specific character of the disease, from only seeing a patient in the last hour of his life—much less, four days after death. Dr. Joseph Smith, the consulting physician (who, as a witness, was a model of manliness and propriety), repudiates and rejects the idea altogether, except in certain cases where the fever is merely symptomatic; as in cases of small pox, measles, &c.; and where the exact character of the disease is rendered manifest by cutaneous eruptions, and by other unequivocal signs.

To strengthen the suggestion, that not the disease but the treatment produced the death, two other witnesses were called—Dr. Rogers, a distinguished surgeon, and Mr. Chilton, a chemist—who is also dignified by the title of Doctor. Indeed, it is worthy of remark, in passing, that while these learned pundits are so frugal in dispensing medical honors—even in name—to the Thomsonians; there is scarcely a private in their battalion that you would not take for a " field-marshal " at least.—Titles are squandered with the most lavish and unsparing hand. Every dentist among them—every chemist—every bleeder —is a doctor; and those only who are among the *obscure* and the *missing*, are their patients. For *those*, gentlemen of the jury, we have looked, and looked in vain. How, and why is this? On one side we have given you the ocular proof of the beneficial results attendant upon our practice. We have examined *scores* of *living* witnesses, all of whom have been reclaimed from the jaws of the tomb—some, after an express abandonment by the regular physician—by the botanical system. We have given them *practice*, they have answered by *theory*. We have produced *our patients*—where are *theirs?* Am I not authorized to conclude that *they* are beyond the reach of a subpœna; and, that before they can be produced, the doctors must condescend to dig—aye, to DIG for them?

Well, still let us hear the doctors: Dr. Rogers, as I have said, conducted the post mortem examination. He removed the stomach and part of the intestines, with the

liquid they contained; which he subsequently confided to
the analysis of Dr. Chilton. This learned and scientific
gentleman, so far as it appears in testimony, never examined the brain, or the heart; those two great seats and
citadels of life. His search is directed only to lobelia;
and accordingly the stomach is his spoil. Well, sir, what
did it contain? The answer is, "I handed it over to
Dr. Chilton, and he detected lobelia"—Heaven save the
mark!—But let us turn to Dr. Chilton, and look to *his*
account:—What did you do, sir? "I applied tests to
the contents of the stomach, after having first evaporated
the liquid to dryness." Well, sir, what did you find?
"I found about seventy-five grains of vegetable matter;
and, I think, but am not prepared to swear, there was
lobelia among it." What test did you apply? "I *tasted*
it, and I thought it tasted like tobacco."—Mirabile dictu!
—Such is the evidence upon which this prosecution is to
be sustained.

It is perfectly well settled, that of all earthly tests the
vegetable tests are the most imperfect; and that of all
vegetable tests, that through taste is the most illusory and
fallacious. Supposing the chemist to speak sooth in this,
—why, the extract from a quid of tobacco; or the mere
decoction of a pinch of snuff; or the saliva from a segar,
would settle the fate of a physician, if found in the stomach of his patient.

But we are told by these learned Thebans—and that
too with a sneer—that we pursue a system laid down by
one Sam Thomson, who sprung from an obscure corner
of the State of Massachusetts, and whose father was a
farmer. Why, gentlemen, who was it that shed the
brightest lustre upon the vast science of astronomy?—
one Dave Rittenhouse, a native of Pennsylvania, who
followed the plough. Who was it that tore the light-
ning from heaven, and the sceptre from tyrants?—one
Ben Franklin, a printer's boy, who protected himself
against the inclemency of the winter by exercise alone,

and lived upon a single roll of bread a day. Who was it—when the veteran armies of Great Britain faltered and fled, in the Indian war—safely conducted the retreat, and secured the remnant of the army, though he had "never set a squadron in the field, nor the division of a battle knew, more than a spinster?"—one George Washington, a Virginia planter. Who was it that shed the brightest halo around the brightest reign that the world ever knew—the reign of Elizabeth—the age of the Raleighs—the Burleighs—the Bacons and the Sydneys?—why it was one Ben Jonson, a quondam apprentice to a bricklayer; and one Will Shakspeare, a peasant boy, and shrewdly suspected of poaching upon his neighbor's deer. Or passing from astronomy, philosophy and poetry, to law: Who was it that rose from low beginnings to be Lord Chief Justice of England?—one Charley Abbot, whose father was a barber. Who was it that rose to be Lord High Chancellor of England?—one Jack Copley, whose father was an American painter. Who was it that became the brightest star in the judicial constellation of Great Britain?—one Phil Yorke, whose father no man knew. Or passing to a still further illustration—Who was it that subjugated three-fourths of Europe, and confident against the world in arms, made the autocrat of all the Russias tremble upon his throne?—one Napoleon, who rose from the station of a corporal to such consummate power—to such dazzling heights—as to enable him to look down upon emperors, kings, princes, and the potentates of the earth—while he unmade them. Let us hear, therefore, no more of one *Sam Thomson*—for although I do not mean to say that there never was a great man among the "wealthy, curled darlings of the nation," yet I do mean to say—and all history sustains the assertion—that luxury and affluence are calculated to enfeeble the mind; and that those therefore who are great in despite of them, would probably be much greater if removed from

their influence. It is a well known fact among gentlemen of the turf, that blooded horses, who for years have
been permitted to browse and career on broken, irregular
and mountainous pastures, have acquired a much greater
muscular strength, and in sportsmen's phrase, better
bottom, than those who are fed upon a level surface: the
application of this, although a physical illustration, is not
difficult. Men whose lives have been an uninterrupted
course of difficulty—a perfect up-hill work, acquire in
time a self-dependence, a self-sufficiency, and a promptitude in every emergency, which those who have been
accustomed to stand for fame on their forefather's feet,
or to lean for all pleasure upon another's breast, never
have known and never can know.

I throw out of consideration, therefore, the name and
the birth-place of the founder of this system, and proceed
to inquire into his works. By his fruits you shall know
him—"Do men gather grapes from thorns, or figs from
thistles?" His notion is, that all disease is the result of
a want of vital power, producing or allowing obstructions
in the system, which nature cannot, from her weakness,
without assistance, remove. He further contends that *fever*
is not disease, but the effort—or to speak more accurately—the evidence of the effort of nature to expel disease; and he strengthens this position by alleging that
chills are the enemies of man resulting in death, unless
superseded or *overcome;* and that they invariably precede
a fever, which fever at the same time manifests the severity of the *attack,* and the power and extent of natural
resistance; that by the relief or diminution of obstructions you aid the fever and assist *nature,* and in the same
proportion diminish the power of the *disease:* until finally
the obstruction being entirely removed by the reproduction of vital power, and the restoration of the equilibrium
of the system, the body is restored to a sound and pristine state.

Now you may call this Thomsonism, or what you

please, it smacks much of philosophy; and it has been followed by practical results of the most beneficial nature to which it may triumphantly appeal. The only objection to it seems to be that it is *new*.

Why this extraordinary objection to everything like innovation; as if nothing could prove good unless it is encrusted or sanctioned by time? The celebrated Dr. Harvey, one of the most distinguished of the medical school, uses language upon this subject which is particularly applicable. Thus he speaks: "By what unaccountable perversity in our frame does it appear, that we set ourselves so much against anything that is new? Can any one behold without scorn, such drones of physicians, who, after the space of so many hundred years' experience and practice of their predecessors, have not detected one single medicine that has the least force directly to prevent, to oppose, or to expel a continued fever? Should any by a more sedulous observation, pretend to make the least step towards the discovery of such remedies, their hatred and envy would swell against him as a legion of devils against virtue. The whole society will dart their malice at him, and torture him with all the calumnies imaginable, without sticking at anything that would destroy him root and branch; for he who professes to be a reformer of the art of physic, must resolve to run the hazard of the martyrdom of his reputation, life and estate."

It is a mistake, sir, to suppose—as the court seem to suppose, from their course of inquiries—that according to this system, there is but *one* remedy for *all* diseases.

There is one remedy for the root or trunk of all diseases; and as when the axe is applied to the body of the tree, the branches share in the fate of the parent stock, and are felled with it: so when the obstruction from which diseases in their various phases and branches spring is eradicated from the system, nature again assumes her empire, and peace and harmony and salubrity prevail where rebellion and discord and disease had previously existed. But there are seventy different kinds of medicine embraced by the Thomsonian *materia medica*—possessed of emetic, diaphoretic, stimulating, sedative and other properties—all of which may be applied in judicious adaptation either severally or in compounds, according to the nature of the disease or the constitution or necessities of the patient.

This is a plain, rational, common sense theory; and with the practical illustrations of its utility which we have supplied from thousands of living witnesses, it is neither to be contemned or rejected. The Thomsonian system is not to be put down by the *sneering* system—and especially by those who are *paid* for sneering. It was never the design of the great Creator of Earth and Heaven—if such a worm as I am may be allowed to imagine what were the inscrutable designs of the *Omniscient*—that recourse should be had to the vast and innumerable compounds of mineral, vegetable and poisonous substances, embraced by the materia medica of the regular faculty, in order to effectuate the cure of his creatures.

Indians live to a great age, even though subjected, as they are, to the greatest exposure. Their only medicines are herbs. Sickness with them is less fatal than with us; and this would appear to lead to the conclusion that more patients die of the *doctor* than the *disease*. But if this were not true, if death were more rife among them, they at least are not subjected to a living and prolonged death; as is the result of calomel, arsenic, antimony, and other mineral poisons.

But, say our adversaries, if the system of Thomson be good, yet "lobelia" is possessed of *poisonous* properties; and therefore may be supposed in this instance to have caused death. This is strange and inconsistent doctrine, coming from that quarter. But it is as unsound and untrue, as strange and inconsistent; there is not a man of them that has ever known it to produce death; and I challenge the district attorney, and his colleague to boot, to turn to any portion of the testimony by which it so appears. Doctor Smith, of Rochester, is the only one of all the witnesses who approaches anything like such a result, and he states that he knew it to have killed a lady who at first had a slight fever, and who told him she took lobelia from a bottle, which he, the doctor, saw on the table.

In the first place this is no testimony at all, as the court intimated, being mere hearsay at the best. In the second place, it was the communication of a deranged woman, though in a supposed lucid interval; and in the third place, the doctor saw the patient in the close of her life; appears to know very little of her disease; and, of consequence, relies more upon fancy than upon facts for his conclusions—of all medical or judicial tests the most feeble and unsatisfactory.

Now, having shown the state of the patient and the probable nature of the disease: what were the prescriptions and the course of treatment adopted by the defendant, as in distinct proof upon this occasion? For the regular consecutive course let us refer to that testimony to which we must all delight to turn—the testimony of Elizabeth Frost. [A portion of the testimony of Miss Frost, describing symptoms and applications was here read.]

Thus it appears, that repeated doses of "composition tea," as it is called, made up of harmless ingredients, were administered to him on the evening of the day upon which he entered the establishment, and that he was then put to bed. The next day he took more tea, and took a vapor bath, which was continued for about ten minutes, tea being administered during its continuance; then he was carefully covered with blankets—conveyed to the bed, and shortly after took a dose of lobelia, and in fifteen or twenty minutes after that, another dose. Occasionally he seemed relieved, and then again relapsed. On Monday "a powerful dose," as it has been called, of lobelia was given; this for a time relieved him. On the evening after the arrival of Dr. Davids and Ulysses French, he got worse; and it would seem from that time until Tuesday evening, when he died, the disease continued to increase. On the afternoon of the last day, the symptoms seemed, however, more favorable, and a gentle perspiration suffused the whole frame. There seemed to be a point where nature made one final effort to throw off disease with some signs of success—when, unluckily, owing to the fears of the brother, Dr. Cheeseman was called in. If the course pursued by Dr. Cheeseman has been correctly stated by the witnesses; and if my views of medical treatment be correct; there was much in it to condemn. I will consider its excuse presently. The clothes were thrown off; the last applications removed; the fire extinguished; the windows thrown open; the doors fanned; and an instantaneous and violent change thus produced in the temperature—the body exposed to the influence of the air—the night damp and bleak.

We do not mean to say that this course was adopted by Dr. Cheeseman from any malevolent or uncharitable purpose. Heaven forbid! But I will ask whether the sudden check of perspiration, attendant upon such treatment, and operating upon a weak frame already having suffered from two relapses, must not necessarily have been followed by pernicious effects. I have always been so taught, and appeal to the medical faculty, for the correctness of the instruction. Dr. Manly, however, informs us, that although ordinarily the check of perspiration may be dangerous, yet it is not so much so, if at all so, while the patient is under the influence of medicine; inasmuch—as I understood the learned doctor—as the medicine forms a counteracting power, which resists external attacks upon the system. There is some philosophy in this—but might not even the conflict be-

tween the medicine and the atmosphere prove fatal to
the patient, where life is reduced to so low an ebb, as in
the case of Tiberius G. French?—in such a condition—

> "That death and nature did contend about him,
> Whether he lived or died."

They say, however, that the facts were not so—that
Dr. Cheeseman did not expose the body, and subject
it to the influence of a chilly atmosphere. It is true
there is some slight variance in the testimony; but there
is substantial consistency, with circumstantial variety,
which ever characterize the highest order of evidence.
Dr. Metcalf, Miss Rae and Mrs. Frost, although they
refer in their testimony to different parts in this last
sad scene (each one having witnessed but a portion of
it), in the effect of their *combined* testimony leave no
question upon this subject. Pardon me while I show
you how entirely they agree. Dr. Metcalf says, that
when Dr. Cheeseman came in first, he threw off the
coverlet, opened the doors, and went away after examining the patient's tongue; that when Dr. Cheeseman
returned with Dr. Sweet, he threw off all the bed covering, raised the sheet to examine the stomach of the
patient, and permitted him so to remain for an improper
length of time—the windows were opened front and
back, as were the room doors and hall doors. Before
Dr. Cheeseman came in, the witness examined the patient
and found him in a gentle perspiration—equally diffused
all over—and thinks, to check a perspiration in this way
must prove fatal.

Miss Rae states, that when the bell rang she let in Dr.
Cheeseman and Mr. French—she opened the chamber door
half way—Dr. Cheeseman opened it all the way—went
to bedside, said he was afraid the patient was too warm
—threw off the top comforter. Dr. Cheeseman then
went for Dr. Smith, and in about fifteen minutes they
came in. Dr. Cheeseman then took all the clothes off

of patient down to the feet—the sheet was then raised and the chest of patient was exposed. Dr. Cheeseman then ordered witness to put out the fire; he then ordered the windows to be let down, which was accordingly done. Dr. Sweet, and Dr. Cheeseman then retired, and subsequently Dr. C. came in and ordered the warm applications to be removed from the feet—the back and front windows were open. The witness then withdrew, and upon coming in again found the patient in a chill, and in a few minutes after he was seized with convulsions of which he died.

Mrs. Phebe Frost, states, that she was present on the evening French died—found him, upon examination, in a moderate perspiration—that after Dr. Cheeseman came in the room was cool—the doors were opened: they appeared to be about to strip the patient and the witness turned her back. It was a damp, foggy evening—the room was made too cool for a person in *health*—shortly after patient went into spasms.

Some attempt, it is true, has been made to contradict these witnesses, but unavailingly. It will be found that they are entirely corroborated by those who profess to oppose them.

One thing is certain from the testimony—and it accords with my theory, and with the Thomsonian system—that a chill immediately followed this exposure, and *that* chill terminated in *death*. This, at least, is a fact; and facts are said to be stubborn things. You have here presented to you, cause and effect—a cause that ceases to be doubtful from the nature of the effect, and the rapidity with which it followed. The abstract hypotheses, therefore, of distinguished members of the faculty, though respectable for their authority, lose all their charm, when tested by actual observation and experience—yet who shall say, notwithstanding these facts, that Dr. Cheeseman killed the patient.

We say that he acted up to the best of his skill and ability. If mistaken, the motive should justify the means. It would indeed have been a proud triumph of science, had the learned physician redeemed the deceased from the cold embrace of death.—But is he to be censured or *indicted* for his failure—certainly not. "In great attempts 'tis glorious e'en to fail." And what attempt is greater than that which is directed to the preservation of human life.

But do you not perceive, gentlemen of the jury, that all that is thus justly said in behalf of Dr. Cheeseman, operates equally in defence of Dr. Frost. No man doubts but that his remedies were prescribed with a view to the restoration of his patient.—Suppose those remedies failed; suppose even they produced death; is there nothing (in a criminal case) in the motive, in the design, with which they are administered, calculated to protect the defendant. If not, wo be unto all the professors of the healing art. The terrors of their responsibility shall unfit them for its due discharge, and they shall either in spite of fate, save the life of their patient, or sacrifice their *own*. Let that be once understood to be the law, and whole hecatombs shall perish, without one helping or alleviating hand. Let that once be understood to be the law, and then show the diploma, that shall prove a panoply against indictments like *this*. Upon this branch of the argument I am the advocate of all physicians, without regard to systems. Systems, will ascertain their respective levels, from unequivocal manifestations of public opinion—but the principle I here contend for, is salutary, and necessary to *all*—is salutary and necessary to the *public*, upon which all must depend for support. It is not as I have said, by persecution, that the one is to be exalted or the other degraded. When did genuine talent, or conscious worth descend to means like this? During the trial of this very cause; one of the brightest luminaries of medical science, in the person of the venerable and lamented Physick, has sunk beneath the horizon of the world, to rise, it is to be hoped, in brighter and in purer realms.—Whence, while among us, was *his* lustre derived?—not from breaking down, but from building up—not from crushing his supposed inferiors (for if that were the case, his foot would have been planted upon the necks of nine-tenths of his profession), but from assisting and stimulating and enlightening all, and borrowing assistance and stimulus, and light *from* all. The truly great man becomes " in men's despite a monarch." He is not merely illustrious from the insignificance of those by whom he is surrounded ; but he shines in reflected as well as original brightness.

If the medicine produced death—which no human being has said, or can say, though *you* are asked to draw that inference from the evidence—then and then only arises the question—

Secondly.—Was there gross ignorance—or culpable neglect on the part of the defendant—*Lata culpa—or Crassa negligentia* in the language of the law.

If the medicine did not produce death—or expedite death—ignorance in administering it, is no subject of punishment under this indictment ; and if it did produce death, and there was competent skill in administering it, it is but mischance, and certainly no felony ; the design being salutary. I repeat it, this doctrine is essential not only to the doctor—but to the patient— it is doctrine founded in universal policy. If a physician is to answer for the effect of his medicines ; and if his skill is to be determined by the life or death of his patient ; medical science, as it has always been admitted to be the most *uncertain* of all sciences, so will it be the most dangerous ; and not a man among the regular or irregular practitioners, is safe. This is a subject to be reflected upon : no man will be willing to place his reputation and liberty in jeopardy, however urgent the occasion, by prescribing in a dangerous disease in which prescriptions are most required, if this is to be the standard by which his practice is to be tested and adjudged. It is, to be sure, the case only of Richard Frost to-day; but it shall exhibit a more shining mark to-morrow. The result is that patients will be allowed to die without an effort to save them; unless the law shall be considered as involving the further absurdity of coercing medical attendance, at the same time that it punishes its want of success. The pernicious operation of this doctrine would be measureless: in future no old woman will dare to give a dose of camomile tea, for fear, that by the remotest probability it may produce death—or death may ensue. Nay, it would—to refine upon the doctrine—be tantamount to suicide to take medicine yourself, without the intervention of medical aid: if death were to be the consequence, it would be *felo de se;* and the rites of Christian burial should be withheld, and in the place thereof

> " You should in ground unsanctified be lodged
> Till the last trumpet."

I have contended under the first proposed point of inquiry, that the medicine did not produce death; and if it did, I contend under the second head of my argument, that it was administered with competent skill, and care. Not skill and care according to an opposing system; which deems nothing skilful without a diploma —nothing careful that does not conform to its own practice. To be *skilful*, according to the views of some, you must give *poisons;* and to be *careful*, you must pay your patients flying visits only—and, at least, be certain to be paid beforehand. In this sense Dr. Frost has neither skill nor care. His medicines were harmless— he remained almost constantly by the bedside of his young friend, and so far from exacting payment in advance, the only compensation or reward for his services that he has ever received—IS THIS PROSECUTION!—It is,

to be sure, more than he expected, but gratitude is boun-
tiful!—it is more than he deserved, but generosity is
munificent!

To resume the consideration of this point—there was,
I maintain, neither ignorance nor neglect. His education and his prior practice were such as to authorize a
conscientious man to administer medicine. No, say our
adversaries, "he was originally a locksmith!" Suppose
he was, does that render him less competent—with fair
opportunities of instruction—of understanding the wards,
and intricacies and mysteries of the physical system?
Many a locksmith might make a physician, though, from
the specimen afforded, it is certainly not every physician that would make a locksmith. "Honor and shame
from no condition rise." No rational man will pretend
to compare the science of medicine with that of the law,
in point of the requisite diversified accomplishments; and
yet I can recall to your honor's memory one of many
instances in which a poor unlettered country boy, having driven his load of hay into the city of Philadelphia,
and being attracted by youthful curiosity or driven by
force of character, into the courts of justice, was so captivated by forensic eloquence as to abandon his rustic
vocation and devote himself at once to the law. In a
few short years where do we find him? On the very
pinnacle of professional glory, looking down upon those
who, standing for fame on their forefather's feet had,
presumed to look down upon him. That man was William Lewis—a profound lawyer—an unequalled advocate.

Recorder.—I knew him well, and he merited all you
have said.

Well then, sir, let us not be taunted with the *locksmith.* Upwards of five years ago, Dr. Frost commenced
his preparatory studies. He directed his attention to
various medical authors, and at length became a student
under Dr. Sweet, an experienced physician connected
with the Thomsonian system. After continuing in the

office of his preceptor for about a year, he opened an infirmary himself; and for three years and more has been in an active and successful practice—I think I may say successful, for it does not appear that he has lost a single patient. How many he has saved, this court room shall testify. Ignorance is not to be inferred from the want of a diploma, or the limited extent of a library. His great study was the book of Nature—

An institute
Of laws eternal—whose unaltered page
No time can change—no copier can corrupt.

Practice and observation were his study, experience his preceptor—and are all these to be broken down, in order that mere theory may be kept up? But let us cast an eye at the evidence his career affords.

Dr. Metcalf, who has been a physician for upwards of ten years, is of opinion that the course pursued by Dr. Frost, as he understood it, was judicious; and he also states the character of Dr. Sweet (with whom Frost studied) for skill and science; and the course of examination to which candidates for admission to practice are subjected before the board of medical censors.

Leonard Kirby states the case of several cures of scarlet fever in his family by Dr. Frost, some years ago.

. Andrew Lockwood lost two children by measles and scarlet fever, while under the treatment of regular physicians. Subsequently two others were taken with the same diseases, and despairing of the regular practice, Dr. Frost was sent for, and both the little sufferers were speedily restored to health.

Valentine Kirby testifies, that he has employed Frost repeatedly in his family—for his wife, his children and himself. In one instance Dr. Anderson attended a child for inflammation of lungs—it got worse—he thought it would not live, and called in Dr. Frost. Under Frost's treatment the child got better. The regular physician

afterwards called and said "continue the drops." He
didn't know Frost had been there. Instead of continuing the drops, he continued the Thomsonian system,
which cured the child, and the regular physician took
the *credit* of it.

I say then, there is no manifestation of culpable neglect, or gross ignorance. The suggestion of rashness
which may be embraced either by the term " neglect," or
"ignorance," should be weighed with great caution—in
the language of Judge Brice in the Maryland trial,
which has been more than once referred to: " Physicians are often obliged to exercise a discretion which to
by-standers and unskilful persons may appear rash and
unfeeling; but which may, nevertheless, be dictated by
the soundest judgment and the kindest feelings toward
the patient, and an anxious desire to promote his re-
covery. To use the language of Lord Hale, ' God forbid
that a failure should subject the unfortunate practitioner
to a criminal prosecution, when he has done the best he
could to effect a cure.' "

Thus, sir, I have considered: first, the question,
whether the medicines, or the course of treatment
combined, produced the death of the deceased; and
in the second place, I have bestowed some attention
upon the allegation of gross ignorance and culpable
neglect. If the prosecution has not succeeded in establishing to the entire satisfaction of the jury, the
affirmative of both propositions, it is impossible, legally
speaking, that the defendant can be convicted:—that is,
if the treatment did not produce death, however ignorant
or unskilful or neglectful it may have been, no conviction
can ensue. For let it be remembered, that the ignorance
and neglect are connected with the treatment; and not
relied upon as substantive or independent grounds of
accusation.

There is another matter, that although I trust it is not
necessary to be enforced upon your minds, in a case like

this, yet it is never utterly to be lost sight of in any criminal case. It is this. That in order to render a verdict of conviction, your minds must be relieved from everything like reasonable doubt; and that doctrine is applicable, not only to the interpretation of the facts, but to the conclusions of law. It is founded in mercy, it is true, but is not unmixed with justice, and a due regard to the protection of the community. It is better, much better, that ninety-nine guilty men should escape, than that one who is innocent should suffer.

The law does not require a sacrifice: it punishes, it is true, where guilt is clearly shown; but it is not that justice delights in the groans of the victim, but that society may be preserved from the influence of evil example, and protected from the encroachments of vice. With the benefit of these reflections, it will be for you, the sworn twelve, to say how far it comports with your sense of duty to pronounce a verdict of guilty against the defendant, now upon his trial. My task is accomplished. Yours, and it is a much more important one, as it affects the character and condition of the defendant, remains to be fulfilled. It is for you to restore him to his reputation, to his family, to his hopes—neither of which he has justly forfeited. It is for you to return him to the affection of a sister; to the arms of an aged and respectable mother; or·to consign him to the cells of a penitentiary, and thereby not only blast his reputation, but also to destroy all those who cling about him, for their consolation and support. This, I may therefore be allowed to say, is a momentous question. It is your province to decide it—and for its decision, you are responsible to yourselves, your country and your God.

During the trial of the preceding case, in which all the medical faculty of New York were enlisted against the professors of the Thomsonian system, the newspaper re-

porters took a very active part in behalf of the prosecution, and carried their zeal so far as to supply questions
to the district attorney and his colleagues, and thereby
interfered most improperly with the propriety and dignity
of a judicial tribunal; this interference at last became so
gross as to compel Mr. Brown, though most reluctantly,
to bring the subject to the public notice of the court,
which he did in the following brief address:—*

Pardon me, may it please your honor, for interrupting the proceedings—I must be pardoned for I speak
under an irresistible impulse, which would seem to carry
with it its own excuse. I trust I am neither "splenitive
nor rash;" but that man who can endure the indecorum
of such an examination as this, in a court of justice,
must be lost to all sense of right—to all obligations of
duty, to all professional or personal respect. I have endured it until patience is no longer a virtue; and now I
feel myself imperatively called upon to express my unqualified reprobation of the course thus pursued. What
a scene is this! what a sorry sight is here presented! a
respectable young man placed at your bar upon a charge
of felonious homicide, surrounded by his parents, by his
relatives, his anxious and sympathetic friends, all absorbed in speechless anxiety; while arrayed on the side
of the prosecution, stands the district attorney, aided
by his learned associates, and supported by hosts of
willing and eager witnesses, standing, as it were, "like
grayhounds in the slip." To all this, sir, I take no objection; it is sanctioned by the law; and the legitimate terrors of the law, we must be, and we are prepared to meet.
Yet is not all this enough!—not only is the witness compelled to submit to a rigid examination by the counsel;
but scores of learned and medical professors, desert for a
time their own science, and here publicly enlist them-

---

selves, to the disgrace of justice, beneath the bloody flag of this prosecution. From every quarter of this vast hall, the constables and the tipstaves, and the bystanders are put into requisition, for the purpose of forwarding written communications and interrogatories to the law officers of the district. Is this dignified?—is it decent?—is it honest? Nay, more, sir,—following up this iniquitous example, and converting the liberty of the press, into the licentiousness of the press, (the heart speaks, and I will not restrain it)—the very stenographers and reporters—to whose industry and skill the community is indebted for the daily notices of this trial—losing sight of the limits of their privilege, also lend their important aid to the learned counsel, and supply them with new inquiries when their own genius may flag. This is bad—very bad, but it is not the worst feature in this anomalous course. Those stenographers are to report their own questions—they are to report the answers to those questions; both questions and answers are subject to the influence of preconceived partizan opinions upon the subject of inquiry; and thus in to-morrow's account of this trial in the public journals, every thing will be exhibited in the most unfavorable light for the defendant: the *printer* is the opposite *counsel*. If the prisoner is to be offered up as a victim, commit him at once to the mob; hand him over to his concealed or avowed enemies; and, instead of subjecting him to these lingering *torments*, let the work of destruction at once be accomplished. But if this be a *trial*—if these be the hallowed precincts of justice—if the law, or life, or liberty be more than a name; let not, I beseech you, let not the record of this important issue be stained and blotted by irregularities like these—at all events, may it please the court, their history shall bear upon its face my humble, but prompt and unequivocal protest.

I am aware, may it please the court, that this is a bold step upon my part: in behalf of an innocent, and an op-

pressed man, it becomes me to be bold—and I should be
a traitor to my trust—to myself—and to my God, were I
capable of weighing mere considerations of personal favor
or advancement, in opposition to the solemn convictions
of conscientious duty. If I enjoy the applause of my
own feelings, I shall not require that of the world—if I
am free from self-reproach—the reproach of others will
lose all its terrors.

Here Mr. Phenix rose and contended that he not only
had the right to the assistance of the medical gentlemen,
and the reporters, but of every individual in the room,
who might think proper to communicate information
upon the subject of the trial, or to propound inquiries—
and he concluded by observing, that the objection of the
defendant's counsel arose from fear that the imperfections
of the Thomsonian system, and the guilt of the defendant, should become matters of notoriety.

Mr. Brown resumed—Sir, I am not afraid of any legal
course—it is a departure from the law that I deprecate,
and fear. There is nothing in the talents of the counsel,
great as they are—there is nothing in the prosecution
rightly conducted, or in "twenty times its stop," that
can appall me. Far, very far from it; and I beg leave to
tell the learned gentleman, who taunts us with our fears,
that he will find much more serious cause for alarm, by
looking closely at home. And I tell him further, sir, so
far am I from deeming this cause in peril, that I possess
the power at any moment—here in the city's eye, of
strangling, yes *strangling* this fondly cherished offspring,
of whose infallibility he boasts.

The court decided that the district attorney had a
right to call in the aid of scientific men, but that it would
be a most indecent exhibition for any one to pass a written question—that "such a proceeding would be a most
improper administration of justice."—The recorder spoke
with considerable warmth, and indirectly rebuked the
medical faculty for their disgraceful conduct.

HOLMES' CASE.

COMMONWEALTH *v.* WILLIAM HOLMES.

SKETCH OF FACTS.

At the April Sessions of the Circuit Court of the United States, a case of absorbing interest was brought to trial—it was a prosecution against William Holmes, for the murder of Francis Askin, and arose out of the following circumstances: The American ship, William Brown, left Liverpool on the 13th of March, 1841, bound for Philadelphia, with a crew of seventeen, and sixty-four passengers—Scotch and Irish emigrants.

About ten o'clock of the night of the 19th of April, when distant two hundred and fifty miles southeast of Cape Race, the vessel struck an iceberg, and filled so rapidly that it was evident she must soon go down. The "long boat" and "jolly boat" were lowered; the captain, second mate, seven of the crew, and one passenger, got into the jolly boat; and the first mate, eight seamen [of whom the prisoner was one,] and thirty-two passengers, got indiscriminately into the long boat; the remaining thirty-one passengers were obliged to remain on board the ship, which in an hour from the time she struck went down, carrying with her every person who had not escaped to one or other of the boats. The long-boat leaked, and all on board were in great jeopardy. The gunwale was within from five to twelve inches of the water, and she was supposed to be too unmanageable to be saved; in a moderate blow she would have been swamped very quickly.

On the following night (Tuesday), after experiencing great hardships and perils, the mate—finding the boat unmanageable, and being in immediate danger from the heavy sea and floating ice—gave the order, which consigned fourteen of the passengers to a watery grave; among whom was Askin, to whom this indictment related. Holmes, the defendant, assisted in the execution of this order, and his participation in the deed was the subject of the indictment.

The trial commenced on the 13th April, 1842, and terminated with a verdict of guilty on the 23d of April. The defendant was sentenced to six months' imprisonment and fine—which latter was remitted by the President, and the defendant discharged November 14th, 1842.

For the United States.

Messrs. OLIVER HOPKINSON, GEO. M. DALLAS, WM. M. MEREDITH.

For the Defence.

Messrs. EDWARD ARMSTRONG, ISAAC HAZLEHURST, DAVID PAUL BROWN.

SPEECH IN HOLMES' CASE.

WITH DEFERENCE TO THE COURT:

How wonderful and mysterious, gentlemen of the jury, are the vicissitudes of human life. How frail and precarious are our best holds upon human happiness. Man, the boasted lord of creation, is the sport of every wind that blows—of every wave that flows. He appears like the grass of the field, flourishes and is cut down—and withers ere the setting sun—like the dews of the morning he sparkles for a brief moment and is exhaled. There is nothing earthly *certain* but *uncertainty*—there is nothing *true*, but HEAVEN.

What a salutary practical commentary, is supplied by the present intensely interesting occasion, upon the truth of this melancholy doctrine. On the thirteenth day of March, in the last year, a staunch and gallant ship, with a competent commander and a noble crew, with sixty-five passengers on board, sailed from the port of Liverpool, destined for that of Philadelphia; a destination, alas! which was never accomplished.

For more than a month, notwithstanding she encountered storms and tempests, she outrode them all; and like a thing of life, held on her way rejoicing.

On the 19th of the succeeding month she arrived in fairer climes and enjoyed more propitious gales: but even then, when every heart throbbed with the anticipated joy of a speedy arrival, the angel of destruction spread his broad black wings above her, and while traversing the ocean with all sails set, at the rate of ten knots an hour, she came into collision with an island of ice, and in a moment her pride was prostrate, and the doomed ship was reduced to an actually sinking condition, affording scarcely time for her unhappy inmates, in the moment of their extremest need, to cry GOD BLESS US. The ocean, her favored element, of which for years she had been the pride, became her sepulchre—and the winds that had borne her upon many a prosperous voyage, sung her last sad, only requiem. Here is a scene strikingly presented, in which the theories of philosophy are reduced at once, to a frightful reality.

But there is still another picture to which I would invite, and upon which I would fasten your attention. On that dreadful night—the crew and half the passengers having taken to the boats—the agonizing voice of a mother is heard even beyond the tumult and the clamor, calling for the preservation of her daughter, who in the consternation of the moment had been forgotten, and remained on board the fated ship. In an instant, you may see a gallant, athletic and powerful sailor, passing hand over hand, by dint of a slender rope, until he regains the vessel. And you may further behold him upon the quarter deck—in the depth of the night, surrounded by the wild and wasteful ocean—with one arm entwined around a sickly and half naked girl, while with the other, he bravely swings himself and his almost lifeless burthen—by means of the " boat tackle falls "—from the stern of the sinking ship into the boat below; and at once restores the child to the open arms and yearning heart of the mother. Yet to-day, I say it to the disgrace of the law, after months of solitary imprisonment, you here see that self same heroic sailor arraigned upon the odious charge of having voluntarily and wantonly deprived a fellow creature of his life; and THAT, gentlemen of the jury, is the charge that I am to argue and you are to determine.

I say this is what you are to determine. It may
not be inappropriate, however, though certainly not
vital to this cause, that I should ask your attention, in
passing to the real subject in controversy, to two other
indictments which stain the records of this court, referring to portions of the same transaction; the first
charging the defendant with murder, which the grand
jury promptly ignoramused—and the second, in the
impotency of disappointed revenge, accusing him of larceny in having stolen *a quilt*, of the alleged value of three
dollars, which charge shared the same fate. You can
form some idea of the dignity of the United States and
its value, while observing how it has been cheapened
by itself. This very quilt, permit me to remind you,
is that which was converted by Holmes into a sail for
the boat, in a moment of the extremest peril, in order
that he might save the lives of those very beings who
gratefully appeared before the grand jury upon the
first opportunity, in order to convict their benefactor of
these imputed crimes: I shall speak of this hereafter—
for the present I merely advert to it, and pass at once
to more important matters.

In approaching the consideration of this case, which
I do with pride, and pleasure, and confidence, I cannot
but express my regret, to adopt a military phrase, that
I am called into conflict, not only with the regular
troops of the United States, but with her recently
enlisted *volunteers.* I am sorry that my gallant friend*
who led on the attack so boldly yesterday—and who is
a legitimate leader everywhere—should so far have returned to his first love, as to desert the white banner
of innocence (under which he has lately so successfully
fought) to engage once more beneath the bloody flag of
such a prosecution as this. Since it is so, however,
let him nail that flag to the mast. We should be

---

* Mr. Dallas.

happy to abide by every principle of civilized warfare;
but in a mortal controversy—in a death struggle like
this—we shall neither ask nor will we receive any
quarter.

This case, in order to embrace all its horrible relations, ought to be decided in a long boat, hundreds of
leagues from the shore, loaded to the very gunwale
with forty-two half naked victims; with provisions only
sufficient to prolong the agonies of famine and of thirst;
with all the elements combined against her; leaking
from below, filling also from above; surrounded by ice;
unmanageable from her condition, and subject to destruction from the least change of the wind and the
waves—the most variable and most terrible of all the
elements. Decided at such a tribunal, nature—intui-
tion—would at once pronounce a verdict, not only of
acquittal, but of commendation. The prisoner might,
it is true, obtain no outward atonement for nine months
of suffering and of obloquy; but he would at least enjoy
the satisfaction always to be derived from a consciousness of rectitude, in which the better part of the world
sympathize, and in which it confides.

Alas! how different is the scene now exhibited.

You sit here, the sworn twelve, the centre of that
society which you represent, surrounded by the sanctions of those laws which for a time you administer—
reposing amidst the comforts and delights of sacred
homes—directed and instructed by a judge, who, being
full of light himself, freely imparts it to all he approaches—to decide upon the impulses and motives of
the prisoner at the bar, launched upon the bosom of
the perilous ocean—surrounded by a thousand deaths
in their most hideous forms, with but one plank between
him and destruction. What sympathies can be inspired
by relative positions, so remote, so opposite as these?

Translate yourselves, if you can, by the power of
imagination, to those scenes, those awful scenes to

which this proceeding refers. Fancy yourselves in a frail barque, encompassed by towers of ice Olympus high, and still magnified by the fear natural to man ; exposed to the bleak and pitiless winds, surrounded by forty wretches as miserable as yourself—deepening your own afflictions by the contagion of grief; removed a hundred leagues from land, and still further removed by a destitution of those means by which alone it could possibly be reached.

Nay, further, superadd to these horrors the apprehension of famine—of storm—bearing assured destruction on its wing; and connect all these with the scenes and terrors of the night just past—enough to appall the stoutest heart and overthrow the firmest brain—and then tell me, not what the defendant should have done, but what the most severe and rigid would have done, in trials and perils and calamities like these. It is easy to scorn the tempest while sporting with the zephyr— to laugh at the ocean while secure from its ravages and horrors—to expatiate upon the harmlessness of ice, while indulging in it, perhaps as a luxury—or to underrate famine in the abundance of your supplies—but may that Power that " rides on the whirlwind and directs the storm," protect you against the sad reality of those afflictions which in their mere theory are often so readily overcome by your self-secure, cold blooded and reckless philosophy. Philosophy readily triumphs over past and future and remote ills; but present and immediate ills grapple closely with the heart, and triumph over philosophy.

Let us now come to those facts which distance and defy all the powers of fancy. Before doing this, however, you will pardon me in examining the legal character of his charge: First, as relates to the act of Congress. Secondly, as regards the inherent defects of the indictment. Thirdly, as respects its inconsistency with the evidence in the cause. I have for the present but a word to say upon each of these subjects, rather to show that they have not been overlooked, than with any intention elaborately to discuss them.

The act of Congress leaves manslaughter where it was at common law, so far as regards its definition—it only modifies its punishment. The punishment is not more than three years, with a penalty not exceeding one thousand dollars. You have been truly told by the opposite counsel that the court may reduce their sentence to a merely nominal punishment. That is the business of the court, however, and after your verdict is found, your influence is extinct. Whether the punishment is to be an hour or a year, it is an infamous punishment; and you should be equally cautious in resting your verdict upon unquestionable and satisfactory proof. I marvel, indeed, that my learned friend, while haranguing you upon the enormity of this offence, should attempt soothing you into a verdict by the suggestion that it would probably be attended with no evil to the defendant. Allow me to deprecate this questionable mercy—it is calculated, if not designed, to seduce you from allegiance to your duties. If the defendant be guilty, he should meet the rigor of the law; if innocent, his rights should not be compromised by the imaginary insignificance of his anticipated punishment. I make no claims upon your charity—my appeals are to your justice.

Now, as to the internal defects of the indictment. The indictment contains four counts for manslaughter. That is, for unlawfully, but without malice, depriving a fellow-creature of his life. Malice would elevate what would otherwise be manslaughter, into murder.

The first count charges the homicide on board of the ship William Brown, belonging to Stephen Baldwin.

The second—on board of a vessel, name unknown, belonging to Stephen Baldwin.

The third and fourth are the same, with the exception

of Thomas Vogel's name being substituted for that of Stephen Baldwin's.

Now, these charges are incompatible with each other, and are calculated to bewilder the prisoner in his defence. They cannot all be true, and as there has been no election on the part of the prosecution, a verdict upon all will involve an inconsistency obviously illegal, if not utterly fatal. The doctrine of Milton, as applied to angelic existences, that, vital in every part, they cannot, but " by annihilation, die," is not true in its application to indictments. They are mortal in every part, and the destruction of one part of a count, is the destruction of all parts of the same count. One count, it is true, does not destroy another when they are at all compatible with each other, and when an election has been made; but when the charges contained in an indictment are, as in this case, totally inconsistent, if the jury should find a verdict of guilty upon the indictment generally, it will be subject to a motion in arrest of judgment, and it can never stand.

Lastly, I say, if the indictment were unquestionable in itself, it is not supported by the proof. I say nothing in regard to the error in the time stated, which, in *some* cases might be fatal, but probably not in *this*. The ship, as appears by the evidence, neither belonged to Baldwin nor Vogel, but to McCrea, who is not even referred to. Baldwin, however, it is said, held a claim to her—a mortgage upon her as collateral security. That does not improve the case of the prosecution. Special property may be sufficient, but it must be special property accompanied by possession; or at all events possession itself, actual or constructive. Suppose a person were indicted for committing a burglary upon the house of A. B., and upon the trial it appeared that the house was the dwelling of E. F., and that the person whose name was introduced into the indictment was merely the mortgagee, certainly the charge could not be sustained for a moment. I merely, for the present, hint at, rather than press these objections. I shall, if necessary—which it probably will not be—have the benefit of them hereafter.

We pass now to the law more immediately connected with the facts of this case. Russell, Paley, Rutherforth, Blackstone, and, above all, Lord Bacon, are the authorities upon which the entire law of the case rests.

As to Puffendorf, Grotius, Heineccius, and others who have been quoted, with all their lofty pretensions, they do not contain as much wisdom or light as may be found upon each and every page of " the wisest and brightest of mankind." So far as regards the present subject, they exhibit more pedantry and casuistry than either learning or common sense.

[The books referred to and the doctrine of self-defence, &c., were here discussed at length.]

I have thus given you the law. There is but little difficulty between us in regard to it. The labor is in the application of the law.

I maintain that a well-founded apprehension of peril to life, justifies self-defence—to the extent of destroying the adversary. The opposite counsel maintain that the peril must be actually inevitable. This I deny, and say that it is enough if it be *honestly* and reasonably *supposed* to be so. An *inevitable* danger I don't understand.

They maintain that the peril must be not only inevitable, but immediate. I answer, it need be neither ; but it must reasonably be supposed to be both.

Suppose—upon an indictment for manslaughter—a plank be measured in court, with square, rule and compass, and it be found that it would have sustained two persons; still, is he, who in his terror, supposes it would not, to be liable to conviction ? Certainly not.

The prosecution contends that if there be a doubt as to the inevitable peril, the defendant is to be convicted. I say it is presumed to have been considered inevitable, from the fact itself; there being no pretence of animosity, but clear evidence of the greatest kindness and sympathy.

They say—that if the danger were inevitable, still the defendant had no right to make selection. To this I reply, that this argument involves the necessity of throw- *all* overboard.

The selection would have been just the same, if they had destroyed those who are living now, and permitted the others to remain.

But say they, lots might have been cast. If the peril were inevitable and immediate, that could not have been done. We hear for the first time of casting lots in a sinking boat—where the question is whether any can be saved, rather than who shall be lost. Lots in cases of famine, where means of subsistence are wanting for the number of the crew, are matters which, horrible as they are, are comparatively familiar to us. But to cast lots to see who shall go first, when all are going, is reserved for the ingenuity of the counsel, who constructs a raft on board of ship, in the depth of the night, with the prospect of her going down before he drives the first nail, or plies the first rope.

Now I have shown, if these views be sound, that apart from the preservation of the rest of the passengers, and themselves, these men could have had no inducement to take life. That the magnanimity, gallantry, and tenderness of Holmes, utterly forbid the idea. That therefore it is honestly and fairly to be inferred, that they apprehended immediate peril, and were sustained by the laws of nature in acting accordingly.

As to the circumstance of Frank Askins offering five guineas to preserve his life till morning, and its being refused; that so far from making against us, makes for us. If they had complied with that request, they must either have sold the lives of all on board for five sovereigns; or have offered conclusive evidence that they did not conceive the peril to be immediate. If they had even received the money, and afterwards deprived him of life; the money itself would have been an indication, either of a corrupt motive, or a reliance on their own security, incompatible with the doctrine for which I contend. It was a terrific deed, to be sure, consider it which way you will; and the very horror of the deed constitutes part of its defence: as it is fairly to be presumed it would not have been resorted to, except in a case of a *horrible* necessity.

The fate of the two sisters, is spoken of with peculiar pathos. I maintain their lives were never sacrificed by the crew.

1st. Because there is no positive proof to that effect—mere loose suggestions or inferences.

2d. Because there was not a hand laid upon any other woman in the boat.

3d. Because never mentioned by witnesses upon previous examinations.

4th. Because the conduct of the sisters shows that it was an act of self-devotion, which is almost admitted indeed; and which adds another bright page to the records of time, exhibiting the fidelity, affection and devotion of a woman's heart.

Considering it in this point of view, its glory is almost equal to its horrors—neither of which is attributable to the defendant.

But it is said, that if the passengers had been allowed to live until the next morning, a ship was at hand.

First—I answer, that the probability was, that they could not have survived the night.

And secondly—that without prescience, they could not know of the ship being at hand.

Now let us look to the next morning. The boat is still filled with water—the peril is not abated, and two more half frozen wretches are removed—some few hours after this, the vessel is discerned, and Holmes, and the passengers, through the instrumentality of Holmes, are saved.

As to the notion that there is any distinction between
sailors and other men, in their natural rights of self-defence, it is not to be tolerated. If the peril were not
imminent, no man has a right to destroy the life of
another for the preservation of his own. If it were imminent and apparently inevitable, any man, without regard to condition, vocation, or degree, had that right.
A state of nature implies the absence of all but natural
law; and natural law is not to be affected by artificial
distinctions. A sailor is upon equality with passengers—
nay he is upon an equality with his captain in emergen-
cies like this.

With these views of the law let us turn to the facts.

On the 13th March, 1841, as has been said, the ship
sailed from Liverpool for Philadelphia—she came in contact with the ice on the 19th of April—and in one hour,
and less, was reduced to a sinking condition.

The captain having unavailingly attempted the pumps,
ordered the boats to be launched from the ship. Thirty-
three passengers and nine sailors entered the long boat,
and the captain, seven sailors and one passenger entered
the jolly boat. The boats were moored at the stern of
the ship, by dint of a ten fathom rope, attached to the
vessel. And in a few minutes the ship sunk forever; the
rope being severed at that very moment by Holmes, who
was posted for that purpose.

The counsel at this point of the case indulged in a
severe and unmeasured attack upon Captain Harris, for
having deserted the vessel; maintaining that he was
bound to have sunk with her—that he has disgraced the
American name by not having done so—and that he
presents by his conduct a shameful contrast to Grace
Darling, who placed her life in peril, to redeem the passengers and crew from a wreck, in the neighborhood of a
light house, of which her father was the keeper.

Now this is all very poetical, very beautiful, and what
embraces both, very gallant on the part of my learned

friend. Rather than take the *laurel* from the brow of
Grace Darling or any other darling, I would wear the
cypress round my own; but you will still allow me to say,
there is a vast difference between an experiment in a life
boat and almost within hail of the shore, and the scene to
which our attention is here called—one hundred leagues
from land—in the darkness of night and surrounded by
icebergs: the captain was not bound to do more than he
did—he was bound to do all that he did. His calmness
and composure in the midst of these horrible scenes
contributed to save the lives of upwards of fifty human
beings; although it is true, that he was not enabled to
rescue those who remained on board of the ship. Their
temporary rescue would have resulted finally in the loss
of *all.*

As to his sacrificing his own life, sympathy for others
forbade it. If he and all of the sailors had perished, so
far from its operating to the benefit of the passengers, it
would have proved their inevitable and total destruction.

But say the gentlemen, why didn't he construct a raft
—he had an hour to do it in. He had no assurance of a
moment—the ship was laden with iron—two columns of
water of the thickness of a man's body, were pouring
through the stem of the ship into her very vitals. And
although nearly an hour elapsed after leaving her, and
before she sunk, how was he to determine upon the probability of her surviving the shock. The learned counsel's
argument is quite consistent throughout the case. He
says a raft should have been constructed because it turned
out that the vessel did not sink for an hour—as he says
that the men should not have perished, because a ship
afterwards hove in sight.

But, it is further said by the learned gentleman, that
the captain might have taken off more of the passengers.
That suggestion is in direct opposition to the evidence.
The gunwales of the boat were within six or eight inches
of the water; a single additional person would have

swamped them—and thus *all* must have perished, perhaps, from an ill-judged effort to save *one*. The conduct of the captain was not only judicious, but humane. If he had returned alongside of the ship he would have been ingulfed by the vortex, produced by her sinking—or, subjected to a calamity scarcely less terrible, by some of the inmates of the ship jumping into the boats. As to the suggestion that he might have at least rescued the children in the ship, that attempt would have resulted in the same consequences—even supposing that the perishing parents would have been willing to sever themselves in this moment of direst emergency, from offspring more precious than even life itself.

I have deemed it my duty to say this much in behalf of an absent man, and a most meritorious and exemplary officer; not that it was by any means essential to the defence, but simply because it was an act of justice. If the captain is so disgracious now in the eyes of the prosecution—so culpable in the eye of the law, why have not our learned adversaries instituted legal proceedings against him, instead of attempting to transfer the burthen of his imputed guilt to the shoulders of the prisoner. The captain's deposition was taken; he was examined in the office of the attorney for the United States—he was within the very jaws of the *Royal Tiger*, yet those jaws did not close upon him, with all their thirst for blood. Now, however, that his march is o'er the mountain wave, the counsel speak of his escape from justice, and the horrible retribution that awaits his return. This is the thunder without the bolt, or the power of Jove to wield it.

We pass now to other scenes. In the morning of the 20th of April, which was ushered in in darkness and in gloom, the two boats separated from each other—the captain and eight others directing their course, in the jolly boat, for Newfoundland, and the mate and thirty-three passengers and crew remaining in the long boat. At the time of the separation, which was on Tuesday morning, the captain directed his first officer, who had left the jolly boat for the long boat, to endeavor to steer for the nearest point of land, which was two hundred and fifty miles off; and then having taken a list of those on board of the long boat, he bade them a melancholy adieu. In parting, the mate begged him to take some of the passengers into the jolly boat; the captain refused it as a matter of impossibility; the mate declared that his boat would sink, or they should have to cast lots; and the captain, clearly acquiescing in that probable necessity, begged that it might be the last resort.

Shortly after the departure of the jolly boat, the sad series of disasters commenced, which terminates in the lamentable catastrophe in which this trial originated. Nothing before this point of time bears directly upon this question, although there is much in the scenes referred to, calculated to touch the most callous heart.

At the time the boats parted company, or shortly after, it was raining heavily—the air was very cold, from the proximity of the ice; and the miserable, half naked passengers were benumbed by exposure and hardships, to which they had been subjected the preceding night. The long boat had leaked from the time she left the ship; the plug had, in some way, been removed, and another was substituted. The second plug was lost, and a variety of expedients were from time to time resorted to to supply its place, as well as to stop the other leaks. Added to this, the long boat was, in her situation, entirely unmanageable. The testimony of the mate and captain, which is not contradicted by any of the witnesses, places this beyond the reach of doubt. Parker, the mate, says—"I have followed the sea for twenty-one years. I think the long boat was too unmanageable to be saved, from the experience I have had. If there had been no leak, I do not think they would have been able to save themselves." Again, upon the cross-examination—"The long boat being unmanageable, I thought she would have sunk the first night. By unmanageable, I mean they could not put her head from one point to another—she was going round like a tub; she was like her own mistress—they could not keep her head any one way, not even for a minute."

And Captain Harris is equally clear and explicit upon the subject, when 'he informs us—"That the long boat leaked, that they attempted to bail, but could not make out anything; they were so thronged in the boat. She would not have supported one half she had in her, had there been a moderate blow, even without a leak. The gunwale was about twelve inches above the surface of the sea."

Again, speaking on the same subject, the captain says —"I found she was unmanageable, and that it was useless for me to waste further time with them—they could not use the oars—they could not steer the boat," &c.

And further—"A very little irregularity in stowage would have capsized the long boat; a moderate flaw would have swamped her very quickly."

On Tuesday it rained heavily all day; the sailors were employed in rowing at times; the passengers took their turns in bailing, and it is perfectly apparent from the proof, that this course continued, with but little intermission or relaxation, until the dreary night closed in. At this time the wind increased, the waves ran high, at times dashing into the boat—depositing ice upon the already half frozen passengers and crew; and at the same time calling for renewed exertion, while impairing the ability to make it. At length, abandoned to despair, the water increasing in the boat, and the peril of death being imminent, and apparently inevitable, a cry of horror is heard from various quarters, exclaiming, "We are sinking! We are sinking!" Then it was that the mate— who, unmurmuringly, had taken his post in the very throat of death, at the command of the captain,—perceiving that everything was reduced to a state of utter hopelessness, and unable longer to repress his emotions, cried out "Help me God—this will not do—men, go to work." The witnesses all agree in regard to these expressions of the mate; some, however, say they were thrice repeated before they were obeyed—and finally, the obedience of the crew was the death of sixteen of the passengers; by which, alone, in all human probability, the remaining seventeen passengers and nine seamen were saved.

Here let us pause, to ascertain, if we can, what were the impulses, the secret impulses, the direct impulses that led to this deplorable catastrophe. I deny, emphatically, the correctness of the doctrine of the prosecution, that if there be any doubts of the sufficiency of the cause which led to the death, the defendant should be convicted. This inverts the whole current of the philosophy of criminal jurisprudence. Doubts of motive—doubts of acts—are always doubts of guilt; and reasonable doubts of guilt must result in acquittal. I am strengthened in this position by the indisputable fact that Holmes, the prisoner, during the whole voyage, was upon the kindest and most harmonious terms with all the passengers; that he preserved the same friendly relation to them after the loss of the ship; that he had perilled his life more than once to preserve them; that he had literally stripped himself of his apparel for their comfort: in short, his desire to save them, seemed to absorb all consideration of mere personal or individual safety. In these circumstances, to suppose anything cruel or wanton upon his part, is to run counter to everything that is possible or natural. I infer, therefore, that he supposed the peril to be imminent and instantaneous, or he never would have complied with the orders of the mate—and that the mate who gave the order, did it under the impression of direct necessity, is too obvious to require or admit of argument.

On Tuesday night, I say, about 10 o'clock, the boat filled with water from above and below; the wind having risen; the waves having increased; the ice accumulating, and the passengers shrieking with horror at the prospect of drowning; the final, fatal order was given. It is not to be supposed that these hardy sons of the sea were unnecessarily alarmed. That Holmes, particularly, was a brave, resolute and deter-termined seaman, as well as a most humane man, no one will venture to deny: that he had but one supposable object, which was to save such as might be saved, is equally clear. I maintain therefore, that the most favorable construction is to be placed upon his motives; and it is justly to be inferred that he acted upon the impression that the danger was imminent, and that death was inevitable to all, except by resorting to those means which he actually adopted. We are told however, that he is not the judge. I ask, who is the judge? There is a vast deal of difference between judging in a storm, and judging of a representation of a storm; and therefore it was that I said, that in order to a righteous determination of this case, your verdict should be rendered in the midst of perils such as have been described, instead of being pronounced while surrounded by all the securities and sanctions of the law. I agree that if you can conceive of any other inducement than the desire of self-preservation, and that of the majority of the passengers, inducing this act—which I defy you to do—you may then imagine that that inducement led to the act, and thereby divest the prisoner of his present defence; but even taking all the statements of the witnesses for the prosecution, highly colored—I will not say disclored—as they are, and torture them as you may, it is impossible for you to arrive at any other conclusion, than that Holmes was actuated by the kindest and most generous influences; and certainly I need not say that kindness and generosity are opposed to wantonness and barbarity. I repeat, then, that in these

circumstances of terror, men are left to their honest determinations.   They are not to resort to mere imaginary
evils as a pretext, nor are they to be *supposed* to resort
to them as a pretext.   If they err in their determination,
according to the rules adopted by a cold system of reasoning, their error, as thus detected, is not to be visited upon
them as a crime.

Suppose two men, occupying perfectly friendly relations
to each other, should be cast away, and both seize the
same plank (to me the favorite illustration), and one
should thrust the other off; would it not be monstrous,
upon the trial of the alleged offender, that the plank
should be brought into court and submitted to some men
of approved skill, and measured and examined by square,
rule and compass—its specific gravity ascertained, and the
possibility of its sufficiency to sustain two men discussed
and decided—and upon the basis of such calculation as
that, the prisoner should be deprived of his liberty or his
life; when, if you had placed the witnesses in his precise
situation, and they had been called upon to act upon a
sudden emergency, they would have done precisely what
he did, and what every principle of natural law abundantly warrants.   It is worse than idle to suppose that in
such a critical juncture as this, men are to cast lots or
toss up for their lives.   In such peril a man makes his
own law with his own right arm.

But, say the learned counsel, had the passengers been
permitted to remain until the morning, they might have
been saved by the Crescent.   I answer, had they remained
a single hour, they would have never seen the morning—
every man, woman and child, would have weltered in the
coral caves of the ocean.   The approach of the Crescent
could not, even in point of fact, have operated to alleviate
their fears—without prescience, they could have anticipated no such relief.   Men are to act upon the past and
the present—the future belongs to God alone.

You are told, however, that the condition of the boat

was not hopeless—that she was on "the great high road of nations," and that there was every prospect of her being picked up. The gentleman speaks of the great high road of nations over the pathless ocean, as if it were the Chesapeake and Delaware canal, in which two vessels could scarcely pass abreast. The "President" steamer, sunk probably upon this great high road, leaving no voice to tell her fate. Surrounded, as the boat was, by mountains of ice, no ship would probably ever have reached her, if steering in that direct course. Fate itself seemed to forbid it—nay, no vessel, says the captain, would have ventured among the ice, had the position of the boat been known; as no commander, however philanthropic, would have so far perilled his own hopes in order to redeem the lives of others. The chances of rescue were entirely too remote then,—ninety-nine chances against one, say the witnesses,—to enter into the calculation of the mate and crew, had their circumstances even been such as to allow them dispassionately to reason upon the subject—but as it was, terror had assumed the throne of reason, passion became judgment, and you know the sequel.

I have now briefly and imperfectly passed over that part of the case upon which your decision must mainly turn; but before I close, let me direct your attention to another circumstance which casts a reflected light upon the matters already adverted to. I refer to the occurrence of the next day—and this leads me to present to your view another picture in this nautical gallery.

On Wednesday, the 21st of April, the morning dawns; yet the sun still shrouds his face amidst shadowy clouds and darkness, from the traces of horror which the past night had left. You may see, gentlemen of the jury, without any extraordinary stretch of fancy, on that awful morning, a small boat, in the centre of the ocean, with a single sailor. apparently engaged in an effort to rig out a sail—baring his brow and his breast to the bleak winds that howl around him, with no one to impart encourage-

ment or aid—deserted by earth and frowned upon by
Heaven. That man was Holmes, the prisoner at the bar.
His mess-mates have sunk exhausted into the bottom of
the boat—the mate is lost in dismay—the passengers are
buried in hopelessness and horror—

> Silent they sit
> All faculties absorbed by black despair;
> The world is banish'd, and the soul is dead
> To earthly sympathy—to earthly care,
> Brooding alone on its eternal fate,
> And prostrate in the presence of its God.

And there amidst this solemn and harrowing scene the
defendant stands, toiling and struggling to the last,—not
for himself, but for those very persons who, having forgotten their *gratitude* with their *danger*, now appear
before you to pay for *their own life*, by depriving their
preserver of *his*. Whether this mode of discharging
obligations shall meet with your approval, it will remain
for your verdict to decide.

I have now done. I am perfectly sensible of the power
of the learned counsel opposed to me; and if this case is
to be determined by the comparative strength or skill of
the advocates, I have much cause for alarm. My gallant
friend who opened the conflict, appeared like Apollo, radiant in his glory—balancing his body, adjusting his bow,
and directing his shaft—*his golden pointed shaft*—at the
very heart of his intended victim. By and by, his colleague, who may be compared to Hercules, will take the
field with his club, and exert all his stupendous powers
to demolish this defence. Still, armed in the panoply of
justice, I entertain no fear, for after all, gentlemen of the
jury, what is a giant when wrapped up in a QUILT?
Against all these odds therefore I stand firmly by the
side of that man, who always stood firmly by others.
The destiny—the worldly destiny, of the prisoner, is now
confided to your hands. Do with him as you would be
done by.

HINCHMAN CASE.

Supreme Court.   July Term, 1848.   *No.* 87.

Morgan Hinchman *v.* Samuel S. Richie et al.

[Extract from "The Forum."]

"The case of Morgan Hinchman against sixteen defendants—persons all of great respectability, and some of them of wealth and influence—was tried in the Supreme Court of Pennsylvania, in March, 1849.   The case awakened great attention ; it commenced on the ninth of March and continued until the seventh of April.

"Morgan Hinchman was a young man of respectable connections, a member of the Society of Friends, residing with a wife and young family of children, in a neighboring county, apparently prosperous and happy.   On the' evening of the fifth of January, 1847, he left his farm to attend the market in Philadelphia.   Before his departure he arranged many little domestic affairs with regularity and care ; and when in Philadelphia, after disposing of' his produce, attended to some business relating to a loan of money, by a mortgage on his farm.   On the morning of the seventh, the transactions occurred which gave rise to the subsequent suit.   At the same hour of that morning—the hour previously fixed upon by, Morgan Hinchman for concluding the negotiation about the mortgage—several of the defendants assembled at the same place, and arrested Morgan Hinchman, after informing him that they were about to take him to the Frankford Lunatic Asylum.   Without repeating the details of the case, it is sufficient to state, that in pursuance of the plans previously laid, and in spite of the resistance of the alleged lunatic, he was carried to the asylum and restrained of his liberty for several months.

17

"It was for a conspiracy, accompained by the overt act of his imprisonment, that an action for damages was brought; the parties charged being not only those actively combined in the arrest, but others, by whom it was alleged, a less active, but equally culpable part, was taken in the proceeding against the plaintiff. It is just, to this statement of the case, to remark that the defendants, one and all, denied, in every way and form, the charge against them. They alleged that Morgan Hinchman was taken to the asylum at the request of his wife and mother; upon the certificate of a very competent medical adviser; and that he was at the time of his arrest, and had been for a long time previous, a lunatic."

The trial of this cause took place before Judge Burnside, one of the judges of the Supreme Court, sitting at Nisi Prius; and although the sessions of the court frequently continued until after eight o'clock P. M., the testimony and speeches of counsel (as has been stated) occupied nearly a month.

After a very able charge from the judge, the case was given to the jury, who, after being "out" five days, found a verdict in favor of the plaintiff, against Samuel S. Richie, Edward Richie, John Lippincott, George M. Elkinton, John M. Whitall, John L. Kite, and Elizabeth R. Shoemaker, and assessed the damages at TEN THOUSAND DOLLARS; and a verdict in favor of the defendants, Philip Garrett, Joshua H. Worthington, Benjamin H. Warder, Thomas Wistar, Jr., William Biddle, John D. Griscom, and Anna W. Hinchman.

Dr. Evans had been previously acquitted at the close of the plaintiff's evidence.

The case was removed to the Supreme Court, *in banc;* but was subsequently settled, without any action by that tribunal.

Counsel for the Plaintiffs.

Messrs. WILLIAM B. REED, SAMUEL H. PERKINS, DAVID PAUL BROWN.

For the Defendants.

Messrs. J. WILLIAMS BIDDLE, CHARLES GIBBONS, GEORGE GRISCOM, HENRY J. WILLIAMS.

SPEECH IN HINCHMAN CASE.

[*Delivered on* GOOD FRIDAY, 1849.]

MAY IT PLEASE YOUR HONOR:

Upon this day, gentlemen of the jury, this HOLY day, while the great masses of the Christian community are devoutly engaged in a public manifestation of pious gratitude for the priceless and free sacrifice which redeemed the fallen family of man, from the miseries of eternal death; it is a melancholy and painful duty, to be compelled to force upon your attention, the persecution and oppression—the cruelty and barbarity—practised, or alleged to be practised (for I take nothing for granted), by a body of professing Christians, lovers of peace, and followers of a meek and lowly Saviour, against an unoffending fellow *man.*

My learned friend, though professional adversary, has ventured, in the close of his remarks, to appeal to you, and to attempt to enlist your sympathies, in behalf of the defendants in this case, closely connected together as they have been from the first to the last, as a solid phalanx, in an unsparing opposition to Morgan Hinchman. Instead of casting an eye of pity or commiseration upon the helpless condition of the plaintiff—upon his destitute and forlorn, degraded and disgraced condition—all his humanity seems to be absorbed by a sympathetic regard for those, whom he professionally represents, and who are the actual *offenders.*

When Pilate (and, it is an apt illustration upon the

present occasion) meanly yielded to the clamors of the multitude, and washing his hands in their presence, surrendered the Saviour of mankind to an unholy and infuriate combination, consoling himself by exclaiming, "I am innocent of the wrongs of this just person;" he adopted by anticipation some portion of the argument resorted to by this defence. He only stood by, forsooth, and did *nothing!* He was innocent of the blood of the accused! But let me tell you now, and it will be a subject for elaborate descant hereafter—let me tell you now, that that man, however elevated or respectable, who stands by patiently and acquiesces in a wrong that is about to be, or has been committed; imparts to the wrong-doer the aid and support of his presence, and thereby participates in· the offence. Although, like Pilate, he may console himself with the operations of washing off external guilt; he shares in that evil, shares in that crime, which he neither endeavored to prevent, nor was disposed to resist or redress. That is my doctrine, and we shall soon see how it will abide the test, when I come to apply it in requisite connection with the different portions of this case, in which that point of inquiry is involved.

May it please your honor, I never had more occasion to entertain confidence in a judicial officer than I have now. I never felt more distinctly or more deeply the necessity for entire reliance upon the integrity of a judge. I think during the progress of this case, however your honor's mind may have wavered—as it is. proper it should do—in relation to certain legal points; yet I have not observed, and I am certain in relation to the discharge of your duties I never shall observe, the slightest vacillation or unsteadiness, in regard to the immutable principles of justice.

It will be my duty, so far as it may be within my power, to relieve you of any doubts hitherto entertained; and if I do not settle beyond cavil or question the entire fallacy of the whole doctrine of the defendauts' counsel; and show that at most it is a mere castle in the air, resting upon no other foundation than fancy, or error; then I will submit as a philosopher ought to do, and calmly encounter the consequence.

Gentlemen of the jury, the extraordinary and unexpected remarks of my learned friend, have forced me somewhat from the order of my proposed argument, but that's not much—I can readily return and pursue it.

I am not, allow me to say—and perhaps it may be somewhat gratifying to you to learn—I am not, may it please your honor, as I presume *you* know, one of that class of advocates, though I speak in no disparagement of others, who seem to conceive the length and the strength of a speech to be synonymous. I shall therefore, if I have measured myself rightly, occupy comparatively but a short time in discharging the duties that have fallen to my allotment. If my argument be to the purpose—if it be efficient, with relation to the nature and results of this case—it cannot be too *short;* and if it be not appropriate to the cause, and calculated to aid you in your deliberations, and secure your arrival at just results, it must certainly be too *long.*

Now, gentlemen, to set out deliberately and composedly upon our journey, in order to proceed regularly through its progress, I take leave simply to make one or two additional observations. My learned friends and colleagues have already prepared the coloring, and sketched with a master hand the different figures in this sad picture, and it only remains for me [and in that I have been somewhat assisted by the last counsel who addressed you for the defendants] to group those figures together; to impart to them the benefit of light and shade, and leave it to your verdict to complete the work, and then submit it to your honor as the judge—and a ripe and good one —to ratify and approve that which shall have been done.

This, as my learned friend has justly told you, is a most

important case. Not as you will perceive at a single glance, with reference to the stupendous magnitude of the pecuniary amount involved; not that it embraces any considerations directly affecting human life; but because it is unparalleled by any proceeding recorded in the annals of American jurisprudence; and because it comprehends those momentous principles—without the sanctity, protection and vindication of which—even life itself would be a burthen and the world a waste. Let me conjure you to think well of this—don't suppose that the question here is merely whether forty thousand dollars are to pass from the pockets and coffers of the wealthy and respectable into the pockets and coffers of the poor and destitute. I scorn to put this case on any such footing. I am not here as a pauper to BEG; and if I were, the last men to whom I would apply to relieve the wants or the necessities of the plaintiff, would be his heartless persecutors and oppressors.

I am here for justice. Answer—shall I *have* it? That is the question. I don't come to steal it. I don't intend, borrowing an example from the defendants, to take it by *force*. I don't come with my corporal's guard—or armed myrmidons, for the purpose of wresting it from you. I come here to demand it; here in this court of *justice*, and I present to you the basis upon which I build my claims. My learned friend has said, and whatever he says, he says well—and skilfully too—that if you give a verdict for the plaintiff, you deeply affect these defendants in the estimation of the community. These respectable men!—I dare say you will suppose it rather strange to call them so in connection with this case; but whether they are respectable, powerful, wealthy, or otherwise, matters nothing to me—and should matter nothing to you. Those are not the vital considerations here. I don't ask them to share their wealth unless we are entitled to it as an idemnity for our wrongs. I invoke no prejudices. I don't desire to oppress them; on the contrary, the whole philosophy of this case is reared upon a very different doctrine. If instead of a legitimate defence, *they talk of respectability*, I give my answer in the words of Samuel Beans,—the venerable individual who has been so much censured here, because he ventured to encounter this self-created autocracy, if I may call it so,—I answer them in *his* simple though powerful language; "Your characters must be very good, if they will resist the flood and current of proof in regard to this transaction, which sets against and overwhelms them." Why, these sage grave men attempt to make character a mere marketable commodity; not that priceless jewel that my learned friend has spoken of. It is to be a mere shield and protection for iniquity and outrage; for that is what I understand to be the practical end and application of the argument. I agree that character is everything. I agree that the human frame is but a tawdry, empty, worthless casket, when that jewel's gone. But where shall this doctrine land us? That's the point. Had Lord Bacon no character? "The wisest, brightest, meanest of mankind?" Had *he* no intellectual, no moral, no national, no universal character?—broad and expansive as nature itself—yet all this did not save him, when he had committed an atrocious wrong, and sullied the pure ermine—the judicial and national glory—of his country. Was not Dr. Dodd a man of high character? Yet all his character could not save him from the gallows. Nay, if you will pardon me, it is pertinent to the time, and I introduce it with becoming reverence for its associations—was not Judas, one of the disciples, a man of character, until he traitorously betrayed his master with a kiss—and basely sold the Redeemer of the world for "thirty pieces."

Character, so far from being a defence, so far from being matter of vindication or protection; where the testimony is calculated to enforce the claims of the plaintiff, is matter of aggravation, disgrace, and confusion. What is there—while I admit and maintain the elevated position

in which character places man—what is there, I say, that
degrades him, even below the lowest deep of odium and
contempt, more than its willing and wanton sacrifice?
Why, was not Lucifer—surnamed the Morning Star—before his fall, one of the brightest spirits among the angelic
hosts? IIe that *then* stood the highest and the purest;
for that plain reason *now* stands the lowest and the blackest. I wish this subject of character distinctly understood. It is a sort of mawkish sentimentality too often
introduced, to lend grace to a desperate defence. It is
like a moon-beam on a thunder cloud, making the gloom
more dreadful. I repeat it, I am disposed to pay as
warm a tribute to the regard in which reputation is held,
as any man. But I have no notion, no idea, sir, that
gentlemen like these, or any other persons, should imagine
that there is any personal hostility on my part towards
them, because I take leave to speak of them as they deserve.

When the principles of this case are fully understood
you will find little or no trouble in disposing of all its details; and, therefore, I shall address myself to principles
rather than details. It is not necessary for me to apply
chemical process, or a microscope, to analyze or detect
every freckle in a man's face, in order to identify him.
So, if I show you the principles that embrace the diversified facts, that have been brought out during the progress
of this laborious and protracted investigation, and which
bear essentially upon this case; and show you, also, that
the grounds that we occupy, and profess to stand upon,
are sound and unshaken; and that our learned friends in
their attempted assaults upon us, labor under a delusion—
to borrow a phrase from Horace, through the quotation
of Mr. Gibbons—"a dear delusion of a raptured mind;"
you will pardon me, when I say *that* will be abundantly
sufficient.

Really, these men must consider that a very slight
matter is a basis for issuing a commission of lunacy, if

their doctrine be correct; and, if the commission be irregularly issued, I suppose it is perfect indemnity, according to their creed, that comfortable quarters in a mad-house are supplied for their victim.

Let us turn to the beautiful picture, prefixed to the accompanying history—written by Dr. Evans upon the moderate compensation of six hundred dollars a year, for one or two flying visits a week. That history has been read here by the counsel, almost in extenso; and certainly " ad nauseam." He tells you that it is a perfect paradise; don't let him ensnare you with "mere springes to catch wood-cock." Would you not now suppose from this poetic, and romantic, and rapturous description of the Frankford Asylum, that it was a perfect Arcadia? See, how well it appears in the engraving, and in print! Only behold the terraces, the lawn, the gravel walks, the flower gardens, roses, deer parks, and everything of the most attractive and alluring character! And all these luxurious indulgences, says our learned friend, are supervised and secured without even the equivalent of a salary. Amazing Philanthropy! How is this! It seems very wonderful! That wonder disappears when you are told that it is not the *fact*. Philip Garret, Dr. Worthington, Dr. Evans, and a whole retinue of keepers are all abundantly paid. I don't mention this as a matter of complaint; but in refutation of their pretensions, which have been introduced as a part of the defence. And I beg leave to say, with all respect and deference to the learned counsel, that it was an abuse of the patience and time of the court and jury, to press so elaborately upon us, the very equivocal and somewhat meretricious attractions of a private mad-house. I wish when you can be brought to think yourselves insane (though, according to the doctor's notions, you will never be *sane*, until then), you would take up your lodgings in this most magnificent boarding house —making, however, the special provision that you shall have the benefit of the habeas corpus act, in case it so turns out that you should be awakened from your slumbers every hour of the night, or nearly beaten to death by some of its civil and courteous inmates. Why, gentlemen of the jury, this outward parade of comfort is only calculated to sharpen the agony of the sufferer. *Do* you—*can* you, suppose, that the free bird, that has been accustomed to scale the blue vault of heaven, when entrapped and consigned to a costly cage, is consoled by the consideration, if I may ascribe consideration to a bird—rather let me say its instinctive emotional feelings? (to borrow something from the doctors.)—Do you suppose, I say, it is comforted by the fact of the cage being of gold; or, will it not rather beat its fluttering little life out against those golden bars, that shut it in from liberty? It is useless, therefore—nay, worse than useless—to resort to these empty lures. I don't care if this asylum were made of "one entire and perfect chrysolite." What does it come to? What is all that to the famished soul, the degraded and debased spirit, the humiliating sense of a two-fold bondage—bondage of the body, attended with *imputed* bondage at least, of the immortal mind.

With these views—thus generally expressed—while, as I have said, I shall not wantonly trespass on your patience, I shall still devote so much time to the proper examination of the essentials of the subject before us, as may be commensurate with its importance, and a becoming respect to this tribunal. It is my duty to discuss it fairly, though freely and fearlessly; and it will then be your duty to determine upon its merits.

I had spoken, gentlemen of the jury, of the general outlines of this case; and I am sure you will not deem it improper that I should return, for a moment, from a slight wandering—into which I have been seduced by the example of others—to its individual and relative conse· quences. It is important to the plaintiff as an unauthorized and cruel abridgement of his liberty—liberty without which "life grows insipid and has lost its relish;" it is important as it bears upon the bodily and mental sufferings to which he was subjected—the exposure and disgrace to which he was causelessly condemned; it is important as it regards the arbitrary assumption and waste of his little property—the result of the honest earnings of a life of toil; but it is infinitely more important in its relative effects—sundering him from the affections and consolations of a beloved wife, to whom my learned friends wish to transfer all responsibility in this case—to the wife, and to the mother!—a fine specimen of professional gallantry!—in order that they might fight under a woman's 'kerchief, and convert it into a shield. I will show you that this cannot avail them. I wish you to stand upon your guard in relation to this ingenious suggestion; and not to suppose, that it originates in anything else than the anxious desire of these defendants to escape just retribution. There sit, sir, the master spirits, who, while they stood behind the scenes and governed others at their will, never, from first to last, have been able to show that the wife of the plaintiff voluntarily threw off her allegiance to her husband. And if they had been able to show it, what can it avail: how does it diminish the horrors of this scene, that the plaintiff, like the wounded bird, should discover upon the shaft by which he perished, a feather from his own wing. This slander upon the wife is an additional aggravation of the outrage upon the husband; and should be so considered and punished by you. This is a sad though an awful mode of getting rid of a prosecution for a conspiracy. The wife of course cannot be questioned —she cannot be a witness: they have nothing, therefore, to do but to throw out such suggestions against a broken-hearted woman—broken-hearted by them—in order to escape responsibility for the ruin they have caused. For I aver, that all the difficulties between this husband and wife, have been produced by them, or some of them. I charge upon them, that it was by their injudicious inter-

meddling, or interfering between two hearts, that Heaven
is presumed to have formed for each other, that a paradise of conjugal love and affection was converted into a
desert. I wish them to bear in mind, if they can derive
no other benefit from these admonitions, the salutary
doctrine, that those whom God unites, man should never
attempt to sunder. Why, sir! I profess to have some
pretty extensive knowledge in respect to matters of this
kind, though, thank Heaven, no experience; and I take
leave to say, that in nine instances out of ten of family
discord, the disunion produced between husband and
wife, is attributable to some cogging, cozening knave,
who, with or without other motives than the mere disposition to do evil and render others as unhappy as himself,
spreads a ruin round: or perhaps, it may be sometimes
properly ascribed to some gossipping old women, who
exercise the prescriptive right of sacrificing human happiness by the decrees of the Areopagus of the tea-table.
They arise in this case from some such causes. And
their authors must be gratified in having succeeded in
dividing the interests and joys of husband and wife, who,
in the pithy language of the law, have " two bodies,
though but one mind." Only sever that mind—the immortal portion of human beings—what confusion, desolation, distress, and destruction, must inevitably be
produced? All this, shocking as it may appear, is to
be traced to the defendants in this case, and their confederates.

You will find, all these deplorable consequences are
really attributable to these defendants. Why what is
the meaning of Samuel Richie's having been out to the
farm a year or two before—which he himself expressly
admits? Has your honor lost sight of that? Richie
and others have pursued this unhappy plaintiff, like a
vulture who never loses the scent of blood. What does
he find when he reaches the farm? He finds Morgan as
sane as he, or any man in this community. He finds him

deeply seated in the respect and affections of a large surrounding neighborhood. And he finds, also, that that was neither the time nor the place to attempt an aggression on the plaintiff's rights. He therefore returns to the city, and waits for a more favorable opportunity to renew his attempt. Opportunities will always be afforded, where there is a disposition to embrace them, however they present themselves.

I say, then, that relatively the effects upon the plaintiff have been ruinous in sundering him from the affections and consolations of his wife; and that these effects are attributable to these defendants. His wife has been really, bodily, taken from him; and my respectable friend, Mr. Griscom, professionally imbued with his client, seems actually astonished that the husband, to use the counsel's own language, "should require his wife for his own purposes!" Heaven save the mark!—whose purposes should he want her for? Is it not wonderful that a man should be taunted in a court of justice, for desiring his own wife? And was it extraordinary that he should not consent to live with a sister-in-law—subject to her direction and control, and liable to be whisked off, at any convenient season, to the asylum again? The plaintiff had never used his wife for any other than a kind and a noble purpose; and therefore he was entitled to her confidence, and I have no doubt, really enjoyed it; for I maintain that you cannot find in any portion of this case, from unquestionable evidence, that she ever complained or murmured against him.

But we are referred to this flighty matter of his attempting to hang himself, as related by old Mrs. Clark; who *admitted* herself to be insane once or twice during her deposition, and who *proved* herself to be insane in every part of it; and who seemed to *consider* the magistrate insane, for correctly reporting her testimony.

We find that when Mrs. Hinchman was spoken to, and the various slanders against her husband repeated, she

promptly and utterly denies them, and avers that they
are without the shadow of a foundation. And this, too,
in the presence of her sister, one of the defendants; and
yet, in spite of this denial, Samuel Richie, in speaking
to Samuel Beans, repeats them again.

[The opposite counsel here remarked, that the story of
the alleged hanging was not alluded to by Mrs. Hinchman.] I did not say that it was expressly alluded to; but
I do say that so far as the slanders related to misconduct
or personal violence, she promptly and with a womanly
spirit utterly denied them.

I have already said that the course of these defendants
was obstructive to the happiness of the wife, as well as
the husband; but it is still more to be deplored in its
effects in separating him from the innocent embraces of
his prattling children—one of whom, at least, he was
doomed never again to see. Indeed no humane man can
listen to the simple history of the wrongs he has sustained, the penalties he has endured, and the sufferings
he has borne, without being convinced of the total inadequacy of language to embellish or exaggerate it. The
plain statement presented to you in the most undisguised,
and unadorned shape—for truth like beauty when least
adorned, is most adorned—would be sufficient to bring
you, if my sympathies instruct me rightly, to a conclusion which would sweep away at once all the defendants'
testimony—so transitory in point of character, and so
unsubstantial in point of worth.

Allow me in the next place, as a matter of vindication—
of what both my learned friends, in their nice sense of
morality, have considered as an anomaly in Ethics—to
refer to the remark of my friend and colleague that " the
effect of insanity in this world's view, absolutely and relatively, was as much to be deplored as even that of
crime itself." You must have observed, gentlemen of the
jury, that Mr. Gibbons occupied a considerable time upon
this subject. It is no doubt, convenient to the defend-

ants' cause, to throw the deformities which it exhibits into the shade, by presenting some collateral subjects on which the mind may more agreeably rest. Both of my opponents tell you, that the remarks of my colleague are utterly incomprehensible, if not reprehensible, in implying the doctrine, that the existence of crime in a parent was not more to be deprecated than imputed insanity. Now, may it please your honor, you seemed rather to adopt the views of the opposite counsel; but if you will hear me for a moment I will satisfy you of their entire fallacy.

My learned friend told you only a melancholy truth: for although, when your honor said there is no criminality in insanity you spoke only the sentiment of your own excellent heart—let us apply the *head* to it. There is no criminality in insanity, it is true, and there *ought* to be no disgrace; but the question is not what *ought* to be, but what there *is,* in this unkind, unsympathetic, and slanderous world. The mere absence of crime is no protection against imputed insanity; which may be called the curse of the burning brow—the curse of the sleepless eye —" to have no creature love you living, nor your memory when dead."

Gentlemen of the jury—What man among you can look at the plaintiff and behold his destitute and forlorn condition, and listen to the simple story of his sufferings, caused by the acts of these men, and can safely return to his avocations till he performs a solemn lustration through the instrumentality of their hoarded gains? What has been his portion? Shrunk from like a pestilence. How has he been treated by these pious defendants, though certified to be sane? Who has taken him by the hand? None but his " paternal relatives "—I borrow the word. What has been the effect of the course pursued towards him by these defendants? The effect has been to defame, to destroy him. I agree there is no crime in insanity; but there is obloquy, worse than crime. For although a son may not wash white the crimson garments of a father, yet he is not compelled to *wear* them ; and he may at least preserve his *own* unspotted and unstained.

But in such a case as this, a case of alleged insanity, do you forget you poison the very fountain of a man's blood—nay, you corrupt the blood of all united with him ;—his children and his children's children, have *that* for an assured inheritance! Speak not to me in regard to this being no disgrace. They all derive it from him, though it should be their only legacy. He does not, Saturn-like, devour his own offspring; but he desecrates them, and deprives them of all honorable and reputable association. I speak to experience. Why, has not your honor adverted to the fact, that although our learned opponents deny the doctrine of my colleagues; they practically adopt it, while they maintain its fallacy. Have not the counsel even inquired, upon this trial, in the cross-examination of our witnesses, whether there was not insanity among the ancestry or relatives of the plaintiff? [Defendants' counsel here interrupt—and assert the question was from the jury.] Mr. Brown replies. Well it was pursued and followed up by the counsel. If it came from the jury, so much the better; they have practically adopted my doctrines before they were mentioned. So may it also be in after days with *his* helpless and innocent *children*—and his children's children—and his name shall be quoted as a living and hereditary curse —a curse that more than kills—down to the last syllable of time.

I speak of this, and I speak of it emphatically, for it is like the iron that enters the soul—like the worm that never dies.

Interrupt me gentlemen—I shall be happy to answer any suggestion—it throws me into no confusion. I will be happy to hear any intimation that may relieve our "*friends*" from their uncomfortable position ; and I wish to contribute to the benefit of these defendants themselves, by teaching them a salutary lesson of future forbearance. Is further proof required? Does not Edward Richie—mark me and refer to your notes if necessary—Does not Edward, in a conversation in relation to putting property in trust with the plaintiff's "paternal relative" —I thank you for teaching me that word—give as a reason for the plaintiff's executing a deed of trust—or for his permitting L. Mifflin, whom they had caused to be created a trustee of his person and estate, to *remain* in control of matters—that Morgan Hinchman would henceforth be suspected and mistrusted, and thereby rendered virtually incompetent to transact his *own* business. That must not be lost sight of. Does he not give as a reason, the very argument that his counsel have condemned? Does he not say, when the plaintiff comes into the world nobody will trust in him—will confide in him? He will be a mere object of scorn and reproach. But his *friends* will be able to manage his property, take care of his wife and children, and do all for him. Do you remember that?

"They pluck out his beard—then throw it in his face." —Extraordinary sagacity—admirable charity—unparalleled friendship!!

Again, my learned antagonist, denying my colleague's doctrine, still tells you: "after the decision of Dr. Kite and committee—the plaintiff no longer walks the streets untainted." Will that do? That comes from the very counsel. Well what has that to do with the argument? —their own report? Does that justify *themselves* in trampling him into his original earth? That's a hard doctrine! That's a monstrous doctrine! May it please your honor, it is a doctrine that you will never sanction. It's a doctrine this jury will never be inclined to approve. *Tainted how?* Why, by the opprobrium of insanity. Thus you perceive while they deny the position assumed by my colleague, they essentially adopt it, as their excuse, for *exacting from an alleged lunatic a deed of trust.* I am amazed! Brought up and educated among them—knowing as I supposed much about them—it seems to me that this is a strange state of things. I am *not* speaking, let it be understood, of the *whole body* now; but they talk of the Pope—*why the Pope's a fool to a Quaker overseer!* Does your honor know how the vote is taken in matters connected with Friends' Discipline? It was indicated in the progress of this cause: There are, say 150 persons present at a meeting—147 vote one way, the three overseers vote the other way—the clerk has nothing to do but put down, that the *weight* of the meeting is against the *majority*—a perfect autocracy, if it was not for its number—it is a divided though reserved power possessing great and illimitable authority. But your honor remembers they did give him a certificate of good standing, recommending him to their unsuspecting brethren of Bucks County—whom you have seen here as witnesses on his behalf—so you see it was the weight of one meeting, against the weight of another meeting.

With your permission, I will now endeavor (having vindicated those united with me professionally) to present to you, under a hasty but orderly argument, some of the characteristic and controlling principles and facts involved in the consideration of this case.

Before I proceed to discuss the question of sanity in its application to the present case, it is necessary that we should understand rather better than the *doctors* appear to do, some of those metaphysical principles, not to say refinements, which are most intimately connected with the immediate subject of our inquiries. Now I do not profess to be more than a mere purveyor of secondary supplies to your honor; but nevertheless, I will give the result in fifteen minutes of what a personal examination in detail, would occupy as many months.

It is unnecessary to remind the court—nevertheless it is not unworthy of your regard—that " man," as the Bible truly and divinely tells us, " is fearfully and wonderfully made." He is composed of qualities somewhat opposite—

nay, directly so, if you please. He consists of different natures, marvellously mixed. In his best condition—with a sound mind every way considered, in a sound body, every way considered—a sound mind in regard to moral influences, and in regard to its intellectual power—and a solid, substantial, and vigorous body—man is very little short of an angel. If the opposite exist in his constitution, he is very little short of a demon.

MIND, as I understand it, and as I took leave to say in the course of my examination of Dr. Evans, in reply to his question—(when he turned cross-examiner, and I turned witness)—MIND, is a term applied to the aggregate of man's intellectual mental powers and faculties. When we speak of the body, we speak of the aggregate of his physical functions, organs, and faculties. And it is, though I cannot dwell upon it, undoubtedly a most interesting portion of this discussion. It is a subject, perhaps, in reference to which there is more anxiety than is occasioned by any other in the entire scope of what may be called metaphysics. Mind is sometimes confounded with the soul; but, sir, it is not the soul. Let us disabuse ourselves on these matters. Mind is not the soul. It is *one* of the *qualities or attributes* or constituents *of* the soul. It belongs to it, it is *of* it. It no longer, or no further, belongs to the *body*, than as it employs the body as a medium of communication with external things in this nether world—otherwise our virtues or vices would not, to any extent, depend upon our intelligence. The mind's own direct communication is with its great Creator. The mind is never *diseased ;* and here I differ from Dr. Wood, and I trust it is the last occasion that I shall have for a difference with a physician in that respect. A physician knows nothing more about the mind, except through the medium of the body, than he does about the moon. But, nevertheless, in the line of his duty—like a lawyer—it is scarcely possible for him to have intercourse with men in their various and different relations, without forming some conclusions on the subject. Yet Dr. Wood tells you that the mind, *he thinks* (though he does not know), *can* be diseased, and the body be sound. May it please your honor, that can never be. The mind is a ray or emanation of the Deity himself. It is *His* miniature resemblance, impressed on man! " 'Tis the Divinity which stirs within us." If the mind could be *diseased,* it follows, of course, it could *die;* and what then becomes of the sublime doctrine of the immortality of the soul? Infidelity and the notion of total annihilation must take its place. Nay, further, if the mind can be diseased, even angels may go mad. This doctrine, *impious* as the thought may be, does not stop short of the derangement of the Sovereign Ruler of the Universe! Omnipotence himself could not escape; for He created man in his own image, and imparted to the creature a ray of his own mind. *He* is the only perfect mind. If the mind—the immortal part of man—can be affected with insanity; insanity shall spread undivided, and extend through the whole celestial system—and Heaven itself might be converted into a lunatic asylum.

The soul, of which I have said the mind is a constituent, is the immortal principle which is connected for a time with the material world, by means of our physical organization. We can have, sir, no *knowledge* of the mind or soul, of *ourselves ;* I mean of its source or origin—for how can finite measure infinite: You might as well attempt to measure the ocean with a thimble. Our *reason* cannot comprehend it: it can only be conceived of through revelation and faith. The only perfect mind, as has been said, is God himself: that great Mind, the source and support of all. "To see ourselves," in the language of Lord Bacon—and this should be written in characters of gold ; " we must not look *up ;* we must look *down.*" The mind is like the eye, which sees not itself, but by reflection—by its action on external objects; by its power of receiving impressions through the physical faculties.

There is, sir—and it is very strange, passing strange—there is a class of materialists who have no notion but that the *pineal* gland—which is in the centre of the structure of the brain, of the form of a pine apple, and about the size of a pea—inasmuch as it is a solitary organ or gland, and all the other organs of the brain are *coupled* as all the senses are ; that, therefore, I say, having—as far as they can discover, with all their ingenuity, no obvious connection or communication with the rest—is the peculiar abode or tenement of the soul. How preposterous! When once we get among these scientific enthusiasts, they play *hocus pocus* with natural simplicity. Though Shakspeare says " the times have been, that, when the brains were out, the man would die:" yet since his time, science has discovered that a great part of the brain may be removed, and even the pineal gland itself, yet the mind or soul remain perfect! Certainly that goes to show that it is not destroyed by mere physical influences alone. The brain, it is true, is the *organ* of sensation ; the channel of communication between the physical and intellectual powers of man. But the brain, though the organ of sensation, is in itself perishable, and insensible. Its wounds are attended with no pain ; and yet the sensibilities to pain in any other part of the system depends upon the brain itself. Only sever the nerve which leads to it, from the injured part, and all consciousness of suffering is lost. Remove the brain, or a large portion of it, the creature may still live, the soul still exist ; but the mind is unable to act upon external objects, as the physical medium of communication is gone. In short, I sum up this doctrine by saying that all minds, as minds—and this is consolatory, sir—all minds originally, are in their capacity alike. The Hottentot, or the idiot, has as much mind as Bacon, or Newton, or Milton, or Shakspeare—or *even* Dr. Wood, or Dr. Evans. But your honor perceives what I am coming at ; they have not the same physical susceptibilities ; the warder is asleep at the portal of the castle, and makes no announcement to the immortal part of man, of the approach of friend or foe. The mind has no sentinel, no outposts, no communication with the external world, from which instruction may be derived as far as regards the temporal concerns of life. It is like, in short—what is it like? It is like (though it is somewhat degrading to be sure), like Morgan Hinchman within the melancholy walls of the Frankford Mad-house. It cannot communicate with anything outside; nothing outside can communicate with it. It is locked up within its cell in Tartarian darkness; it is not susceptible of instruction; it is not susceptible of the heavenly light of liberty ; it is not sensible of anything but the vacuity of its own solitary immortality. To give a simple illustration of the perversion of thought, by diseased physical functions, I can refer to a case which your honor has been familiar with—a remarkable instance. A man who has had a paralysis, will either not know men with whom he has been familiar, or will call men by wrong names; say yes, when he means, no; as was the case with a very learned and estimable friend of yours, who when he meant to affirm anything, said " no ;" and when he would deny a thing, said " yes." Do you suppose his mind was changed? Not at all ; the functions or faculties that joined him with external matter were destroyed or perverted. [Judge Burnside remarks, I made his will for him, and a very good will it was. Mr. Brown replies, he was a man, sir, not only good in WILL, but in DEED; it is well he did not fall into the hands of the defendants.] In the case of persons affected with paralysis, the functions of the body, instead of furnishing the facilities for intercourse between the soul and this external world, are perverted, obtunded, or destroyed ; " and the state of man, like to a little kingdom, suffers then the nature of an insurrection." Not that those persons have lost their mind, but that their mind is misrepresented by the imperfect or diseased, organs of the body ; which communicate false impressions, or convey impressions falsely. The communication with the governing principle being lost or perverted, every function or faculty runs into licentiousness and confusion; and all the harmonies of the mental, moral, and physical structure become,

> " Like sweet bells jangled—
> Out of tune, and harsh—"

But I pass on. I have a word to say as to *moral* insanity. It is a new theory—who understands it—emotional insanity! Has not your honor been astonished by this doctrine? Why it is like some of the French dancing; it is like what Addison calls a "regular confusion;" it is like the polka; it is like all the frippery, sir, of the French schools—though I am an admirer of them—full of phantastic inventions! *They* are full of jimcrackery—*moral* insanity! Our friends, are plain citizens, grave men—they ought to look before they leap, or they will fall into mazes, from which even Ariadne's clue could never extricate them. Why it's neither fish, flesh, nor red herring! but something among them all! I will tell you what moral insanity is—it is that corruption of the moral faculties which is the result of long continued crime, becoming, by habit, too strong for rational or conscientious control. That's what it is; and that is not a matter which puts a man in the mad-house, it puts him in the *penitentiary*. I believe Dr. Wood said that moral insanity often exists without intellectual—and without the body being diseased. How can that be? there is no moral insanity, unless it affect the immortal mind: talking of morals without mind is ridiculous—perfectly ridiculous. You might as well talk of the morals of a dead body. Moral insanity is nothing more than a division formed by metaphysicians, of intellectual insanity. They place it in the heart, because the heart is termed the throne of the passions; they don't allow it to be attributed to the head or the mind, without which man's affectious or passions are nothing at all! I have thought proper to advert to these things, because they are interesting; and not altogether unimportant in the use that is given them. I must shortly advert to a more admirable science, which I trust we understand quite as well. Though before passing on, permit me to say I have been disappointed! surprised! confounded! at the sequel of that magnificent volume whose preface promised so much wisdom. I did suppose, that the gentleman who could write such a romantic history of the deer parks and flower gardens of an asylum, might have devoted *some* portion of his leisure to metaphysical pursuits— "*utile cum dulce*"—which would have appeared to much better advantage when exhibited on this occasion.

Having thus cursorily discussed the metaphysical portion of this question, the next subject in order, and more important, though not more interesting, is THE LAW—the greatest of all earthly sciences, and embracing quite as much metaphysics, quite as much of the important relations of every earthly science, as any other. It is the QUEEN of the temporal sciences; those that are directed to explain the knowledge of the Creator, are *above* comparison—above ROYALTY.

Now, it will be my duty, and I hope my learned opponents will pardon me, to show—not that they are quite as much misled as the doctors themselves, in what they deem their peculiar province, but that they are very egregiously mistaken. Indeed I thought they might for a time, have led your honor into their views, until by accident they stumbled upon the case reported in Binney —which promulgated the doctrine of want of probable cause and malice—which doctrine I aver to you has, so far as the purposes of our present inquiries go, no more to do with it than the Copernicau system. They make that their defence—their turning point; and if I take that poor refuge away—dispel that delusion—they have no pillow upon which to rest their disconsolate heads.

Didn't you observe that our learned friends "caught a Tartar," in reading the authority referred to. It was read for *one* purpose, but unfortunately it has in it a principle which destroys the *whole* defence. Now, sir, although the observation is not remarkable for its modesty—for which *lawyers* you know are remarkable; nevertheless, I may be permitted to say, that I profess to understand the doctrine which has been applied to this branch of the case as fully as it can be understood—for that requires no Solomon. I understand it, and your honor understands it; and by comparing notes we shall all understand it better. Now, sir, what is a *conspiracy?*—because we must begin here—there is no managing an argument by jumping into the middle of it. A conspiracy, gentlemen of the jury, is not half so complicated as you might suppose. It is the agreement of two or more persons to do an unlawful act; or it is an agreement of an equal number of persons—that is, two or more—to do a lawful act in an unlawful manner. To show you what is necessary to establish a conspiracy, though I don't wish to pause to read books, I refer you to 2 Russell, p. 697, edition of 1845. I don't intend to read it, because your honor understands it as well as Mr. Russell; but it is sometimes a facility to give you the page, which may save you the trouble of research. Now allow me to tell you that any person who is art or part, either in doing, or conspiring to do, an unlawful act; or is art or part in adopting an unlawful manner of doing a lawful act, is a conspirator.

It is not necessary, as his honor will tell you, that an act should be done. I am now speaking of the criminal character of conspiracy. It is not necessary that an act should be done at all. Nay, if the act be a felony, the conspiracy is lost utterly; for being but a misdemeanor it is merged in the graver offence. It is the *agreement* to do the act which constitutes the crime. Your honor will perceive the beautiful philosophy of the law—not like the metaphysical moonshine that is introduced here.

The whole law, and especially the criminal law, consists of a system of checks and safeguards. It is the protection of the community against vice—and subserves the *divine law* in forming, guarding and inducing virtue, in man. That is the basis of it—build upon that—the object is not to punish; the object is to prevent or reform. What does it do? As long as man keeps his design within his heart—within his breast—though it be of demoniac gloom and blackness, of course human tribunals cannot suspect it, and cannot affect it. He is left to the punishment of the Omnipotent; "for darkness and light are both alike to Him." *He* alone can pry into the deep recesses of the sinner's bosom; drag forth the secret motive from its hiding place, and expose it to the reproaches of an affrighted and horror-stricken world. What can man do in such a case? I can tell you what he *can* do, and what he *does* do. The moment that, by the slightest whisper, the inward workings and purposes of the culprit's mind are communicated to the officer of justice, he becomes amenable to justice. Beautiful system! Here is a man who *intends* to take the life of another; his motive and his purpose are known only to that power that can fathom the ocean. The motive *there* is equal to the act —it is the act *itself.* The motive *here* is nothing, till it be accompanied by the act; because it cannot be detected. If a man having the design, simply say, I will take the life of A. B. (though he may have been plotting it for years), he is taken before a judicial officer and is bound over; the incipient impress of the devil is detected in him. Upon this system of checks, the guilty purpose is noticed, and he is prevented from sinking lower in the gulf of crime. He is not punished, for he cannot be indicted; he has done no act; he cannot be indicted for *saying* he will do a thing; he is only bound over to keep the peace; no laws go farther. But still observe the admirable system of the law.: the moment he communicates that design to Mr. Richie; and Mr. Richie

unites with him in the design ; and that becomes known
—though they do not take a single step towards it—they
are both subject to be indicted and punished for an infamous crime. See how the law checks the downward
course of guilt.

The action on the case, in the nature of a writ of conspiracy, is one of our ancient inheritances. It has nothing to do with the doctrine of criminal conspiracy.

Now, sir, to the difference which your honor has somewhat anticipated. In a criminal court, the mere agreement, without any act, can be punished and has been
punished a thousand times. In a civil court, the mere
agreement without any act, cannot be noticed. I ask
your ratification (his honor nods), you will give it; I
have only to suggest it. How can you punish it in a
civil court? You proceed for *damages*, if a man has conspired in malice. If two persons have agreed corruptly
together, and institute proceedings before a magistrate,
that is the overt act. They may be punished in a civil
court, because it produces injury; but as long as the conspiracy rests as a naked conspiracy—a mere *agreement*—so
long it is not punishable in any way by a civil tribunal.
It is not there actionable at all. But to make it so, it is
necessary some injurious act should be done. Now, sir,
what is the force of the case of Munns and Dupont, and
the two cases quoted by my learned opponent, Mr. Griscom—who certainly said as much as could have been said
in a bad cause. They have no importance at all, permit
me to say. They have not a particle more to do with
this issue, than with the law in relation to ejectments; or
any other utterly irrelative matter.

I say, may it please your honor, that the whole of this
doctrine is settled in a work adverted to, but not fully
read, by my learned friend, Mr. Perkins—the best work
known to the law—I refer to, 1st Williams' Saunders, page
230. If your honor will permit it to be handed to you,
you will find at page 230 (in the notes which consist of

some two or three pages in the case of Skinner *v.* Gunton
and Lyon), the whole doctrine most admirably laid down,
with all the necessary references and authorities. There
is one feature that may strike you, as a little remarkable: though your honor is a ripe and experienced lawyer, these things do not always occur in the practice of
one short life. You know that in an action on the case,
in the nature of a writ of conspiracy, you can convict
one person, where there are but two charged. Go into a
criminal court, indict two persons for a conspiracy, for
the purpose of testing this matter—acquit one—and you
acquit the other. Does not that satisfy any man of the
distinction between the character of the two cases; and
to show your honor the soundness of the doctrine, I present to you a very brief reference to Buller's Nisi Prius,
page 14: "If the action be brought against several, and
one only be found guilty, it is sufficient. There is considerable difference between this form of action on the
case, and the old writ of conspiracy." If I were to read
all day, I should only come to the same result. I'm not
in favor of reading books in public places; a man's study
is perhaps the best place; but I'll just refer to page 230
of the same book, which has been alluded to—Williams'
Saunders, page 230—in refutation of their entire doctrine
in respect to civil actions for conspiracy, sounding in
damages. In criminal cases, the conspiracy to do a wrong
is punishable, although the wrong be not accomplished;
but in civil cases, twenty thousand conspiracies amount
to nothing, without positive, or constructive injury, to the
party. The injury, therefore, is the ground of the action,
although the confederacy may be matter of aggravation.

In a criminal case, I repeat it, at least *two* must conspire, and one cannot be convicted without the other. In
a civil case, a verdict may be found against any one, or all
of the defendants.

This is "Crowner's Quest Law," and every tyro, or neo-
phyte, is bound to know it.

But they contend we are obliged to prove malice, and want of probable cause, as well as·confederacy. *That* I will defeat just as readily as the other position they have ventured to assume. Not, that it is very important, for they are both proved *here*, as I shall satisfy you, ere I have done with the case. But it is not necessary that *either* should be proved, as they are inherent to the act itself.

The act itself sufficiently implies malice. The operation of the theory—as your honor will perceive with your perspicacity—is that these defendants cannot get relief from rumors that *they* themselves put in circulation. Malice is no where more necessary than in murder; yet, if—according to the Spanish custom in some of the West India Islands—a felon runs *a muck;* and strikes dead any or every other man in his way, for the gratification of some demoniacal principle, or some fanatical impulse, and he is arrested and brought before a judicial tribunal to answer for his deeds—must I prove malice? Why, sir, I have nothing to do but to point to the dead body—to hold up the bloody dagger—and all nature with her thousand voices exclaims, malice!—malice!!—malice!!!—and the matter's done—the question's settled. It is no answer to say—one of the victims was his twin brother, sprung from the same loins, with whom he had always been on the most intimate terms; and another was a man he never knew or saw—and *could* he entertain malice? The law says your acts—and it is not necessary to go beyond *them* —speak of malice, "and manifest a heart regardless of social duty and fatally bent upon mischief." It's no answer to say he was ignorant of the law. Ignorance of the law excuses no man. Malice is not always confined to the blood-thirsty, or hasty in disposition. It sometimes contrives its snares in secret, and watches long years for its opportunity to revenge some fancied slight or unforgiven offence; and sometimes it is a reckless, careless indifference to the just rights of our fellow men. In some

instances *this* may be culpable; and the law says to the
culprit—your felon hand was directed against all laws,
human and divine, as well as against the ordinary light
of reason, and you must expia'e your offence upon the
gallows!

There is a wide distinction between the case cited by
our learned opponents, and the case we are engaged in
adjudicating: a difference very interesting, very important, and easily distinguished. The case they quoted, was
an action for malicious prosecution; to which the doctrine
of malice, and want of probable cause, is applicable. Here
it is *not* necessary to be proved. Why, your honor knows
it is not necessary to prove anything in connection with
slanderous words—in themselves actionable. The action
for malicious prosecution (to which their argument is
solely applicable), is brought against those, who have
sought to punish the plaintiff, by resorting to legal process. Then the law takes care of its own. In the case of
Munns and Dupont—and a thousand other cases that
might be mentioned—the law says: you have appealed to
the law—you have made oath—you have issued your
warrant—you have arrested this man—brought him to
trial, and it happens either by mischance, accident, or in
some way, the charge fails, and he escapes; but it is contrary to the policy of the law that he should turn upon
his pursuer. In such a case the law presumes there was
no malice. I won't allow—says Justice—my temple to
be converted into an arena, for conflict between a man
who has prosecuted, *according to law*, from good and allowable motives, and the person who for want of proof,
has escaped by the clemency or charity of the law. I
won't—says Justice—raise a presumption against an individual who has resorted for protection to my hallowed
temples. We presume *everything in favor of the man who
confides in the law*. Now I am sure I make myself understood. But, may it please your honor, it is a widely different matter, when *instead of proceeding under the law*, a

body of men *take the law into their own hands. It is only the man who wields the* SWORD *of the law, that enjoys protection from the* SHIELD *of the law.* That is the sum total of the whole doctrine. The men who employ their *own* swords, or their *private* daggers, for their *private* purposes—defying the law, and trampling upon it—appeal in vain, in their extremity, for the application of those principles, that *they* only are entitled to, whose resort has been to *legal means.* Show me a case, sir, in which the want of probable cause, or malice—as being necessary to be proved—ever arose, where the original arrest was an illegal one! Shall it be tolerated, may it please your honor—to bring this suggestion closely upon the heels of these defendants —that half a dozen men shall seize you, without oath or warrant, with impunity (while half a dozen of their confederates shall watch for you in the neighborhood) and bear you away to a *private* mad-house? Why, what said Mr. Allen, one of these managers, produced here as a witness for these defendants—and who, by-the-by, seems as cold and heartless as the marble mortar he has so long pounded with his pestle? Having been brought up in his drug shop among preserved reptiles, and "alligators stuffed," he seems to have imbibed some portion of the venom, that once actuated his companions. He says, in answer to your honor's inquiry, that on the mere certificate of any doctor whatever, no matter how obtained, he would consign me, or any one of the hundreds in this court room, to incarceration in this private prison near Frankford. Yes, on his affirmation, he declares he would! He did not blink the question—take us all! Remember this, gentlemen of the jury. (Defendants' counsel remind Mr. Brown that the witness said he would require a bond.) Mr. B. continues: Yes, a bond of indemnity—a bond to pay three or six dollars a week. What do they care for the law? All he cares for is the bond; that's right, old Shylock,—stick to "the bond."

And shall we now be told—will any man maintain,

when such men are brought into a court of justice—that they may fold their arms and say, " Well, here we are, now you must prove a *want of probable* cause, and *malice;* you never saw some of us before! No! (says the law) I don't know you; you are outlaws; you are not the children of the law; the presumptions of the law are not in *favor* of you, but they are *against* you—and all your kith, kin, kidney, and companions. That, I understand, is the doctrine to be applied to this arrest; which was not committed under authority, but in open, direct, bold, barefaced violation of that law, which is your pro- tection and mine—nay, which is also the protection of these very defendants; resembling, in that respect, the beneficence of the sun of Heaven, which smiles alike upon the poor and the rich, the weak and the powerful, the oppressed and their oppressors. The law is the protection of the very men who have ventured to violate it; and it will be a dark day for them if the principles could be established that they now contend for. They would be among the first to feel the effects of that whirlwind of passion, that would inevitably break forth. Let them beware how they ask your sanction to a doctrine that will destroy those great ties, that bind together and protect society. They know not how soon, in the circling changes of life, they may be subject to its application. The prosperous of to-day—pass but a few years—are oftimes the lowly; seeking the shelter of that very law which throws its impartial protection over its meanest subjects. Such is the beneficence, the wisdom of the law —such the justice of the law; which is but the handmaid of that divine law which flows from the throne or seat of God himself.

Now, sir, I will show you with a single authority, that the decision is as I have stated; and that is the one which my friend ran afoul of. It is the opinion of one of the best men that ever sat on the bench; and perhaps as bright as any other. It will be found page 172 of 1st

Binney. "It seems that in an action on the case in the nature of conspiracy, it is not necessary to declare, that the conspiracy was without probable cause." Here, too, was a regular and formal charge, preferred in the form of an affidavit, in a legitimate tribunal. I ask them to show me any case, where the arrest was *without* authority, in which anything was said about probable cause. It would be converting the temple of justice into a private arena for gladitors, " The defendant's counsel have based their arguments on the first point (*i. e.*, in regard to probable cause), on this position, that the analogy between actions for a malicious prosecution and the present action is so great as to warrant the conclusion that the declarations should be alike, in alleging the want of probable cause. There is, however, a considerable difference between these actions. The action for malicious prosecution being founded on a malicious proceeding by the defendant in a court of justice, there is more reason for alleging and proving in that action, than in this, that there was no probable cause for the prosecution; for where legal process is issued, the presumption, *prima facie*, must be, that the proceeding was proper."

We presume malice, *prima facie*, and put it upon the opposite party to remove the presumption, by proving probable cause, and want of malice. There is no use of a man's enjoying the benefit of the presumption of the law, if he is bound to prove it. The character of the pre-sumption throws the necessity for exculpatory proof on the opposite party. What they have to do is, not to call on *us* to prove all that took place in their orgies; in their different meetings; in their grand divans, in which the plot to cleave down this man's liberty was laid. Let *them* show anything calculated to *justify* them; for nothing short of *justification* answers in the pleadings of this case. Let them even show anything to mitigate the offence, and not resort to matters of this sort. They presume their victim insane, and want us to prove all

that took place in their secret meetings. It is out of the
question. It cannot be.

(Judge B. Suppose the jury be of the opinion that the
man was in a state of partial insanity, and this man was
arrested from pure motives, and not with a view to pecuniary gain?)

My answer is this—(because it must be qualified) if
that partial insanity were of such a character as to render
the arrest imperative, in order to the protection of life or
limb; or to forestall impending danger; then I hold them
excused. But would your honor apply it to the case of
a harmless· and unoffending citizen, who for seven years,
under the very eyes of these men, and from their hands,
receives certficates of competency and sufficiency? Why
they never doubt his sanity, until he gets money; until
the trust was revoked. I do not mean to say that where
the man is raving, you should not be permitted to arrest
him, for his benefit or for the safety of the community;
nor do I mean to say that it necessarily follows that you
do a wrong act where you arrest him without a warrant;
but I do mean to say that when you do arrest him, you
must make good the charge. If you do it, you do it at
your peril. Do it in a legal mode, the law is your shield
—but don't go into the highways and by-ways, to seek
evidence, which, if true, was utterly unknown to you at
the time. What your motives are, you best know:
prove that yourselves! Show there was an actual neces·
sity. Show the man was guilty—show he was insane—
show why the character of his guilt, or insanity, required
this disregard of the law. Show that there was no time
to take him with authority. All these enter into the application of the principle. One of these points is decided
in the case at p. 452, Watt's Reports; where the doctrine
is fully laid down. But where the man has a known
residence where he may be found; shall he be waylaid and
arrested, without authority? Why, may it please your
honor, this would be the most hazardous doctrine that

ever was known. You may *not* arrest a man without cause.

A police officer may arrest; but let him look to the bill of rights, and not break down the constitutional protection of the citizens, for the purpose of meeting fancied exigencies. If, on the contrary, you proceed, on your own responsibility—with the intimation that you must abide the consequences—must do it at your peril—then you will do it only when you feel secured. Why, sir, the king of England himself— I don't know what the queen might do, for women assume many responsibilities,—the king would not dare to do what our puritanical and peaceful Friends have done. Does it not strike you all with astonishment, that the descendants of Penn—as Mr. Gibbons called them—and the great-grandfathers of Penn— as my friend Griscom has considered them—(Mr. Griscom interrupts, and says it was great-grandchildren) no—let it be grandfathers, for the other is not ancient enough for prescription—is it not wonderful, sir, that the first offence of this kind (for aught we know) should be perpetrated by the peaceful—the pious—the professed lovers of the meek and lowly Saviour; and that Mr. Gibbons, who seems to misunderstand the application of the doctrine to this case—

("Hear it, ye heavens, and wonder while ye hear it,")

should compare these gentlemen to the *good Samaritan,* who found a wounded traveller upon the wayside, and poured oil and balm into his wounds? He made a mistake; they were the highwaymen that *wounded the traveller.* There is the difficulty, and all the trouble we have is in the proper application of the text. *Who* wounded him but *themselves?* What oil and balm did they pour into his lacerated heart? Was it balm, to withdraw him from his children's consolations; to sever him from his wife; to imprison him, and doom him night after night

to his melancholy cell ; to interrupt him hour after hour
during the period allowed to sleep—if such a man could
sleep in such a situation ? They tell you in the next
breath that he requires *repose ;* and for that purpose they
put him in a cell where he is awakened every hour!
Admirable consistency !

First impressions are correct : and when your honor
said you could not trust yourself to speak of this case as
you felt, you could hardly restrain your indignation—it
was your first impression. Resort may be had to ingenious suggestions, and escape may be hoped for; but whenever you find them ensconcing themselves behind the
arras, there is some mischief! According to the Spanish
proverb: when you find a man who wears a long cloak
you cannot tell what it conceals, it is true, but you may
know from the cloak itself that it is evil. That is sound
reason—here they all are *cloaking* together. When I
come to another part of the case, I will show you that
there never was a more fantastic defence, than that which
was exhibited here, if I understand it. Why, don't you
perceive that this defence never existed—even in fancy—
until after the action was brought ?

The defence, in order to exist availingly, should have
existed before—look at that. By sounding the trumpet
of a retreating army, they can gather all the stragglers.
Notwithstanding they fought him out of his pocket, they
did not stop there—thus showing their malice and hatred
—they fought him after he was declared to be *sane.*
They pay a lawyer for resisting him in getting his own
property—out of his own funds. My learned friend says
that Philip Garret, in taking Morgan Hinchman in, and
then confining him, had no art or part in the concern.
May it please your honor, when does a defendant partici-
pate—I may as well dispose of that now. Men may conspire together; and if a man come in at the eleventh
hour, he is answerable for all done before. (*Judge.*—Suppose he is not in the conspiracy, but does some collateral

act—not of a nature to prove part of it—he is not answerable at all.) I know your honor likes fairness and openness, and I am not going to strain any point. It comes to this; if he was not one of them he is not answerable. But your honor will see that if two men, or twenty men, in different parts of this wide-spread city are all doing similar acts at the same time, against the same individual, who lives in the centre; when the law comes to try them, their simultaneous acts prove their guilt: because the law cannot understand how twenty men, twenty miles asunder, could act exactly alike, with reference to the same person, unless by concert. Your honor will perceive, that I have said when a man comes in at the eleventh hour he is a conspirator; but if a man come in at the first hour, and with others concoct and concert a plan of injury; and then he is not seen till after its completion, he is answerable for all that takes place. It is the same heart, the same motive; and whether he raises his hands to carry out the motive or design, is of no consideration or regard. So of a man who lives in California; he may be, though out of the jurisdiction of this court, a conspirator with a man here. Men in different countries may be conspirators. It does not matter where they reside—when they come in—what portion of the wrong has been done by them—they are answerable from the beginning to the end. Those who come in *last*, adopt the acts from the beginning; and constructively conform to the motives of others, and are answerable. Nay, more than that, sir, I take leave to say, that if a dozen men assemble around three armed men ; and these armed men present their weapons to the breast of an intended victim ; and the other twelve do nothing—say nothing— and harm nobody; they may wash their hands as they please, the law makes them guilty: for their physical force operates to destroy or defeat the intention of self-defence, that may, of right, exist in the other party. It is not necessary the men should act. If you had thought

of defending yourself against one man, what hope have
you against such a number? Though they do no act,
they promote the aggression. They were bound to prevent it, and he who does not is answerable.

These men have trampled upon the bill of rights, and
violated constitutional protection; they are all implicated;
whether all were present and all united in the immediate
design, as is undoubtedly the case, it matters not. It is in
vain they refer to the wife and mother; it is in vain they
attempt to screen themselves behind a petticoat (for that
is part of their valor, and it is admirable to be sure); it is
in vain they assert their ignorance of the law. No man
is permitted to be ignorant of the law, and of the rights
of individuals. With three counsel in Doylestown, and
one in Philadelphia—four lawyers—and still be ignorant,
almost passes belief. These men seize me; take me to the
asylum; keep me there for six months; allow my child to
die; sell my property, and then say "we were *ignorant!*"
Who is to pay for your ignorance? You must pay for it
yourselves. There are no excuses, except the proof of
their insanity, or *that* of the plaintiff. I could prove them
insane more clearly than they prove Morgan Hinchman
to be so; sending Mr. White—a respectable man; impos-
ing on him, and making him the wretched pander of a
lie, to deceive a man, who they say was insane, by making an appointment with him to buy his property. Are
these the characteristics of just men? It appears to me,
that it is an extravagant notion, to say the least of it.
Although ignorance is poetically said to be "bliss;" it will
be found in point of law, to be a troublesome companion.
It is certain that so far from justification, it is in many
instances, a gross aggravation of the offence. Now, sir, I
say, for the purpose of meeting the gentlemen; if Morgan Hinchman were in a deluded or doubtful state, they
had no right to arrest him in this manner—away from his
friends, away from his home, in another county than that
of his residence, without any legal authority, and without

actual necessity—which is the only substitute for authority. The law utterly abhors a proceeding like this. If he were a criminal, they would not dare to arrest him in this way; and to say that they heard slanders about him; and to bring such a man as Matlack—a living anachronism—who cannot correctly remember anything within five years, and who forgets the time of his own marriage—for the purpose of swelling the slanders. He finds Mr. Hinchman always sane when he wants him to lend him $1,250; but not sane when he requires him to pay it back again.

I don't wish to travel out of this case for the purpose of dragging in these matters; there is, heaven knows, enough to do, in what belongs to the case. I say, if he were a criminal, they would not have dared to arrest him in this way; making themselves magistrates, witnesses, bailiffs, judges, executioners—everything. Let me test it. This will be a fair test to you : suppose when they came to arrest Morgan Hinchman—even with Mr. George M. Elkinton, the Napoleon of this train-band! who speaks "true cannon powder," when he says—" There is no use of talking any longer, if thee is not going, we will force thee,"—suppose, notwithstanding this leader of the Spartan band—so " bloody, bold, and resolute,"—Morgan Hinchman had said, " Gentlemen, I don't understand this; I shall not go;" and he had felled each one of the six, successively to the earth, and they had prosecuted him; what would be the result? His honor would tell you that after he had knocked them *down*, he ought to have kicked them *out*. It may have been sport to them, but to the plaintiff it was death. Suppose you should be awakened from your slumbers as by a thunder-clap from a cloudless sky, and find yourself surrounded by your hunters, and told that you are sick—you think you are well, and say, " I am not sick, and I am the best judge of the matter." " Well, but we shall give thee repose," and yet you were interrupted every hour of the night.

" Well, but I don't want to go—I have business to attend
to." And I'll show you at a proper time, how beautifully the business of Morgan Hinchman was arranged.

Can any one contend, that you may be violently seized,
and remorselessly and legally borne away, to the melancholy cells of a common mad-house ?—It is madness to
assert it.

I say, gentlemen of the jury—and we move step by
step, desiring at the same time some little impress may be
made in the progress of the journey,—suppose they had
gone there armed with the law—with a warrant, accompanied by a police officer, acting under a regular deputa-
tion ; and then had arrested him—he would not have dared
to lay his finger on them. That goes to strengthen the
opinion previously suggested, that the law protects those
acting in the name of the law; and punishes those who
attempt resistance to its authority. It is true that individual oppression is rarely so abhorrent, rarely so odious,
as when it stalks forth decorated in the sacred habili-
ments of the law. But still there is one condition of
things more odious than that—where it is perpetrated
without the sanction of the law—where it not only does
injury to the individual, but exhibits and furnishes an example to the community, which teaches them to imitate
the outrage, instead of adopting virtue and the law as
their standard. It is, therefore, important—(I can't refer
to it too often, for I consider it a vital matter)—that you
should distinguish, between what men do of themselves,
against the general principles of civil society ; and what
they do under the law with the law's authority, and with
the law's shield. I cannot exhibit it more strongly, than
by showing, that in one case he would be justified in
kicking *them* down stairs; and in the other case, *they*
would be justified in taking *him*, whether he was right or
wrong, in obedience to their official mandate. They may
kill him if he resist. But if they had killed this man, he
resisting, there is but one result—it would have been

murder—" murder most foul as in the best it is, but this most foul, base and unnatural." Your honor says truly, it would have been murder, simply because it was not under authority; and *he* was authorized to resist, if *they* were not authorized to punish. If he had died in resisting these unauthorized attacks, they would have been malefactors, and must swing for it. I don't know that I shall have occasion to return to this, but I wish it to be impressed upon your minds, in order that you may know, when you hear the law spoken of, that it is your protection, only while acting in obedience to it. The shield is turned into a sword, when you become violators of public peace, order, and law. I say then, summing this up: it is plain, if this doctrine be sound, that the proceeding was *wrong* from the beginning, being founded in *wrong;* and I say further that no subsequent proceeding, could make it *right.* This is another point that runs counter to our friend's position. You cannot impart life to a dead body. There is no Promethean spark that can revivify that frame, in which life is once extinct. An act that is void (not merely *voidable*),—an act that is void as this was— an act that is worse than void—that is *criminal,* as this was—can never be restored to pristine health and purity. But if it *could*—and here is another point—I further say, that every subsequent step was as illegal as the first. If the wholesome ear cannot impart life to a blasted brother: certainly the corrupt ear cannot restore health. The petition was all wrong—the commission was all wrong—the inquest was all wrong. The mode of summoning the jury, I will show you at a future time, was *wrong*—I use no harsher term. All contributing to show how strong, operative, and diffusive were the principles of this conspiracy. The want of a seal was defective—the affidavit was defective; and the continued confinement in the asylum was a superadded outrage.

Why, if we had even admitted that he was insane—did your honor not observe a peculiarity here: Dr. Evans

says, the plaintiff was convalescent early in February—
that was before some of the letters were written. Then
why did they keep him there till the 7th of July? Now,
that is the doctor's evidence. What is the object of it?
There is no other mode of accounting for the sanity of
the letters, than by his being convalescent in February?
Why is he kept five months afterwards? Do you mark
that—I only ask the question now—I will answer it
by and by.

The learned judge, to whom I bow with deference, has
said: "that as the inquisition has been set aside, it is as
though it had never been." It will be a dark day when
the opposite doctrine shall be tolerated—when original
wrong may, under the wing of the law, be purged into
pristine health and soundness. *Once* wrong, it is *always*
wrong. Its foundation is too weak, to sustain any defence, however light and ærial, that is built upon it. It
has been quashed and set aside for original defects. It *is*
as though it had never been, so far as regards the defence.
They can have no protection from it. But it is not as
though it had never been, so far as regards the *plaintiff's*
case. The very machinery that they have resorted to, for
the purpose of imparting vigor to their puny bantling, is
evidence of their malice—of their connection with the
transaction; and their connection with subsequent matters is a proof of original combination. Still they recur,
(whenever they are hemmed in by difficulties of this character) to the old suggestion, so well argued by my friend
Mr. Williams—"that they performed different parts, and
came in at different times." I answer, they *came* in: it
does not matter when they came in, or what *part* they
acted. It does not matter whether in this drama they
were stars or supernumeraries—kings or servants—they
all contribute to swell the *dramatis personæ*—they all perform their respective parts—all contribute to disturb
domestic sanctity, and must all bear the penalty. Now,
gentlemen of the jury, after discussing almost every prin-

ciple that is embraced, or can be embraced in this case—
though not applying it, because that must be reserved for
the minute consideration of facts—after all this, we come
to what is considered the essence of the cause. My learned
friend and professional antagonist, Mr. Gibbons—inverting the natural order of things—has commenced with his
conclusion ; and has concluded where, I think, he would
have more properly commenced.—That however is a matter of choice—a matter of judgment. He may be right. I
shall take another course, and shall ask you to ratify it, and
unite with me in its pursuit, beginning with the unlawful
arrest, the character of which I have shown, and tracing
the plaintiff by the current of time down to the period
when the proceedings against him, under the commission
of lunacy, were quashed. Having gone over this part, I
shall next examine the alleged ground upon which the
arrest was made, and on which the confinement was continued down to the 7th of July, 1847. You will bear in
mind that the confinement would have continued until
this day—heaven knows how much longer—if it had not
been for the interposition of Benjamin Hinchman, and
the subsequent escape of Morgan Hinchman—he having
withdrawn his parole. They tell you they never allowed
patients to go, until the parties that placed them there,
came for them. You know that the mother, herself,
differed from Dr. Evans ; and entered into an argument
to show that her son should not be set free—the first instance on record, established against this most estimable
lady : equal to the Countess of Macclesfield herself, who
pursued her own child to death, dooming him to famine,
while she was rolling in the luxury and opulence of
Eastern magnificence. This lady, whose heart should
have overflowed with joy, and who should have been the
first to suggest that it was probable her son was recovered—
when Dr. Evans said he was about to be discharged—expresses doubts whether it was proper. Now while the tears
of a *paternal* relative flow down manly cheeks—and while

no man that listens can fail to feel,—where was the glist-
ening moisture of the eye exhibited by a mother, in the
attempt to demolish the character of her own child. I
suppose " Grief drank the offering ere it reached the eye."
There is no other mode of accounting for it. Again, the
fair sister smiles—looks on and smiles—and enjoys this
proceeding, under the protection of the adversaries of her
brother ; and never sheds a drop of sympathetic dew from
her bright eyes, to improve the roses on her cheek. Look
at these things. And then another sister, *condoling* with
him: Heaven spare me and mine, from such condolence,
should condolence be required. " There is a *cant* condolence that gives more pain to the afflicted mind than open
scorn !" Such was the character of her letter. I think
I never knew more obduracy, in a matter calculated to
enliven and invigorate all the springs of the human heart—
than was exhibited there. My learned friend, Mr. Gibbons, complains of an honorable, high-minded man, who
has done nothing but venture to stem the torrent of persecution in behalf of a brother's son ; and turning upon
him, stigmatizes him as a "*paternal relative*, who shed his
dramatic tears." It comes well from that quarter. There
was not a man in this assembly that was not more moved
by the plaintiff's injuries, than the mother that bore him—
Not one. I am perfectly willing to pay all homage to the
feelings of a woman's breast that it is entitled to; and
remember I say nothing against her—it is not my business. I know nothing of her character. A woman may
have a marble heart ; and yet may be an honest, prudent,
careful woman, in good standing. I should be mad, and
put in a mad-house, if I were to create an issue of that
kind. But I will venture to say, that the course pursued
by these persons—whether stimulated by affection or fear
or hatred, I don't care which—operated, like thrusting an
ice-bolt through your hearts. Theory is one thing ; woman's love is a delightful theory ; but inverted love—love
sprung from hate that is engendered by the dislike of

relatives for nearly eighteen years; these things corrupt
the genial current of a woman's affections. When she—
owing a divided duty—comes to be supported by her
daughters, in opposition to her son; it is only a comparison of relative affections. In addition, she was endorsed
by the whole confederacy. To manifest some regard for
their authority, she burns *his* letters. Is this fair? Burning them within one week,—*since the cause came on!* I
am not going to say that she is guilty of treason; but I
do say, when you put all these things together, you must
perceive that there is a most unkind, not to say cruel,
disposition towards Morgan Hinchman; occasioned either
by alienated affection; by his having lived apart from her
after the miserable affair of the apple tree; or by a preference for her other children, or a stronger adherence to
the monthly meeting and board of managers of the asylum. It is plain—for no man denies it—no cloak can
cover it, the evidence proclaims it—that she acts in *concert* with the avowed adversaries of her son.

I wish, as I have said, to pursue the chronological order
of events, in the discussion of facts. Time is said to be
the discoverer of all things : and the most judicious mode
that can be adopted, where you have a case of any en-
tanglement, is to take it up in the order of time, and each
successive step will be explained by that which precedes;
and thus you will have a regular course of deduction.
Your honor knows, we all know, let a man be embarrassed in investigation, if he has the dates, and order of
the events, it is a perfect Ariadne's clue, that enables
him to escape without difficulty. That's my practice—it
answers me—and I presume it answers others.

In the result of the course which is thus proposed, I
shall show you, that this is a most wanton and high-
handed attack upon the plaintiff's rights; further aggravated by the obdurate character and course of the defence,
and those engaged in it—further aggravated by mental
reservations at which you were astonished!—further

aggravated by the concealment of papers, and the denial
of well-known and important facts, by these reputable
men!—honorable men!

No man that has any pretensions to respectability, denies his own hand. Any one that wears a clean shirt,
would scorn such quibbling and evasion, as have been
exhibited here by witnesses on the part of this defence!
Why, I assure you, there never was such an opportunity
for a cross-examination; your honor has perceived it, but
not wishing to weary you, I have sometimes passed it by.
The evasive character of the whole defence—signatures
denied—orders denied—minutes kept back—records viti-
ated and altered—burning letters—aye, our letters which
would have proved our sanity—burnt during the progress
of this very case! And such testimony! On the surface
it is smiling and beautiful, but, when you dive below—I
won't say it is " filled with dead men's bones," but it still
resembles very much " a whited sepulchre."

Let me give an instance. There was a reputable gentleman as high as the highest, Mr. Scattergood—one of the
managers of this asylum—and as respectable as any man
among them. Your honor will remember that Mr.
Warder had put himself upon the court for a discharge,
upon the inability on our part to prove, that he signed
the order—by virtue of which the plaintiff was confined;
and the ground of his application was that *he never signed
the order! That* I say nothing about. But gentlemen
of the jury, when Mr. Scattergood was called on the
other side; and, by a mere random shot—for I assure you,
I had no idea what would be the answer—I happened to
ask, " Sir, do you know who signed the order of admission?" He said, " No, I do not." I then proceeded,
" Did you ever speak to Benjamin H. Warder on that
subject?" Says he to the judge, " Am I bound to answer
that question?" " To be sure you are." " Well, yes—I
did." My next question was, " Did he not admit to you
that *he* signed the order?" " Am I bound to answer

that question?" "To be sure you are," replies the court. "*Well—he did.*" Now you can see the difficulties we have to wade through in regard to the snow-bank, &c. (Though that melted some half dozen years ago, it is treasured up to swell the catalogue of this man's eccentricities.) And here, I may as well remark, in all my experience I never knew equal mental reservation. Here is an honorable, high-minded man, who tells me he does *not know*, when he *does* know! That would be nothing; but by refusing or declining the questions that followed, it is *evident* he knew what was required from him; and when driven to the wall, he confesses that Benjamin Warder himself, told him that he had signed that very order. Well, now, what do *you* say. A man affirmed to tell the *whole truth!*—a strict professor! So with Dinah Taylor— I wish you would call her *Diana*—a beautiful name, and a beautiful woman, and all the most beautiful things should be put together. Well, what does Diana do? Why she gives you a terrible account; making this man out to be mad, because he drove her through a snow-bank. When she was examined here, as to where the snow-bank was; it was in the middle of the street, or on the side of the street. What did he drive you through for? Why to bring me to the curbstone. Fire and fury!—is this the manner in which we are to be baffled? This is all true, no doubt. I do not impute any direct falsity to it—Heaven forbid! but it is given in such a *sly manner*—which, I know, his honor abhors. There is no moral difference between purposely evading a question, and a positive untruth. So again, I could go through a dozen occurrences of a similar nature. This shows why letters were burnt; it shows why certain portions of the correspondence can be got, and others not. It is a very extraordinary case, let men speak of it as they will. I don't think this system of strategy belongs to the original school of Friends; or else I do not understand its character.

Having exhibited a brief summary of the grievances and wrongs of the plaintiff; I shall leave it to you, through the medium of your verdict, to indemnify the plaintiff—to teach the defendants a lesson of obedience to the law, and exhibit an example to benefit others.

Now, sir, I go to the evening of the 5th of January, 1847. On that evening, neither dreading nor thinking harm, in pursuance of his ordinary business, the plaintiff leaves his farm in Plumstead, in a neighboring county, to attend the market in this city. Before his departure —and all this must be noted—having recently employed some new hands, he gave directions to his agent or superintendent to keep them closely to work ; to give proper attention to the cattle—for the righteous man is merciful to his beast,—and with his ordinary kindness, and with the expectation of returning in forty-eight little hours, he bade a tender farewell to his innocent children—one of whom, he was destined never again to see. Look at that first stage in our progress. I will not embarrass or perplex you, by introducing anything that does not relate to the subject. He left upon the farm, an affectionate wife and three prattling infants—those for whose comfort and prosperity, in his own language—in the language of his letter, which speaks with the most miraculous organ of his sanity—those for whom he had endured privations, those for whom he "would freely have borne all his toils." That is the language of his letters. Could he at that moment,—carry your mind back to that point of time— could he at that moment, have entertained any presentiment of what was about to befall him, within forty-eight little hours, the echo of that simple word FAREWELL, would have sounded like the knell of departed joys—departed, never, never to return. Farewell, he might have added, for six long, lingering months, to be spent in the gloomy recess of a *mad-house*, where he could never get a glimpse of liberty. As to his family, that is too tender a subject to speak of now. It is the last touch of this pic-

turc, of almost unparalleled woe. Bring it to yourselves!
—that is the test? Place *yourselves* in his position, if
imagination can reach as far; or does it distance the conception of your minds?

He arrives at Philadelphia; attends to his duties faithfully; disposes of his produce; regularly collects his rents;
prepares to see his agent, Mr. Saurman; and renews a negotiation with Ezra Smith with regard to a loan of $3,000,
which was to be procured for him at an interest of 5 per
cent., for the purpose of relieving his farm. There is no
act without its reason—and a consistent, proper and judicious one. Do not all these facts, corresponding and concurring, make out the perfect sanity of the plaintiff?
Does he borrow money at an excessive interest? No—he
borrows like a prudent man, like an honest man, to meet
an approaching debt due in April; with an eye to thrift
he borrows it, at one per cent. less than his former contract. He makes his arrangements in a formal, profitable, orderly, and discreet way. Where is the man here,
who could have done it better? If a man act appropriately in the business in which he is concerned—in all its
branches, and never fails to indicate a just comprehension
of his position: what other evidence can you have of his
sanity than that? I don't mean a *single* instance, in *all*
its instances—in all method—in all his relations. If any
man—if Morgan Hinchman—is to be declared a lunatic
on such evidence; there is not a man in Bucks county,
says one of the witnesses (John Rich), that cannot be declared insane. There was nothing insane in this step:
there was no "wasting" of his estate, as they have sworn.
If there were any fault in him at all, it was rather too
much nicety, too much calculation, but no "wasting;" on
the contrary, as I have said, his course was characterized
by ordinary intelligence, thrift, prudence, and precaution.
Whatever little anxiety he exhibited, may it please your
honor, about this time, was perfectly natural. These things
explain each other. All of these matters, which have

been conjured up for the purpose of indicating insanity, are perfectly natural and rational. There was a judgment of $1,000, in favor of Heston falling due the 1st of April, 1847; and the mortgage to Brown, which he desired to pay at that time. Is it unnatural that he should show some little ordinary anxiety? Is that evidence against his reason; or is it not evidence in support of it? They will give you these detached matters without any circumstances of explanation. Most men can be proved mad by such means. I say, *he* must be a madman, or worse, who will endeavor, on such a basis, to build up the suspicion of insanity.

The conversation held with Michener (I don't speak of *recantation* Michener—I speak of lawyer Michener), a short time before the plaintiff left his quiet home, showed clearly what were his means of payment; and whatever fears were entertained, as to the payment by Hinchman, were dispelled. He explained satisfactorily the sources of his getting money; and satisfied the claimant by an exhibition that has never been denied—corresponding with the statement, since verified—that he was perfectly competent to pay the original sum owed by him; and Mr. Michener being satisfied, would never have pressed it, but for this calamity, which brought ruin upon his house. But they say, what did we get of his property—did we not give it back to him? Aye! you fought to the last— you fought and paid lawyers out of his estate—*to keep him out of his estate.* Is that giving back his property—is that a matter of mere dollars and cents. You have sold his entire property and stock; as well as broken him up root and branch: and do you talk about giving him back his property; you might as well give him back the body of his child, robbed of life, and ask him to console himself in the contemplation of his own irremediable loss. This is an abuse, an aggravation of the offence.

Then the ridiculous matter, that is brought into the case!—selling two pounds of butter, because he wished to collect money to pay a bond (every little helps); and taking the clover seed to Dr. Noble—which Mrs. Noble did not understand! These are wonderful indications of the want of sanity: clover being scarce with the doctor, who was on a farm, and money being scarce with Morgan, it was natural for one to wish to sell it, and I don't know whether it did not turn out that the other bought it. This is a very dangerous scheme—to cast your drag-nets over eight years of any man's life.

Then, again, his desire to make sale of his Marshall street property, to pay off his mortgage! His great passion was his farm. Collecting every cent that was due, is reconcilable with a correct and sound view of his pecuniary condition at that time. Well, then again, please to call to mind Mrs. Wright's testimony—a harmless, unoffending, estimable woman, I have no doubt; I have not a word to say in regard to that. She says he came hastily into her house. To be sure he did; he was in a hurry to leave town; he had business to do; he had seen Mr. Bispham; he was going to Mr. Pepper's, still bent on that one absorbing object. Mr. Pepper is not in; and he returns and takes his dinner at Mrs. Wright's, and there ventures to count his money—there is certainly no harm in that. He was a young man; he was just about departing to the farm, and there were a thousand matters to induce him to count his money—at all events, it was entirely consistent with sanity. All these matters belong to the same category, and receive the same explanation. He expects, as you remember, to overtake Mr. Smith at Jenkintown; and, with a prudence that is remarkable, so arranges it, that, if he does not happen to overtake him at Jenkintown, Mr. Smith and the lender of the money, are to meet him at his place in a few days; when the money is to be loaned, the circumstances are to be explained, and the security is to be given. Can there be anything more regular or right? This is on the 6th, the

day before the eventful morning when he was robbed of
every object dear in life.

I may mention, properly, in this connection, that this
was no hallucination. The lender, by this very appointment, came down with the money; and the whole projected scheme would have been accomplished (it being
some eight or ten days after the period that I have referred to), when he is met with the astounding intelligence
that Morgan Hinchman is a madman. Now, sir, bringing these matters to a focus, you will understand what
their bearing is. The plaintiff could have paid off his
mortgage; he could have relieved himself from his anxiety; his money was all ready; he had but a thousand
dollars to take care of. He would have gone on prosper-
ously, and been a blessing to his family; and having his
liberty, would have still toiled, at the expense of every
possible earthly convenience to himself, for the benefit of
his wife and little ones.

After these events of the afternoon of the 6th, new
actors present themselves on the stage—the scene shifts.
A grand divan is to be held at Mrs. Hinchman's on the
night of the 6th. The mother, Elizabeth Shoemaker,
Anna W. Hinchman, Edward Richie, Samuel Richie
and Mrs. Hinchman, were there. Bear that in mind—the
number of *six* is a fatal number here, it seems—they have
moved in sixes altogether—six when they arrested him—
six in the inquisition—six everywhere—an *even* number,
but an *odd* undertaking. Of the particulars of their deliberation we are not distinctly informed; and we must
therefore look to the practical results, to understand what
they *determined* to do, from what they *have* done. I can
only say for the honor of the wife, and woman's love,
that when Margaretta Hinchman was subsequently asked:
" did she ever consent in word, thought or deed to the
perpetration of this outrage upon her husband"—the
father of her children—she said " she never did." It runs

counter to the current of the feelings of every noble woman.

Elizabeth Shoemaker says that Morgan *lost* his memory: he was one entire memory. He seemed to concentrate all that ever passed under his knowledge; and he acted correctly with reference to it. That is the reason why I asked Dr. Evans the question—will not a man who has a delusion, as you say, gambol from his subjects; misconceive or misrepresent what he has done or said, just before? "Yes, that is considered the great test." Sirs, no *physician* ever supplied that test. Shakspeare supplied the test;—a man whose mind embraced all things—whose genius pervaded everything,—who was a better chemist— a better metaphysician—a better lawyer—a better doctor —a better gardener—a better everything than almost any man,—nay not almost, that is short justice,—*than* any other man. What does he say? He gives two tests. I .will not go to Horace, for he is not fit to hold a candle to Shakspeare. He gives you two tests. The first is, quickness of pulse. Hamlet's mother plays the same prank that is played here, and sends her son—not to the asylum, but to England—for his insanity. See how he answers when accused by his mother, of ecstacy—which signifies insanity—

> "*Ecstacy !*
> My pulse, as yours, doth temperately keep time,
> And makes as healthful music, it is not madness,
> That I have uttered : bring me to the test,
> And I the matter will reword ; which madness
> Would gambol from."

Two of the best tests known to metaphysicians—one a strictly medical test—the great excitement of the pulse— the other *re-wording* of the matter. And sir, there is a remarkable case—which I know your honor will take pleasure in referring to, or in allowing me to refer to—related by Sir Henry Halford, physician to George III, and the head of the medical faculty, at one time, through-

out the world. He tells you that he never would have
been able to detect insanity, if he had not applied the test
that Shakspeare gives. He begins it, by the by, with
this very quotation from Shakspeare. (Reads from Halford's Essays.)

Saturday.—May it please your honor: the time allotted
to complete, or rather to terminate—for it may scarcely
be considered, complete—the course of the investigation
originally proposed to you, is too *short*, to tell you *how*
short it is. And, therefore, gentlemen of the jury, without resuming the former course of observations—except so
far as it may be absolutely necessary in order to its continuance—without attempting to review it in any way
(considering that " by gone is by gone"); I shall address
myself to that which remains. I have but a single remark to make—and that rather in the way of apology—
and that is,that you must not suppose that I have overlooked many matters to which I may not particularly advert; but that you should be inclined to excuse the omission, when you bear in mind that it is attributable in a
great measure, to the desire to contribute to your comfort
or convenience. The time is short, sir, as has been said;
but I am not certain that it is not adequate to the necessary purposes of the argument.

You may remember, gentlemen, I took leave of you
yesterday, after having adverted to the grand divan, assembled at the house of Mrs. Eliza Hinchman upon the
night of the 6th. I only recur to that as a sort of start-
ing point for the course I am now about to pursue; and
for the purpose of asking you to bear in mind that of the
six assembled at that time, there were Edward Richie,
Samuel Richie, Anna W. Hinchman, and Elizabeth Shoemaker, four defendants. The mother was there; she is
not one of the defendants; and the wife was there—she
is not embraced.

Now, gentlemen, the next stage in our journey presents
a new scene. Immediately from the house of Eliza Hinch-

man, where these four persons were assembled, Edward
and Samuel Richie proceeded to the house of Mr. White;
and they induce Mr. White to join with them in the effort
to secure Morgan Hinchman, although as Mr. White himself says, he "never saw anything irregular in Morgan
Hinchman in his life." They induce him to call at the
house of Robert Richie, the father. He does not succeed in finding him. Edward and Samuel Richie, who
figure at every point, go with him next to the tavern.
Now where there are bad beginnings—where there are
hypocritical schemes resorted to—depend upon it, in nine
instances out of ten, the sequel will be worthy of the introduction.

They build the whole proceeding upon his sanity, while
they accuse him of insanity. Well knowing that there
had been a negotiation between Mr. White and Mr.
Hinchman, months before, in relation to the house in
Marshall street, they suggest to Mr. White to make that
the basis for the postponement of Mr. Hinchman's departure to the next morning; in order that they may then arrest him. What do you say to this? There is no mental
reservation about it: I will venture to go so far as that.
But, is not there a scheme, a plot, a combination; or indication of pre-existing conspiracy? Mr. White goes in,
sir, and comes out, and does not find Morgan Hinchman.
It is the night before poor Morgan's departure—exhausted
and worn out with the course of the day's events, or loss
of rest the preceding night, incurred in his line of duty,
he is reposing upon a buffalo skin, which rests upon a bench,
and Mr. White did not perceive him. Then comes in Mrs.
Richie, while the other Mr. Richie, being a sentinel, is
looking in at the window—just recall this scene.—Mr.
Richie discovers him; and instead of going up like a
man and a Christian, and employing some measures for the
purpose of ascertaining whether the suggestions that had
been made in relation to his sanity, were well founded—for
it does not appear that he had had any intercourse with him

for months—instead of going up and saying, " Morgan, I wish to have some conversation with you," and then talking over matters to satisfy his mind ; he skulks and shrinks, and dare not encounter the eye of his victim. Thus " consicence doth make cowards of us all." Mr. White is to do the work; for being innocent, he is bold. He acts upon the suggestions of Samuel Richie—who figures most unfavorably in every branch and scene of this transaction, from beginning to end. Mr. White rouses Mr. Hinchman, shakes hands with him—the old habit of *betraying with a kiss*, having grown into disuse. How did he look ? Perfectly well. Was there anything irregular about him ? Nothing at all. Did he talk rationally ? Entirely so. When you spoke of the house, did he remember the arrangements previously suggested ? Yes, sir, he told me I had better buy the house. Now, may it please your honor, you may make any man crazy when the wind is north-northwest ; but when it is southerly, he may distinguish between " a hawk and a handsaw." Still, there is not a man that I have the honor to address, that, embracing eight years of his life, can exhibit a course of character more consistent with honesty ; and one portion more consistent with another ; and more entirely adapted to right reason, than the plaintiff has done. Well, he makes the appointment, and what does our friend, Mr. Williams, say to this ?—for whatever he says is entitled to regard—but this is rather an astonishing manifestation of candor ! He says they don't deny that this was a contrivance—a scheme. No! they don't deny it ; because we have Mr. White to prove it. This is another specimen of liberality. So, Mr. Scattergood doesn't deny that Benjamin Warder signed the order—after we had got the fact from him. Mr. Benjamin Warder doesn't deny it—after Mr. Scattergood proved it. I want you to understand this.—If you once understand it, you will have no difficulty in relieving yourself from embarrassment.

Now does the gentleman ask me for a motive ? Why

the very lust of power, in little men, is a sufficient motive for nine-tenths of what they do. Has that never struck you?—their very desire of playing the despot—the desire for notoriety in consigning a fellow man to a public or any other institution—the desire of notoriety in a profession of charity, in interposing to assist the wife—as they would have us to understand—the wife who had not one particle to do with the matter! But there are other motives that, in the progress of my remarks—without making them now distinct and independent subjects of inquiry—will present themselves clearly to the mind.

The next morning, who comes? Why they were drumming up all the recruits. You ask me to show that there was a combination. By some strange influences, at all events—some sullen influences, as they will prove to be—*these* six men all assemble punctually at eight o'clock. How do they come together? Do you want me to prove that they sat in conclave—that they pre-arranged that Mr. Elkinton was to play the Napoleon of this iron band—that he was to be the leader—that when force was necessary, he was to suggest it—that Mr. Whitall was to play police officer, assisted by Mr. Edward Richie, who was posted inside of the prison? We are forced to suppose, from all this, that it was well understood by the friends—it was very systematic either for good or evil. There they were—I have gone through with what was said, and I mean to go through with it again. The remarks of Morgan Hinchman, his remonstrance, his desire to settle up some pending transactions in relation to property—nothing will do—you must go; and if you won't go willingly, you must go by force. One takes him on one side, another on the other, and drag him down stairs—there, says my learned friend, " he placed his hand upon the bar;" that is very true. But he *seized* the bar, and attempted resisting as far as he could with propriety; because, let the battle end as it would, he would be the sufferer in public estimation—he would have cloven down

his own character; for come what must, the people would
understand that he was an alleged madman. He was
sensible enough for that; besides he was in the hands of
the overseers—that was enough; he was " cribb'd, cabin'd,
and confined." Well, what do they do? They wrench
him away with violence; they force him into what ? Into
his own carriage, says our learned friend. Is that a mitigation of the offence? A man's carriage is valuable only
to him, if I understand it rightly, because he goes in it
when he pleases, and comes out when he pleases. Does it
diminish the enormity of the crime, sir, that at the same
time they control his person, they exercise control over
his property? Is it not rather an aggravation of the
original offence? Why, allow me to say, gentlemen of
the jury, that those horses, had they been sentient beings,
would have blushed at the occupation in which they
were engaged. Yet these gentlemen, said to be respectable, and to a certain extent entitled to regard—by virtue
of the power which they had been accustomed to exercise
—and in the reliance that they had been accustomed to
repose upon the confederated strength of the institution,
or its character, if you please—actually do such things in
public view and in broad, blushing daylight, as any ruffian in the land, would shrink to look upon.

They take him, sir—six of them—(Mr. Whitall and
Mr. Richie are charioteers by turns) and they deposit
him in the asylum; which has been so beautifully depicted
to you—with deer parks, delightful grounds and gravel
walks, its springs and fountains, and all that—a course
of exhibition that has been resorted to for the purpose of
seducing you from your fealty to the law. This is very
captivating—it resembles the beautiful plumage of the
peacock; but when you come to the substantial portion
of the argument, and the ground upon which it rests,
you will be disgusted with its odious and abhorrent legs.
A beautiful paradise! a paradise surrounding, or enclos-
ing, if you please, Hesperian fruit! All this is charming!

but, do you see the dragon beneath it? Do you look into the cells and see the wreck and ruin of the human mind? Do you see the course of treatment, or confinement, calculated to produce results with any man who is sane; as terrifying as those produced by a visitation of Providence?

However, I come there. Now fancy to yourselves the condition of this man—within twenty-four, or forty-eight short hours, translated from his happy home, without premonition, or even implication of notice—deceived, deluded and betrayed, by craft, artifice, and hypocrisy in every shape. Imagine if you can, for a moment, that condition to be yours. What have you to say to it?

When the curtain next rises where, alas! do you find him?—The inmate of a melancholy mad-house! He goes into the day-room, buffeted, tortured in body—and in mind. The very first thing that he does, as if the fates were pouring all their quiver on him—he seeks to rest himself; to remove his boots; when the gruff keeper tells him it is contrary to rule—within one hour after he is received in this hospitable receptacle. What does he do? He mildly excuses himself by stating his sufferings. Why, says Mr. Biddle, he does not rave, or break out, as was natural, into any storm or tempest of fury. No, they had put him past that. It is lucky that he does not. Suppose that he had shown excitement, what would have been the result? They say when he does *anything* he must be mad; when he does *nothing*, he must be mad; if he is quiet, he is moody; if he talks, he is excited; if he is inclined to sleep after a day of toil, that is an indication of his insanity; if he wake up and looks a little wild, he is stark, staring mad. Look at these things, once for all. I cannot pause to go over them. Nay, more than that, if he make a speech in Quaker meeting—if he has the hardihood to speak for one minute (the shortest speech, I believe, on record) before these anointed elders and overseers, and looks frightened—and Heaven knows he had cause—Ezra Comfort doesn't understand him, and thinks

it was very incoherent and wild. I should like to see the
incoherency of a speech of one minute. As to looking
wild, I have no doubt any man summoned before such a
tribunal as that, would look wild—where they don't decide
according to the views of the majority, though there
should be *one hundred and fifty* to *three ;* but according to
the *weight* of the meeting, that is in favor of the *three ;* thus
inverting the whole republican order.   That is not all.
Look at Priscilla Jones, a tower of strength in herself,
and an old maid—I don't speak of it as a reproach, but
for the purpose of explaining some of her fantastic
notions. She goes to meeting, and sees Morgan going
there also. He picks up his boys in the fields, and they
have no hats on. That is a most extraordinary and unpardonable offence. If each of them had come with
twenty hats on—like Knickerbocker's Heroine, with
twenty petticoats—it would have been all right, no doubt;
but to come *without* is unpardonable. He proposes to
take her home ; she does not seem much inclined, but at
last concludes to go with him. Then, because there is
something refractory in the horse, on account of some dis-
arrangement in the harness, he gets out on *one* side to
arrange it ; and as might have been expected, she gets out
on the *other*. This is most ridiculous ; but it is not my
fault. And this forms one of the items, which contribute
to make up the sad melancholy insanity of Morgan
Hinchman. What else ? Why, says my learned friend,
he goes to Mrs. Jones' house at ten o'clock. Now, gentlemen of the jury, are all the acts of his life to be tortured
in this way—perverted and misconstrued for the purpose
of extorting proof against this unhappy man ? Where
else should he go ? He was remote from a tavern ; and
besides being a sober man, he does not wish to go there ;
and if he had, that would have been considered a strong
mark of insanity, for there is no escaping them—it is
impossible.

Well, he goes there and takes his supper—I shall be

careful not to take my supper in Bucks county, *out* of a tavern. He goes to bed. Wonderful to relate! He gets up in the morning, and rises before any other one in the house; then this good lady—I won't call her old, that is an unpardonable sin, too—hearing him walking about, takes for granted there is something wrong. When he came she was given to understand, that he, fully intent upon speculation, was desirous to see Mr. Brown in regard to a purchase. Perfectly reasonable and right! And being desirous of seeing him; before beat of drum, in the morning, after having enjoyed the hospitality of the family, he anxiously moves back and forth until this lady comes down, when he declares his design. Then what does he say? " *I should have gone away without waiting for you, but I thought you would think me crazy*"—a very ordinary phrase—"*and therefore I have remained.*" Gracious powers! if that is to be the course by which insanity is to be established, good-bye to security in man. I am not going through all these matters—I merely cursorily advert to them. I ask *you* to examine them, and carry out the thought I suggested in the former part of my argument, which is this; that none of these things were known or thought of, at the time this arrest was made; but having by a false step involved themselves in difficulty irremediable, they have sounded their trumpet through the ranks of their confederates, and brought forward a sort of *ex post facto* history of the transaction, upon which they attempt to sustain a most flagitious course, adopted by them in regard to this plaintiff. That is the true interpretation. I will not return to it again. My object is now to interweave into the web of this case every one of these defendants; without making the inquiry as to their identification with the primary outrage, a subject of independent consideration.

He is consigned to a maniac's cell. There are *special* orders for his *strict* confinement—he is not left upon the general rules of discipline—he is not left in the ordinary way—he is not left upon the certificate of his physician. Don't be led astray, and induced to believe that Dr. Kite was ever *his* physician.   Dr. Kite was one of his persecutors.   Dr. Kite was the man who united with the mother in the original communication to the meeting, with regard to the affair of the apple tree.   Dr. Kite was the man, together with Mr. Willits (the tall gentleman whom you may remember), who waited upon Morgan over and over again.   Mr. Willits stated, as the result of the conversation he had with Morgan, that he was refractory and would *palliate*—that is he would not confess!   He would not confess—(most extraordinary system of jurisprudence!)—because he would not confess the crime, but would deny it, they thought he was incorrigible.   "He said he was to blame, and regretted it; but what they *charged* was not right."   They reported, in a prejudicial state, to the meeting; but strange to say, the meeting certify, subsequently, that he was a member in good standing.   What is the meaning of this?   They are not "tricks upon travellers," but tricks of one meeting on another.   Don't let us be misapprehended.   They certify him to be a member in good standing; which they never should have done if they had not thought him so.   However, Dr. Kite prepares his certificate.   Under that, Morgan Hinchman is confined as an insane man.   Now this certificate of Dr. Kite has no *bobtail*—no such appendage as is required, setting forth residence, age, disease, symptoms, &c.   It shows a most unholy haste.   There is that in it which is most truly extraordinary.   He knows Morgan Hinchman to be *insane*—he *knows* it; and yet he has not seen Morgan Hinchman for four months, as he subsequently confesses.   When he was called upon, and was asked to explain how he could sign a certificate of that character, stating "that he knew Morgan Hinchman was insane," he says he knew perfectly well six months ago that *he would become mad* just about that time.   Look at this.   It is a very serious matter, gentlemen.   It is

nothing to be certified into a mad-house in our *present*
condition; but to be certified by anticipation or prospect,
or even retrospect, is a little too much. Suppose they alleged what was the condition of his body; then we should
have had something to have laid our fingers upon, instead of engaging in metaphysical discussions. But to
this moment nobody has shown that he was ever *sick.*
Perhaps that was a crime—that he never had occasion for
the doctors. It is true, they made him sick, as well they
might, after he was confined in the asylum; but until he
got there, I ask any one to show me where is the human
being, medical or otherwise, who has ever rendered him
a service as a physician.

They take the plaintiff's account in the hospital, for
the purpose of showing the state of his body; and at
that time they contend he was *mad.* When you understand that he was appealed to (towards the *close* of his
confinement), to acquiesce in the views of the doctors—
" that the moment he admitted that he was insane, they
would consider him sane,"—you may suppose Morgan
Hinchman was sane enough to know, that if he did not
comply with their theory, he never would be released at
all. Here is Dr. Kite's certificate; and where Benjamin
Warder signed it, Heaven only knows. Mr. Bettle never
saw that order until it was brought to town. There is
much mischief here. Mr. Bettle says he has no recollection of ever having signed such an order of admission.
Now observe the management. He is not brought in, as
long as the question could be agitated whether Mr.
Warder signed it or not. But the moment Mr. Scattergood puts it beyond the necessity or reach of argument,
they introduce Mr. Bettle. And it is most remarkable
that Mr. Bettle, who appears to have signed it, did not
remember that he ever signed it at all; or that Mr.
Warder had anything to do with it. I don't consider
that an overruling circumstance. But I want to show
you what the memory of man is. After the lapse of two

years—while he professes to state words and minute circumstances—he forgets that he signed his name to the paper in question, when it makes adverse to the interest of the cause. Benjamin Warder undoubtedly signed it; and Benjamin Warder is not to escape. He is one of the persons to whom Mrs. Hinchman sent an invitation to the grand divan. If you will connect probable cause with the actual effect, you will have no difficulty in understanding it. The agent of Elizabeth Clarke, a woman who has figured in another scene—the individual who interposed to rescue Mrs. Dinah Taylor from the terrors of a snow bank.

They seem to suppose that in the establishment of conspiracy, it is necessary that we should bring every man in contact with another, to show joint guilt. It is no such thing. I will convict six men of conspiracy, and never show that they were together—that they ever *actually* communicated one with another. Your honor may perhaps remember the famous case, decided by Lord Mansfield, where a family of card makers was in a prosperous business; and it happened that some rival artisans in their line, regularly had glue put into their paste pot. Each one of the six was shown to have been separately concerned; but no man knew of any correspondence between them. The relationship that existed in this case was manifested by the consistency of the conduct of the whole six. They were all engaged in the same medium; prosecuting the same purpose; although they were never seen together; being of the same family, engaged in the same trade; and in the same rivalry: when you combine all these together, you cannot fail drawing the inference that they were combined together. So it is in respect to this case. We are not to be eluded in this way.

But to return. The plaintiff is, as I have said, deposited in a mad-house by this certificate—by this interference on the part of the gentlemen, in the way that I have

stated—and there he remains for six long months. He is
kept in strict confinement—more strictly confined than
any other man in that house. Remember that. Mr.
Garrett says, in excuse for that strictness, that such were
the *orders of his friends.* This is a matter my learned opponent seems to have forgotten. Undue strictness—unusual severity, applied to a man in his condition, by the
order of his FRIENDS. This is the declaration of Mr. Garrett, one of the agents, binding upon him; and showing
the general character of the transaction. And when you
come to the admission, "that it had been a mere family
quarrel, and if he would arrange his property, there
would be no more of it," or something to that effect; the
secret is all out. Here he remains night after night,
month after month, as I have said, in worse than a char-
nel house; surrounded by the fragments, if I may use the
phrase, not of the *body*, but of the immortal mind. His
condition rendered more intolerable from his not sharing
in any of the delusions of those by whom he was surrounded. He, a sane man, encompassed by gibbering
idiots and raving maniacs—enough to *drive* any man mad
—for there is something contagious in moral insanity, as
in other diseases. There, alas! he sits—

> No pleasing memory left—forgotten quite
> All former scenes of dear delight.
> *Connubial* love—parental joy,
> No sympathies like these *his* mind employ,
> —But all is dark within—all furious black *Despair.*

Let us step out of the mad-house for a moment, and
see how his mother is engaged. She goes on the 8th, in
the evening (the day after he was confined), to Mr. Eli K.
Price. (Interrupted by opposite counsel.) "The petition
was sworn to on the 9th." That will do. That is coming
to the "chalk." I only want something definite. Does
not your honor remember that it was part of the argument, that the wife, accompanying Mrs. Hinchman, went

to Eli K. Price, and there witnessed the oath to the petition, thus making herself guilty of moral perjury? Mrs.
Morgan Hinchman was safely at Morgan Hinchman's
farm on the 9th, in company with Mr. Richie. (Interrupted by counsel for defendants.) I have no wish to
steal any conquest. I wish to come at it fairly. I say
that Forkner and his wife, and Hall, all say, that Samuel
Richie, Mrs. Hinchman, and Elizabeth Shoemaker,
arrived on sixth day (which is the 8th of the month);
and that Samuel Richie remained there until the next
Monday, or second day. How could Mrs. Morgan Hinchman be present with Mrs. Eliza Hinchman at the time of
taking this oath on the 9th, at Philadelphia, when she
was at Doylestown, which is twenty miles off? It was
executed on the 9th. (Discussion between the counsel.)
The argument of my learned friend was, that Mrs. Morgan Hinchman was guilty of moral perjury, because she
stood by and approved of it. Now Mrs. Morgan Hinchman was twenty-five miles off on the 9th. How then
could she approve of it on the 9th? That was the bulk
of his argument. If this can be answered, I am ready to
hear the answer now, or at any time. And yet she is said
to be guilty of moral perjury for joining in an oath—an
oath which she never knew of. There is nothing that
can be relied upon, in this inconstant, transitory world.
See what memory is, when it comes to words and to
dates. All that argument, goes for nothing. She never
did approve of it. I am anxious to retrieve an honest,
artless woman from the imputations of injustice. These
things were carried on in secret—covertly carried on.

When they arrive at Plumstead, what else takes place?
Why, do you forget? They say that Elizabeth Shoemaker had nothing to do with it. I will show you that
she was as active as almost any other person engaged in
the matter. Don't you remember the whispering conversation between Elizabeth Shoemaker and Samuel
Richie; in which she objected to sending Forkner to

the almshouse, because it might lead to disclosures? Do you remember that? You see I am interweaving these people as I proceed. When Forkner and Richie go to the asylum, Forkner asks Samuel Richie to be permitted to see Morgan.   Richie told Forkner that he was " down there,"—whether he pointed to the south, or in a more dangerous direction, I do not know. But, when questioned more particularly, he said he was in the asylum— that Morgan was to be considered a dead man. I was about to say, I almost wish he could have been so con sidered. Death would have been a blessing to him. " That he was to be considered as though his horses had run away with him and killed him ;" and the inference was that Mr. Richie was to be the executor. He was certainly consigned to a living death. How far he would be justified in being executor, I will leave to others.

Well, sir, they go to the asylum ; there a very touching scene is presented.—Jesse asked to be permitted to see him. What harm could there have been, according to the strictest discipline? No, he cannot be allowed to see him. Why not? because " he has got his head shaved, or he may be having it shaved now." Look at this— very insignificant, to be sure, but making against them, when it tends to show what were the motives, and what the direction of these motives. Well, while they were talking, this man, Forkner, not being allowed to go in, looking up into the second story, saw poor Morgan, looking, not through an iron grating, but through panes of glass with iron sashes. I give you this as the most favorable exhibition you can have of the institution. Morgan signified that he would like him to go round and come in at another gate.   Just then Mr. Richie came out ; and poor Forkner says he was moved to tears in seeing Morgan appearing exactly as he always had. That is his simple mode of expressing it. He said to Samuel Richie, in the fulness of his heart, " I would give ten dollars, poor as I am, to have one minute's conversation with Morgan."

There is a manifestation, not of the feelings of a cultivated man, but of an unsophisticated man, retaining those warm emotions that were infused into him by his Creator. "No, you cannot do that;" and he is carried off.

Next, the defendants go through all this machinery in relation to the sale of his property—killing the hog, not the fatted calf—returning and disposing of the property with an unholy haste. There is an entire mastery exercised over that farm by Samuel Richie and the rest— every thing meddled with and. managed by them; this poor, heart-broken woman scarcely comprehending what had been done or what was about to be done, could not oppose any resistance to the power by which she was controlled. Here they are acting upon—remember that—the supposition that "Morgan's horses had run off with him, and killed him,"—instead of *their* running away with *him* and *horses*—and they go on using the property as if it were their own. But that is not all—after, may it please your honor, they have got the affidavit—that has been made so much of by Mr. Williams—it is forwarded to Doylestown; and Mr. Du Bois, in the month of February, obtained from the court the appointment of John D. Michener as the commissioner. John D. Michener, as that commissioner, received the commission, on the night it was granted, from Samuel Richie himself. Don't you see how they are connected? we cannot move an inch with one, without running foul of another. I cannot trace all their dark and secret meanderings; but what they do in public is what we can trace—and there is no room for any other inference than that they were associated, soul and body, in this case. What does Mr. Michener do? He comes down immediately, and arrives upon the evening of the 4th, and takes up his lodgings at the house of Mrs. Hinchman; and in the morning she accompanies him to Mr. Wm. Biddle, one of her friends and one of these defendants—and Wm. Biddle accompanies the commissioner, with that commission in his hand, down to Eli K. Price, and there he takes leave of them. Now they say Wm. Biddle had nothing to do with it—*that* is something to do with it. But if you will look to the language of Mr. Biddle, when the certificate of the recantation of John D. Michener was read in the house of Elizabeth Shoemaker, you will bear in mind that he says—and nothing is stronger than a man's own declaration:—" I would have thee,"—resuming the character of the INQUISITOR, and turning to Morgan, who had just escaped from his confinement in the asylum—"I would have thee and thy uncle" (this respectable man, Mr. Samuel Fisher, who has not escaped them), " I would have thee and thy uncle understand that *I have been concerned in this matter from beginning to end*"—will that do ? " And I would have thee further understand that *I am determined to see it out.*" Now the only question is, whether you will let him see it out. This is no imagination, there is his own testimony; there is his own avowal. Well, sir, what then ? Why, they say, that Wm. Biddle was not improperly placed upon that inquest; I only say to you that Mr. Thomas Wistar said that *they* had appointed Mr. Wm. Biddle, Mordecai L. Dawson, and Edward Bonsall, three of their own friends ; and that the list had been handed to the deputy sheriff—I suppose Mr. Wolf. I say to you further, that Edward Richie stated, Wm. Biddle had drawn up the list, and that he (Richie) carried it to John L. Wolf. I hope that has not escaped your honor's attention. Upon the result, produced by the concentration of all these facts upon the point under consideration—not taking any insulated circumstances into consideration—what question can there be ? But I will show it to you besides. There is no man who has more respect for the word of a respectable man, than I have, and the sheriff is a respectable man. They bring the sheriff—not the deputy sheriff—for the purpose of showing that he appointed Wm. Biddle, Mordecai L. Dawson, and Edward Bonsall, without any suggestion from any body ; and yet, as you will find from his testimony, he thinks Mr. Wolf did recommend Mr. Bonsall, as being the son of an old superintendent—but when he is called upon two years after the event, how can you expect any officer, who has been but two months in his post, surrounded with diversified scenes and cases, to remember exactly what took place in the course of that morning, when he was first called to make an inquisition? He gives you nothing explanatory of the case, but refers you to John L. Wolf, with whom this paper, as I suppose, had been left the day before.

I come to another topic. Is it not perfectly certain that the sheriff said, he never appointed those gentlemen upon any inquest, *before?* Is it not equally certain that he never appointed them on any inquest *after?* Is that denied? No! How is that? Is it not a little remarkable? Is it not wonderful? Is it not miraculous, that never having been appointed before, and never afterwards, his mind should fix upon Bonsall, Biddle, and Dawson, the very names designated by Thomas Wistar and Edward Richie; and that he should travel the distance of half a mile for the purpose of selecting them ; and that he should select among them the very man that fifteen minutes before had gone down to the office of the counsel for the petitioner?

(The sheriff's cross-examination and examination was here read.)

Well, now, you observe exactly what is the operation of this reasoning. I said that it was probable that Mr. Wolf made the suggestion to Mr. Lelar, and my friends sustain that view ; for the sheriff himself says after two years have elapsed, he can remember enough to say that he thinks it *probable* Mr. John L. Wolf suggested to him that "there was Mr. Bonsall." Is not this a most extraordinary chapter of *accidents?* Edward Richie stating that he had served this list upon Wolf; and that list consisting of men who were never selected before or after! But what is a little more extraordinary—it is proved that William Biddle expressed some *surprise* at his appointment! What is the meaning of this? What is the meaning of moral acquiescence, and moral perjury? What is the meaning of the suggestion that Mrs. Hinchman was guilty of moral perjury when in Doylestown, while the mother took the affidavit? What is the meaning of Mr. Biddle being surprised at being called upon, if he had written out the list, or if he had been named on it before, or when in Price's office, on that particular business? If you can attribute this to the " error of the moon," and result of chance; you can go further in credulity than any twelve men I have ever known. Remember that, and see whether you believe that this was all news to Mr. Biddle; go further, and inquire whether you are to believe Mr. Biddle or not, when he said he had been engaged in the business from beginning to end.

But, however this inquisition was formed, is there not an obvious omission here upon so critical a turning point? Where is Mr. Wolf? He is within trumpet sound of this place. He is probably within the hearing of my voice at this time. He is the deputy sheriff; he is one of the individuals who, it is thought, made the suggestion: he could answer at once whether he received such a communication from Edward Richie. They very conveniently shove by him, and shuffle up the sheriff, to the top of the pack of their witnesses.

(Mr. Williams interrupts.) " Why did *you* not produce him?" (Mr. Brown continues.) Why did we not produce him! We had been already sufficiently in your care and keeping; we had no idea of going into the enemy's camp to gather up recruits. Why did not *you* bring him? it was necessary to himself—it was necessary to the character of his office—it was vitally necessary to the support of the defence; and with all these inducements I marvel much that you could resist them. They can't answer that, it is impossible—and thus, it is therefore sustained abundantly by proof, as it was originally asserted, to be a combination extending so far as not only to corrupt every generous feeling, but sap the sacred foundations of the law. Men who are to sit as judges, creating themselves— I have not a word further to say to that. *You shall speak for me.*

(Mr. Biddle interrupts to say that there are seven deputies, and that Mr. Wolf is not the only one.) *Bring* the seven deputies; and there are *seven* reasons why you should bring them. I supposed when you said, " deputy," you meant Mr. Wolf. There are sub-deputies—that is not what I speak of—I mean the acting deputy. Mr. Lelar speaks of Mr. Wolf as his deputy—he says he was his factotum—Mr. Wolf himself had deputies. Some of his deputies were Mr. Richie and Mr. Biddle. Now, gentlemen, whether rightly or wrongly, they have got their jury.

They call it an INQUISITION. How appropriate, though how terrible the name. MERCIFUL HEAVEN! Let Spain no longer be abused—no longer revile that benighted region for her folly and fanaticism—no longer reproach her for her chains, her racks, and her tortures, and all the accursed machinery of human wretchedness, and human degradation—since here, in this boasted land of equality here, in this hospitable asylum from persecution and oppression—here, in this thrice glorious and sacred sanctuary of enlightened liberty and equal rights—if principles like these are to be tolerated, advocated, or allowed, every doctor is a spy—every lawyer an inquisitor—every superintendent a jailor—every citizen a victim, and every domicile a dungeon. (Loud applause, which his honor could scarcely restrain.*)

---

* Reporter.

An INQUISITION, sir! Let us see how conformable were its proceedings to its character. How conformable to its title, was the nature of its principles. They are, partly, self-constituted judges. Sir, this is a matter of concern—a matter of deep concern. They go out in their carriages—a sort of triumphal parade—to determine upon the destiny of a fellow man, professedly a friend. Three, as we say, self-constituted—three, if you please, chosen by the sheriff—attended by counsel, and prepared for an *ex-parte* hearing, preparatory to an *auto-da-fe;* and wonderful to relate, according to the evidence of some of the witnesses, the two Richies, Dr. Griscom, Dr. Worthington, are all examined; and they *then* resort to the form of sending for the poor victim! This is worse than the inquisition—it surpasses it in injustice and cruelty!—when you have one-half of the judges made up of the prosecutors, it's rather strange they should be unwilling to face the man they came to condemn.

You may remember, yesterday I stated to you, that his honor was perfectly right, in saying that " the inquisition was dead and gone." And you may remember also, I suggested, that it was dead and gone so far as it was calculated to supply aid to the defence—but it is living and operative *against* these defendants. Well, they have all been examined, as I stated—Edward Richie, Samuel Richie, Dr. Griscom, and Dr. Worthington—and then Morgan Hinchman was sent for.

In broken-hearted obedience he enters. Now what does he do? He asks for counsel. Is it conceded to him? No! He is away from hundreds and thousands of those who knew him—he is in a comparatively strange county, surrounded by his spoilers—by those very men who had arrested him, and they acting as witnesses. What he said, no man can know! One of my learned friends, Mr. Price—and it is remarkable—has given in evidence what took place when they got the account of his property—he got it from Morgan, when Morgan comes out! He talks of his property, and they make that evidence of his insanity—at the same time that they incorporate his statement, as evidence, in their report!—[There is no getting clear of these people, who involve in the proof of insanity, exhibitions of great absurdity.]—It is perfectly obvious that Morgan Hinchman was apprised that they inquired after his property, and he could not do less than speak of his property. He speaks of it as it is—they act upon his information, which is true, and then urge the information against him, as evidence of madness. If *he* were mad in giving it, *they* were mad in taking it.

He says, "what is this about?" Why! says Eli K. Price, "a number of the friends have come to inquire"—(not to hold an inquest) "as to thy health." There is not a man that has the hardihood to tell him, candidly, what they are assembled for—surrounded as they are with keepers. At last he says, "I think it seems to be an inquisition of lunacy"—he understands it, taken suddenly as he was—"and I would like to have counsel,"—"but ain't I thy friend?" "Certainly; but you are the counsel of the opposite party, and I cannot put friendship in opposition to professional interest, I want my *own* counsel." "Art thou not satisfied with me?" "Yes, I *have* been, except in one instance, and that was in a case in which thee compromised a debt, instead of getting the *whole* debt." What more can you want? wherever you touch him he is sane. They can't answer him, so they *turn him out of the room*—the best mode of getting out of a bad argument. They disgrace even the inquisition. Look well to it—they pass judgment. Look at that record—look at the words: "Morgan Hinchman is a lunatic, and has been a lunatic for ———— last past." Mr. Price tells you it was drawn up in this city. I only revert to it to show the preconceived intention. He was declared a lunatic in Mr. Price's office. What is judgment, after execution? What, to kill a man first, and then try him afterwards! I don't wish to pause upon this; but I ask you to turn your attention to it, and to remember that you and yours, hold your liberty, your life, your sacred reputation—more valuable than both—by the tenure of a spider's web, if this doctrine is to be tolerated or indulged. You will have no protection; the charter of your rights is an empty boast, and in the hour of trial your imaginary security vanishes.

After this,—they pass back to the farm; sell out his property; account with the commissioner; and subsequently appoint Mr. Lloyd Mifflin committee of his person and estate: they dispose of his property, and rend and deracinate him!—pay counsel fees out of his own estate—a matter totally unnecessary—and having conveyed his person to captivity, they sell out his last hopes.

Well, there he slumbers; no, not slumbers—decays in the asylum; nobody interposes; nobody knows of his condition. His *uncle* knows nothing about it—his uncle, who had been seven years in the Legislature, and was well known to Mrs. Hinchman and others of the party. And Samuel Fisher, and Samuel Webb and wife—Samuel Webb, with whom he served his apprenticeship—nobody, relative or friend—none of his neighbors—no human being—is called, or allowed, or noticed, to interpose in his behalf; sacrificed as he was in the morning of his days, and doomed to eternal shame. Even Charles Shoemaker was not informed. It however happens that Mr. Hinchman is apprised of his nephew being in the asylum at Frankford. Then, with all the promptitude of a man of business, he goes himself to the asylum, and inquires in relation to the matter; and in the course of his conversation with the defendants, ascertains that it is the result of a mere contrivance. He subsequently gives the defendants to understand that this cannot be continued—that he will try the potential effect of the habeas corpus. Now it is their turn to be taught something like reason; they seemed to consider it previously a mere matter of despotism. Look to this; take notice here, for I cannot dwell upon it; my allotment of time will not permit it.

Well, when the property is sold, what then? Thomas Wistar is at the place—he was there only for the sale—when Miss Shoemaker came, they carried away a part of the furniture, and distributed this poor man's garments, and they leave nothing to be found. They make a sale upon his farm—take an inventory, and do everything, affectedly with form—pay all expenses for what they have done, or what was done for them, out of the estate. But what more? Morgan Hinchman subsequently escapes from the asylum, and applies to the court for the purpose of having the original commission against him rescinded, and the whole proceeding quashed. Was not he sane then? They say they had cured him? What do they do? They thrust Lloyd Mifflin into the forefront of the battle; and in pursuance of their design to have the control of his property, they attempt resisting the application of a sane man to rescind a commission of lunacy. You ask for motive! Can it be stronger? [Favor me with the testimony of Mr. Benjamin Hinchman.]

It was also argued by Richie, that Morgan having been in the asylum as a lunatic, he could do nothing with his property; and he had better make a deed of trust, or leave it in the hands of Lloyd Mifflin, the present committee. Mr. Hinchman said, " Why, if he is a *sane* man, I don't see why he should not have his property; if *insane*, what is your deed of trust good for?" Well, says Richie, either let him make a deed of trust, or let it remain in the hands of his committee, Lloyd Mifflin. (Mr. Benjamin Hinchman's testimony was read.)

I connect that matter with Dr. Worthington's remark in relation to his property. I connect it with the fact of Wistar being Mifflin's security. I connect it with Mr. Garrett's declaration, and I show that the object was to keep the property from Morgan. What is plainer, when Edward Richie distinctly states, " if you do that, you may come out, and be a sane man." It is as plain as it can be. They follow that up until he regains his liberty from the asylum ; and even afterwards, they still hold on to his property, and take his money to pay counsel, to keep him out of it. Can you look upon these things and misunderstand them ?

Mr. Richie paid all the expenses, board, counsel and all, out of the plaintiff's own money ; but Mr. Duboissays, apart from the money he received from Mr. Mifflin, or Mr. Richie, he received a fee from Mr. Wistar in the whole matter. Then comes Mr. Lloyd Mifflin, and tells the uncle that he (the plaintiff) had better not attempt reclaiming his property, but leave it with him ; because *they* would either prove him insane, or so blacken his character that he could not walk the streets. Can they account for that ? Does it not indicate the nature of the whole transaction ? Does it not unfold the motive much more clearly than I could ? It is plain and obvious, and cannot be denied, or misunderstoood.

I leave you, gentlemen, to do the rest of this work. Take the notes—Think of them. Judge of men's thoughts by their actions, the only earthly test ; and tell me whether a doubt can remain upon your minds. Take what they themselves have *said;* take what they have *done.* They were all influenced by the same motive and same spirit, from first to last. Tell me, if you can, when was it that the occurrences of life involved a more unnatural confederacy, or produced worse consequences ? Don't mistake this case. It is not merely the case of Morgan Hinchman ; you may blot his unit out of the sum of life ; but do not stab society ! Do not immolate the laws under which you live, which protect you, by which you are protected, and to which you are to turn for security. Look well to that. You are the guardians of it. Don't suppose, because time is not allotted to discuss it, that every portion of this case is not attributed to the same design. You shall discuss it for me. It is a work of justice. It is a work of mercy, too, and upon its accomplishment depend the interests of the land.

There are a few isolated remarks of the defendant's counsel (which, in my rapid flight, have not been distinctly noticed), that before I conclude, demand a moment's attention. I hasten to the period when our joint labors are to be terminated ; and to be crowned, I hope, by the consciousness and consolation, of having faithfully discharged our duty.

The learned gentleman says, we must show the defendants *knew* him (the plaintiff), to be perfectly sane at the time of the capture. Not so. That refers as much to the condition of *their* minds as to *his*. The defendants must show that they at *least* had satisfactory evidence, or knowledge, of his *insanity*. That is the only mitigation of their offence. *They* know upon what grounds they acted—*they* can show what were their inducements ; and if they show unreasonable, or inadequate inducements, wo betide their defence.

Again, he says : " that if there was reasonable ground to suppose that the plaintiff required medical treatment, none of the defendants can be guilty." He forgets that the illegality of *manner* in the arrest, as well as the *arrest itself*, may be the subject of conviction for conspiracy— and he further forgets that they have not shown—consistently with a fair view of the evidence—that the defendant required such medical treatment as they have thought proper to apply.

It is said they had the opinion of a reputable physician : —the report of Friends : the finding of the inquest : the consent of Warder and Biddle. Why, some of these are the grounds of complaint ; and others were the mere measures resorted to, *ex post facto*, for the purpose of giving a semblance of justification for the original outrage. But we have included Dr. Evans and Anna Hinchman, and Benjamin Warder. They were properly included. Apparently at least, they were parties. Suppose we had sued one, then we should have been told, according to their doctrine, that a conspiracy required more. Suppose only two—then we should be told, it is a great hardship,—that others were as guilty as they. Why didn't we include White? Because it was ascertained that he was imposed upon—did nothing but make the appointment—and obviously disapproved of *that;* and was necessary as a witness in order to explain the treachery resorted to.

But we give Morgan Hinchman's letter and statements in evidence!—" *only in rebuttal.*" Which was perfectly right. They attempt proving him insane by his letters. He burnt none; but exhibits all in his possession for your candid examination.

I set aside the settlement in 1840, or consultation with Judge Stroud. What has that to do with the issue? You are not to settle mere questions of property—individual or domestic controversies or difficulties. The application to my distinguished and excellent friend, Judge Stroud, certainly implies no want of sanity; nor was the object of that application incompatible with sound reason, or the exigency of the occasion.

I have now considered the more prominent arguments of my learned friend. I have vindicated, as far as necessary, the views of my respected colleagues. I have discussed the doctrine of insanity—as relates to the mind, or as connected with the diseases of the body—and I have endeavored to show you that in reference to neither, had the defendants any sufficient ground for the course they have adopted.

In addition to this I have shown that we are not called upon to prove the existence of malice, or the want of probable cause, in a case of this character ; that if we were, they are both fairly to be inferred from the nature of the aggression ; and that the absence of the former and the existence of the latter, must be subjects of satisfactory proof, by the defendants themselves.

I have further briefly glanced at the defendant's testimony, in order to prove its inadequacy to such proof, when justly examined. And I have now to say, in conclusion, as I have said before, that these defendants cannot escape, by showing that there were others concerned, as guilty as themselves, though not embraced in this suit. That they cannot escape by their character—by the importance of the lunatic asylum—by the prospective liabilities which it may incur—by the rumors in regard to the plaintiff, which may have either been set afoot by them, or otherwise originated—by the gossip of old maids, or the phantasies of married women—by the report of Dr. Kite, or the endorsement of Dr. Worthington or Dr. Griscom—by a commission irregularly issued, or an inquisition illegally executed—by a secret conclave at the farm of Mrs. Eliza Hinchman, nor by skulking behind the mother and wife for protection. None of these resorts will afford them any aid; and all that remains, therefore, to be determined, is the amount of the damages—and upon that, gentlemen of the jury, it is your peculiar and exclusive province to decide.

But a few words on the subject of damages, and I have done. You shall adjust the *amount.* I take leave to say, sir, that after having examined the account, you will find that when Morgan Hinchman married Miss Margaretta Shoemaker, his fortune was equal to hers in every respect. They make it less, because they take the price of the stocks at their quoted rates originally; whereas it was much *less,* and they remained in the hands of a trustee, and there diminished, until they had been reduced one-fifth of their original value. That is called *his* wasting—it had been *wasted* before it came into his hands. This was a most artful course to establish incompetency. What do his neighbors think of Morgan Hinchman? Do they think him an incompetent man? They thought he was a "cute" man. He drew up the instruments for all the neighbors. He was a gem, in that neighborhood—everybody relied on him. But because he could not calculate farther than any other man ; because he could not "look into the womb of time, and see which seed would grow, and which would not ;" he must be considered a madman. Look at that marble palace down the street,* with able, sagacious and distinguished men at its head. What did they foresee? You all relied upon them. Yet *they*, and you—and *all*, were deceived! Why, vicissitude is the lot of human transactions—that which seems the most prosperous, is often our ruin. Our penalties are often our blessings. So does Providence dispense all things—" man proposes, and God disposes."

But what are his damages? Why, says my learned friends, didn't they *restore* the property—that fragment that remained with them after the sale—after all these expenses, after all these liabilities were deducted, after the breaking up of his household—didn't they *restore* the remnant—except the farm, which they still hold. What does that come to; when a man's farm and house have been stripped and desecrated? They take the jewel, and cast the empty casket at our feet,' and say, take that and rejoice. Is the restoration of the dead body a consolation when the life is torn away? Is the brand of imputed insanity resting upon his brow, like the mark of Cain, to travel with him through life; to be compensated by figures? Well, look to that? Is that the mode in which they account? I consider the pecuniary amount as comparatively nothing. How do they account to you for the months of solitary imprisonment? How do they account to you for the present sufferings of this man? How do they account for the continued estrangement of his wife? How do they account for robbing him of his children—for staining his character, making him a figure for the hand of scorn " to point his slow unmoving finger at?" Are these nothing? How—for the nights of torture, waking him hourly, though he stood in want of

* Formerly the United States Bank.
22

sleep? How—for the restraint upon his liberty, in refusing communication with the external world? They say he is insane—*even now!* Take his letters, written at the very witching time—(I have not time to read them)—and tell me if the whole college of physicians could write or reason more soundly—take them all and tell me what they come to. Nay, take the testimony of the defendants themselves. They resemble men who walk backwards to destruction; and who look upon the sun or stars, to the last.

I ask you to indemnify him—to signify your sense of the wrongs and injuries to which he has been wantonly subjected—by the character of your verdict. I ask you only to indemnify him as far as you *can;* because *entire* indemnity never can be reached. A cureless wound has been inflicted; for which "there is no balm in Gilead; there is no physician there,"—speaking in the temporal application of the phrase. But do what you can—the law demands it from you—individual right appeals to you for it, and every consideration it awakens, in the minds or consciences of men, imperiously lays claim to it. But it is not only in regard to *him* that you are called to give it: I ask for it in regard to the defendants themselves. It is not more necessary in the dispensations of justice, may it please your honor, that the injured should be indemnified, than that the offenders should be punished. I ask you, then, to teach them a lesson; if not through their hearts, through the salutary medium of the pocket, which is a little *lower.* Do as you would wish to be done by. All these matters enter into the consideration of this case. Give them to understand that a harmless, helpless, inoffensive individual may not in broad blushing daylight, as I have said, be arrested—either by a military band or by *friends,* more remorseless than a military band—and taken to a mad-house, and there incarcerated. Let them understand that this enormity, continued for six long, lingering months, shall escape, uncondemned; and you establish an example in the contemplation of which the community shall be corrupted, and the whole world may weep tears of blood. I leave this matter to you: I don't ask you to bring it home to yourselves and look at it through the painful medium of your wives, and with reference to your children; but to regard it with respect to blighted prospects in times to come, and blighted fortunes in times past. I ask you to look at it as calm dispassionate men will do, as *all* just men *must* do,—determined that " JUSTICE SHALL BE DONE THOUGH THE HEAVENS SHOULD FALL."

SMITH'S CASE.

COMMONWEALTH OF PENNSYLVANIA v. THOMAS WASHING-
TON SMITH.

In the Court of Oyer and Terminer, held at Philadelphia.
January Sessions, 1858.

CHARGED WITH MURDER.

INTRODUCTION.

The history of this case is one of the most painfully sad
records of human suffering and human wrong—culmi-
nating in a terrible human sacrifice—that the annals of
any time can furnish. The material facts, however, are
so clearly set forth in the following pages, that it is only
necessary here to state, that after a trial that lasted two
weeks, the defendant was "acquitted."

For the Commonwealth.
District Attorneys — J. P. LOUGHEAD and WM. B.
MANN.

For the Defendant.
Messrs. M. RUSSELL THAYER and DAVID PAUL BROWN.

(340)

SPEECH IN SMITH'S CASE.

WITH DEFERENCE TO YOUR HONORS,
GENTLEMEN OF THE JURY:

After a painful, deeply interesting, and unusually protracted course of investigation, you and I are about to separate. Your time has been well employed; and that patience and attention which you have exhibited from the commencement of this cause have been well bestowed. Time and toil, properly considered, are of little value when they are compared with the importance of eternity. Time is nothing—justice is all.

Justice is much talked of, but not always well understood. Her temperament has been resembled to that of the lamb rather than that of the lion—to the dove rather than the vulture. In her human administration—to say nothing of her celestial properties—she is dignified, calm, mild, moderate, and even merciful. She bears a sword, it is true, which indicates that offenders against her holy edicts must be punished; but even when she inflicts the blow, she does it reluctantly, and for salutary, and not for vindictive purposes. She mingles her sighs with those of her victim, and returns him groan for groan. While bearing the sword in one hand, she holds the scales in the other, wherein to weigh the actions, the vices, the virtues, and the motives of men. When those scales are equiponderant, she drops a tear into that of the accused, and the commonwealth's kicks the beam.

Some thirty-five years ago—perhaps before your honors were born—I had the distinction, being then a very young man, to discuss an important case of homicide (indeed every case of homicide is important, whether it involve the fate of the low or lofty), in this very court. At that time, I observed an emblematic figure or effigy of justice, placed immediately over the judgment seat. In the *left* hand she bore *uneven* scales; and in the *right*, an equivocal sort of implement, which appeared to resemble a trowel, or a butcher's *cleaver!* Instead of wearing her white and immaculate robes, it struck me as most remarkable, particularly in a court of *criminal jurisprudence*, that she should be covered from head to foot with GILT (*guilt*). That figure, I find, still remains; but in looking at her now, I perceive the scales are gone, the cleaver has also been removed—and if I were suspicious, bearing in mind the sanguinary doctrines of the commonwealth, I might readily suppose that it had been transferred, together with the notes of Mr. Bulkley, to the tender mercies of the prosecuting counsel.

In a case like this, allow me to observe, there has rarely been exhibited such undue severity against a defendant engaged in a struggle for his life, as has marked the course of the prosecution. Nevertheless, we guard the citadel of human life, and we will maintain our posts until the last, even though our own lives should be the forfeit.

Permit me further to say, that if I had changed places with the officers of the State, I would at once, with my views of this cause, after hearing the testimony—as I should answer to the JUDGE of judges—have promptly abandoned the prosecution, and that too, if urged on by twenty commonwealths. No commonwealth should stand between my conscience and myself: no commonwealth can stand between my conscience and my God.

In the course of this trial too, the State, not depending alone upon her own strength, or that of her official functionaries, has been surrounded by a trio of herculean representatives from Tamaqua; so that at one time we were almost appalled at the anticipation (knowing our friend's fondness for the *antiquities* of the law) that he was about to revive the ancient and obsolete mode of trial, called "the wager of battle:" in such a physical rencontre the defendant would have had as much to fear, as he now has to hope, in his *legal* and *moral* defence.

The public prosecutors, I repeat it, while they have conducted this case with great ability, and I am compelled to add, with unexampled zeal, have, it is true, professed some sympathy for the defendant, and spoken of their own impartiality.—*Professions* are nothing to me, I look to the *action* of men.

The counsel may have bedecked their brows with laurels; but it is the business of my colleague and myself, with your aid, gentlemen of the jury, to prevent these laurels from being imbued or nurtured by the blood of an innocent man. The honors that spring from cruelty or severity, are ever questionable in their birth, and at the best but of a precarious and short duration. But one thing at least is true, their remembrance shall be perpetuated in the groans and agonies of those whom they have oppressed. Power is desirable, it is laudable, when used for a laudable purpose; but it is most pernicious, not to say culpable, when applied to unjust ends.

> "It is excellent to have a giant's strength,
> But it is tyrannous to use it like a giant."

We now take leave, for a time, of the commonwealth and its officers, and turn to a more agreeable subject. My learned friend and colleague, in the discharge of his duty, has reflected great light upon this cause and great honor upon himself. By his industry and talents he has removed all impediments (there were no obstacles) which had been temporarily thrown in our way; and almost all that remains to me, is to deepen the impressions he has made, by treading in his footsteps. It is certainly no difficult task, to pursue any path in which he has been the pioneer.

A single other preliminary word to *you*, gentlemen of the jury: However this case may eventuate, you will bear with you, in withdrawing from your present public functions, not merely the thanks of this honorable court for your patience and attention during this important and vital trial, and the thanks of the humble advocate who now appeals to you; but you will bear with you, what is beyond all praise and all price, the grateful acknowledgments of lacerated, bleeding and broken hearts. You will bear with you, also, what the world's applause cannot give, nor its censures take away—the consolatory consciousness of having faithfully and fearlessly performed your duty.

For myself, allow me to say, if I should close a forensic career of more than forty years, by the successful vindication of the prisoner at the bar; if not the crowning *glory*—better than the crowning glory—it would be the crowning *happiness* of an arduous, laborious, and diversified professional life. But the mind of man is so mysteriously constituted, that in moments and matters of the deepest interest and anxiety, it often becomes impaired in its exercise and efforts, in the very consciousness of its responsibility; and in its desire to do *most*, it accomplishes the *least*. In the language of the unhappy prisoner, our very " hopes are hopeless"—our very wishes give us not our wish.

When I look at the unfortunate defendant, blasted, as it were, in the very prime of his life, the spring-tide of his existence—when I behold his pale, fragile, affectionate, and self-devoted sister clinging to him, as the tendril clings to its support, beautifying it with its verdure, and refreshing it with its shade—when I cast a retrospective view over all that *he* has suffered, and all the sufferings in which *she* has shared; and when I bear in mind that all this load of grief appeals to me, at least in part, for alleviation; you must pardon me for saying, that I almost shrink from the appeal. "I tremble, and confess myself a coward"—not, heaven knows, from a want of sympathy—not from a want of will—but from the fear that the warmth of that sympathy, and the earnestness of that will, may defeat the exercise of those abilities which are so urgently and imperatively demanded.

⅄ *Your* condition, however, gentlemen of the jury, painful as it is, is far more enviable than *mine*. To you is delegated a portion of the attribute of Omnipotence: you are his Fates: you hold his life in your hands: you control his temporal, if not his eternal destinies: you can avoid what I can only deprecate—his condemnation: you can secure what I can only solicit—his acquittal. Upon you, therefore, the hopes of this unhappy man must mainly rest, and to you we solemnly and confidently commit the result of this deeply interesting and most momentous cause; at the same time earnestly beseeching you ever to bear in mind, that—

> " Human power doth then seem likest God's,
> When mercy seasons justice."

Now, gentlemen of the jury, to come to the case:— This indictment charges Thomas Washington Smith with the murder of Richard Carter, on the 4th day of November, 1857. The ordinary defences of murder, generally consist in the denial of the *act* of homicide; or in the denial of the death, as the *consequence* of the act; or the mitigation of the alleged degree of felonious homicide, arising from the cause that produced it; or the allegation of mental irresponsibility, in excuse of the crime charged, whatever may have been the imputed offence.

Such, I say, are the ordinary defences. In this case, however, we do not deny the act, nor do we deny that it produced death. Both of these are fatal and unquestionable truths. Except, therefore, for the sake of adherence to formal and technical propriety, no proofs thus far, would have been required by us from the commonwealth. Our defence rests on widely different grounds.

If we were astute, and it were necessary, we might show
you that, if the defendant were as sane as Solomon (I
don't mean as *wise*), this could be no more, according to
the evidence, than the very least degree, of the least and
last order, of felonious homicide. I shall just intimate a
thought on that subject, rather to show that we might
rely upon it, if necessary ; though at the same time disa-
vowing all such intention. I shall skim over, rather than
argue it, and then come to the main ground of our reliance.

There are three kinds of felonious homicide in Pennsylvania :—

Murder in the first degree.

Murder in the second degree ; and

Manslaughter.

Prior to the year 1795, there were but two grades of
felonious homicide—as the English law then existed in
all its rigor, in this State. At that time, William Brad-
ford immortalized his name, by the amelioration of this
portion of the criminal code, whereby the second degree
of murder was introduced ; and in the introduction of
which the Legislature provided : " That all murder perpetrated in the commission, or attempt to commit robbery,
rape, burglary, or arson, or by poison, or lying in wait, or
any wilful, deliberate, *and* premeditated killing, shall be
deemed murder in the first degree ; and all other *murder*
shall be murder in the second degree.

Remember, it is all other *murder*, not all other *killing*.
If it were all other killing, it would render our code
more sanguinary than the British code ; and elevate the
crime of manslaughter into, murder of the second degree.
The intention of this law was clearly (as both murder in
the first, and second degree, require malice), to discriminate between the grades or species of malice ; and to
regulate the offence accordingly.

The terms " wilful, deliberate and premeditated,"—
particularly when we associate with them, as connected

with, and as illustrative of, their character, the terms
" poison and lying in wait,"—can leave no doubt as to
the truth of my position ; and I take leave, therefore, to
say, that when Dougherty was convicted of murder,
upon the plausible doctrine of Chief Justice McKean;
and also when Lieutenant Smith was convicted by the
same doctrine of Judge Rush—that, " as he struck the
blow, it must therefore have been wilful ; and if it was
wilful, and he intended to kill, it must have been deliberate; and if the deliberation was for a single moment, it
amounted to premeditation "—so that the act became
" wilful, deliberate, and premeditated !"—I take leave to
dissent, *toto cœlo*, from the law and the logic of those distinguished jurists. Again: " If the defendant has time
to think, and did intend to kill, for a moment, as well as
an hour or a day, it is a deliberate, wilful and premeditated killing, and murder in the first degree, within the
act of Assembly."

Now, if it were not for the high authority of this doctrine, I should hold it to be sheerly absurd, and utterly
opposed to the humane spirit of the enactment in ques·
tion. First: What is meant by a moment ? It is an indefinite lapse of time. Horace speaks of "a moment of
an hour." Legal matters should be definite, particularly
when life depends upon the construction. What might
be wilful, deliberate and premeditated in one man, might
not be so in another. Are the workings of the mind of
an excited man, and the limit allowed to *cooling time*, to
be fixed by a learned judge, who is never permitted to
become excited—who is calm and dispassionate from
habit and necessity? Is he to determine when reason
resumes her throne—when, with him, she has never been
known to lose it ? If this be the case, why then, a man
who, at one moment has his nose pulled, and the next
moment kills his assailant (which can amount to no more
than manslaughter), upon this dicta of the judges that—
" as he had the will to do it, he had the thought to

prompt the will—and if he could think one moment before the blow, he premeditated the blow"—every manslaughter would be at *least*, murder in the second degree. In short, there could be no manslaughter; unless you take from the alleged offender, at the same time, the will to strike and the ability to think—that is, unman him entirely, and deprive him of the powers of a sentient being—of which, let me say, if he were thus utterly deprived, he could commit no offence at all, as he would no longer be a responsible being.

My notion is, then, that in order to murder, there must be such manifestations as clearly imply a " heart regardless of social duty, and fatally bent upon mischief." I do not mean to say, that the plan of destruction shall exist for a day, or even for an hour; but I do mean to say, that it is incumbent upon the commonwealth clearly to show its pre-existence, in order to establish what the law calls *malice*. *Poison* requires the preparation or concoction, and administration of the destructive drug; it is for the most part prepared in the absence of the intended victim; it is an evidence of *will, deliberation,* and *premeditation*, that cannot be disputed. *Lying in wait*, belongs to the same category of offences; the very term *wait*, implies time for will, deliberation, and premeditation; and as "all other kinds of wilful, deliberate, and premeditated murder," clearly refer to the *motive* and *malice* of the cases adverted to; it of course follows that a sudden exigency, producing an instantaneous excitement of mind, whether it be in the shape of a blow, a wrong, or an insult, or whatever you please, is not embraced by those terms which designate murder in the first degree.

The law of England describes murder as the " taking the life of any reasonable creature, with malice aforethought, either *express* or *implied*." Our law does not recognize this doctrine. *Implied* malice with us, is never more than *murder* in the second degree; and although *express malice* amounts to murder in the first degree, the Legislature has taken care to define what shall constitute express malice, by the terms " wilful, deliberate and premeditated."

Now, may it please your honors, do not encounter me, by telling me how you have decided ; or what preconceived notions may have taken lodgment in your minds ; but come to the question with your best reasoning, and with all the lights you can bring to bear upon it ; and before you break into the " bloody house of life," be conscientiously and well assured that you do so upon the warrant of the law.

It matters not what has been decided—if erroneously decided : you are not the scapegoats or pack-horses to carry off all the errors that may have crept into the administration of justice : let those who have committed them answer for them. We are engaged in the case of The Commonwealth v. Smith—you are the judges—this is the jury in his case—I am the counsel—this is the law —and I ask your decision on this law, derived directly from the Legislature, and especially applicable to this case. Do not, by imaginary analogies, or supposed similarities in other cases, as decided by other judges, be betrayed into errors upon the subject which is now immediately before you. No two cases exactly alike—or to which the law equally related—were ever yet known ; and therefore by confounding one case with another—the past with the present—and applying the same law equally to both, you may do great and irremediable wrong.

I say, then, that if this defendant was perfectly himself, it is legally impossible, even if the provocation was not the tithe of what it is—and what I shall show it to have been—to convict him of more than murder in the second degree.

And I will show you with regard to the exact state of the provocation—though he was as sane as any judge or juryman that I address—that the offence, at most was but MANSLAUGHTER. And further I will show you, with reference to the state of his mind at the time; and the cruel injuries and outrages he had sustained; and the peculiar sensibilities of the man, and his inherited infirmities; that he is totally irresponsible to the law for the death of his betrayer.

But to resume—having marshalled you the way that I am going—how is it worse than manslaughter—apart from the alleviating features suggested in my third point?

A man, returning to his home, detects an adulterer in the " manner "—he immediately rushes forth for a weapon and strikes him dead—he *thinks*—he knows it is his *wife*—he knows the *betrayer*—he knows it is his *own house*, and his *own rights* that are violated: he wills—he deliberates—he premeditates. According to the judicial notions referred to, he is guilty of murder; yet that has never been held to be more than manslaughter, even if he kill both. And if it were a rape, and the ravisher were slain, it is excusable homicide—on the principle that the wife and the husband have reciprocal rights of defence; and that in defending her he defends himself.

Well, then, as slaying the adulterer in the act of crime, can be no more than manslaughter—and as it is reduced to that third grade of felonious homicide, by the excitement—if we show you a state of excitement produced in the human mind, equal and greater than that of a husband who detects his wife with the adulterer: does it require an argument from me to show, that the greater the excitement the greater the mitigation of the crime? Let us, in this part of the case, suppose (as has been said) Mr. Smith to be as sane as any man I address, and as composed as any man could be who had been subjected to the same injury; and I will show, that time, which heals slight wounds, causes those that are deeper and more mortal in their character, to gangrene and destroy; in other words, that excitement arising from some injuries is aggravated by every succeeding day and hour.

Anger, is said to be "a brief madness," and it is upon that hypothesis that the law mitigates homicide from murder to manslaughter, where the fatal blow is provoked by the original assault or provocation. Should not that excuse be at least equally available when the party slain —having originally assumed the mask of a friend, and under that disguise utterly ruined the hapless defendant— induced him to marry his offcast mistress; concealed the connection for months; allowed it to burst upon him— and to burst upon a censorious world of a sudden—in the midst of his hopes—in the very bloom of his affections; and thus consign him at once, while surrounded with all the charms of life, to worse than annihilation, to remediless and fathomless ruin. Ruin to him—to his— to every one who clung to him, or to whom he clung.

The man who strikes an adulterer dead, is partially excused for the deed, by the enormity of the offence thus punished. He is not excused because he is insane, but because even sanity itself would prompt the blow. But suppose the blow were not inflicted at the moment,—that the unhappy husband buried for a time his griefs and his wrongs in his own bosom, like a pent. up earthquake or volcano,—brooded upon it in ceaseless agony—saw it in every human face—saw it in his blasted hopes— inhaled it in the air he breathed—felt it in his "heart of hearts," month after month, and hour after hour, until it utterly absorbed or enthralled his better nature —gaining strength with progress, and finally overpowering all mental resistance—his one, sole, fearful, fatal—inseparable thought. Is that man sane—can he be sane. Would not the *imagination* of such a picture almost drive a sensitive man mad. What think you, then, would be the effect of this sad reality of woe? What law would you apply to it?—by what law was it contemplated?—What human law punishes this manifold wrong, or redresses this unparalleled injury? There is but one law, which, while it prompts, sanctions the vengeful blow—the great universal and irrevocable LAW OF NATURE. —A law which even religion seems to recognize, when we are told in Proverbs, that " Jealousy is the rage of a man, therefore he will not spare in the day of vengeance."

This leads me to consider the facts of this case, as bearing upon the state of the defendant's mind on the 4th day of November, 1857, when this offence is alleged to have been committed; and as also, at the same time, imparting aid to the defence, by reflecting light upon the legal positions that have been already assumed.

It has been truly said, gentlemen of the jury, that there is nothing in the romance of the drama that can compare with the sad realities of human life. Look, now, at this case, which is at once an illustration and an enforcement of these doctrines. Why the fates and the furies combined, could never weave a blacker or a more terrific web than that which is here presented!—a horrible pall, which seems to shroud all the actors in this bloody tragedy! But let me not anticipate, but turn your attention to the lamentable story.

Richard Carter arrived in this country, from England, some twenty-five years ago. He took up his residence in the neighborhood of Tamaqua, where he continued for many years. The district attorney has told you, that by a course of successful industry he acquired a large fortune; that he had many excellent qualities, and an extensive circle of friends. Let us see how he deserved these commendations. The fortune he had made, instead of being applied to virtuous purposes was dedicated to vice—and to come to this very case, was the means relied upon to procure the prostitution of the daughter of his friend, his partner, and I might almost say his brother, John McCauley.

In the year 1856, this man, who had acquired his wealth among us, applies to Mr. McCauley for the privilege of adopting or taking charge of his daughter,—at

that time a budding girl, unpolluted even by the atmosphere of a corrupt and corrupting world. The father,
relying upon his honor, complies with his request. Carter assumes to himself, ostensibly, the paternal duties in
relation to her; and upon leaving her father, promises to
make her a "finished lady;" and so he DID—that promise
he kept literally—she is *finished* for all the valuable purposes of this life—*finished*, almost, in regard to the hopes
of future salvation—such being the influence which temporal ruin sometimes produces upon our eternal hopes.

He places her at a respectable female college in an ad-
joining State. She remains there some months. In the
month of July he sends his summons to those in charge
of the college, to permit her to visit the city of Philadelphia; she accordingly arrives, and he receives her at
Jones' Hotel. There, this man—a professed father, having
adopted this child, and having refined her sensibilities
through instruction, and thereby rendered the crime into
which he betrayed her doubly deplorable,—in the night
time,—at the hour of midnight,—the poor girl being un-
well, and the door left open for the use of her nurse (as
no man can doubt, except the district attorney)—this
modern Tarquin, "this remorseless, lecherous, treacherous, kindless villain" approaches, and finally enters her
chamber, and there commits—merciful heaven, what
shall I call it? It is adultery, at the least; it approaches a rape—indeed, it is almost an incest! This is
the man who is eulogized and applauded to the very echo
by the district attorney. This is the man over whose
ashes the commonwealth weeps; and to conceal whose
crimes the commonwealth spreads her immaculate and
impervious mantle—I wish I could plant flowers on his
grave, but they would only wither. If a man forty-eight
years old; holding the position of a father; professing to
be a guardian and a benefactor; receiving an innocent girl
into his charge, in double trust from her parent, can be

capable of committing such a crime as this!—he exceeds
all limits of penitence,—all hope of mercy!   Let him

> " Never pray more : abandon all remorse ;
> On horror's head ! horrors accumulate !
> Do deeds to make Heaven weep,—all earth amaz'd.
> For nothing can he to damnation add—
> Greater than that."

The defendant's acquaintance with Miss McCauley, or
rather his first interview, took place some time in the
spring of, I think it was May, 1856.—It was then, as you
will remember, that he said "She was a girl that filled
his eye."   He had been a traveller North and South,—
and, as he expressed himself, had determined that, in
choosing a help-mate for life he would neither take a
Northern nor a Southern lady, but one from the Key-
stone State, as combining the warmth of the South with
the strength of the North.   Well, as we have said, he sees
Miss McCauley, and she makes an impression upon his
too sensitive and susceptible heart.   He is, however, soon
drawn away by his occupation—and perhaps time might
have obliterated this impression, but that in the month
of August, 1856, while employed in pursuit of his business in New York, he is visited by his sister, who informs him that Miss McCauley had written to him, and
had requested her to inquire whether he had received the
letter.   This, let it be remembered, was after the intercourse with Carter, at Jones' Hotel.   Time is the great
discoverer.   It is but a month after she has been deflow-
ered.   This poor, unsuspecting young man is overjoyed at
the idea of having captivated a blooming young girl, by
whom he had been so deeply impressed at a first and
single interview.   He has never received the letter, but
the recollection of her beauty is agreeably brought back
to his mind by this indication that there is at least one
person in the world besides the sister—who now clings
around him—to whom his welfare is not indifferent.

Now observe the delicacy, the respect, the inborn gentleness of the prisoner—he does not write directly to Miss McCauley, but addresses his letter to Tamaqua, to the care of Richard Carter.

After this, in the month of December, Carter, Miss McCauley, Miss Smith and the defendant are found in Philadelphia, at the Madison House. At this period she is nearly five months gone with child—a matter perfectly well known to Carter, and of course to her. At this very time she exhibits the engagement ring, and apprises Mr. Carter of her intention to be married to the defendant. In addition to this, it is clearly established by subsequent interviews and conversations, that he had full knowledge of it, and that it met his approval. What is the meaning of Carter's coming to town to dine with Smith—going to church with him and the ladies—asking for the postponement of the marriage for a few days, in order that his presence might give it more form, ceremony and sanction? And yet the district attorney says that he, Carter, never knew of it, and considered it as a joke. I should consider an argument of this character, in the face of such facts as these, and the subsequent ratification of the marriage, as the worst sort of a joke,— a joke calculated to bring into ridicule both truth and justice.

Smith does not postpone the marriage; he did not feel bound by the suggestions of Mr. Carter in relation to it. To use his own language, he did not marry her for pecuniary advantage, or in reference to Mr. Carter's wealth— he married her for her own wealth, and as the daughter of a poor man. But, we are told, Carter wrote a letter to her, intimating, that she had better not get married, knowing her "*situation.*" This shows two things:—First, that he was the father of her child, as *we aver.*—Secondly, that he knew of the intended marriage, which *they deny.* The writing of that letter clearly confirms the paternity of the child, and as clearly shows his knowledge of the intended

marriage.   This letter is shown to the defendant while in
the full tide of hope and happiness.   Surprise has been
expressed that it did not put him on his guard ; there are
many reasons why it should not put him on his guard.
In the first place, nothing is so blind as love.   In the
second place, its very exhibition by his betrothed, would
have closed his eyes, if they were as keen as an eagle's.
In the third place, if he had been lynx-eyed, what could
he have seen—being innocent himself—incompatible with
the innocence of the woman of his affections, in the terms
" *your situation ?*"   Certainly, that does not imply an
adulterous connection.   Well, then, in these circumstances,
no human voice forbidding, and all apparently approving,
on the 16th day of December, 1856, they were married.
Was ever matrimony, for a time, more blessed with seem-
ing happiness ; and on his part, with more pure and noble
kindness of heart, or more marked devotion to the partner of his bosom?   Certainly never.   At home or abroad
he is still the same.   You may remember, that while on
a brief sojourn in New York—whither his business had
drawn him—he spoke rapturously of his conjugal bliss—
of his having brought all his wanderings to a close ; that
he was about now to settle down in domestic peace, and
in companionship with a virtuous woman, and his first
love   You .will remember, gentlemen of the jury, the
touching little incident of his removing the miniature of
his wife from beneath his pillow, and repeatedly and
rapturously kissing it ; and then, when detected in this
spontaneous manifestation of his feelings, by one of his
friends who was present, concealing it in his bosom, to
rest upon his heart.

> " If Heaven had made him such another world,
>   Of one entire and perfect chrysolite !
>   He'd not have sold *her* for it."

Permit me now to present to you, gentlemen, as the
shadow to this bright picture, a scene of misery, of con-

jugal and domestic misery—such as you have rarely, if ever, been condemned to witness.

He at length returns from New York, and scarcely returns, when he is suddenly informed that his wife is in the peril incident to a premature birth. This is on the 10th of April, 1857. Full of anxiety, he rushes to Mrs. Leonard and her husband, to inquire what is to be done with the embryo-birth. He wishes also to know the probable extent of his wife's danger; his anxieties and his sensibilities are excited to the highest possible degree; all his hopes are centred in her; all his fears relate to her;— he prepares the nurse; introduces Mrs. Leonard; rushes for the doctor; congregates around him almost all that he knew; summons them for *what;* to relieve his beloved wife from peril!—and there they stand, living witnesses to her unsuspected degradation, and his undying infamy! There they stand, to prove his wife a *wanton;* and himself a wretch, unfit to crawl upon the earth! There are the Leonards—the nurse—the doctor—the sister—and the domestics of the establishment—all witnesses of this most deplorable scene!

When he goes for the doctor and consults him, he inquires, after what period of gestation a child might be born alive? " Well," replies the doctor, " it might live possibly at six months; but at seven or eight months its living would be quite probable." " Alas! then," says Smith, " I am childless, and there is no hope, as I have been married less than four months." The doctor goes to the room of the patient, prepared for an abortion; and upon examination ascertains, to his surprise, that she has reached her full term! He returns home. In a few hours poor Smith rushes again after him, and upon the doctor's second visit, this faithless woman is delivered of a child of full nine months' gestation! Look, for a moment, at this melancholy picture! Look at the accumulated horrors which distract his brain! Look at the publicity which he, himself, has contributed to give to this story of disgrace and woe!

The doctor attempts to cheer him, by saying "you are not the first man who has been presented with a child in so short a time after marriage."—"But," says Smith, fully comprehending this insinuation, "I tell you, I have been married less than four months, and I never knew my wife until after the sanctions of my marriage. Indeed, whatever may have been my faults through life—and they may have been many—I can truly say, I have never been guilty of illicit intercourse." Thus circumstanced, tell me, ye severest, what could he have done?

> " Had it pleased heaven—
>   To try him with afflictions ; had it rained
>   All kinds of sores and shames on his bare head—
>   Steep'd him in poverty to the very lips—
>   Given to captivity him and his utmost hopes ;
>   He should have found, in some part of his soul,
>   A drop of patience :—But, alas ! to make him
>   A fixed figure for the time of scorn
>   To point his slow unmoving finger at !—
>   Yet, could he bear that too—well, very well !
>   But there ! where he had garnered up his heart—
>   Where, either he must live or bear no life !
>   The fountain, from the which his current runs,
>   Or else dries up ; to be discarded thence !
>   Turn thy complexion *there*,
>   Patience, thou young and rose-lipp'd cherubim—
>   Aye ! *there* look grim as hell !"

Do you remember the description of the nurse? Do you remember how he fell, in an instant, from the topmost to the lowest round of ambition and love? Still, his gentleness and his kindness, in this terrific shock, at least, partially remained. When about to desert these scenes of his former joy; upon being asked by his wife, if he would take the wedding-ring he had given her, and the Bible, which he had presented to her, "No," was the reply, "I leave the former as a memento of my affection, and I leave the latter for the improvement of your future life, and your consolation for what has passed." Call to mind, if you please, the description of the scenes transacted in that room. He threw himself across his trunk, while preparing for his departure, and wept as no man ever wept. The nurse says: " In all her experience, she never witnessed, before, such a scene of sadness, agony, wretchedness, and horror !" This untutored description was the very perfection of eloquence, springing spontaneously from the heart.

Almost immediately after this appalling discovery, the defendant forwards a letter to his sister,—that lovely and devoted girl, who now clings so closely to him, in his hour of extremest need. He beseeches her to come up, for God's sake! Immediately, upon the wings of affection, she flies to him. She finds him in the lowest depths of grief—he embraces her—weeps upon her bosom—begs of her to control him, and to act for him ; and being totally incapable of self-government, he relinquishes himself entirely to her guidance. He tells her he has been most grossly deceived ; that his honor is in the dust ; that he would as soon have suspected the angels of heaven of a wrong, as his wife. "Oh, God! how I loved her, how I worshipped her,—and this is my reward!" His sister endeavors to console him, telling him he must rise in his manhood and strive to outlive his difficulties ; that there was seldom a life pictured so dark as to admit of no ray of hope. She refers him to the only source of true consolation, to which he replies: " Would you not have a man feel when he has his heart taken from his living body ?" and then, in broken sentences, adds, through his sobs and groans. " I was born to misery—my life has been one of continued sorrow—I have known what it was to be a fatherless boy—I have known the sorrows of orphanage— I have been a houseless wanderer in a strange land—I have buried most of my kindred—I have stood by the grave of my mother—one of the purest spirits ever lent to earth—no son ever idolized a mother as I did mine—but all my life-sorrows are nothing to this! This is the grave of all my hopes—ah! merciful God, why was I born to such a fate! This grief, says the witness, continued with little abatement until the evening of the day, when he tore himself away from this scene of his agony and disgrace.

Where do we find him next? It would, indeed, be difficult to trace him in his erratic course—he passes back and forth in his devious career—sometimes in Washington—then among the mountains of Virginia—then at Baltimore—then at North-east—then at New York. Wherever he went, he fancied he moved with the indelible mark of Cain upon his brow! like Cain he wandered a vagabond and a fugitive upon the face of the earth—like Cain he sought death, while death seemed to flee from him.

He seeks, at length, relief from Mr. Townsend; but even there he finds that the law affords no relief for one in his hapless condition. He grows daily worse and worse. His constitution is ruined, his nervous system destroyed—his heart is broken—and he resigns himself to one horrible and absorbing thought, which sways the entire empire of his mind. He conceives that he is hunted wherever he goes, by his betrayer and his spies—surrounded by them in Washington—pursued by them in Baltimore—and threatened by them in Philadelphia. All these scenes and circumstances have been minutely related by the witnesses examined in this cause. Finally, laboring under this delusion—a delusion arising from the actual, the unparalleled sufferings to which he had been doomed for the last six months—he again reaches this city in the latter part of October, 1857.

The state of his mind, as manifested by his conduct,—produced directly by the wreck which his sorrows had made—has been so graphically described by Murphy, Davis, Campbell, and others who speak of his condition, within less than three days of the time of this lamentable catastrophe, as to leave no doubt upon the mind of any man who is not himself mǎd, that the prisoner was, at that period, an irresponsible agent. The voice of reason was either no longer heard, or heard through a false and perverted medium. The will, which may appropriately be called the executive officer of reason, had lost its power and control. It was overthrown or so subjugated, as to play the pander to those delusions of mind, which it was utterly unable to resist.

We do not contend for the exemption of *intensity of passion*, from punishment—though there might be something in the horrors of this case to excuse even that: what we contend for, is simply this, that where passion and delusion too (whether that delusion arise from actual, or imaginary, suffering), combine together against the reason and the will, and thereby overthrow all mental government and moral restraint, that there is no responsibility for anything that may be done under the impulses arising from this deranged condition of both body and mind. There is not a madman, in a lunatic asylum, whose insanity is not to be referred to this disorganization—to this revolution in the moral and mental structure—to this rebellion, as it may be called, of a man against himself: his *reason* is not extinct; but instead of swaying the government, it becomes subordinate; and passion and illusion usurp its sceptre. This is what I call *insanity!* Do you ask me for its manifestations? I will answer you—for I profess to know as much upon that subject as any of the witnesses; or as any of the books exhibit that have been presented here before you. If I show you a man, who has lived the consistent and holy life of a professor of the gospel; at peace with all mankind, and what is better, at peace with heaven—full of warm affections, and lively sensibilities—meek and modest as it becomes the vicegerent of the Lord to be; and all of a sudden—or after having passed through the heaviest of all earthly afflic-

tions—you see that selfsame man playing the recreant
and the ruffian; profaning the Almighty; trampling upon
his laws, and cursing and swearing without excuse or
apparent provocation!—What would you say of that
man? Would you pronounce him sane or insane? These
are manifestations of insanity: the sudden, total and
anomalous transition from all that was moral and virtuous, to all that is vicious and devilish!

"Now look upon that picture, and on this;" compare
them and see whether they correspond or differ. The
mind, of all wonders, is the most wonderful; and the
complicated machinery of the body through which it
operates, and by which it manifests itself, is scarcely less
wonderful—the former is of Heaven, the latter of earth—
the former is immortal; but by that very immortality it
dignifies its tenement of clay. Where they act in concert—where the emotions of the heart and the dictates of
the head are in unison—entire and perfect harmony pre-
vails; but in the conflicts of the passions of the human
heart with the intellectual government, disorder and mis-
rule in both, are the terrible result—both are consequently
enfeebled: or if, finally, the morbid affections of the
heart should acquire the ascendancy over the intellectual
powers, reason, as I have said, must necessarily be overthrown.

But again: so fearfully and wonderfully are we made,
that by the excessive indulgence of an unrestrained, morbid passion; or by an insurmountable obstacle suddenly
checking that indulgence, insanity is equally likely to ensue. A check to the ruling passion of pride, of love, of
hope, of patriotism, of ambition—an utter check, when
those passions are at their highest tide—will cause them
(to use a strong figure) to overflow the banks of reason,
and spread around them destruction and desolation!
This is what is called *monomania*—and is characterized
by the ruling, or despotic propensity. Why did Lord
Castlereagh destroy himself? Why did Mr. Whitbread

destroy himself? both prime ministers of England—because they were so ensnared by political wiles as to be defeated in the objects of their ambition; they became mad; and suicide was the result. Why did Sir Samuel Romilly take his own life?—a man of the highest intellect and the warmest heart—who was at once a public and a private example—while revelling upon the very summit of distinction, and professional honor: he was bereft of the partner of his bosom. His ruling passion was resisted; life became no longer of any value; and he terminated it with his own hand. The coroner's inquest placed all these deaths to the account of insanity.

Come we now "to the last scene of all, that ends this strange, eventful story." On the fourth day of November, 1857, at about five o'clock in the afternoon, Smith presents himself at the parlor of the St. Lawrence Hotel. At half past four, of the same day, you find him at the store of Mr. Davis, in Walnut street, below Fourth. There is nothing from which we could infer that he visited the hotel with any design, or that he even knew that Carter was there. The weapons were not *prepared:* it has been proved they were generally worn, almost as a part of himself, in his travelling agencies. Those, let it be remembered, were the very weapons that, out of distrust of his own self-control, he had, sometime before this, deposited with Mr. Brinton; expressing the desire that he should hold them in safe keeping, and not surrender them again to the owner even if he should beg and pray for them—as he was *afraid*—mark that word, that if he should encounter the man who had betrayed and ruined him, he might be impelled, resistlessly, to commit some act of violence. Possessed of these weapons, as I have said, he encounters his adversary—a powerful, bold, bad man. As he approaches him, in a mild and modest way —according to the statement of the nephew—Mr. Carter "seemed not to know him;"—*seemed not to know the wretch he had made!!* He must have known him, notwithstanding the change, perfectly well. He knew him well in December; he knew him well on Good Friday, but a little week before the birth of the child; and he must have haunted his sleeping and his waking thoughts ever since, if he had any conscience to influence his dreams, or to stimulate his reflections. This very cold-blooded inso-lence and cruelty, was enough to rouse the lion in any man, sane or mad! They are seated on the sofa beside each other, conversing in a subdued tone; so as to render it impossible for the defence to extract from any of the inmates of the hotel, who were present at the time, even a single word, from which we might guess at the nature of their conversation. We are merely told, by the nephew, that Carter "*smiled.*" Gracious Heavens! could that man smile amidst the wreck and ruin he had made!

Exactly what took place between them none shall say, but you may imagine—nay, you are *bound* to infer, from the affected want of recognition, and that lurid smile, that he taunted the man he had betrayed.. Was this, think you, a smile of benevolence—of sympathy—of con-dolence; or was it the smile of a demon in contemplating the agonies of his victim. You may judge of it partly from the result that follows. Had he denied—had he ex-plained his iniquities—had he poured balm into the heart he had lacerated, this deplorable event might not have taken place.—Everything tends to show that his conduct opened the wounds which time had scarcely cicatrized; and produced an impulsive and involuntary act, which deprived him of his life, and has brought the defendant, borne to the earth, with unmerited odium and grief, to abide this fearful charge. There is, however, a Provi-dence even in the fall of a sparrow; and we are relieved from all doubt, upon that subject, by the unintentional disclosures derived through the commonwealth itself. The district attorneys, perhaps, will hardly choose to remember a fact, which had been brought out not by the will, but by the blundering, of the prosecution. It was

the very important fact testified by Lieutenant Deckhart
—their own witness (while they endeavored to extract
from him the confessions of the prisoner, in order to a
conviction), that the prisoner in his conversation remarked, he " had done justice between God and man ;"
and then added, referring to the conversation with Carter
on the sofa, " *he had even the audacity to tell me he was going
to see my sister !*" Do our friends on the other side *now* remember this ? Do the jury remember this ? That is the
spark that exploded the magazine ! If he had been ten
times *sane;* excited by his past wrongs, it would have
driven him *mad;* but *being mad*, and this being connected
in his distracted thoughts, with the monomania under
which he labored, it tended directly to that catastrophe
which is the subject of this indictment. [Here, District
Attorney Mann, interrupting the speaker, observed, " There
was no such evidence given, as I remember." Mr. Brown,
" Look to your notes, it will be found in the evidence of
the lieutenant of police, who conveyed the defendant to
prison." The counsel, examining their notes, admit it is
there.]

Immediately after the threat of Carter to visit the sister of the defendant (showing that my view of its effect
is right), they simultaneously spring to their feet—and instantly Carter receives a ball in his heart. Then, turning
from his victim, with that glaring and remarkable expression of the eye which was noticed by all the witnesses, the prisoner declares that he " will surrender to no
one but an officer of the law." No doubt that even here,
he was governed by the illusion that he was surrounded
by Carter's spies. This is just the conduct of a maniac.
If this had been the act of a calculating avenger, would
it have been suspended or deferred for six long months ?
Would he not have gone to Tamaqua ? Is Tamaqua at
the opposite end of the world ? Could not the act have
been perpetrated there, without the probability of affecting his own life ; in the by-ways of the country, in the

concealments of ravines and coal-pits? Is it to be doubted, that a man who had even a malicious mind to direct him, would have sought his own destruction; when it might have been readily avoided, and his vengeance rendered equally sure? To say that he was bent upon a double-death, is to give up one-half of the argument of his sanity. In short, it is almost conclusive, with the other proofs, of his *total insanity.* But they tell us that we are bound to *prove* insanity—to prove it clearly—and to show it existed on the 4th of November—and at the very moment of the commission of this act. We have done so. We have shown it, in its incipient stages, months prior to the act. We strengthened that proof, by evidence of the ancestral taint of insanity in the mother's, and in the father's line. We have traced him down to the very day, almost the very hour, when the act was perpetrated. We have shown you that his monomania culminated at that time—and that his reason was dethroned; and we have given you the immediate, proximate and exciting cause of that dethronement. Our defence then is, that he was morally and mentally irresponsible—and that this irresponsibility was produced by the very man who was its victim!

Allow me here to say, that I am utterly amazed that the commonwealth's counsel should have been so puzzled and perplexed with the doctrines of monomania; and that they should have conceived, that because insanity is exhibited in reference to one illusion, it follows that that illusion does not indicate a *general* unsoundness of mind. The human mind is not like a piece of mechanism, wherein one wheel may turn the wrong way, without impairing all the others. In the mind, it may be said, if the expression be allowable, that the one wheel turns wrong, because all the others are more or less out of harmony or order. It is, in short, from the general infirmity, that monomania is produced; which, in its turn, re-infects the rest, and at times would seem to transfer its own de-

ranged character, if we may use the phrase, to the entire
mental machine. When a mortification is detected at
the extreme end of the finger, a skilful pathologist
knows at once that there is danger to human life—that
the disease is not merely local, but is, or will become, constitutional;—and when a cancer, in the smallest shape,
presents itself on the surface of the human frame, it loses
its insignificance when it is remembered as a denotement
of its having spread its destructive fibres through every
portion of the vital system, riding as it does, upon the
blood—which is the life of man.

The most clear, simple, and beautiful illustration of the
doctrine for which we contend—and it is marvellous that
it was overlooked by the learned gentlemen—is derived
from the loftiest human intellect the world ever knew,
and presented in the insanity of King Lear; to which, at
the risk of being considered too poetical, and too enthusiastic in my admiration of the author, I shall take leave
to refer. There are two books which I shall never be
afraid or ashamed to quote, and which are worth more
than all the authorities—whether *bound* in calf or *lined*
with calf—that have here been arrayed in support of the
prosecution. The first is the Bible—the foundation of our
eternal hopes: the second is Shakspeare—the great ex-
pounder of all the springs and motives of human action.

The earliest indication of the approaching mental infirmity of the aged king, is in the interview with his
daughters, in which he discards Cordelia from his heart,
from her supposed want of filial affection; and then
divides his kingdom between Goneril and Regan, as a
reward for their professions of devoted love. When,
subsequently, these ungrateful daughters lop off their
father's retainers,—abridge his comforts,—deny his authority,—and punish his friends; then it is that the
whole current of his feelings, or his passions, is turned
back upon itself; and his insanity is displayed more fully
than as originally exhibited. He becomes, then, a mono-

maniac, under the direct influence of the rebellion of his children : the unexpected discovery of which, is the immediate and exciting cause. We have neither time, nor disposition, minutely to trace the progress of his mental alienation; but in support of the theory assumed in this part of our argument, and in refutation of the fallacies of the commonwealth, let us refer to his language while indulging in his maniacal ravings, and when exposed to the peltings of the ·pitiless storm.

> "Spit fire ! spout rain !
> Nor rain, wind, thunder, fire, are *my daughters;*
> I tax not you, you elements, with unkindness,
> *I never gave you kingdom, call'd you children;*
> *You owe me no subscription;* why then let fall
> Your horrible pleasure;—here I stand your slave,
> A poor, infirm, weak, and despised old man :—
> *But yet I call you servile ministers,*
> *That have with two pernicious daughters joined*
> Your high engender'd battles, 'gainst a head
> So old and white as this. O ! O ! 'tis foul !"

What say our learned friends now? Do they maintain that there can be no illusion growing out of facts? Do they say that there can be no reason in madness? "No matter and impertinency mixed ?" If they do, they have my answer as thus derived from the knowledge of one, whose authority has never been disputed.

But they tell us that he was not·so mad but that he knew RIGHT from WRONG. We do not utterly deny that. He may have known right from wrong, as respects matters not connected with his monomania; but you must remember that he conceived he "was doing God a service" in ridding the earth of his betrayer—in his own language that, " *God would smile upon it.*" Now, this, our learned friends will not say, is a discrimination between right and wrong: and as concurrent and coincident with this, you will bear in mind, that he was perpetually haunted by the notion that Carter had united with spies for his destruction, and was ruthlessly attempting his life. That may have been all an erroneous fancy or an illusion; but what then becomes of the prosecution: they maintain that the illusion is necessary in order to exempt him from punishment; and the only way in which they attempt to extricate themselves from this dilemma is, by suggesting that all his sufferings were real, and therefore not illusory. Have the gentlemen forgotten that illusions may spring out of realities? Does not their Bible teach them that "persecution will make even a wise man mad?" Suffering was the *cause*, and delusion was the *effect;* and the two combined produced this fearful result. The doctrine of right and wrong, however, is exploded; and I am inclined to believe that those who originally adopted it, could hardly have discriminated between them.

In the Monograph on "Mental Unsoundness," by Dr. Morton Stillé and Mr. Wharton, this test is laid down to be absurd, and almost impossible—and in this doctrine, the highest psychological, and physiological authorities concur. 1st. "The *right* and *wrong* test," say they "can never be rightly applied, because it rests in the *conscience*, which no human eye can penetrate. 2d. It is useless, even if possible, as almost every case of decided insanity is accompanied with a moral sense." In illustration of this doctrine, a man named John Billman, confined in the penitentiary for horse stealing, murdered his keeper in circumstances of great brutality, and with so much ingenuity as to elude suspicions of his intention, and almost concealed his flight: he hung a noose on the outside of the small window, which is placed in the door of the cell to enable persons to look in; he then induced the keeper to put his head entirely through, in order to look at something on the floor directly at the foot of the door; the noose was then drawn, and but for an accident, the man would have been suffocated. Notwithstanding this attempt, the same keeper was inveigled into the cell, alone, a few days afterwards, on the pretence of Billman being sick, and was then killed. Billman then undressed him —changed clothes with him—placed him on the bed in such a position as to present the appearance of his being there, himself—traversed, in his assumed garb, the corridor—with an unconcerned air, addressed a careless question to the gate-keeper, and sauntered listlessly down the street, on which the gate opened. He was, however, soon caught; but his insanity was so indisputable, that the prosecuting authorities, after having instituted a careful and skilful examination, became convinced of his irresponsibility, and united, upon the trial, in asking a verdict of acquittal. He afterwards disclosed the fact, of his having several years back murdered his father; in circumstances which he detailed with great minuteness, and which, upon inquiry, were found to be true. The father had been strangled in his bed—the son was arrested for the crime, but so artfully had he contrived the homicide, that by means of an *alibi*—got up by a rapid ride at midnight, and a feigned sleep in a chamber, into which he had clambered by a window—he was acquitted. Here there was not only a sense of guilt, but a keen appreciation of the consequences of exposure, and an abundance of evidence of a long harbored intention, and intelligent design.

Again, when Martin set fire to Yorkminster, a conversation took place at a neighboring lunatic asylum, in reference to this topic. The question was, whether Martin would be hanged; and in its discussion, one madman announced to the others, a position in which they all acquiesced, that Martin would not be hanged, because he was "one of themselves."

It certainly will not be maintained, that the consciousness of the legal relations of crime, such as these cases exhibit, confers responsibility, where it does not otherwise exist.

There is one other case, with which our illustrations on

this subject will close, and which, perhaps, is more extraordinary than either of those referred to, the case of
Wiley Williams, which is to be found in the second volume of the "Forum," page 477.

Williams was a gentleman from the South, and had
been about a year in the Blockley Asylum; having made
his escape, he wrote to counsel, wishing to know what
legal redress could be obtained for his unjust confinement,
ruined prospects, &c. In his letter he thus reasons: "If
I cannot obtain redress I will shoot Dr. Kirkbride for
having imprisoned me; and should I be tried for murder,
my defence will be this—if I am mad, as he said, I cannot commit a crime; if I am not mad, the deceased deserved death for having deprived me of liberty, and
blighted my hopes." Following up this design, he shortly
after introduced himself into the enclosure of the garden
of the asylum, mounted into a tree, and as Dr. Kirkbride
passed, shot him in the head; but happily the contents of
the gun lodged chiefly in the rim of the doctor's hat, and
the result was comparatively harmless. Williams was
afterwards tried in this very court, for an assault and
battery with intent to kill; but his insanity being established, as he predicted, he was acquitted, and ordered
into strict custody in the penitentiary--where he shortly
after died, having never been restored to reason.

But the counsel have further expressed their surprise,
at what they call the suddenness of this monomania.
1st. Let us inquire—was it so sudden? Remember, he
was prepared for it—it run in his very blood; he had
reached the very time of life when it disclosed itself in
his father; his predisposition; his age; the exciting
cause; all cohered and united together to bring upon
him "the curse of the burning brow, and the sleepless
eye." For six month he had labored under the influence
of his afflictions; his deplorable condition could, therefore, scarcely be said to be sudden, though the act might
be sudden that eventually arose from it; and the cause

might be sudden that impelled the act, which was directly connected with his monomania. Talk of suddenness— read your books—meditate upon human nature—its frailties and its weaknesses. Did you never hear—the only case that I think it necessary to refer to—of the unfortunate young man who, being engaged in a sporting expedition, shot his nearest and his dearest friend, and went mad upon that subject *on the instant;* and ever after spoke of little else than the calamity which brought him to this most unhappy condition. According to our friend's notion, he could not have been mad: first, because it was too sudden; secondly, because the origin of his madness still dwelt deep in his memory.

The best view of the character and causes of insanity, is to be found in Dr. Burrows' Commentaries, page 9, which runs thus: "Every impression on the sensorium, through the external senses, and every passion in excess, may become a moral cause of insanity. Thus, all, however opposite, act as exciting causes, and will produce this result. Joy and grief, pleasure and pain, love and hatred, courage and fear, temperance and ebriety, may have the same effect. Vices, also, which occasion changes in the physical constitution. All impressions that affect the feelings are conveyed to the sensorium, and operate according to the degree of constitutional susceptibility, and the nature and force of the impression. The action of the heart is correspondent with the impression, and reacts upon the brain and nervous system. Hence there are two impressions; the one primitive, affecting the sensorium; the other consecutive, but simultaneously affecting the heart. Thus the nervous and vascular systems are both implicated; and in this manner moral impressions become causes of insanity. The moral cause is, therefore, always the remote cause; the physical, the proximate—or that state of the cerebral functions, which immediately precedes, the peculiar action denominated maniacal. A frequent cause of madness, is suffering the mind to dwell too long on one particular train of thought, whether the subject be *real* or *imaginary*."

You will perceive, by a retrospect of the evidence, that we have shown clearly, *hereditary insanity*, in the prisoner's family. We have shown also, that the physical conformation and keen susceptibilities of the defendant, rendered him peculiarly liable to the influence of exciting causes, calculated to develop this disease. We have shown you, that in his happiness, his joy became *transport—* that his whole soul seemed to be occupied by the object of his affections ; that his prospects were not clouded by a single anticipation of sorrow ; that his imaginary bliss was perfect ; and that such continued to be his condition of unalloyed happiness down to the 10th day of April, 1857. We have shown you that by the occurrences of that dark day, all his enjoyments and bright prospects were swept away, like the beams of the morning, by the wings of the tempest! That the revulsion, the shock, was so great, as to change from that moment the entire character of the man. His nervous system is utterly destroyed—the generosity of his nature is converted into hatred and suspicion—he becomes moody, morose, and misanthropic—all his thoughts are concentrated upon one idea—*the betrayer of his confidence,* which, " like the raven o'er the infected house, bodes ill to all." For six long months he finds no relief to this torture—relief did I say, —his torments are rather increased, and every additional hour is freighted with superadded horror !

During his sad and wayward course, the very sympathetic efforts resorted to by his friends in vain endeavors to administer to his relief, defeat their own purpose, and serve only to probe the wounds of his bleeding heart—to remind him of what *he was,* and of what *he is.*

There are afflictions for which there is no consolation— " no balm in Gilead—no physician there :" their only temporal cure is the grave. We are told that he sought that grave, and *that* even, was denied him ! In this con-

dition of mind and body, of brain and heart; do you require an elaborate argument from me, to satisfy you that
he was utterly irresponsible for any act committed by
him, having a direct connection—an almost immediate
connection—with the great source of his controlling
griefs. The argument that should satisfy any man upon
this subject, is that which is abundantly supplied by the
conduct of the defendant, from the day of this disaster
down to the catastrophe which is the subject of this
charge. You can have no difficulty, assuredly, in finding
that he was a monomaniac on the 4th of November, 1857.
But, say the opposite counsel, you must show that he was
such, at the very time of the perpetration of this deed.
How do we show that? for I agree we are bound to show
it. We clearly prove by Albright, their own witness, and
I am happy to say, a man of unquestionable veracity, by
whom the prisoner was arrested within five minutes of
the perpetration of the fell deed—say at five o'clock—that
at the time of the arrest " the prisoner looked very wild
out of the eyes—was apparently very nervous—his frame
shook—his agitation continued, and he looked like an insane man." Now, on the night of the same day, and on
the very next day, in his cell, both of the doctors speak of
him as being of an unsound condition of mind ; and one
of them refers, if not both, to physical symptoms, which
unerringly contribute to support that opinion.

Now, if we prove a man to be insane an hour before
the commission of an act; and then prove him to be insane within an hour after the commission of the act; and
then follow that up, by showing that the unsoundness of
his mind continued for several consecutive days:- do we
not prove as clearly, as though an angel spoke, that he
was insane at the time of perpetrating the injury ? Then,
having done all that, it is conclusive ; and we may now
turn triumphantly to the opposite counsel, to whom we
have thus transferred the laboring oar, and call upon
them to show—which they are bound to do—that at the

time of the offence complained of, the prisoner enjoyed an unclouded *lucid* interval,—if they fail in that, there is no hope in them.

They seem to acknowledge that this obligation rests upon them, for they have made an effort—and heaven and earth shall witness a most *wretched* effort—to discharge it. They offer what they call rebutting evidence for that purpose. What is their rebuttal? It seems to be a farce, tacked to a tragedy. They have called some half dozen witnesses, to whom the prisoner was utterly unknown; who had never seen him before, much less been acquainted with his habits, his sensibilities, his general demeanor. No one of them having observed him more than five minutes, and even then, with the most unfavorable opportunities for judgment or opinion, they state what! " that they did not see he was insane,"—and with a little more conversation than "yes" or "no," they observe nothing remarkable in the state of his mind! Why, if these men will visit Dr. Kirkbride's asylum— even with ten times the opportunities which they have enjoyed in this instance, and with a very natural suspicion of insanity—they would mistake every madman, probably for a superintendent, or a profound philosopher; and turn them all loose again upon the world. Men who judge thus, or men who confide in such judgment, may be congratulated upon the improbability of ever becoming insane themselves,—" folly, folly, is only free!"

Having thus briefly and imperfectly endeavored to establish our positions, and to overturn those of the prosecution—with what success you shall determine—I have now done. The prisoner is in your hands. I ask no mercy for him. I had almost said I disdain it—but be merciful to yourselves. By his conviction, it is true, you abridge *his* sufferings, but may you not promote and aggravate your *own*. Can you reflect upon such a verdict, without being hereafter haunted by the " compunctious visitings of conscience." If you think you can, why strike at once his unit out of the sum of life.   And when, after your labors are terminated, you return again to your firesides to enjoy the charms of your domestic circle—the blessings of your household gods; then tell your anxious wives and children, who assemble around you, while you relate the lamentable history of this trial—tell them of "one who loved not wisely—but too well;" tell them of the pollution of female innocence—the betrayal of confiding friendship; tell them of the prisoner's blighted hopes —his wounded honor—his ruined fortunes and his shattered reason; tell them how he trusted, and how he was deceived; and when your hearers, with tearful eyes and trembling lips, earnestly inquire what relief you afforded for all these monstrous and most unheard of wrongs; tell them—if you *dare*, that to requite him for all these sufferings, for all these shames, YOU! YOU!! CONSIGNED HIM TO A FELON'S IGNOMINIOUS GRAVE.

WEAVER'S CASE.

THE STATE OF DELAWARE v. ISAAC H. WEAVER.

CHARGED WITH MURDER.

The trial of this case lasted nearly a week, and resulted in a verdict of " not guilty."

For the State.
Attorney General GEORGE P. FISHER.

For the Defendant.
Messrs. GEORGE B. RODNEY, of New Castle, Delaware, and DAVID PAUL BROWN.

SPEECH IN WEAVER'S CASE.

WITH SUBMISSION TO THE COURT:

This case, gentlemen of the jury, has been so elaborately and ably argued by the learned gentlemen who have preceded me, that if you will give me your patient attention, so as that which I say may be clearly understood and properly applied, I will promise you, in the outset, not to trespass unnecessarily on your time. Indeed the exhaustion of this protracted trial, would almost seem to forbid it; yet, notwithstanding that exhaustion, in approaching this case I may truly say, that I feel just as I desire to feel, in addressing a body of men, in relation to whom I occupy the position I now do in regard to you—that of a comparative, if not an utter, stranger. I have no apprehensions of the result; for, with an enlightened court, an honest jury and a good cause, what scope is there for fear? Still, the fatigues of such a trial as this, and the natural influence of advancing years, admonish me of the prudence and propriety of withdrawing from deeply interesting and absorbing questions of this character, and leaving the turbulence and anxiety of the forensic field to younger, and abler, and more aspiring men to battle and to bustle in. Yet, may it please your honors, I do not know that a professional man can die better than in harness—in the faithful fulfilment of his duties to his oppressed fellow-creatures; which duties, we are divinely taught, largely contribute to the discharge of those obligations which we owe to a higher and heavenlier sphere.

I do not forget, sirs, in speaking thus, that I am not here to speak *of* myself, or *for* myself, but *of* and *for* the unhappy prisoner at the bar—unhappy, even if innocent—for his future life, unjust as it would be, will still be blurred and blasted by the recorded imputations of this day : doubly unhappy, if guilty—for your verdict must then consign him either to an ignominious death upon the gallows, or a protracted, lingering, living death, during the whole course of his temporal career, within the melancholy cells of a common jail. Were the choice mine, the speedier the termination of existence, the better ! Life is only desirable, so long as it remains undivested of all that makes life precious. Death is a blessing, when it terminates the scene of infamy and hopeless suffering, and transfers a man to that tribunal which is omnipotent, and that judgment which is infallible—where his actions and his motives can never be misinterpreted or misunderstood.

All that I can expect from you, gentlemen of the jury, as human agents, is to exercise human intelligence, and to give me a fair and impartial hearing; and, while you decide like fate, to feel like men. But how can you commensurately feel for the condition of this boy—for his father, now hanging over him—for, I almost am afraid to mention it—for that absent mother, in her condition of insupportable suspense; while the hope of that father, and the joy of that mother's heart, are awaiting the impending blow which must consign them all to one common ruin? Your sympathies never can appreciate justly the agonies of this scene. You may be fathers, it is true, and feel like parents; but you regard the prisoner as a child of others, not as your own. Sympathy falls far short of that actual experience, the lessons of which are only to be taught through the medium of selfish sufferings; and heaven forbid that you should ever be subjected to such experience.

How precarious, gentlemen of the jury, how dangerous

is the condition of youth—puzzled with mazes and perplexed with errors—with none of those safeguards to rely upon, which age and experience alone can supply—launched like a skiff upon a stormy ocean, with full sail; without helm or rudder, chart or compass, star or pilot, to enlighten or direct it in its course. This simple case furnishes a fearful, practical and painful commentary on the truth of this doctrine.

But, to approach the cause. Who is the defendant, and what is the case? You see before you, a youth of eighteen summers—just budding into manhood—a father's hope and a mother's joy—charged with precocious guilt—with having imbrued his almost infant hands in the blood of a human being—a class-mate—a friend and a brother; one with whom he had lived for years upon terms of familiarity, harmony and affection; and one, the untimely loss of whom, no one can mourn more than himself. Such then is the prisoner. Such the charge which this indictment prefers against him.

Now, what is the lamentable history—what the melancholy facts of this case, which call for discussion by the counsel, and which must finally appeal to you, the sworn twelve, for a decision? At the age of fourteen, in the year 1854, the prisoner at the bar, a native of Maryland, was placed by his parents at the Newark College of this State, for moral and literary instruction. Passing through the usual gradations of college life, we find him on the 30th day of March, 1858, in the junior class, rapidly approaching his matriculation. At this time, in the various classes of this institution, there were some thirty or forty other students; all, or nearly all, older than himself; among whom was the deceased—at that period a member of the senior class. These two young men had their chambers at the college, but boarded, together with some fifteen others, at the house of Mr. Platt, a respectable gentleman, and one of the trustees of the seminary. There, and thus, they lived, on kind and friendly terms, down to the fatal day to which our attention is more especially to be directed,—the 80th day of March, 1858. They were members of the same society, inmates of the same house, ate at the same table, and lived like brothers; notwithstanding the feeble and cruel effort on the part of the State—and which recoiled upon the State—to establish animosity between them.

Before considering the events of that day, it is proper, and may be profitable, that we should advert to some antecedent matters introduced by the evidence, having relation to this charge; and tending to show that evil may sometimes spring from the mere sportiveness and impulsiveness of the young, who, in the exuberance and excitement of their feelings, too often overlook or disregard the restraints of reason.

It would seem that for many years it had been usual (a usage certainly "more honored in the breach than the observance") at the periods allotted for public exercises, for the excluded students by way of raillery, or amusement, or satire, to resort to sham programmes, ridiculing the pretensions of the different candidates for public favor. This, though certainly rough sport, had always previously been taken in good part, and seemed to serve chiefly to relieve the monotony of college life. Certainly, no one ever imagined that any evil would result from it; and yet, as you will find, DEATH attended the sequel.

A public exhibition by a portion of two of the classes, was appointed for this eventful—this fatal day. The programme and announcement of the performance were made public, and a sham or burlesque programme was also prepared for distribution, and deposited in the room of Mr. Harrington, under double lock and key. About twelve o'clock of this day (the existence of these sham programmes having been· discovered), those who were opposed to them, determined to destroy them; and while the others were absent from the college, at their respective boarding houses, the work of destruction commenced

—commenced only to end in the loss of life, and in the consequent institution of those proceedings, which have occupied our anxious attention for the last four days.

On that day—in those circumstances—while Hazel, one of the students, stood sentinel, a committee of five of Mr. Roach's party, suddenly present themselves at the door of Mr. Harrington's chamber. They first attempt picking the lock, that not succeeding, they violently burst open the door; then break open the bureau drawer, and finally prize open and rifle the trunk, where the offensive programmes were found. These programmes are forthwith conveyed, first to Miles' room on the third story, then to Higgins' room on the second story, the door of which they locked and barricaded. In the meanwhile, these proceedings are reported to the absent students, of both parties, who immediately and in great haste repair to the scene of outrage and conflict. Mr. Roach, appears to have been the leader of those opposed to the sham programmes; and it will be remembered, as stated by one of the witnesses, that the very morning before, he showed great excitement, and prophetically declared, that if he once got possession of the programmes, they only should be taken from him over his dead body:—this suggestion, as we have seen, became a prediction. One might almost see the finger of Providence in every page of human life, but we do not seek for it, and either it is not seen or not regarded.

But to resume. Friends and foes having reached the college, rush into Higgins' chamber, Roach and Harrington entering abreast: a conflict, a scuffle, a row or an affray was the result, in which Harrington, Roach, Miles, Giles and Frazier became most conspicuous.

A mass of the programmes was thrown into the stove, saturated with camphene, or other inflammable fluid; the can was cast upon the floor; a part of the burning papers was rescued from the flames and trampled under foot; the fluid took fire; the combustibles in the room were in flames, and the whole college edifice was in danger ; and here, in the midst of this outrageous scene, in a room fifteen feet square, are some twenty belligerent young men, divided into parties and struggling for mastery.

This scene of commotion lasts from two to five minutes —no one pretends that it continued longer—and towards its close, Mr. Roach leaves the room, and is traced to the front door, where he faints from the loss of blood, and in less'than an hour, he expires. These are the melancholy outlines of this sad story.

Mr. Harrington, Mr. Giles, and young Weaver are charged with the homicide ; the two former have been released under the *habeas corpus*, and the last is now upon his trial, and awaits his doom from your hands: THE CHARGE IS MURDER.

We are thus brought, before entering more particularly into the facts at present, to a brief consideration of the law ; and you will allow me to say in the outset, that there is one matter, which, unless it be established beyond the reach of a reasonable doubt, there is nothing for any branch of the law to take hold of, under this issue—I mean the fact of the prisoner having struck the fatal blow : unless that be ascertained, there can be no neces- . sity for discussing the degrees of guilt. We are not called upon, on behalf of the defendant, to show who *did* strike the blow; that is the business of the State, which they cannot transfer to us ; and if they fail in it, your verdict belongs to the defendant.

I repeat, then, if Weaver did not strike the blow, it is nothing; if that fact is even doubtful, it is nothing; but let me further say, if'he undoubtedly *did* so strike, it is not murder ; and that I will maintain until my dying day.

This brings us at once to the attorney general's argument upon the law. He begins, as the prosecution *always* begins, with the common law ; it is the most serviceable, because it is the most bloody ; yet, surely, it has not much to do with the present question, except that the decisions under it have been resorted to for the purpose of interpreting the provisions of your statute, which, according to my view, could have been readily understood of themselves. And, indeed, in regard to the statute, there ought to be no difference of construction between us. Murder, is killing with express malice aforethought. Murder in the second degree, is killing with implied malice aforethought. Manslaughter, is killing from provocation or hot blood, which implies a *want* of malice.

Now, what is *malice aforethought?* it is a preconceived and express intention to kill—that is to say, the facts must show, or in other words *express*, that the defendant, at the time of perpetrating the act, harbored the design to take life, clearly and beyond all reasonable doubt. If that be not clearly and conclusively shown, no killing can be more than murder in the second degree—a conviction of which, substitutes for death upon the gallows, imprisonment for life in the penitentiary. Remember, murder in the *second* degree *also* requires malice aforethought; but it differs from murder in the first degree, by excluding the *intention to kill*. As regards this point in our case, we shall contend that upon the facts of the case, there was not only no intention to kill, but no malice; and we shall further contend, that if there was no malice, but if a blow was struck in an affray or in the heat of blood, or in a quarrel or struggle that lasted but two minutes, the offence can in no possibility exceed manslaughter. Bear in mind, I am speaking of it now upon the strained presumption that the defendant struck the blow, which the prosecution has not shown, and cannot show; and the omission or inability to show which, entitles the prisoner to an entire acquittal.

Pardon a few words more in regard to the law, as explanatory of what I have said, and as addressed directly to the court. First, then : a *mere* homicide is but murder in the second degree. If the prosecution would *elevate* it

to murder in the first degree, it must establish former
threats or grudges, or unequivocal attendant circumstances, showing a predetermination to kill; or if the defendant would *reduce* it to manslaughter—sudden impulse
arising from a sudden fight or provocation, producing hot
blood, and evincing want of premeditation and want of
malice, must be shown by him.

Having thus given you a *general* outline of the *circumstances*, and presented the principles of the LAW which
must govern the results of this trial; in order that those
principles may be legitimately brought to bear upon the
salient and vital points of the evidence, I must beg you
to indulge me, while, for your instruction and the benefit
of the prisoner, I again, and somewhat more particularly,
crave your attention to the testimony.

The whole *time* essentially embraced in this case, so far
as regards the perpetration of the offence, is from *two* to
five minutes; and the whole *space* to which our attention
is to be directed *during* that time, and with reference to
this offence, is the chamber of Higgins. Now, within
that *time* and *place*, who ever saw Weaver? Miles is the
only witness who saw him; and he states that when he
saw him coming into the room, he, the prisoner, was from
four to six feet from Roach—with other persons between
them—and without any weapon that was seen. That
from that time, considering Weaver but a small boy, who
could do no harm, no further attention was paid to him,
nor was it known at what time he withdrew. Although
then it was supposed that Weaver could not do much
harm, it is *now* attempted to transfer to him all the harm
that was done—to make him, in short, the scape-goat to
bear away all the offences of the college.

He was not intimately connected with either of the
parties: it is not shown that he was even concerned in
the concoction of the programme, or that he felt more
than a boyish interest in the agitations of the moment.
We do not impute falsehood to those witnesses who have
25

testified against him, certainly; but let it be remembered that they were all swearing themselves out of a scrape, and although they would not voluntarily perjure themselves for the whole State, yet, when their own feelings were interested, and their own positions affected, it was very natural, I do not say commendable, that they should favorably incline to themselves—each one being desirous to clear his own skirts.

But, as has been said, after the lapse of two minutes, Roach leaves that room, wounded and bleeding. No man living contends, or no man living proves, that Weaver was there then—nor that he came out of the room afterwards—nor that he was in the room for a single minute. Still, the State alleges he was guilty of murder—they substitute fancy for fact—they look upon this scene with jaundiced eyes; nay, not jaundiced eyes, for that would exhibit yellow tints, but with cruel, gloating, and *blood-shot* eyes; and they cry out before you with united voice, blood, blood—hot, reeking, youthful blood!—and they call upon you to play the panders, or the butchers, to cater to their sanguinary and depraved appetites. Well, if they must have blood, and you cannot resist their appeals, let them prove the prisoner's guilt, and then gratify their desires to their heart's content.

Poor Roach passes, or was taken, as has been said, to the front of the building, and in an hour was no more.

One of the witnesses tells us, that he saw young Weaver at that time *do*—what, allow me to say, he never *would* have done, if guilty—kneel down by the side of the dying victim, and in a mournful and peculiar voice, speak to Roach, and ask him if he was dead; and this young scion of a witness, also testifies, that there was something very remarkable, at that time, in the tone of the prisoner's voice—that it was mournful. Why! what, let me ask, should it have been? What could it have been? when contemplating a youthful companion, his associate for years while in the agonies of departing life.

But to turn to another, yet closely connected portion of this case: The KNIFE is a great scare-crow. Had it not been for the knife—this knife which has been flourished about by the prosecution from the first to the last of this drama—Weaver would never have been thought of, certainly never would have been suspected; but because he had been in possession of this knife for several months, it is now supposed or contended that he must be the guilty actor in this bloody scene. Yet, strange to say, the other knife—the anomalous knife—the mysterious knife, that was present at the witching time and place, and has never appeared since—but when last heard of, was thrown into the coal-box in Higgins' room—the learned counsel for the State thinks, is of no consequence whatever. Be this as it may, *that* knife, at least, was never in Weaver's hands, and I shall not, therefore, dwell upon it. It is not my business to convict the guilty—but to acquit the innocent.

But when enthusiastic, and learned young men, become enlisted under the flag of the commonwealth, as adjuncts of the attorney general, they see but one side of the question, and rush onward under the influence of excitement and strong impulse, aided, as in the present instance, by distinguished talents, to the accomplishment of the work of death. When my young friend, who opened the argument on the part of the State, shall bear upon his brow the impress of a few additional years, his enthusiasm will grow cooler—his arguments become more liberal—though certainly never better. Thank heaven! I never occupied the same relative position to a prisoner that he does. I cannot, therefore, perhaps, justly sympathize with him; but I must say, that with my views, I would not, if I could, have prosecuted this case as it has been prosecuted, for the value of the entire State of Delaware.

But, to return again to the melancholy details: after the deceased had remained bleeding for the space of thirty minutes, he approaches the last confines of life, in technical language, he is in *articulo mortis.* Dr. Cooper, Dr. Ferris, Professor Porter, and other estimable persons are surrounding him in his last agonies—and then it is—as Dr. Cooper says, and he is supported by all the rest—in full consciousness, that the "dying declarations" were made. Those were fearful declarations, undoubtedly. I am among those, however, who do not accord to ordinary dying declarations that full faith which I am disposed to repose upon testimony when it undergoes the various and severe tests, to which a living and present witness is subjected. I have no doubt but that the dying man spoke the truth, that is to say, that he believed all that he said; but I much doubt the *accuracy* of what he said. Judging from the uncertainty of all that took place in the room— the clouded or smoky memories of all who testified—the suddenness, the confusion, the irritation, the complication that existed at the time; I should deem it very hazardous to rely upon the statement of any man, living or dying. I do not incline, therefore, to adopt this implication of Harrington—nor do I use the dying declarations for any other purpose than to show, that while Roach designated, according to his impression, the perpetrator of the deed, he never referred to the *prisoner* in any manner; and virtually negatived the idea that Weaver was the perpetrator. If Weaver ever stood before him (and it is said he was wounded in front), would not the accused have been seen?—or if Weaver stood alongside or in the rear of him, would not the weapon have been so seen, as to refer to the party that held it? I pass from this painful portion of the subject, simply strengthening my position, by referring to the testimony of Dr. Cooper, who says, that Roach being a very tall man, and the youthful prisoner but little over five feet in height, he did not think it probable that the latter could have inflicted the wound upon the former, without, in some way, elevating himself above his natural height. It is clear that Mr. Roach never saw Weaver in the room—and I summon him from his grave as a witness for this defence.

But the counsel for the State object to these dying declarations, because the victim was so *near his death*—this is strange doctrine!—*that*—if I understand the matter rightly—is the very time when such declarations are alone valuable. It is not in health, or in hope, that they are to be taken. It is when a man is dying, or he thinks it, that they alone become evidence—or in the language of Chief Baron Eyre, "when every hope in this world is gone—when every motive to falsehood is silenced, and when the mind is induced by the most powerful considerations to speak the truth—a situation so solemn and so awful, is considered by the law as creating an obligation equal to that which is imposed by a positive oath, administered in a court of justice."

But they further say, that the deceased, at the time, had not sufficient possession of his mental faculties. That is an extraordinary argument, and directly opposed to the medical evidence—and tends only to show, that they are willing to make *one* man mad, in order to convict *another* of murder.

What next—still Weaver and the knife!—this is the whole burthen of the charge. It is said, that Weaver went to his room and washed his knife—but again, I ask where is the evidence of it? There was no unquestionable blood in the room, anywhere—no mark—no " damned spot." One witness, it is true, says, there was what he *supposed* to be blood on the towel: that might all have been, consistently with the ordinary accidents or incidents of life, even if it had actually been blood. But why was not that supposed blood analyzed, or examined microscopically, chemically, or otherwise—that it might have been ascertained whether it *was* or *was not* blood?

Again, as regards the knife: it has been said it was found in Weaver's trunk. If you are going to make the

defendant out a felon by forced construction, give him at
least the benefit of the ordinary craft and cunning of a
felon.   If he had used that knife to kill Roach, would he
have taken the dagger to his own room, to marshal his
pursuers the way to his detection? would he have left it
there exposed in an unlocked trunk? would he not have
thrown it into the creek that ran near by? or would he
not have concealed it in some one of a thousand ways, or a
thousand places, where it never could have appeared in
evidence against him?   It has not been proved that the
stain on the guard of the knife, was blood at all; and it
has certainly not been proved that it was human blood:
and if both *had* been proven, Mr. Wilson has shown you,
that it must have been produced by having been handled
by Mr. Evans, after having first been seen *spotless*, by
himself.   The language of the witness runs thus:—"I am
positive, that, when after the death of the deceased, I
looked at the knife, there was no blood on the guard;
but subsequently Mr. Evans handled the knife, his hand
being then bloody—and I then saw blood on the guard,
and I am positive that the blood on the guard came
off of Mr. Evans' hand.   There is no kind of doubt
in my mind, that the blood was not on the knife when
I first took it in my hands, nor is there any kind of
doubt in my mind, that the blood on the guard came off
of Evans' hand."

Then, as to the SHEATH, the inside of which is said to
exhibit traces of blood—that is not denied, but it is explained by us, by showing that prior to last Christmas,
that knife was used by Wm. Adams, a young man of
Baltimore, in killing a ferocious dog; and that after
having been imperfectly wiped, it was thrust into this
sheath, and thereby left those stains, which the Commonwealth's counsel have made so much of.   They could
readily have tested the accuracy of that evidence, without following poor Adams from one end of Baltimore to
another, up and down and crosswise, in a sort of wild

goose chase, in order to overtake him in falsehood. Why did not they prove it human blood? It could easily have been done; for in this enlightened day, science can readily discriminate between the blood of brutes and the blood of man.

But there is another word I have to say in regard to this matter, to show that it was neither the *hand* of the prisoner, nor the prisoner's *weapon*, that produced this fatal wound; and I infer *that* from the character of the wound itself,—such a knife as this might have produced death, but it did not produce the wound in the present instance, inasmuch as the form of the knife is totally inconsistent with the character of the wound. Dr. Cooper says, that he probed the wound to the depth of two inches, with his finger, and that the wound was of equal width: now look at that knife—for more than two inches above the point, it diminishes gradually more than one-half the width of the blade— so that the wound inflicted would have gradually nar-rowed, until it reached its termination. And it is not straining a point, to say—though I no not rest upon it— that it is quite as probable that the knife which was thrown into the coal pit in Higgins' room, produced the wound, as that *this* is the guilty instrument.

The jury will have observed, that in the discussion of this case, I have made no reference whatever to the very doubtful and equivocal confessions of the prisoner, as testified to by Hudders and Bradley—bearing relation as they do, of father-in-law and son-in-law—and neither recommended by that relation—by their own characters, nor by the character and nature of their statement, to favorable consideration, or reliance. One of them seems to be contradicted by others; and it would rather appear that he has contradicted himself. At all events he professes motives, which are not in entire consistency with his conduct upon the present occasion. He was directly contradicted before the coroner's inquest, by the defendant himself; who stated to his teeth, that the witness had misunderstood or misrepresented what he, the prisoner, had said. Nor was this all: this young man, without friends or advisers, immediately calls upon Hudders, and boldly states to him, that the language used—"that he believed he had struck the deceased with a knife,"—was not a true representation of what took place; but that the language *actually* used was, "that he feared the possession of the knife would be calculated to *implicate* him in the affair." Without, however, pausing upon this branch of the subject, I simply refer you, in relation to it, to what has been said, and so well said, by my learned and able colleague, Mr. Rodney. He has presented it so clearly, so fully, and so cogently before you, as to obviate the necessity for any further remarks of mine. A strong man strikes a strong blow, and one that generally serves its turn, without occasion for repetition. I have no disposition to travel over the same field that has already been so fully beaten. If you think that the flimsy statements made by these men, or the imaginative account given by Constable, are sufficient to resist the reasoning that has been urged against them, and to induce you to convict the prisoner, nothing that I could say would be calculated to forestall his doom.

In my argument, as you must have perceived, I have avoided as far as possible, those points of discussion which I conceived to have been satisfactorily disposed of. The case is almost too narrow, perhaps, in its essentials, for two, to move abreast; and I have therefore satisfied myself with the humble task of a gleaner, collecting the scraps, or the grain, which may have fallen by the way-side—so that nothing may be lost that may prove available to the defendant in this death-struggle.

My humble task is now done—however feeble it may be, it at least possesses the merit of frankness, of candor, and of brevity. I have urged nothing upon *you*, but what my own feelings and my own reason have urged upon *me*, under the deep responsibilities imposed by the investigation of this case. I pray you not to resist that which has been said, from the notion, I fear too generally entertained, that counsel often act under influences inconsistent with impartiality or sincerity:— this, let me tell you, is an erroneous notion. There is no class of citizens, not even excluding the clergy themselves, that are more faithful to their duties, or more sensible to the high obligations of moral honesty and professional honor, than an approved and well deserving member of the bar. His duties are often of the loftiest and most momentous character. They involve property, liberty, reputation, and as in the present case, life itself. And in relation to the discharge of all those obligations, a lawyer, as properly understood, never proves recreant to his trust.

The case is now in your hands. Having been estranged from your families, probably for more than the usual length of time; after pronouncing your verdict upon this fearful issue, you will return to them again—again to enjoy their smiles, and to share in their consolations and their happiness; and when you shall retire to your repose, after the labors, and toils, and privations you have passed through, that repose, we trust, will be sweetened by the consciousness of having this day faithfully fulfilled the pledges, which you have solemnly assumed, by pronouncing the verdict of "Not Guilty."

Table of Contents.